J. Willis
Sardin
5/2024

The
One
Red Brick

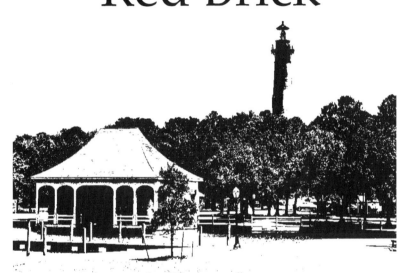

J. Willis Sanders

BUGGS ISLAND BOOKS

Printed in the United States of America
Cover art by BookCoverZone.com

By J. Willis Sanders
Learn more about these books at
https://jwillissanders.wixsite.com/writer

The Eliza Gray Series
The Colors of Eliza Gray
The Colors of Denver Andrews
The Colors of Tess Gray

The Forgiveness Quilt: An Amish Christmas Carol
The Easter Prayer: An Amish Easter Story

The Clara Engelman Series
Clara's Mourning
Clara's Courtship
Clara's Choice

The Essence of Emmaline Strong

The Outer Banks of North Carolina Series
The Diary of Carlo Cipriani
If the Sunrise Forgets Tomorrow
Love, Jake
The One Red Brick

The Hope Series
The Coincidence of Hope
The Yearning of Hope
The Gift of Hope

Writing as J. D. James
Reid Stone: Hard as Stone
Reid Stone: Red Rage

.

Praise for The Outer Banks of North Carolina Series
https://www.amazon.com/gp/product/B098P67LJB

The Diary of Carlo Cipriani

"This is fascinating tale of survival, both of shipwrecked sailors and of how wild horses came to live on the Outer Banks. I enjoyed the characters and the character development, as well."

"The heartfelt descriptions of the characters brings them to life and bids you to follow their stories. There is life and love, despair and grief that eventually give way to hope for the future. A well written, intriguing story that bids me to learn more about the Outer Banks."

"Many twists and turns, lots of tragedy but always hope. At several points you are not sure what is real and what is the narrators madness due to his loneliness. A very satisfying resolution answers all our questions."

If the Sunrise Forgets Tomorrow

"What a captivating book. I read it in 2 sittings because we just couldn't put it down. Brought tears to my eyes!"

"This book was captivating and it was difficult for me to put it down. If you like a touch of history and have a love for Ocracoke, this is a great book to read. It was very descriptive and made me feel like I was there. Virginia and Ruby are typical sisters who are loving each other one minute and the next they are disagreeing. I enjoyed the strength they displayed as they overcame many obstacles. A Great Read!"

"To be honest, I wasn't certain I would enjoy this book. I've read other books at in the Outer Banks and a lot of them seem to be sloppily written and just capitalizing on the setting to prey on die-hard OBX readers. I was pleasantly surprised to find it very well written and descriptive. It was easy to visualize the island, the characters, and the story as it all unfolded. I would recommend checking it out!"

Foreword

If you've ever visited the Outer Banks of North Carolina, you likely know about the Currituck Lighthouse and the renovated art deco retreat of Edward and Marie Knight, now called the Whalehead Club. If that's the case, you know both are located in Corolla, the setting for this story.

I love the Outer Banks for many reasons, but I especially love its history. Most of this story takes place from 1908 on, and that time frame includes World War I, known back then and in this book as the "The Great War." The same time period, unfortunately, is also known for the horrors of the Spanish Flu. Talk about two occurrences for the mind of a fiction author to weave into a book!

Also back then, the landscape of Corolla was quite different. No dunes attempted to stop the Atlantic, and bare sand extended to the lighthouse. Although vegetation grew there in the form of sparse brush and trees, it was nothing like today, with it thickly covering many areas.

I mention these things because I took the liberty of adding dunes and groves of live oaks, those twisted trees of the Outer Banks, to my setting of Corolla. I did so to add description to the place, plus to give it more of the amazing ambiance it has now.

Regardless of those liberties, much of this book is true as it concerns the Whalehead Club, called "Corolla Island" by Edward and Marie Knight at its completion in 1925. If you've not toured it, please do. The renovation team did a wonderful job.

Whether any murders took place in the Corolla Island boathouse, I have no idea. Regardless, I can imagine a lover's tryst or two occurring there by some of the wealthy guests who visited over the years. There are also legends of ghosts in the area. Whether you believe in ghosts or not, it's intriguing to consider.

I also took liberties with creating past sheriffs of Currituck County. If you know the actual names of any of the real ones from back then, please don't be alarmed at the differences. Fiction, after all, is formed in the imagination of the author, and we do what we must for the sake of the story.

Another liberty I was forced to take was this book's cover. As you may have noticed, the landscape from the beach to the lighthouse is not hilly like on the cover, but it does convey the feeling I wanted it to have, which is a serious and somber Chester as a boy. Suffice it to say, buying book covers is a tricky proposition, so we authors must sometimes make compromises. Thank you for understanding.

Finally, as you'll soon learn, this story is much more than a murder mystery or a love story. Like I hope with all of my books, it's something to stir the mind into considering who, what, and why we are. If we do those things, it likely makes us better people, and I hate to think of a world where no one tries to be a better person.

Thank you for reading.
J. Willis Sanders
February 20, 2024

Pronunciation Guide

Two names in this story may confuse readers, and no one likes to be confused. As you'll read, the names are used for specific reasons, so I really wanted to include them.

The first name is Maurea, which is a type of sea snail. It's pronounced Maw-ree-uh.

The second name is Mirlande, a Haitian name. One meaning of it is "shining sea."

It's pronunciation is a bit more complicated than Maurea. From a pronunciation guide I found online, Mir is pronounced like "we're," and lande is pronounced like "land," with the emphasis on "Me're."

Given that, we have Me're-land. Also, the guide sounded as if "land" had a bit of on "o" sound to it, like "lond." If that's the case, it could be pronounced "Me're-lond."

While I'm at it, we might as well cover the proper pronunciation of Corolla.

"No," I say, smiling, "it's not the same as the Toyota car." It's Kuh-rah-lah.

Yes, I freely admit to pronouncing it incorrectly for most of my life. Live and learn, right?

I hope this guide helps as you read. It certainly helped me.

J. Willis Sanders

Dedication

Dedicated to everyone who has, does, and will love the Outer Banks of North Carolina.

You understand its attraction. You understand its nature. You understand the solace it shares with its amazing sunrises, miraculous sunsets, and the pull of its tides.

In each of us lives an infinitesimal bit of the Outer Banks of North Carolina. Like my dear wife and I, as long as we are able, we will never fail to return.

J.W.S.

The
One
Red Brick

Forgiveness is one of the most significant ideals a person can practice. Forgiveness mends relationships, saves marriages, prevents wars, and ends hate.

As bright as the stars, as illuminating as the sun, as deep as any ocean, to set aside hate, to set aside blame, to set aside the wrongs of the past in the name of hope, is likely the most shining example of humanity's existence.

Sheriff Maurea Sandifer
Currituck County, North Carolina
December, 2011

The One Red Brick

When I was just a girl, the first time I assumed the worst about someone, my dad corrected me right away. He said because we don't know what or who shaped a person's life, we owe people the benefit of the doubt. He was quite adamant about it, but he didn't say why. Then, as I got older, he explained it with this story.

To start with, this isn't a standard murder mystery. Like so many murders, these were ignited by a love story. *Unlike* so many murders, these took over eighty years to get closure. Needless to say, though it must be said anyway, it's a story I'll remember for the rest of my life, along with the lesson Dad taught me.

Because of his suggestion of giving people the benefit of the doubt, I sometimes hope to meet a person who embodies so much innate goodness that any of their faults hardly seem worth mentioning. As sheriff of Currituck County, North Carolina, and as a human, I've yet to meet such a person, including myself. Maybe my expectations are too high, or maybe I'm influenced by my job and my desire for justice. When most of the people you deal with in this line of work have so many faults that their goodness hardly seems worth mentioning, or is completely non-existent, you tend to feel that way, which leads me to the body lying in the sand at my feet.

1

I've always wondered when this death would occur. If everything I've read and heard about this story is true, it was only a matter of time. Then again, since the body is here and the cause of death is obvious, maybe this person's faults have faded to where the good *is* worth mentioning. After all, Dad's lesson about giving someone the benefit of the doubt might apply here.

For the record, it's November 2011, and my name is Maurea Sandifer, great-great granddaughter of Amos Sandifer. Amos was interim sheriff of Currituck County in 1928, when two people were murdered in the boathouse at Corolla Island, now called The Whalehead Club.

Unlike now, with crime more common, the murders were a huge sensation back then. The deaths of two people—one a young man from a prominent northern family, the other a local woman without any family whatsoever—both engaged to marry other people—had caused a stir, and stirs in the small Outer Banks community of Corolla, North Carolina, were frowned upon.

The murders also affected my great-great grandfather deeply, even to the point of one of his sons, my great grandfather, Harry, naming my grandfather Chester, after the main character in this story. Also, Amos did become the full-time sheriff, and Harry and Chester eventually became sheriffs of Currituck County as well. My dad chose not to become the county's sheriff, but he did keep the story alive. Amos even wrote a book about the murders and about Chester, entitled *Chester Pinkham: The Personification of Character.* It covered Chester's life in Corolla and how he loved the area, loved all of its creatures, how his greatest love would remain anonymous. Amos told Chester he might write a book about him, and people would know who his greatest love was anyway. Chester told him he didn't care.

Dad said his relatives became sheriffs because they wanted to serve Currituck County's citizens. He also admitted to them wanting to access the records of the boathouse murders whenever they pleased. I admit to reading them a number of times myself, and I can't help wondering about this case because the murder weapon was never found. Regardless, the coroner found particles of red brick in the head wounds. This created the assumption that a missing brick from the Currituck Lighthouse, known to some familiar with the case as The One Red Brick, was used to beat the two victims to death.

The assumption, because of Chester's relationship with the victims and how he lived a short walk from the Currituck Lighthouse, was he killed them with The One Red Brick.

I despise assumptions. All it takes to convict an innocent person of a crime is circumstance, hearsay, and a convenient person to accuse. Sure, jury trials are supposed to consist of an impartial group of people who will look at the evidence and nothing but the evidence. Nevertheless, people are fallible, and concerning Chester Pinkham, my family—both those still alive and those passed on—have had our doubts about him committing the murders.

We've had those doubts for a number of reasons, most of all because Chester was one of those people who embodied so much goodness that any of his faults hardly seem worth mentioning.

Now, as I stand over this body lying in the sand at the base of one of five gravestones, I believe those doubts even more.

The gravestones are located behind Chester's collapsing wood shack in Corolla, North Carolina. The shack is up a rise from the shimmering waters of the Currituck Sound. If I look east, through the twisted live oak trees surrounding this shack and the graves, I can see the red brick Currituck Lighthouse. If I look south, through more of those same twisted trees, I can see the magnificent retreat built by Edward and Marie-Louise Knight, where the boathouse is located to one side of a large lagoon.

I don't study the body. Instead, I study the five pitiful gravestones. Chester and his parents spent their lives here, and they shared their love of the area with him. Alice and Abner's deaths were too tragic to consider, yet here they lie. To imagine how much they loved their son would bring me to tears if I let it. It still does when I read Amos's book and hear unprinted parts of Chester's story from my dad, passed down by our relatives.

Chester, I want to believe, lives on somehow. He would've been 103 yesterday, on his birthday. I hope he's found solace in Corolla over the years, in the wildlife, in the sunrises and sunsets, in his memories of good times long gone.

As I return to the body at my feet, I have a feeling he's near. Other people think the same thing, and I'll get to that later in this book.

Along with Chester and my namesake, Maurea Applewhite, I'll also mention the existence of a third person in this tragedy, a young woman known simply as Mirlande. In the next three chapters, you'll learn the circumstances of their births, plus some of what influenced the parts they played in the murders, so I want to make sure you understand where my short preamble is leading.

The main thing is for Chester's story, especially the tragic parts he couldn't have known, to be told as closely as possible as to how he believed it all unfolded.

And this is how we begin.

He is Perfect in Every Way

Corolla, North Carolina
1908

In a rocking chair by the fireplace with her knitting, Alice Pinkham studied her husband. A fisherman by birth, a woodcarver by trade, he steadied the duck decoy in his lap. With one hand supporting the head, the other holding one of his many carving tools, he carefully incised slitted nostrils into the beak. Done with that task, he looked up at her from beside his workbench on the other side of the fireplace. A kerosene lantern hung from a rafter overhead, pooling a circle of yellow light over them both, him straddling the wooden bench he had crafted for his trade.

Outside their home, within a grove of live oaks not far from the Currituck Sound, a gale, not quite a nor'easter, whistled in the branches. Alice couldn't see the finger of light from the Currituck Lighthouse's massive red-brick form, but she knew it was piercing the winter storm's fine haze of snow, warning ships to be wary of the slender strip of sand that created the northernmost Outer Banks of North Carolina. She and Abner were born near the town of Corolla. No doubt they would die here too, like their parents had. If not from a hurricane like them, or from old age, who knew what might take them? She could die tonight and him tomorrow. For herself, childbirth took many a mother in the early 20th century. For him, worry could do the same, particularly worry about her labor, which had started an hour ago.

The muscles in his throat tightened with a hard swallow, visible because he was so thin. He licked his lips, either in preparation to say something or nothing. Seconds passed. Instead of speaking, he lowered his head again, likely praying for her and the baby, especially since she wanted him to help with the delivery. A length of black hair fell across his forehead. He fingered it back and raised the knife to the decoy again, this time to define a wingtip folded across its back. Lamplight glinted in his hazel eyes. She preferred calling them aquamarine, for they reminded her of the Atlantic.

In a million different ways, Alice Pinkham, formerly Alice Avon, adored Abner Pinkham.

From the first day they met in the one-room Corolla schoolhouse as first graders, his gentle but firm demeanor had captured her heart. This happened when he punched the class bully who made fun of her brown eyes and brown hair and dark complexion by saying she looked like a skinny dog turd. Sometimes, like her papa had said, good men were forced to do bad things. In this case, Abner went a little overboard by kicking the bully in the testicles too. To drive the point home, Alice followed up with a kick of her own. Regardless of their explanations to the teacher, their actions earned them a suspension. Regardless of the suspension, their parents understood. They even met and discussed the matter, saying Alice and Abner were wonderful children and how both families should spend more time together.

Over the years, whether during fishing or crabbing or shelling outings at the Atlantic or the sound, Sunday lunches after church, or simply strolling the live oaks while watching the astounding sunsets over the Currituck, Alice grew to adore Abner's love of nature. His papa had given him a magnifying glass. Apart from burning his own arm with it on a scalding summer afternoon, he soon learned to use it to study anything and everything he could find, either along the beach, the sound, the marsh, or in the groves of live oaks.

"Look here," he told Alice, on one such journey to the beach as eight-year-olds, kneeling to hold the glass over the ribs of a fish skeleton tangled within a mat of salty smelling seaweed.

She knelt beside him. "It's just a fish skeleton. We see them all the time."

He pointed to a tiny ghost crab perched on the vertebrae, the claws picking and bringing invisible morsels to its mouth. "You know those rich people who come here to hunt ducks? They're like this crab. It's inside this fish's ribs, like it's in a cage."

Alice didn't know what Abner meant. Her own papa guided hunters, and he was grateful for the money he earned by doing so. "What do you mean, Abner? I don't understand."

"Well," he said, turning his head to peer at her, "I should've said this crab is like those hunters who won't clean their shotguns. Papa says when some hunters get back in from the sound, they clean and oil their shotguns. The others, though, ask their guides to do it. Papa says a person who won't do for themselves is no better than a crab picking bones. They depend on others. They just don't know it because they're inside a cage of their own making. He says the same thing for anyone who won't work to feed their families. Remember old Scrimshaw Adams? He had eighteen children with three women, and he wouldn't hit a lick at a water moccasin to take care of any of them. All he was good for was making children and drinking spirits. If not for the minister and several people in Corolla helping out, those women and children would've gone hungry."

Alice still didn't understand the connection to the crab. Although Abner was always saying similar things, it didn't take long until he changed the subject.

"Look here," he said a few minutes later, holding the magnifying glass over a white feather with brown edges. "This is from a Sanderling."

Alice knew these birds. They flitted with invisible wingbeats over the waves until they found a stretch of sand to their liking. Then they flared to a landing just above the tide line, marked with lacy strings of foam. They might preen, working their long, narrow beaks beneath their wings. They might run around on backward-kneed legs, which resembled a pair of broken sea oat stalks. They also might chatter at each other, possibly asking who would first chase the retreating foam while probing the sand for whatever tiny morsels of food they could find. Then, as if an agreement had been reached, they all would scurry toward the surf, driving their beaks into the glistening surface like oceanic woodpeckers carving out a nest in the trunk of a dead tree.

Abner raised the feather, turning it this way and that as his aquamarine eyes studied it through the glass. He never said anything when he studied feathers. It was as if he were absorbing each and every detail down to the molecular level. He loved big words, said his mama taught them to him from a biology book about the shore.

At thirteen, he and Alice started holding hands. At fifteen, they experimented with kisses. At sixteen, she refused his proposal, saying they were too young. He wiped his forehead with relief. "I was just testing you. I want to have a better job than fishing to support a wife as wonderful as you'll be." This was another reason she adored him, one of those millions of reasons. A man who wanted to take care of his family was a man to admire.

This led to making migratory waterfowl decoys: Blue-winged Teal, Green-winged Teal, American Black Duck, Northern Shoveler, Northern Pintail, and Red-breasted Merganser to name a few; then, of course, Canada Geese, Snow Geese, and Tundra Swans. After that came the elusive Wood Duck, of which he only made one because he hated to help hunters take them: a male in flight that now hung over their bed.

Before they were married in 1906, Abner claimed, despite the guffaws from hunters of the time, that collectors would eventually clamor for waterfowl decoys. "It might take years," he often said, "but it'll happen. Even if we're dead and buried, our children will be able to sell our decoys."

Alice loved his description of their marriage. Everything, down to the minutiae of each moment, was never "his" nor "hers" —it was "ours," yet another of those million reasons she adored him.

Another labor contraction, possibly a bit sooner than the last, made her wince. It was strange, the things one thought of while having a son or a daughter, already loved.

Abner set the decoy on the bench. At the door, he looked outside, letting in a blast of frigid air. "Still snowing," he muttered, his voice frightened and worried and as cold as the wind. He closed the door and returned to his seat. Fear etched the corners of his eyes, evidenced by his deepening crow's feet. "You're larger, Alice. I hope we don't need a doctor."

Despite the rising sound of the howling winter storm, Alice heard the unsaid part of his sentence: "You're larger *than the last time*, Alice."

In the yellow lamplight, his eyes found hers, but no comfort passed between them. Snow rarely occurred to this degree on the Outer Banks, but on two nights like this, they had lost three babies. The first, a son, came into the world crying as if he hated them, only to pass in the night a week later. Babies two and three, twin daughters, were born prematurely, each clutching the other as if in fear of their coming demise. The first baby had been brought into the world by a midwife, the twins by a doctor. Since none had survived, Alice was placing her trust in God and in Abner.

"The world is evil," he said unexpectedly. "People are selfish and our babies knew it. Many are no better than the hunters who come here for sport instead of for food. They live for the moment. Their emotions are as immature as a child's. Our babies don't care to be born into a world where people strut and preen as if they have the coloration of a Wood Duck. They do it on the mainland with their fancy automobiles and fancy clothes. Many hunters do it here, posing for photographs with their ducks. Then they ignore them. At least the guides save them for food. I pity the world our children and great-grandchildren will inherit. I doubt it will be worth living in then. Thank the good Lord we live out here. I suppose we can keep it at bay for a while yet."

Alice didn't care for this kind of talk. Abner's worry about the baby likely contributed to it, along with his worry about their income.

Despite his admiration for men who properly cared for their families, she knew he considered himself a failure. He spent hour after hour perfecting his decoys and trying to sell them to wealthy hunters as collector items. Once, to show the extent of his skills, he carved a decoy to resemble a dead Snow Goose, complete with dots of red paint on the white breast to mimic the punctures from shotgun pellets. He hid it in a sack and took it out on a hunt when a guide, sick with a fever, stopped by to ask him to take his place. At the end of the day, after the hunters posed for a photograph, Abner took the decoy from the sack and held it out straight by the neck.

Several hunters laughed. One, an old geezer from somewhere in the Midwest, poked the goose. "Why, that thing is frozen hard as a rock."

Abner wrapped his knuckles against the decoy. "It's wood. I made it. Wouldn't you like to admire it over the mantle of your fireplace back home?"

The man, shrewd businessman that he was, asked the price. He then squinted at Abner's sum of ten dollars. "Do you take me for a fool? I didn't make my money by spending it on luxuries like a fake dead goose." He took out a wallet and offered a dollar. Abner, needing a pane of glass to replace one at home, broken when he threw a dull carving knife through it, accepted the dollar. At this point, he knew his best bet was to make decoys to secure his children's future instead of his and Alice's present. Therefore he started guiding fisherman in the spring and hunters in the fall and winter, making decoys in what spare time remained.

Alice rarely despised anything, but she despised the lack of appreciation for her husband's God given skills. She also despised how she had just wet her dress, her water having broken. After working herself up from the unstable rocking chair, she dropped her knitting to a small table between her and Abner. "We better boil water and get out those sheets we tore into rags. My water just broke."

Abner leapt from the bench. He helped her to bed and hung a cast iron pot filled with water over the fire, gathered the rags and sat on the bedside. "How far apart are the contractions?"

Another one of those millions of reasons Alice adored him was his knowledge of human biology, as well as shoreside biology, both taught from his mother. "It'll be a while yet." She patted his pillow. "Lie down and rest while you can."

He did so. Placing a tentative hand on her rounded abdomen, he chuckled. "You mean lie down and rest before the screaming starts."

"Yes," she said, smiling at him while elbowing his ribs.

His hand rubbed her belly. "I think this baby will be all right." He closed his eyes like Alice had suggested.

Another thing she despised was how Abner thought he was a failure from losing their parents in the hurricane. She didn't blame him at all. He couldn't help it if their houses were built on lower areas of the sound's shore than this one. To keep the sound from washing their houses away when the wind from hurricanes pushed the vast waters of the Currituck inland, all three were built on pilings. Unfortunately for their parents, along with their houses being built on lower areas, the pilings supporting their houses weren't tall enough. This allowed the sound, driven by the wind, to explode them as if a bomb had gone off beneath each one. All that night, while the roaring wind and driving rain screeched through Corolla like a banshee, Abner could do nothing but stand at the window and wring his hands, praying prayer after prayer.

To make matters worse, like many locals drowned that night, the bodies of their parents were never found. When the community held a gathering to remember the dead, Abner refused to go, saying he should be dead too because he couldn't save his loved ones. Sometimes blessings are needed to bring a person back to life after a tragedy. Alice knew this, so when she told him of her pregnancy, she was grateful for how it brought him out of his melancholy.

"Boy or girl, I'll teach either everything I know," Abner said, beaming a smile. Then, after kissing Alice, he added, "And of course, sweetheart, you'll do the same. What a fine life we'll give our child—an amazing life—a life filled with love—a life filled with love for our amazing home and all of nature surrounding it, from the sea to the sound."

About thirty minutes apart, according to the clock on the fireplace mantle, the contractions allowed Alice to doze between them. Like with her first babies, the pain resembled the cramps from her monthly cycles, a dull pain in her lower stomach.

When they woke her, she listened to the wind whistle in the live oaks. How many centuries had it taken their limbs to twist like reaching, grasping hands toward the west, deformed by the prevailing winds?

No, deformed wasn't the correct word. Their majestic yet intriguing shapes held an appeal few trees on the Outer Banks could match. Mainlanders sometimes said they resembled monsters. When Abner heard this, he eyed them with disdain. Later at home, he never failed to share his feelings. "Those who only search the outer self are the monsters. The human race isn't perfect, nor do those trees fit what those idiotic mainlanders consider the ideal for a tree. Regardless, God created us all the same, and He considers us all beautiful."

Alice knew Abner also thought the same of nature. When their income allowed it, he ordered picture books with examples of birds and beasts and flora and fauna from all over the world. Still, no matter how many books he ordered, or how many pictures he studied, his favorite place was the place of his birth, the Outer Banks of North Carolina.

"Why climb a mountain when I can see the mountains of the Atlantic?" he would ask. "Why trek a desert when I can stand with my feet in the hot sand of our beaches? Why visit a jungle and listen to the whine of mosquitos when they ring in our ears here on summer nights? Why watch a herd of horses gallop the western plains when our Spanish Mustangs are just a short walk away? Why fish any other ocean when our waters offer a plentiful bounty? Why hunt anywhere else when ducks and geese darken our skies each autumn?"

Yet another one of those millions of reasons Alice adored Abner, his enthusiasm concerning their home matched hers, and as he had mentioned earlier, she planned to teach their child to love it too.

The water in the cast iron pot hanging over the fireplace steamed. The embers had burned down, illuminating the immediate area with a glow resembling sunsets over the Currituck Sound.

The contractions came closer. At the next one, the clock on the mantle said fifteen minutes apart. Maybe sleep had hidden the time between the former and the latter.

Above the bed, the Wood Duck hung motionless: a multicolored talisman of nature to guard their child, beauty in feathered form, sleek and graceful yet short and stocky, its yellow bill held straight and true with character and purpose.

Although Abner never claimed it, Alice thought his character came from his love of nature. "Nature never fails," he often said. "Humans fail continuously. I understand that to a degree, because too many allow emotions to rule them. My point is for us to at least recognize this and try ... just try ... is that too much to ask? For example," he would continue, "if our child reaches his or her teenage years, the hormones will be roiling like a hurricane. If, however, we teach them how the consequences of their actions can create hardships in their lives, I would hope with all my heart that they would—at the very least—try to think before they act. Unlike animals, we can do that, yet our ability to reason, when animals react with instinct, too often fails us. Then we're left to scratch our heads while looking around for someone to blame for the misfortunes of our own making."

These observations—Alice didn't call them rants because they made sense—came with each of her pregnancies, evidence of his concern for their child's future. Like with the example of Scrimshaw Adams and the three women who accepted him regardless of his low character, Abner's observations held merit. Also, he felt so strongly about such things because he genuinely cared about other people, and he didn't believe material things made anyone truly happy. True happiness, he often told her, came from having gratitude for the simplest things in life, even if one of those things was surviving another day on the Outer Banks.

Alice may have dozed again, or may have not, for an intense contraction raised her from the bed. Abner bolted upright, his black hair sticking out at wild angles. "What? Is it time? Is it time, Alice?"

"It's getting closer. Stoke the fire so the water will boil."

Abner did so, looking back at her as he did, eyes wide with concern.

The flames soon rose, brightening the room. A cloud of steam enveloped the water. The wind whistled in the oaks. The Wood Duck trembled from a draft hissing in at the top of the door.

To sterilize a pair of scissors for the umbilical cord, Albert dipped them in the boiling water. He then piled the rags at the foot of the bed.

A contraction clenched Alice's teeth. A guttural moan filled her throat. Abner supported her back as the spasm raised her from the bed. Hours passed. The pains came at closer and closer intervals. The wind went from a whistle to a moan to a shriek, mirroring Alice's own shrieks.

Abner pulled the table from between the chairs to the bed and set the lamp on it. He raised her knees and nightgown. Alice was grateful he had bought a book on birthing a baby. He looked from between her legs to her. "You're doing a fine job, Alice. It won't be long now."

The Wood Duck trembled again, hinting at the day Abner proposed. His father owned an ancient canoe, the canvas painted hunter green, the wooden ribs yellowed with age and crusted white with salt. Like most everything on the Outer Banks, time and age takes its toll. Although Alice loved paddling too, he climbed into the stern, insisting he do so on this trip.

They set off across the Currituck. He told her how he loved her brunette hair streaked with sun, how golden her tan was, how her bare legs, short though shapely, made him feel like a Spanish stallion chasing a mare along the beach. She told him she wasn't at all attractive and he agreed, grinning, then saying he loved her soul all the more.

She would never admit it to him, but his thin frame and narrow face, so the girls of the community had said, were why none had ever been interested in him. Alice didn't mind his appearance one whit, for she loved his soul like he loved hers.

His tan, though, as golden as hers, created the appearance of a tawny statue, wiry and sinewy when he went without his shirt like he did now. The tendons inside his elbows flexed with each paddle stroke. The muscles in his chest tightened and relaxed, tightened and relaxed. He stuck his tongue out at her. "I see you salivating over my manly form, Alice. Shame on you."

Lying back in the bow, trying to stay cool on the August-hot afternoon by letting one foot trace a V in the sound, Alice kicked water at him. "Just wait until our honeymoon, Mr. Stallion. This mare won't need a saddle, if you know what I mean."

Easy to embarrass when she teased him so blatantly about sex, Abner glanced away, his cheeks turning scarlet. A few paddle strokes later, he faced her again. His eyes moved up and down the length of her, and his tongue darted out to lick his lips. Despite her short stature and plain features, plus their attitudes about inner beauty being more important than outer beauty, his attention made her feel as if she were the most desirable woman in the world.

Another pain, this one much closer to the last, clenched Alice's middle. She gripped her knees and rose, pushing for all she was worth. Beads of sweat popped on her forehead and ran into her bulging eyes, stinging them. Her scream joined the whistling wind, adding her note of agony to its voice. Done with the effort, she collapsed to the pillow.

Worry creased Abner's forehead. "Once more should do it, but the head seems larger than our other babies' heads."

Feeling the next contraction, Alice panted like a rabid dog and gripped her knees again. This birth felt nothing like her other babies. This child felt like it was ripping her womanhood apart. Sensing another death, she clamped her eyes shut. From within her mind came the blurred vision of five tombstones behind their home. Already there, two were to commemorate the loss of their babies. Two were for her and Abner when they passed, hopefully far into the future. On the fifth, between a canoe and the profile of a Labrador Retriever, both inscribed into the granite, no name identified the corpse. Nothing was there except a single word: Beloved.

A great gush of hot liquid burst from her, and she fell back to the pillow, chest heaving from the effort. "Abner," she gasped, "why isn't—"

"I'm sorry, Alice, something's wrong with him. His left hand only has two fingers and a thumb, and it's smaller than the right. His head ... well, it's—"

"But why isn't he crying? Is he dead?" She raised up in time to see Abner pop the baby's bottom. His forehead was taller than usual, not sloped like their last babies' foreheads, which explained the birth's difficulty. Despite his lack of sound, his hands reached for her. She pressed him to her chest, the umbilical trailing like a length of blue rope.

Abner tied the cord with a piece of boiled string and cut it. Alice settled on the pillow and strained to expel the afterbirth. He used the rags to staunch the bleeding. "I'm afraid you tore, Alice. His head was so big."

She told him to stitch it like in his book. He boiled a needle and thread from her sewing basket and went to work, moving the lamp closer and squinting as he did. The dark length of hair fell across his forehead several times. He swept it back each time, huffing angrily.

Alice used the rags to clean her son. She thought his forehead was a mark of intelligence. She thought his left hand was a mark of nature, demure yet intriguing, while his right hand was a mark of strength, perfectly formed and flexing with confidence.

"Chester," she said. "Chester Pinkham, no middle name. He is perfect in every way."

"The world won't think so," Abner mumbled, clearly upset by the night's turn of events.

Alice wanted to kick him, but he might miss a stitch. "Since when have we cared what the world thinks, Abner Jay Pinkham? The world, in my view, has gone to Hades anyway. I can't imagine a happier life here in Corolla. A simple life. A life where we have everything we need and some of what we desire. Isn't that right?"

Abner set needle and thread aside. He joined her on the bed to study his son. Alice took his hand and placed his pinky into Chester's right hand. The fingers closed, gripping tightly. She placed her own pinky into his left hand. The fingers there closed too, just as tightly.

Abner chuckled. "Look at you, Chester, a fighter from day one." He kissed Alice. "You're absolutely right, he's perfect."

"He certainly is. Like you said, though, the world won't think so. That means we'll teach him to ignore the world and its wicked ways. As we well know, beauty—including character— dwells in the heart and soul, and we'll make sure Chester knows to ignore the cruel voices of a world gone to Hades."

Abner kissed his son's head. "You're right, Alice. He is perfect in every way."

Over their heads, the Wood Duck trembled, yet no gust of wind had shuddered the door.

Throughout the night, as her family dozed, Alice woke several times to wonder about the five tombstones. The one with the canoe and Labrador Retriever might be Chester's, but how far in the future had it been placed there? As dreadful as the thought was, she could see her and Abner having nothing but Beloved incised into it. No matter how hard she tried to recall the dream, it refused her, like a door slamming in her face to hide a secret.

The wind had calmed. The embers in the fireplace crackled. The lamp glowed with comfort. Chester nursed confidently. Abner slept the sleep of a loving father, a slight smile on his lips.

What a perfect life, an amazing life. As Alice caressed the dark fuzz on her son's head, then fingered the length of hair across her husband's forehead, blessed sleep took her.

Yes, she thought, *he is perfect in every way.*

And Then There Was She

Richmond, Virginia
1908

When Wilbur J. Applewhite proposed to Catherine T. Stanley of the Richmond, Virginia, Stanleys, he knew he would be marrying above his position. His mother, Elizabeth—Lizzie because she loved Jane Austen's *Pride and Prejudice*—taught literature in the county high school. His father, Theodore— Theo because he liked things concise—taught math and science at the same school.

Catherine's parents, however, enjoyed the rank of high society in Richmond's inner circles. Howard M. Mooney— Howard because the name had been passed down for several generations—owned one of the largest tobacco businesses in the east. Astoria—Astoria because she thought it sounded like royalty—did her utmost to carry out what she considered her duties as the wife of a wealthy man, which was simply to *appear* to be the wife of a wealthy man. Whenever she did this, by throwing expensive parties—soirees she called them—at their four-story mansion, Howard privately called her Ass instead of Astoria.

Sitting at the desk in his study, Wilbur couldn't imagine why he was thinking of his and Catherine's parents. Perhaps it was how they had gotten along amazingly well despite their societal differences. Perhaps it was how a sonless Howard had groomed Wilbur to run the family business. Perhaps it was how the Stanleys had invited his parents on a Mediterranean cruise last month in October, and the ship had sunk in the Atlantic in a hurricane, leaving him and Catherine as adult orphans without siblings, the owners of both the mansion and the business and wealthy beyond belief.

The tobacco in Wilbur's pipe no longer glowed. He lit a match and touched the flame to the bowl. After several satisfying puffs, he sipped thirty-year-old scotch from Howard's whiskey cabinet.

No, indeed, Wilbur couldn't imagine why he was thinking of his and Catherine's parents when she was upstairs in their bedroom with a doctor and a midwife, shrieking as if she were the hurricane that had sunk the ship with their parents on it.

He puffed and sipped, sipped and puffed, anxious about his wife's condition, despite his wife's condition.

"Must we have it?" she begged, two months after their honeymoon. "I'll either have none or a dozen. I don't care to have a dozen, so why start now?"

Wilbur noted how *we* had changed to *her*, or to be precise, *I*, meaning Catherine either wanted none or a dozen children, meaning she wanted none, meaning he wished they had discussed the subject before they married, because he wanted at least two, maybe three or four, but certainly not a dozen. After all, it was 1908, and certain things, like prophylactics, could control how many children a couple had.

Another hurricanish shriek—Wilbur knew what they sounded like from his and his dad's experience with one during a duck hunting trip to Corolla, North Carolina—came from upstairs, reverberating throughout the mansion and causing

Wilbur to strangle on a sip of scotch as he faced a streetside window. He sputtered and wiped his lips with a handkerchief from his pants pocket, sipped and puffed again. The shrieks weren't close enough to merit a baby anytime soon, so said his experience with his stillborn brother.

Missing his parents desperately, he watched a fine snow sift through the leafless limbs of the maples in the yard. His parents loved this time of year, including Thanksgiving, Christmas, and New Year's Day. Dad made sure to read *A Christmas Carol* by Charles Dickens at least once during the season, sometimes more. Mom made sure to do the same with the story of Christ's birth in Luke, from the Bible. Although they were academics, they were believers. Although Catherine didn't believe, she believed in nature, and this was why Wilbur, a believer like his parents, adored her.

They met in the spring of 1904. He was twenty-two, recently graduated with a degree in English literature. She was eighteen, starting college without knowing what to study. When he first saw her, she was studying a young man with a cigarette hanging from his plump lips. She was pinching a lit one between the index and middle fingers of her right hand, the hand to one side of her cheek, the other fingers folded to her palm, the wrist at the same angle as that of a hired waiter or waitress offering a tray with several glasses to a tuxedoed buffoon at one of Astoria's soirees.

Wilbur, done with a job interview for a teaching position at the same school where his parents taught, was strolling the banks of the James River. Catherine and the man were standing within a grove of pecan trees beside the roiling water, the leaves barely greening the branches. Sunlight pierced them and illuminated her hair, yellow and bobbed like one of those girls who danced the Grizzly Bear. It was an apt name for the situation, for Catherine let out a roar, slapped the man's face, kneed him in the crotch and, growling ferociously, snatched a dead limb from one of the pecan trees. As she raised it above the man's head, which he had conveniently lowered while he clutched his crotch and groaned pitifully, Wilbur ran to her and grabbed the branch before she could bash the man's brains out. "Whoa there," he said, huffing from his run, "you can't bash that man's brains out. You've already ruined his ability to father a child, isn't that enough?"

She jerked the branch, still held by Wilbur. "Gimme that. He deserves to have his brains bashed out for what he said."

Despite the chaotic scene, Wilbur admired her figure. Tall and slender and rounded, she fit the green, ankle-length dress perfectly. Along with it, she wore a white sweater for the cool spring day. He caught the faint hint of perfume, not the least bit hidden by cigarette smell. "Can you tell me what he said," he asked, "or is it too embarrassing? I don't care to embarrass a lady."

Still groaning and holding his crotch, the man twisted his head toward them. "She acts like she's all that. Says she's been to Greece."

"What's that got to do with it?" Wilbur asked.

Again, Catherine jerked the branch. "I said gimme. He asked if he could bugger me."

Wilbur knew that word from some of his English literature books. He faced the man. "Are you British?"

"I'm Greek."

Confusion found a home in Wilbur's brain. "Say what?"

Catherine jerked the branch again. "He says they do that in Greece. I told him we're in America, to forget it. He pressed the issue so I pressed *my* issue. I'm not doing *that* with any man."

"Have you known each other long?" Wilbur asked, not wanting to interject himself into a relationship.

"A day," the man said, easing himself upright.

"A day too much," Catherine said, jerking the branch again.

Wilbur stepped between the man and her. "Ma'am, we just met, and I already admire you in a million different ways. Please, if you drop this branch, I'd love to take you out to dinner."

"Good," the man said. "Maybe she'll let *you* bugger her."

In one smooth motion, Wilbur snatched the branch from Catherine and whirled around to bash the man's brains out. Unfortunately—or fortunately, depending on a person's perspective about murder—he only succeeded in knocking the man out, evidenced by his even breathing and the lack of brains protruding from beneath his thick mop of black hair as he lay in the grass beneath the pecan trees.

"I don't see any brains," Catherine said, stepping to Wilbur's side and peering down at the man. "Why aren't there any brains? I want brains. Can't you hit him again so I can have brains?"

Wilbur eyed her. "Wouldn't you rather have dinner with me?"

"We're in Virginia, we call it supper. Don't you like my drawl? Why don't you drawl? Say y'all. Can you say y'all?"

"I will at dinner. How about it?"

She looped her arm within his. Leading him away past the man, she kicked him in the ribs, grinned when he groaned, and smiled at Wilbur. "Dinner sounds wonderful, but only if you call it supper."

Gazing into the greenest eyes he had ever seen, Wilbur patted her hand. "Why, that sounds fine, y'all. Supper it is." He tried his best to say supper like she said supper, an extremely southern drawl of "sahppah." The word flowed thickly off his lips, as if each letter were molasses.

Again reverberating, this time a tad higher in pitch than a hurricane, Catherine shrieked. Wilbur glanced at his pocket watch. Seven minutes between contractions. He had a few minutes yet.

From the time he called Catherine "y'all" and dinner "sahppah," they met every few days, either strolling the banks of the James River, taking a drive into the country for a picnic, or making love in discrete locations at those two places. Lucky for Wilbur, a friend had suggested prophylactics, for Catherine's ardor was such that she hadn't seemed concerned about such things as limiting the number of children they might have, despite her insistence after their marriage on having none or a dozen.

On one of these afternoons, on a quilt in the shade of an oak at the edge of a field, as he lay with his head in her lap while she fed him strawberries, both naked after making love, she asked what he thought about the mountains instead of the ocean because he talked about it so much. Wilbur's first thought was how he had become accustomed to lying outdoors naked, having surpassed his believer's shame at lying outdoors naked, or just being naked around Catherine. His second thought was how his believer's attitude had eased concerning his guilt about making love, fornication as some called it, before marriage. His third thought was how their drive in the Blue Ridge Mountains two weekends ago had been wonderful, but he'd rather drive along the sandy road at Corolla, North Carolina, preferably to one of the hunt clubs where hunters took ducks and geese. He told Catherine this third thought. She preferred the mountains, the crisp air even during summer, the valleys, the waterfalls, the curving dirt roads, the country stores where one could get a bottle of pop and a bag of peanuts, bought from a snaggle-toothed old man in stained coveralls who winked at her. She also confessed to liking the mountains better than the ocean because of the time they had swam naked in a pool at the base of a waterfall, making love in the water after, this time without a prophylactic. This was when Wilbur fell in love with her love of nature, and he was determined to have her fall in love with his love of the ocean, particularly along the Outer Banks of North Carolina.

He planned to do this soon, but two months after they made love in the pool at the base of the waterfall, he had to drive her to a hospital on one of their dates. The doctor said it was a miscarriage. In tears, Wilbur asked why she hadn't told him she was pregnant. Not in tears, she said her math was terrible, meaning she hadn't missed missing her period. From then on until their honeymoon, after they were married in the spring of 1908, she made sure they used prophylactics and so did he, at least until she agreed to have the one child.

Thinking back on it now, as Wilbur took turns sipping scotch and puffing the pipe while listening for the next shriek, maybe the miscarriage was why she only wanted one child or a dozen, although it made no sense to him whatsoever because he was sure she wanted none. Also, maybe the trauma of the miscarriage was why she wanted to have the baby at home instead of at the hospital. He could certainly understand that.

The heavy footsteps of the heavy midwife thudded down the stairs. The doctor's shoes, for he was toothpick thin, didn't thud. Wilbur set the pipe in an ashtray on his desk, downed the scotch, and hurried toward the stairs as the midwife appeared, chest heaving. "It's time, Mr. Applewhite," she said, wheezing cigarette breath in his face.

He followed her up the stairs, wondering why the shrieking had stopped. The midwife had given no hint, but her tone had been positive. She stopped several times to catch her breath, grasping the banister and leaning over to pant like an asthmatic dog Wilbur once had. Mom said the dog had asthma. Dad said she fed the dog too many sweets. Their neighbor, a farm veterinarian who specialized in dairy cows and draft horses, flatly stated the dog, a bowlegged dachshund, was the fattest dog he had ever seen.

When Wilbur entered the bedroom, the doctor smiled, evidenced by his walrus moustache curving upward. "Applewhite, Applewhite," he said, waving a bony hand toward the bed. "Everything is fine, come see."

Wilbur went to search the covers. Sweat covered Catherine's face to the point of not beading, a sheen of wetness illuminated by the chandelier overhead. She was as wet as that time in the pool beneath the waterfall. Her complexion, red as the proverbial beet, was splotched with white. She grasped his arm. "Did you hear me screaming? I told you none or a dozen when I really meant none. Why didn't we talk about this more before we got married? Is it too late now?"

Wilbur refused to reply. She tended toward drama, having acted in several plays as a child. "Where's the baby?" he begged. "I don't see a baby. Where's the baby?" This was the first time he realized they had repeating sentences in common, like she had done with the Greek man and his brains, and he fell out of love with her the tiniest bit because he hated repeating things.

She drew back the covers to reveal a tiny baby swaddled in a blanket, saying it was a girl. "Oh," Wilbur said, a soft sound that was hardly more than a puff of air.

Yellow fuzz graced her head. An upturned nose graced her face. Hints of dimples decorated the corners of her mouth. Either that or she didn't care for breast milk.

"Oh," Wilbur puffed again. "Oh, isn't she so … so … so …" He realized, despite all the books he had read and loved, or read and disliked, he couldn't find the words to describe the overwhelming sense of astonishment that flooded his heart.

The tiny fingers closed and opened, closed and opened. He offered his right pinky to her right hand, and she clutched it tightly.

"Oh," Wilbur said again. "I'm your daddy, and I love you very, very much." He kissed Catherine's forehead. "And I love Mommy very, very much too."

"Mommy is *not* very happy," Catherine groaned. "I hurt all over and I never want to make love again."

The midwife clucked her tongue. The doctor chuckled. "Oh, you'll be up to that in no time." He chuckled once more. "In no time at all."

Wilbur knelt by the bed and kissed his daughter's cheek. Out of thin—or perhaps salty—air, the beach at Corolla gifted him a name. "Maurea … Maurea Lynn Applewhite," he crooned. "A Maurea is a type of sea snail with a spiral shell that will protect you for all of your life, sweetheart." He kissed her again, feeling so profound a love he thought he would die. "And then there was she," he said softly, barely saying it at all.

Happy with the birth, the doctor packed his bag. *Two fine parents and a fine baby girl,* he thought. *It doesn't get any better than this.*

The midwife placed several bloody rags in a basin. *One good parent and one bad,* she thought. *It doesn't get any worse than this.*

Wilbur kissed Maurea's cheek again. *Wealth and position have ruined many a child,* he thought, *but I won't let it ruin my Maurea.*

Catherine frowned at the silly name her husband had given his daughter. *If it's the last thing I do,* she thought, *I'll make him pay for this.*

Puckering at the sour taste of hot milk in her mouth, Maurea vomited. If she could've formed a thought or thoughts within her brand new brain, it would've been this: *Who is this woman? Why did she frown at me before that handsome man who smells of scotch and pipe tobacco came up the stairs? I'm their new daughter, so why doesn't she love me like he loves me?*

Tentatively, gradually, she grew used to the milk. Her heart beat solidly within the tiny chest. Her blood coursed decisively within the veins and arteries.

And the last thing she felt and heard before her eyes closed in sleep was her papa's lips kissing her forehead and him whispering sweetly, "Maurea, my darling Maurea. And then there was she."

She Should've Died

Port-au-Prince, Haiti
1908

The woman waiting near the docks was born without a name. Beside her, wearing a wrinkled white dress to her ankles, the white as dingy as the gray sky spitting rain, her companion, Lovely, ran a hand over her rounded belly. It was eight months after the rape, so they needed to be as far away as possible from the coffee plantation and the Creole excuse of a man who had forced himself on Lovely.

Two cloth bags at their feet held all their possessions. A rusted tin box in the pocket of the woman's dress held all their money. Two hearts held the hopes of finding a land to live where workers were treated better than both here and in Africa, where their ancestors were enslaved, seemingly since time began.

The woman tucked the loose end of the cloth wrapped around Lovely's head. If not, if her curls fell across her shoulders and down her back, some man might snatch her away, despite the child waiting to be born.

Milling around the women, the mix of Creole and non-Creole people stopped and studied the ship. This was better than looking at Lovely. Of Creole birth, her light skin, high forehead, and green eyes, along with a Spanish nose and high cheekbones, might make one of the men ask her to marry him. The woman, being Lovely's aunt, resembled her in a way, and she had often used her appearance to gain favors at the plantation. She had done so with the Creole who had raped Lovely, which made the situation even more disgusting. The plantation owner lived in England, leaving his taskmaster to run everything. In the case of the female workers at the plantation, the Creole bastard had ruined them.

Although he had bided his time with Lovely, he had known her as an infant. Ten years old at the time, present at her birth with the woman as the midwife to her sister, Hazel, he had named her Lovely, and a dying Hazel hadn't objected. The woman saw no harm in it, having yet to gain a favor from anyone. Regardless, she began to practice voodoo in her spare time, a rarity on a coffee plantation. Now, instead of favors, she preferred the suffering of those who would harm her. In her estimation, almost everyone wanted to harm someone.

A man and a woman, both astride donkeys with huge baskets on their sides, went by. The first donkey raised its tail, and several clods of manure thudded to the wooden planks. The second donkey did nothing.

A gust of wind rattled the ship's rigging. The name on the bow, *Promise*, was likely a lie. In the woman's experience, both women and men, whether poor or wealthy, whether plantation owners or not, lied every chance they got. Lying wasn't a sin she aspired to, although revenge was.

In a way, she hated Lovely for killing her own mother and the woman's sister. In a way, she didn't. Hazel had slept with whoever she could regardless of how well she lived. Their former taskmaster, a man from Australia, gave her money and food and even set her up in the best shanty on the plantation. It wasn't enough for Hazel, who worked in town at night as a prostitute. "I'll get rich and run my own plantation," she often said. It had taken her death and sixteen years to find her money, hidden beneath a loose floorboard that had shifted beneath the woman's knees as she searched under the bed for one of her sandals yesterday. Now, not only could she leave Haiti, she could get Lovely away from that Creole bastard who had raped her and gotten her with child.

Aboard the ship, several men in dark pants and dingy white shirts lowered a walkway. At the top, a man in blue uniform pants and a white shirt took money from passengers and shoved it into a cloth sack. When he told the woman the amount, she plopped both fares into his hand. Satisfied, he shoved the money into the sack, and she and Lovely followed the other passengers along the deck and down a set of steps. Below the hull, in a shadowed hall, a man showed them their quarters.

Her and Lovely's room, little more than a closet with bunk beds, stank of rum and sweat. Lovely set her bag on the lower bunk. The corn husk mattress rattled, scaring a huge rat out of a hole in the end. Wide eyed, Lovely screamed, and the rat scampered into a hole in a dark corner.

The woman lit an oil lamp hanging from a wall. They had no window and no chairs. At least a short ladder would help her into the upper bunk. Lovely, over her fright, lay on the bunk, the corn husks crackling. "How long will it take to get there, Aunt?"

The woman didn't mind Lovely calling her Aunt, especially in English. She despised Haiti and anything to do with it, her reason for teaching Lovely English. She couldn't have taken being called Mother. Mother meant Hazel, and Hazel had been the daughter of the devil himself.

"I don't know where *there* is," she said, her tone aggravated. "I don't know where this ship will stop. I *do* know I want us to go farther than Florida."

"What other states are there?" Lovely asked innocently.

"I only know as far as North Carolina." The woman paused. "That might be far enough."

Lovely stood from the bunk. "I need to pee."

The woman pointed toward a brass pot in a corner. The lamp's orange light barely glinted off it. "That's a spittoon," she said. "Do your business there." The woman climbed the ladder to her own crackling corn husk mattress.

Lovely returned to the bunk. "What do you know about North Carolina, Aunt?"

"I know it doesn't have a Creole bastard in it."

"Besides that?"

"I know you're too old to ask so many questions. Try to rest."

"It's just midday."

"Try anyway."

The corn husk mattress crunched as Lovely lay down again. The woman listened to the thud of footsteps outside the door and overhead, to the murmur of voices in the rooms flanking this one, to the cry of sea gulls growing louder and then fading as they moved across the sky. She dozed off and on, rose to use the spittoon and dozed again.

The next time she woke, the room listed to the right. They must be in the open ocean, the wind billowing the sails, Haiti at their backs.

From the bag at the foot of her bunk, she took out a voodoo doll. Sewing a black hat to its head, she smiled at the resemblance to their taskmaster, the Creole bastard. She took out a second doll, this one incomplete. She had considered making it resemble the plantation owner in England, or at least his clothing, which might work. Instead, she might make it resemble Lovely. Her niece had too many of Hazel's ways. The woman put this doll away and took out one of two long hatpins, stolen from an English lady one day in Port-au-Prince years ago. She lay the Creole bastard on the bed, drew back the pin, and stabbed it through his chest. Whether it worked or not, she didn't care. The satisfaction of doing it was enough. With Lovely, however, if her doll didn't work, a knife to the throat or a shove over the ship's rail, no doubt, would work. The key was if she asked too many questions during the voyage.

The *Promise* stopped in the Florida Keys for provisions. The woman and Lovely stayed below, taking food in their room when it was offered. No one offered to empty the stinking spittoon, so the woman dumped it over the stern when needed.

On one of these trips, an Englishman, evidenced by his strong accent, wished her good day and asked her business. She replied her business was none of his and asked why, curious why he asked.

"I was wondering about your attire, specifically why you wrap your head like an Arab. I also wonder why that enormous hat pin is sticking out of it." He paused. His brown eyes searched her face. "You're very dark. Are you from Africa by chance? I've always wanted to visit but haven't gotten around to it, don't you know."

The woman asked if he was married and had a family. She didn't care to ruin a family. He said no to both questions. That night she sewed a piece of white cloth to the Creole doll to make it appear like the Englishman's suit and stabbed it with the hat pin. The next morning, as she dumped the pot over the stern, she overheard someone saying the Englishman died in the night, possibly from a heart attack, so a supposed doctor had said.

Nodding with satisfaction at the deaths of both the Englishman and the Creole bastard, she returned to the room and continued to sew on the Lovely voodoo doll. She might not need it or she might, but it didn't hurt to have it ready. She also cut the stitches on the Creole bastard doll to make a smaller one. If the baby cried as much as Lovely talked, it might need a hat pin through its chest too. This went against her feelings in a way. She loved babies, but only quiet ones. Perhaps Lovely's baby would be a quiet one. They needed something fresh and new to begin what she hoped would be their equally fresh and new lives in America.

In South Carolina, the *Promise* let passengers both off and on. Lovely joined the woman at the stern, where they watched Charleston fade to a pinpoint. In Norfolk, Virginia, the woman asked a passenger what the smallest town on the coast of North Carolina was, not mentioning her hate for large cities like Norfolk and Port-au-Prince, where people like that Englishman were too nosy for their own good. The passenger suggested Corolla, then suggested a ride there on a fishing vessel, which would take something called the Intracoastal Waterway to the Currituck Sound and Corolla. The woman led Lovely to a decrepit dock to a decrepit vessel to a decrepit two-man crew. The dock's half-rotten boards creaked and sank with their footsteps. The vessel's white paint was peeling. The oily-haired men swallowed tobacco juice instead of spitting it over the side. A fair amount of the brown liquid stained their beards.

Hour after hour, the boat's diesel engine thrummed while the stinking exhaust threatened nausea. Black water passed to each side. Turtles sunned on logs. The men ate saltine crackers and something called Vienna Sausages from tin cans. They washed the bites down with swallows of beer from brown bottles. The woman and Lovely nibbled the offered saltine crackers but didn't drink the offered beer for fear of not having a place to pee. The men did have the courtesy to pee on the other side of the boat's wheelhouse, evidenced by how their streams of urine dribbled into the black water, followed by their zippers zipping.

Finally, at a dock within sight of a red-brick lighthouse, the women left the vessel. Before the vessel left, the woman asked the men the directions to the nearest church, and both men pointed. Seeing Lovely's condition, the pastor offered them the use of a one-room home a half-mile north of the lighthouse, saying he would only charge fifty cents a month rent, including wood for the pot-bellied stove. Grateful for his kindness, the woman gave him enough money for a year, asked where she could buy food, and thanked him when he directed her to the general store.

Only when the door of the house had closed, the stove had warmed them, a counter had held canned vegetables, a loaf of bread, a pail of water from a well, and they observed two beds on the floor instead of two bunk beds, did they take time to relax.

"Thank goodness," Lovely said, dropping to the bed.

The woman agreed. "How do you feel? Any pains yet?"

"Do they have any doctors here? It's 1908, shouldn't they have doctors here? This place is like a desert, just some crooked trees and water on both sides. I doubt they have doctors here."

The woman considered the Lovely voodoo doll in her bag. "I helped your mother have you. I can help you."

"She died. That's not helping."

The woman considered the doll again. Then she realized the baby would need to be weaned before she used the hat pin on Lovely, and weaning would take at least a year. "Your mother wasn't healthy and you are. You'll be fine." The woman didn't add the rest: *If you stop talking so much.*

That night, after a meal of canned beans and slices of bread toasted in a pan on the pot-bellied stove, Lovely woke to say her water had broken. In the excitement of leaving Haiti, along with the ship and fishing vessel journeys, the woman thought she might've miscalculated the time they had been on the Atlantic and the Currituck. Regardless, the baby would be born on this frigid night, the wind whistling in those crooked-limbed trees surrounding the house, the smell of woodsmoke seeping from a crack in the woodstove's piping.

The woman ripped up an old dress and lay out a length of string for the umbilical cord, added water to an ancient cast-iron pot, blackened with age, and sterilized everything like she had before Hazel gave birth to Lovely.

The woman returned to bed. Lovely rose on her elbows and glared at her, black ringlets cascading down her back. "Are you going to let me die like you let my mother die?"

Grateful for only one sentence instead of several, the woman rolled over on the pillow to face the stunning face, illuminated by the yellow glow of an oil lamp on the table, where they had left their canned food and packages of bread. "You just started your labor. You'll wake me when it's close."

"How will I wake you if I'm asleep?"

"Are you having pains yet?"

"No."

"You will."

"When?"

"Maybe tonight. Maybe tomorrow. It's not the same for everyone."

"How long did it take for my mother?"

The woman eyed the head of the hat pin in her head wrap, on the same table as their food and the lamp. "You talk too much and I need to rest. You need to rest too. You're going to need your strength to push the baby out."

Lovely dropped to the pillow. Her well-defined lips, the lips of her Spanish ancestors, pushed in and out, in and out, the same lips that likely had intrigued the Creole bastard. "I wonder if she'll look like me."

The woman clenched her teeth. "You don't want a girl. A girl might look like you. A girl like you will be trouble."

"Why?"

"You're too beautiful. That's why the Creole took you. That's why I took you away from Haiti. If you have a daughter that looks like you, she'll make men do things they normally wouldn't. You don't want that."

"It's not a woman's fault when men do things they shouldn't." Lovely paused, as if recalling something. "My mother made her own misery. That's what you told me."

"She did. She used her beauty as a weapon against weak men for their money."

"You call it a weapon. I call it being smart."

"Being dead isn't smart. Do you want to die like she did, before it's your time?"

The wind whistled in the trees. The smoke puffed from the crack in the stove's piping. Lovely said nothing.

"Well?" the woman asked.

"I think you killed her," Lovely said.

"Go to sleep."

"I think you killed her."

The woman eyed the hat pin. "Go to sleep."

The green eyes closed. Beneath the white nightgown, the small bosom, now swollen from the pregnancy, soon rose and fell with the rhythm of sleep.

The woman envied Lovely. Given the right circumstances, she could be a queen in some distant land. Perhaps they could better their circumstances in America, perhaps not. The most important thing was to leave Haiti.

The woman rose to pee in a white chamber pot in a corner. The pastor hadn't mentioned it, but its use, evidenced by brown stains inside and the faint smell, was obvious. There was an outhouse tucked behind this house in the trees. Maybe the chamber pot was for when it was cold or raining.

She slept in fits and starts, awakened by the combined sounds of the whistling wind and the clattering of tree branches. If she listened—really listened—she could imagine the screams of other women in labor this night. Those women might be rich or poor, near or far. Their babies might affect each other, or they might not. Lovely's baby might even affect them, although there was no way to know how.

Yes, those babies born this night might have untold effects on each other, the woman knew. The question was whether she would be alive to see them. It was even possible, remotely as it may seem, for some or all of them to die and be buried on this very strip of North Carolina sand called the Outer Banks.

The thought made her shiver. As she did, Lovely bolted upright in bed, eyes wide like twin moons. "What did you tell me about death?" she blurted. "Something about voodoo."

The woman frowned in disgust. Lovely rarely asked concise questions. "What do you mean exactly?"

"How to predict when you might die."

"It's not Haitian. An American said a person might feel a chill if an animal walked across the place where you would be buried."

Lovely shivered. She rubbed her arms. "A chill woke me. Two of them. I think that means an animal walked over the place where my child and I will be buried."

Within the continuous whistling of the wind, a sudden gust blew down the stovepipe. Acting like a bellows, it pulsed the glowing embers, visible through two holes near the top, like a pair of demon eyes.

The woman shivered but said nothing, yet fear twisted her guts. Not only had that animal walked across the two graves of Lovely and her baby, it had walked across hers.

They returned to their pillows. Moments passed. The woman faced the window to look for the sunrise in the blackest night she had ever seen, even blacker than when Hazel died. Never had a night lasted so long.

Lovely cried out. The woman threw Lovely's blanket back and raised the wick on the lamp, held it high and gasped. Hazel's sins had cursed them all. The top of the baby's head, covered in dark hair like the mother's, was visible between those two long legs, and without the first hint of pain except for that single cry. In a gush of blood, the baby burst from the birth canal. Lovely, her back arched upward with effort, collapsed to the bed. "Is she alive? Why isn't she crying?"

The woman cut the cord and tied it, then cleaned the baby with the strips of the torn dress. *She should've died,* she thought. *She's exactly like her mother, and she will hunt men exactly like Hazel hunted men. She should've died.*

When she started to place her palm over the mouth and nose of the squirming bundle, now wrapped in a sheet, the baby let go with a pitiful wail, prompting tears from the woman's eyes—tears and pity. She placed the baby within Lovely's arms. "You have a fine daughter. She's the image of her mother."

"I'll name her Mirlande," Lovely said. "Mirlande means—"

"I know what it means," the woman said. "It means 'wonderful.'" *But I doubt this is the case with this one.*

By the light of the rising sun, surprised by snow covering the ground, the woman burned the bloody rags and afterbirth, then scrambled eggs. Every so often she watched Lovely and the baby. Cuddled in her loving embrace, snuffling and rooting like a piglet, Mirlande nursed greedily.

Outside, the woman dumped the chamber pot in the outhouse. Although those crooked trees, stooped with their reaching claw-limbs as if seeking a throat to strangle surrounded her, beams of yellow light streamed down from the east, illuminating a thin layer of snow now sparkling on the sand.

Yes, it may be a new day, but it was the same old story for Hazel and Lovely—and now Mirlande.

She should've died.

Always Looking Back

As I wrote this book, I often wondered what readers would think of the three main characters after learning how they came into the world. Chester, of course, had a rough start in life, but his parents would lead him along the best path possible. Maurea's path, as you've read, is bound to take several twists and turns. Mirlande's path, though, is not the least bit normal, but despite how things seem for her, her mother had a good heart.

Now, since I'm familiar with this story, it was a shock to hear of Maurea Applewhite moving to Aydlett, North Carolina, in the later years of her life. Then, when I heard she had bought land on the shores of the Currituck Sound and built a house almost directly across from Corolla, my shock disappeared.

She moved to Aydlett and built the house on the shores of the Currituck to be as close to Chester as possible, but not so close she would have to face her part in his story.

And here's where we learn who she has become eighty-three years after the murders in the Corolla Island boathouse. Then, after this chapter, we'll learn the same thing about Chester.

By the way, to help readers keep up with the story, which is extremely important, all the chapters with the 103-year-old versions of Chester and Maurea, except the next to the last one, will be entitled *Irene*, and you'll find out why in the first chapter with that name. Most of the other chapters will be about

Chester, Maurea, and Mirlande's youth, as well as their interactions over the years. We'll also take side trips into the points of view of other pertinent characters with parts in this tragedy, including my great-great grandfather, so please pay attention. You don't want to miss a thing.

It's the fall of 2011. Standing in the marsh on the western shore of the Currituck Sound, Maurea Lynn Applewhite rubs the fluff from a cattail head. She studies it for a moment, pinches the silky material between her fingertips, and presses it to her cheek. When memories become too clear, she raises her hand and flicks the bits of downy white into the breeze.

With a hazy burst of recognition, she realizes it's August. She'll be 103 come November, not that it matters. Waiting is all she's done for most of her life.

Warm and sticky from the humidity, her underarms are smelly and sour. Cool and wet from the sound, her toes wiggle in the muck. Hot and uncomfortable from the midday sun, the wide-brimmed hat should've been left in the house.

Perched on a bobbing cattail stalk, a Red-winged Blackbird calls its shrill *kree-kree, kree-kree, kree-kree,* yet another memory to burn within the fading embers of her mind.

Out on the rippling waters of the Currituck, a fisherman in a skiff pulls crab pots.

This isn't another memory to burn. That would be the boy on his dock, the boards gray and twisted with age, his pet pelican, Pete, perched on the last piling to the right. The boy's black hair fell across his large forehead and shined in the morning sun. His blue coveralls hung on his stick-thin frame. Like the rest of him, his bare feet, having absorbed ten years' worth of North Carolina summers, were tanned almost bronze.

He pulled a single crab pot from the sound. Water dripped from the wire mesh as he dumped the scuttling blue creatures into a pail, their claws waving defiantly. Seeing Maurea threading cattail stalks on the path along the sound from where Corolla Island would be built years later, he raised his deformed hand—and burst into a trillion bits of ash. They clouded the air, swirled around Pete. Then they formed a waterspout, until individual bits of ash broke away to rise into the sky to blend with the blue and disappear, followed by the rest. Yes, this scene, like those ashes, are another trillion bits of memories to burn within the fading embers of her mind.

Although other memories are present, they simply smolder, for she can picture these without excessive regret: a green canoe cutting the Currituck; a Wood Duck decoy hanging over a bed; a flight of snow geese on a winter day, their wings swirling snow as they came in for a landing, their webbed feet touching down, their wakes cresting behind them, their incessant honking. She can bear other memories too, but to think of too many at once creates a hole in her heart, where the waterfall of her life crashes into the pool of her sorrow. Eventually, maybe that waterfall will drown those embers, if only to allow her some peace. Only death will do that, though, and even then she isn't sure.

Behind her and the four acres she bought twenty years ago, her closest neighbor's lawn mower roars into life. Minutes later, the scent of mown grass blends with the breeze. She should've bought ten acres, fifty, a hundred. Neighbors are fine until they gossip, and she's sure they gossip about her.

"I think so," Velma Morefield would say, holding her toy poodle while whispering to Terry Bloom. "I looked it up on the library PC."

Terry, her pink nails freshly manicured, snorts. "When did you start calling the library computer a PC? Are you trying to become knowledgeable, Velma? You'll never become knowledgeable in Aydlett. We're too laid back to become knowledgeable."

The poodle yips at a squirrel climbing a tree. Terry loves squirrels. She has posts around her back yard with platforms holding ears of dried corn for them to eat. She does it as a pastime since Harold died. He enjoyed his pellet gun, so she does it to spite him.

Velma hates squirrels. They get into her garden. She was having an affair with Harold, who left her his pellet gun. She would shoot the squirrels off their ears of corn if she could, but her retired arms aren't strong enough to cock the thing. Cackling insanely, she aims an arthritic middle finger at Blue Hair Terry. "How's my sign language, you old bag? I learned that on the library's PC too."

Terry's cackle joins Velma's. "Not bad, not bad. I know that sign myself." She glances around conspiratorially. "I think so too. Quite the uproar for Corolla and Currituck County in 1928, don'tcha know. That Chester Pinkham murdering those two people."

"How do you know he did it?" Velma says, petting Pissy Lou's head. She got the poodle's name from when Pissy gets excited during thunderstorms and pees in Velma's lap. Velma now makes her wear diapers when a cloud comes up.

"I'm just repeating what the library PC said." Terry smirks. "I go to the library too, don'tcha know."

Velma thinks Terry's vocabulary should be good enough to not say 'don'tcha know" all the time if she visits the library. Like her friend did a minute ago, she looks around conspiratorially.

"I think the Applewhite woman's mother did it. That's what I think."

"You've got a point," Terry says. "Proud families and all. Money and wealth, don'tcha know. I bet that mother was a proud one, all right. Didn't think her poo smelled like other folks' poo. You know how it is."

Velma holds in a grin, glad to not hear another "don'tcha know" after her friend's last "don'tcha know." "I know *exactly* how it is." She pauses. "Don'tcha know."

Maurea turns to face her twenty acres, wooded except for the one acre with her home on it. No one mows grass. No one gossips. She's not sure if she has Alzheimer's or not. Her doctor in Elizabeth City says she's as fit as the proverbial fiddle, might even live to 110. She considers him a quack.

Maybe her longevity is because of her routine. Walking three miles a day every day, barring weather, for seventy years, might help her heart. Plinking at squirrels with her .22 pistol since she moved here, missing on purpose of course, might help her concentration. Taking out her kayak every afternoon, barring weather also, might help her wind.

She wades from the sound. At the house, she uses the garden hose to rinse the stinky muck from her feet. Inside, she makes a turkey sandwich, pours white wine, and sits at the patio table on the front porch, which faces the Currituck. On the table, a pair of binoculars waits for rain. Without rain, she can't bear to study the Currituck Lighthouse's red brick form. Regardless, even with the binoculars, even on a clear day, it's only a shimmering tower in the distance. That's what she gets for buying low power binoculars on purpose. It's the same for the yellow exterior of Corolla Island, now the Whalehead Club. As she's discovered over the years, looking at things too clearly leads to clarity, and too much clarity leads to sleepless nights and lighting cigarettes one after another. It also leads to empty bottles of wine, and she gave up binging on cigarettes and wine in her forties.

The afternoon lingers. The sun pulses heat from the center of the sky. Instead of one Red-winged Blackbird, two bob on cattail stalks. They refuse to call because the heat has drained them of their voices. Sweat trickles from beneath Maurea's underarms. She forgot deodorant this morning, evidenced by the odor. It isn't like she was going to the grocery today, or to the Grandy Greenhouse for a frozen yogurt with peaches mixed in, what they call a "Flurry." She licks her lips at the thought but doesn't get up. "Clean your plate," Mother demands. "Your father doesn't buy food so Cook can throw it in the waste bin."

Maurea finishes the turkey sandwich, gulping the wine after. In the kitchen, she refills the glass and takes a pack of cigarettes and a lighter from her purse. On the porch again, she lights the cigarette and watches the tip glow red as her lungs fill. Cancer would be a relief, a stroke a miracle. Not a heart attack, though. She's had enough heartache to last an eternity. Not Alzheimer's either. No lingering death for her. Make it quick, clean, and painful. She laughs at the idiocy of her drunken idea. Cancer and strokes aren't necessarily quick and clean, nor is Alzheimer's. Laughter is what a third bottle of wine does for her—everything is funny whether it is or not. Her life isn't funny, not a single minute of it.

Three times she tried marriage. Whether she loved those men or not didn't matter. Whether they were after her dowry or not didn't matter. After Mother blessedly committed suicide in 1979 at the age of seventy-three, Maurea's last husband, Alexander, had definitely been after the inheritance. Papa, having had oral cancer from his pipe habit and liver issues from his whiskey habit—no doubt from dealing with Mother for all those years—died in his sleep in 1969 at age sixty-three. Mother had been off on one of her flings. Maurea could've shot her for it. Suicide by pistol was fitting. Maurea didn't attend the funeral, although perhaps she should've. Bringing someone into the world is important. The realization of guilt is important. Forgiveness is important too, but Maurea ran out forgiveness for her mother a long time ago.

She fills another glass, lights another cigarette. Sweet wine hides the bitterness of life. Smoke hides the bitterness of regret. One day, like with Mother, a bullet might hide it all.

Leander, Maurea's first try at marriage, which took place in 1938, lasted three months. Love cannot be shared when its first kiss lingers. He was a gentle soul like Chester, but Leander couldn't handle the long absences, nor the drinking. A non-smoker, one of the reasons she married him, he couldn't handle her smoking either. "Why are you smoking?" he asked, lying back on his pillow after their first failed attempt at relations on the first night of their honeymoon at Nags Head. " You never smoked before."

Standing by the window, beyond which the Atlantic roiled and churned beneath the sliver of a fingernail moon, Maurea refused to face him. Why face someone who called sex "relations?" For her, sex, except for one night, had never related to anyone. It was a physical act perpetuated by the drive for either progeny or pleasure, both of which she would never experience again.

Leander crossed his arms. Maurea knew this without facing him. He and Mother shared that habit and she despised it. Chester never did it, so why should Leander? She took a long drag from the cigarette. Her exhale battered the glass, spread like blue silk over a bed beneath a Wood Duck decoy. "It's sex, Leander. Just call it what it is."

"I thought you were a virgin. Why is there no blood on the sheets?"

Leander considered virginity a treasure to withhold until love. Or had he said marriage? In their case, no treasure had revealed itself. "I might've lied," Maurea said, hating that part of Mother in her. Mother lied at will, or whenever she felt like it, which was constantly. Feigning guilt, she returned to bed. Feigning drowsiness, Leander rolled over and turned the lamp off. Feigning fairness, the divorce lawyers talked both parties into signing a no-fault decree.

The second man to attempt to steal her heart from the past, John lasted two years, four months, three days, seven hours, and thirty-two seconds. His reason was simple. He wanted a family and she didn't. Well, she had lied about that too, for she *couldn't* have a family. Specifically, she couldn't have children, meaning she couldn't have babies, meaning she couldn't get pregnant. Rather, she could get pregnant but she would miscarry at three months on the dot. Something her doctor said about a previous procedure bungling her plumbing. He thought he had a sense of humor. He did not.

Given the chance, John might've made a good father. He took the chance with another woman, prompting the divorce. Maurea signed the no-fault decree regardless.

Above the cattails at the edge of the Currituck, a single dragonfly hovers and then flits away, likely to ensnare a mosquito for supper. In the pine tags at the edge of the yard, a single cricket starts to chirp its evening song. Beyond the eastern horizon, above the entire strip of sand called the Outer Banks, the sky transforms from azure overhead, to purple further down, to indigo blue, to—

In the pouch beneath Maurea's right eye, a single tear pools.

She misses Papa. Doctors say Alzheimer's patients retain long term memories. Is it possible to retain them from birth? Like that dragonfly, *And then there was she* hovers and flits within her mind. Throughout his life his voice carried the warmth of love and acceptance despite her faults. Sweet like molasses but not too thick of a southern accent, it comforted her on many a night: "Buck up, Little Snail. You've got to have a thicker shell than that. Life's too short for regrets. Things work out for the best, you know. Chester made his choice and you've got to make yours. I wish all that had never happened, horrible to think of it. Life moves on whether we want it to or not. You'll be good as new in no time."

He could never comfort himself when Mother went off on one of her flings. Although Maurea tried to help him and herself, she never knew if she helped him or not. As far as comforting herself, she knew she was a lost cause.

After the nightmare at Corolla, he stayed busy at work, returning to the business of tobacco. Waterfowl hunting lost its appeal. He still enjoyed nature, but not on the Outer Banks.

In the spring, summer, or fall, whenever a fling possessed Mother, he and Maurea might lower the top on the 1930 Buick Phaeton, its paint a sandy beige, and take turns driving to the Blue Ridge Mountains from Richmond. Day trips included scrambled egg and bacon sandwiches cooked at home and eaten on the road, washed down with swallows of fresh-squeezed orange juice from a Mason jar. As the hours passed, with views of blue peaks and misty valleys, they stopped for a picnic lunch beside gurgling brooks, where sunlight shimmered on water-wet stones. This menu might contain leftovers from a previous supper, pridefully created by Cook: ham or turkey sandwiches, fried chicken or roast beef, each enjoyed with potato salad, their favorite, followed with banana pudding or blackberry cobbler, if in season. Naps while serenaded with the crooning babble of one of those brooks might follow, though sometimes they might hike a trail to a waterfall. If it were summer, swimsuits would allow an icy dip in the pool at the bottom of a waterfall. By the end of these day trips, the sun would've kissed their cheeks golden. Weary from their activities, the drive home at dusk left them yawning and talking to keep awake.

Weekend trips were similar, except they would stop in towns tucked into valleys and hollows and look for antique furniture. If they found a piece, they would admire it for a while and drive to the next place. The house was full of the stuff, so why buy more? Picnics followed. If they found a brook with someone fly fishing, they enjoyed the skill, maybe offered the angler a sandwich, and went on their way. Nights were the best, especially in spring. If it didn't rain, they slept in hammocks strung between trees. If it rained, they slept in the car, serenaded by the dull thud of the drops striking the cloth roof.

To Maurea, except for her days spent at Corolla before everything went so terribly wrong, the times with Papa were the best of her life. As far as she was concerned, Mother could have fling after fling and never return, because Papa had found happiness in another woman's arms.

Like a black silk coverlet, darkness spreads over the endless expanse of the Currituck. The single cricket beneath the pines is joined by a veritable chorus of crickets. The breeze shifts, lapping waves against the cattails, whisperings of long gone days never to return.

When the lights of Corolla and Duck wink on, including those sparkling pinpoints over twenty miles south to the Wright Memorial Bridge, where vehicle headlights shine their way both to and from the Outer Banks, Maurea watches through slitted eyes. No, she can't see all those lights, but she can imagine them—imagine the children who can't wait for the beach, the adults who can't wait for vacation, the business owners who can't wait to share tourism's profits, both in Currituck and Dare Counties.

To think she missed the Wright Brothers first flight by being born five years too late saddens her. "On this day," history might've said, "December 7, 1903, at 10:35 on a blustery morning, Maurea Lynn Applewhite was present." Perhaps she could've been their assistant, delving into the innards of the Wright Flyer's engine, or designing its wooden frame, or sewing the cloth covering its wings, or stringing the wire holding it all together.

What a remarkable time to be alive, yet she has been alive at other remarkable times, some tragic, some equally remarkable.

Of course, as always for Maurea, tragedy is her constant companion. She was eight when the United States entered World War I—known as The Great War back then—in 1917, nine when the Spanish Flu struck. To a degree, both were offset when women gained the right to vote in 1919, and when Amelia Earhart became the first woman to fly solo across the Atlantic in 1932. Then those positives were offset with the negative of the Japanese bombing Pearl Harbor on December 7, 1941, and the United States joining World War II the next day.

At thirty-three-years old then, Maurea, with patriotic fervor, went to airplane mechanic's school. Papa, even at fifty-eight, wanted to join the war effort, so he retooled the business to make airplane parts. Mother, of course, took no interest in such things, her interest being to continue flings.

When the war ended, Maurea married John. When John ended, she returned home to Papa and the Blue Ridge. When Papa died, she met Alexander. When Mother put a bullet through her brain, she married Alexander. When Alexander ended, she sold the business, shared the inheritance with Papa's mistress, and built her home in Aydlett—by hand—by herself— even the wiring and plumbing—although a man had to bore the well and install the septic system.

She took to fishing the Currituck, bought a skiff and a twenty-five horsepower Mercury outboard for it, went for flounder and trout for supper. Tomatoes and lettuce and cucumbers from her garden made delicious tossed salads. White wine, of course, made for delicious beverages, followed by a single after-supper cigarette on the porch.

The darkness continues to embrace the Currituck. One by one, the crickets stop chirping. Sometimes later—Maurea doesn't know when due to dozing—she considers going for a drive to the Outer Banks. Once a month, midmornings usually, sometimes at sunrise, she does so now. The Buick's tires thump across the expansion joints on the Wright Memorial Bridge. Its beige hood rises and falls like a galloping Spanish Mustang. These drives include visits to burgeoning shops and restaurants, needed for the equally burgeoning tourist trade.

On occasion, when her mind wanders, she ends up at the ferry terminal to Ocracoke Island. Kitty Hawk, Kill Devil Hills, and Nags Head passed with notice. The Bodie Island Lighthouse and Oregon Inlet did not. Sometimes she recalls Rodanthe, Waves, and Salvo, sometimes not. Sometimes she recalls the black and white spiral of the Cape Hatteras Lighthouse and one of her favorite book stores, Buxton Village Books, sometimes not.

The ferry arrives. The Buick thumps off the metal ramp. Over the dunes, to the left of the two-lane blacktop, the Ocracoke beaches offer pristine views. She never faces the right.

The aquamarine Atlantic holds her attention like an imperfect hand holds a perfect one.

Seafood at one of the restaurants for lunch. A stroll along Silver Lake Harbor. Visit Books to be Red, another favorite book store. Drive to the British Cemetery. Read the words on the plaques commemorating the four seaman of the HMS Bedfordshire, sunk in May 1942 by the German submarine U 558. Return to the blacktop. Stop to gather shells while strolling the beach. Laugh at the backward-kneed antics of the sanderlings as they chase the lacy surf while prodding the sand for their supper with pencil-thin beaks.

On the return trip, when she nears the intersection of Highway 12 and 158, when the choice between continuing north to Corolla or continuing west to Aydlett presents the usual dilemma, the seafood rises in her throat. North is death and facing her past. West delays both.

At home again. Wine and cigarettes, cigarettes and wine. Sometimes tears, sometimes hiccupping sobs.

It takes a thunderstorm before she raises the binoculars toward Corolla. If she's lucky—very, very lucky—the storm arrives when enough time has passed to clear her emotions. If not, just the sight of the binoculars makes her hands shake.

A single cricket offers a single chirp. Maurea's slitted eyes widen. She dumps the wine bottles in the trash, washes the glass. Bathroom then bed. Bed then wake. Wake then do it all over again.

The night smothers her. Her life smothers her. Why not take the .22 pistol and put an end to it? Press the cold barrel to her temple and squeeze the trigger? Do it slowly because she deserves the anticipation of death?

She won't do that. She's too much of a coward. She's *always* been a coward.

This is her existence, the one her choice created, too afraid to live and too afraid to die, and she can't help wondering when and where and how it will all come crashing down.

Always Looking Forward

Corolla, North Carolina
2011

On the circular walkway at the top of the Currituck Lighthouse, his hands gripping the black-painted rail, Chester Pinkham surveys his domain.

To his left, his beloved Atlantic Ocean reaches to the horizon. To his right, his beloved Currituck Sound reaches to the North Carolina mainland. To the south, Corolla and Duck end and the highway continues toward Kitty Hawk, over twenty miles in the distance.

He circles the walkway until he faces north, where Corolla and the road ends a few miles away, leaving nothing but the beach and a fence that contains the descendants of the original herd of Spanish horses, also known as "Mustangs." Further north lies the community of Carova, which can only be reached with four-wheel drive vehicles or a long walk.

He then faces west again. On a rise, a short walk from the sound's edge, obscured by a thick grove of live oaks, his home of almost 103 years isn't much more than a pile of rotten lumber and rusted tin roofing. Tied to one of the remaining pilings from his parent's pier, his green canoe hides within the cattails. Given time and the elements, nor'easters and hurricanes, salt spray and wind-driven sand, nothing survives the Outer Banks forever.

Below him, the footsteps of the first tourists ring on the spiraling metal steps. These must be first-timers, for their silence reflects their reverence for this grand old lighthouse and its history. A man and woman and two children tentatively step out onto the walkway. Eyes dart left and right. Throats make hard swallows. The height of the walkway, nearly 150 feet, tends to make people do that.

Chester prefers climbing the steps as soon as the doors open. Then he can have some time alone, before too many tourists crowd his space. They ignore him, though. He's thin enough to ignore, old enough to ignore. Children might occasionally look his way. Children notice everything.

The rising sun illuminates the Whalehead Club, giving its yellow paint a golden hue. It also illuminates the nine yellow dormers along the steeply pitched roof of bluish-green copper shingles, replaced during the renovation, plus its five chimneys. Chester, of course, prefers the name Edward Knight gave it upon completion in 1925: Corolla Island.

The children, a boy and a girl, maybe three years apart in age, somewhere around fourteen give or take, ignore the smart phones in their hands. The Outer Banks maintains that effect on people. Their parents, around forty or so, hold hands. The Outer Banks maintains that effect on people too.

Despite how they don't notice Chester, he tugs the brim of Daddy's old hunting cap down over his forehead, a habit from his childhood days when children called him Moby Dick. It didn't bother him then and it doesn't bother him now. He knows the subconscious is a difficult thing to control.

Then there were the older boys who called him a sea monster, who started the rumors of him swimming to docks in the night to sneak inside homes and eat babies and children. They did this because of his deformed left hand. Missing the middle and index fingers, it resembled a crab's claw more than a hand, hence the rumor of him eating babies like a crab tears morsels of tender flesh from the bodies of dead fish.

"Don't let that bother you," Daddy said. "Your mother and I know you and the good Lord knows you. That's your only concern."

"Listen to your father," Mommy said, glancing over her shoulder from beside the fireplace. Steam rose from the black kettle of simmering flounder stew, filling the cozy home with the aromas of carrots, potatoes, onions, and celery, plus dill and oregano, all from their garden. Done stirring, she clanked the lid back down, left the spoon on the table by the fireplace, and hugged Chester. "When you were born, we thought you were perfect. We still think that, so don't give your worries another thought." She held him at arm's length and touched the center of his chest with a fingertip. "Who you are is determined by your heart and God's love. It's also determined by the love your daddy and I have for you. Listening to anyone who tries to tell you otherwise will only end with you doubting yourself. Never, ever, for as long as you live, doubt yourself. It takes character to ignore words meant to harm, and character is what your daddy and I want you to have."

Leaning his stomach against the black railing, the boy aims his phone at the Atlantic and clicks a picture. The girl follows suit, and they both show their parents the photographs.

Chester hopes their parents are fine parents like his were. The parents of some of the children at school were bullies too. Daddy spoke to them about it but nothing changed, which is why he and Mommy taught him the lesson of not listening to bullies—probably one of the best lessons of his life. Otherwise,

Moby Dick, the Monster with the Crab Hand, might've actually eaten a bully or three.

The footsteps of more tourists ring the metal steps. When the group comes up, he goes down, treading the stairs lightly on the balls of his feet, like his younger self used to do.

The August sun meets him at the exit. He doesn't mind the heat or the cold. They're just other aspects of nature to enjoy.

One of his favorite pastimes is strolling the beach during a thunderstorm. Lightning and thunder thrills him. Nor'easters and hurricanes thrill him. Being pelted by wind-driven sand thrills him. Swimming the high tide as waves crash and churn thrills him. Besides, it isn't like he can live forever. Even the Outer Banks will succumb eventually, wiped away by wind, the surf and, if nothing else, time.

During the last hurricane that roared directly over the northern Outer Banks, Chester, physically fit from his life of fishing, canoeing, and swimming the sound and the surf, stripped off his faded blue coveralls, his dingy white shirt, his worn and scuffed leather work boots, and plunged into the ocean. After a few strokes into the foaming surf, he started screaming without knowing why and didn't stop until exhaustion drove him back to shore.

In front of the lighthouse, tourists wait in line. He hurries past them. On the way to Corolla Island, a glimpse of the pink painted boathouse with its curved roof makes him turn away. He's never been able to near it, and he can't near it now. Passing it, he hurries to an arched bridge, which crosses the channel that links the boathouse lagoon to the Currituck Sound. In 1922, back when Edward Collins Knight Jr. hired Daniel Peckham to build Corolla Island, he had the boathouse pond and the channel dredged to form an island. He also had the sand dumped to the island to form the rise upon which the huge retreat now stands.

These are the lengths love will reach, lengths Chester is familiar with.

Edward Knight loved his wife, Louise, and Louise shared his passion for waterfowl hunting. Since the clubs in the area wouldn't allow women as members, the Knights designed their own retreat from the mainland, thumbing their noses at outdated traditions.

Chester crosses the bridge. On the lush lawn, he steps over the droppings of Canada Geese. Like at the lighthouse, except beneath the porch of Corolla Island, a line of tourists forms at the front door, waiting to pay the fee.

Just an old man no one will notice, he goes around back and slips inside, and the ages vanish. He hears the murmurs of the wealthy. The men talk of hunting and fishing. The women talk of children and their dreams for them. For some, no future spouse can be too rich or too perfect. Love is an afterthought. Feelings are something to ignore. Duty to family and progeny is all.

"Take a lover for that sentimental balderdash," a woman whispers, nearing her scarlet lips to the ear of another woman, who wears blood-red rubies on her lobes.

The whispering woman is Catherine Applewhite, and Chester despises her. She's older now, here years after The Great War and the Spanish Flue ravaged the earth.

It's the fall of 1927, two years after Corolla Island was built, one year before everything went so terribly wrong in the boat house. Chester and Maurea and Mirlande are eighteen years old, all born on the same night, all linked in some perverse version of fate. Of all his regrets, Mirlande is one of them.

Whenever he and Maurea sneak away from everyone, they also sneak away from Mirlande.

As far as Catherine Applewhite, she calls these gatherings *soirees*. Like this specific soiree, Maurea and Chester had snuck out to the beach, leaving poor Wilbur trying to avoid the embarrassment of having a wife with the morals of a house cat in heat. Why he stayed with her, no one knew. Duty, Chester thought. Guilt, Maurea thought. Wilbur likely thought his leaving would abandon her to learn the ways of Catherine, since men rarely earned custody of children in divorce proceedings.

The crowd fades, their voices too. The smell of cigar smoke and perfume dissipates. Laughter and whispers and the delicate clink of glasses echo off the walls until it all dies a quiet death. The tour guide and visitors stroll past Chester. None acknowledge his presence. He's just an old man, maybe someone who tends the grounds, maybe someone who rakes and shovels goose droppings out of walkways and picks up gum wrappers and cigarette butts.

In Edward Knight's office, the tour guide's voice—her name tag read Margaret when she passed—echoes off the walls. "Here we have Mr. Knight's safe. It's quite large, as you see. Although it resembles a wooden cabinet with the patina gone dark, it's actually made of cast iron."

Since the renovation in 2002, Chester's seen and heard this tour dozens of times, so he doesn't follow it. He also worked here from 1925 until 1928, so he knows the house better than the average person. Yes, this grand old place fills his heart, but he often wishes a hurricane would blow the boathouse away, taking its history and his memories with it.

Margaret's shoes shuffle on the cork flooring as she turns and points out the light fixtures attached to the walls. "These sconces and globes are by Louis Comfort Tiffany. The colors on each globe were created by applying acid to remove one of three layers of colored glass, plus a sharp tool when needed. This left the green, upturned leaves of a water lily."

The tour continues with information about the kitchen and its pink ceramic tiles, used for the cook, Miss Rose. There's one white tile because of the Moorish tile installer tradition that said a room shouldn't be perfect because only God is perfect.

In the library, to the right of the huge room, Louise Knight's custom made Steinway piano beckons fingertips. Over the fireplace, a portrait of Mr. Knight offers genteel hospitality. In the corners of the doorframes, water lily carvings offer examples of the Art Nouveau trend throughout the rooms. To the left, five window frames with four panes each—two short rectangles at the top, two long rectangles at the bottom—offer an astounding view of the sun-sparkled surface of the Currituck Sound.

Much of the furniture is gone, but Chester recalls a gaming table and chairs, with other chairs and a sofa, also in the Art Nouveau style.

Margaret also mentions the electrical panel by the basement door, adding how this area of Currituck County lacked electricity until 1955. Therefore the Knights used generated power for Corolla Island, which allowed running water. Chester wishes he had running water, both now and as a child. As Daddy often joked, they had running water; they just had to run to the well to get it.

The tour moves to the basement, evidenced by shoes thudding the stairs. There, Margaret describes the cases filled with hunting memorabilia, including how wealthy hunters from the north came to the Outer Banks to hunt waterfowl migrating the Atlantic Flyway. One of the displays holds the tools for making decoys, like Daddy's tools at home that [63]

Chester still uses. She also talks about the Knight's separate bedrooms upstairs, plus the guest and servants' quarters.

Chester remembers one of those bedrooms well, for he used to sneak up the stairs to visit Maurea at night. She always covered a giggle when he softly shut the door behind him, saying Mother would kill them both if she caught them. Most of the time, though, they met on the beach, weather permitting. If not, they would stay inside, sometimes talking, sometimes reading, sometimes lying on the bed to dream of flying to a place where no one, especially her mother, judged them for their relationship.

Bored of the tour, Chester leaves for the beach. Being August, hordes of tourists descend upon the sand like fleas on Goldie, a Labrador Retriever his family once had. Lucky for Goldie, Chester swam with her in the sound every few days to wash away as many fleas as possible.

Chester hurries past the boathouse, along the asphalt driveway, and takes a left in the grass beside Highway 12. He's determined to make the long walk to see the Wild Spanish Mustangs that frequent Carova. Still, the first part of the journey, in the shade of the live oaks lining the highway, is a good way to distract him from the ghosts of his past.

Up ahead, a young woman on a bicycle comes his way. Her blonde hair streaming behind her makes Chester stop. When she gets close enough, her green eyes make him look away. As she passes, the aroma of her shampoo, floral and sweet, brings a hard exhale to clear his nose. If he doesn't know any better, she's Maurea, and she's definitely not Maurea.

Clenching his teeth, he whirls around to go home. He's had enough memories for today. What he needs is a hurricane. What he needs is to scream. What he needs is—

A gust of wind swirls sand up from the shoulder of the road. It billows into a grit-filled cloud around him, each grain a nightmare he wishes he, Maurea, and Mirlande could've avoided.

The half-rotten door to his home groans on rusted hinges. Near to tears, he falls to the bed. Mommy's ghost stirs flounder stew in a cast iron pot over the fireplace. The yellow flames lick the black pot's bottom. The embers pop and crackle. Daddy's ghost reads a book on psychology. The rocking chair creaks softly. From the table at his side, where the family Bible waits, lamplight illuminates his aquamarine eyes.

Chester weeps until nightfall. He doesn't eat. He doesn't sleep. Eventually, like a school of bluefish forcing baitfish from the ocean to the beach to rip them to shreds in a feeding frenzy, dreams tear at what he knows is his fragile psyche.

His desire to know where Maurea is overwhelms him. If she were dead he would know it. He's as sure of this as he is the tides, for her soul tugs at his soul with the same unending pull, always west. They are 102 years old, soon to be 103. He understands why she left, understands why she can't return. He's tried canoeing to the mainland. Regardless, when he gets a mile from shore, his strength fails him. He even tried walking to Kitty Hawk and crossing the Wright Memorial Bridge, but a few miles past Duck, his legs weakened until he had to stop. Then, when he turned back toward Corolla, they miraculously regained their strength. He once considered hitchhiking. His hand raised well enough, but when he tried to aim his thumb south down Highway 12, the joint refused to flex.

It's obvious. They weren't meant to be together in life, so maybe they were meant to be together in death.

Like each morning, he wakes as the first light of dawn illuminates the Currituck Sound. The embers in the fireplace are stoked. The rising wind presses through a crack in a wall. The Wood Duck decoy pirouettes on the fishing line.

This is his existence, the one his choice created. He's too afraid to live and too afraid to die, and he can't help wondering when and where and how it will all come crashing down.

The Stranger, the Monster, and the Yellow-Haired Girl

Corolla, North Carolina
1913

In the one-room house within sight of the Currituck Sound, Mirlande finished a plate of scrambled eggs and crab meat. Across the table, Mommy and Auntie did the same.

Mommy took the plates to a basin and washed them. She wore a plain cotton dress. Similar to what Mirlande wore, its threadbare hem, more yellow than its former white, reached her ankles. Long, black hair draped her back with loose curls.

Auntie refilled a cup of herbal tea and returned to the table. She wore a similar dress to Mommy's, except it was faded blue, and she always kept her head wrapped with a length of white cloth that came from a place she called Haiti.

Outside, as the day brightened through the window, the normal routine of strengthening wind, evidenced by the rustling of tree branches, hadn't arrived yet.

Mommy finished the dishes, refilled her cup also, and returned to the table. Her green eyes, like Mirlande's, glittered. Sometimes they glittered with anger. In the case of a customer at the general store, a bearded fellow with a crooked nose and tobacco juice seeping from the right side of his mouth, her eyes would glitter with malice. Mommy hated nothing more than men making comments about taking her to bed. Mirlande didn't understand such a thing. Sleep was a way to escape the boring existence of this rickety old house.

Although the almost constant wind didn't murmur outside, the cluck of chickens did. Desiring to visit her friends, Mirlande climbed down from the chair and donned a threadbare jacket, a gift from the pastor.

"No chickens today," Auntie said, her voice squeaking like the home's rusted door hinges.

"That's right," Mommy said, rising from the table. "It's November, and today's your fifth birthday. Since it's much nicer outside than the night you were born, we're taking you to see the beach."

"And the ocean," Auntie said, taking her cup to the basin.

Mirlande peered at them in turn. "The ocean?"

"And the beach," Mommy said, wrapping a thick shawl around her shoulders. "We've never taken you there."

Mirlande donned the jacket. "Where is it?"

"It's beyond the road by the store and the post office." Auntie donned a shawl like Mommy's. "You asked us what that roaring noise was one day when the wind was up. It's the ocean."

"Nooo, Auntie," Mirlande whined. "It scared me."

There's nothing to be afraid of." Auntie knelt to pin Mirlande's hair up and cover it with a red bandana. "Not unless we see a monster. We're going early so we don't see any."

Auntie had often talked of monsters: sea monsters that swallowed sailors whole, with huge heads and a hole in the top that plumed water into the sky; sky monsters, with white wings like sharp knives to slice a certain little girl's heart into shreds;

land monsters, their coarse voices that sang songs of love and then betrayed those who were entranced.

Trusting her auntie and mommy, Mirlande followed them outside. Although the slight breeze carried a chill, the sunshine hinted the warmth of the new day. They took the path through the crooked trees, through thick vines and brush, and left both, arriving at the sandy track that split both sides of the village.

"'Crawlo,'" Mirlande said to no one in particular, mimicking the word Mommy and Auntie called this place.

"Kuh-rah-lah," Mommy corrected.

Mirlande ignored her. "Crawlo."

Auntie swiveled her head left and right. "Wait, a wagon is coming."

A horse and wagon, its salt-stained boards white in the sun, rattled by. The driver ignored them. The aroma of fish passed with the wagon.

Mommy ran after the wagon and snatched a flounder from a basket in back. She returned and hid it beneath a bush beside the sandy track. "Just what the fisherman ordered, flounder for your birthday supper."

Mirlande nodded. She loved flounder cooked in a cast iron pan with butter and bits of crabmeat.

On the other side of the sandy track lined with wagon wheel ruts, they entered a path like the one leading to their house. This path was mostly sand, with only a bush or some tall grass or a twisted tree here and there.

Step after step, as the roaring sound ahead grew louder, she clutched Mommy's hand. She told her not to worry, but Auntie cackled. "That's right, the monsters are waiting." Mommy told Auntie to hush, told Mirlande she was teasing, told her she would love the beach and the ocean.

Still clutching Mommy's hand, Mirlande stuck her tongue out at Auntie. "You're a bad old woman."

"That's right," Auntie said, baring her teeth in a wicked grin. "Bad enough to kill every monster we might meet."

Mirlande knew what she meant. Late at night, when the orange flame of the kerosene lamp flickered over the table at the rickety house, she had peeked from bed to see Auntie making doll after doll. Some wore dresses, some wore nothing. Done with one, she would either give it to Mirlande to play with in the morning or stab it with a hatpin, grinning with what didn't look like happiness.

Once, when she caught Mirlande watching her, she whispered for her to come over. "This," she said, tapping the doll with a fingertip, "is that man who called us trash when we were looking through the trash at the store that time. I never saw him before. I think he might've been one of the hunters who come for ducks and geese."

Mirlande didn't know how to answer. Although she didn't like to be called trash, she didn't like digging through trash for food either. At least Mommy and Auntie didn't take the food with maggots in it.

The sandy path came to a low rise, like a small hill. At its crest, sparse grass waved in the breeze. On the other side of the hill, the noise that had scared Mirlande now made her run toward it. As she topped the rise, she stopped, eyes widening at the sight. Looking back at Mommy and Auntie, she waved them on, then turned to face more water than she had ever seen in her life, even more than beyond the path to the water where they caught those blue crabs to eat. Mommy and Auntie joined her and no one said anything. They simply watched and listened and tasted and felt the power of all this blue water, tinted green in places, waves cresting and curling with foam like when Mirlande used soap to wash her hands before meals. Jabbing a finger toward the crashing water, she tugged Mommy's hand. "Oh, oh, Mommy. Look! Look!"

"I know," Mommy said. "I like it too." She kicked off her shoes. "The sun's warming the sand. Let's see what the water feels like."

Mirlande plopped down on her behind, pulled her shoes off and stood. Auntie left her shoes on, complaining about not liking sand between her toes, and they started across the wide beach.

On the way, Mirlande stopped to point at something in the sand, and Mommy picked it up. "It's a shell."

"What's a shell?" Mirlande asked, blinking up at Mommy because of the bright sun over her head.

"Some of the creatures in the sea live in shells. It protects them from other creatures."

"Which is a good lesson for us," Auntie said. "You two are too pretty for your own good. You need to be hard like a shell to keep the men away."

"She's just a child," Mommy said. "Leave her alone."

Auntie's lips tightened. "She's here because of that Creole bastard, remember? I should've kept a tighter rein on you when he was snooping about."

"Don't say that word. I keep telling you, how many times do I have to tell you?"

Auntie touched the head of a long pin in her head wrap. "You talk too much. How many times do I have to tell *you?*"

Mirlande left the fussing women. They averaged three arguments a day. Mommy's scrambled eggs were either too hard or too soft. If she fried them, they were either too runny or not runny enough. She didn't keep the sand swept from the rickety house. She talked to Jeff, the son of the owner of the general store, too much. On and on and on it went.

At the water's edge, Mirlande stopped to wiggle her toes in the wet sand. Foam covered her feet as the water whispered past them. It retreated down the slight incline, leaving her feeling as if she were sinking. The breeze gusted. During her run, her curls had left the bandana and had fallen from her temples, and the breeze swirled them around her face like a dark curtain.

Behind her, Mommy and Auntie were still fussing. Auntie touched the hat pin again. Mommy raised her hand as if to slap her.

Despite the beautiful blue water tinged with green, despite the white wings of gulls slashing by, despite the sunshine warming cheeks and lips, the fussing forced Mirlande to finger tears from the corners of her eyes.

Mommy was nice but Auntie was mean. What made her like that, she never said. She had made dolls for play, though, and Mirlande loved them. Once, while Auntie was going through some of the other dolls, she said one was the pastor, one was the clerk at the store, and one was the clerk at the post office. This happened when Mommy was away. Auntie said if these men ever did anything wrong, they would get what they deserved.

Another time, when Mommy was away and Auntie was in the outhouse, Mirlande looked through the basket of sewing things that also held the dolls. In the bottom, beneath needles and thread and thimbles and bits of cloth, she found a doll that resembled Mommy. This made Mirlande worry. When would Mommy get what she deserved for all the things Auntie said she did wrong?

To her right, voices drew her attention. A boy and his Mommy and his Daddy were running toward the water. They all were laughing, all were smiling, all were loving each other with their whole hearts.

Mirlande looked behind her. Mommy and Auntie had gone back to the hill of sand and were sitting at its base, fingers waggling, faces scowling.

Although the boy's family made her a little sad because she envied their happiness, they made her glad to know such happiness existed.

She ran down the beach, feet splashing in the surf, curls bouncing along her cheeks. Small birds, brown and backward-kneed, scattered before her. She had to meet the boy and his family—*had* to.

In a cottage rented from one of his hunting friends, Wilbur watched Catherine drive away. Always on the go, she wanted to brave the sandy track down to Kitty Hawk, supposedly to see a friend who said she would be there for a few days. Speechless that she would leave right after breakfast on Maurea's fifth birthday, he refused to let it ruin the day.

Dawdling over pancakes, Maurea drank milk. Wilbur dabbed the milk moustache away from her upper lip, then drank coffee. "Papa," she said, "why did Mother leave? It's my birthday. She didn't even say goodbye."

Of all of Catherine's shortcomings so far, this was the worst. If he didn't know any better, and he didn't, her so-called friend was a man instead of a woman. Another shortcoming was they only shared a bedroom when she wanted a conjugal visit, and that was so rare as to be nonexistent.

The standard excuse was a headache, followed by that time of the month, or complaints of Maurea tiring her out while he was at the office. He knew this to be a lie. Since Catherine spent so little time with their daughter, he had hired what Jane Austin's stories called a "governess." Catherine fumed because of the young woman's beauty, which rivaled hers in every way, even more because of her kindness to Maurea and her fondness for cooking when they visited Corolla. Of course, Wilbur's relentless wife preferred Cook's cooking to any concoction from Patsy's hand.

A redhead to Catherine's yellow, freckles like the Milky Way galaxy on a clear night over the Atlantic, a slender figure to Catherine's full one, an open smile to Catherine's tight-lipped grimaces, Patsy's Irish background lightened the moods of both Wilbur and Maurea. Even now she was asking if she needed more butter or syrup or milk, to which Maurea shook her head. "I'll brush my teeth. Then Papa can give me my birthday present." She faced Wilbur. "Isn't that right, Papa?"

In the middle of a swallow of Patsy's delicious coffee, he gulped it down. "It certainly is, Little Snail." He set the cup in the saucer. "It might not be quite a surprise, though. Do you remember coming here before? You were just two then."

Maurea looked around the room, her yellow ponytail swirling about her shoulders. "Um, maybe." She went to the side window. "I remember those crooked trees. Mother said they were monsters. She said they would get me if I wasn't good."

Patsy cleared the dishes. "I love those trees. They would make the perfect place to hang a hammock."

Wilbur suggested Maurea brush her teeth. He went to the window facing the wide expanse of beach. The cottage was located about a quarter mile south of the Currituck Lighthouse.

Last night, after everyone had gone to bed, he had stood here to watch the finger of light probing the sky over the Atlantic. He imagined it waggling at ships to warn their captains against risking the shallower coastal waters, like when Catherine waggled her finger at him like she always did when he slipped into her bedroom. "Not tonight. I'm tired from that ridiculous daughter of yours and all her shenanigans."

How quickly Maurea had gone from *theirs* to *his*. What a disaster of a marriage, one where all the things they had in common had left after Maurea was born. If not for his solemn vows, he would take Maurea elsewhere and start another life, away from all the pain.

Evidenced by the clatter of dishes in the basin, Patsy finished them and joined him. "I know I've only been with you six months, but it breaks my heart to see your wife treat you and Maurea so terribly. If there's anything I can do to comfort you, anything at all …"

The soft southern drawl—not as southern as Catherine's, thank goodness—turned Wilbur to those lovely sea-green eyes. Thank goodness, too, that the shade was more hazel than green. If they had been the same as Catherine's, Patsy's concern would carry no more sincerity than cattail fluff in a hurricane.

She touched his arm. "Really, Mr. Applewhite. Anything at all."

From toward the bathroom down the hall, the patter of leather flats on heart pine floors warned of Maurea's approach. Patsy returned to the basin to dry the dishes. Wilbur returned to a chair at the table to remove his slippers. Doing so, he told Maurea how her birthday surprise involved being barefoot, so she removed her shoes. She then waited, calm and patient unlike Catherine, who flitted around like a flock of sanderlings over the waves.

Realizing it was Sunday, Wilbur knew something was different about November in Corolla, for no shotgun blasts disturbed the morning. Most visiting hunters spent Sundays traveling either from here to home or to home from here. He and his dad had certainly done plenty of that before his death. Sadly, those days were long gone now.

Not that Maurea was to blame for the current state of his marriage, but Wilbur had certainly hoped it would turn out differently. Patsy's offer of comfort tempted him, especially when Catherine stayed overnight with this friend or that friend, whoever they might be. Perhaps he was too trusting. They said their marriage vows, and he took them seriously as well as solemnly. He rubbed his wrinkled forehead. If that were true, why consider Patsy's offer? Regardless of the question, he knew why. He missed hugs and kisses and the warmth of a woman at his side in bed, whether they made love or not.

Maurea grasped his hand. "What's wrong, Papa? Your eyes are wet."

"Oh, it's just this salt air, Little Snail." Wilbur stood, thinking how he needed a shell to protect himself from the trials of an unhappy marriage.

Patsy removed her shoes and asked if she could join them. Wilbur had mentioned Maurea's birthday surprise to her in private, so he waved her toward the door.

After they descended the steps to the path to the beach, Maurea pointed at the Currituck Lighthouse in the distance, behind them and to the right. "When can we climb it, Papa? You said we could."

Wilbur knew one of the keepers, so he intended to ask. "Maybe another time. I need to talk with my friend first."

"Ok, but where's my birthday surprise?"

He pointed toward the beach. "Do you remember yet?"

"Maybe."

"I didn't know if you would, so I'm taking you here now. It's a special place, Little Snail. Almost as special as you."

"I saw it from the windows. Why do I have to see it now?"

At the hint of Catherine's negativity in his daughter, Wilbur paused. God help her if Catherine's influence reared its ugly head later in life. He had brought Maurea here to teach her how special nature was in person, not while looking at it through windows like in the clothing shops of downtown Richmond. If she could have the same enjoyment of nature as he did, which Catherine once did and didn't have now, it might keep his little snail from becoming like her mother when the time to find love came along.

He knelt before Maurea and peered into her eyes. "Nature is meant to be enjoyed outside, not inside. If you let it into your heart, you'll always be amazed by it." Standing, he took her by the hand. "Let's go see."

On his other side, Patsy's shoulder brushed his. "Your wife doesn't deserve you, Mr. Applewhite," she whispered. "You're a wonderful father." She hesitated. Silent words trembled on her lips. "I … I wish …"

The sincerity in her eyes touched Wilbur. Since Catherine had transformed into a wife who no longer cared for her husband, much less loved him, he wished certain things too. Would it be so wrong to find comfort in Patsy's willing arms? No sooner than the question entered his mind, he answered it. Like his parents now dead, he was a Christian, and even considering such things could doom his soul.

Patsy added nothing more and neither did he, content with the warmth of his dear daughter's hand within his.

He told them to watch for sandspurs near the brush on both sides of the path, adding how the tiny balls filled with hooked stickers would burrow into the sole of a foot if stepped on. Upon hearing this warning, Maurea moved ahead to the center of the path while Patsy moved closer, slowing her speed and holding Wilbur back with her hand on his arm. "I meant what I said, Mr. Applewhite … Wilbur. I've come to care for you and Maurea a great deal. If your wife doesn't want both of you, I would do everything in my power to make you a fine wife and Maurea a fine mother." She leaned closer, lips nearing his ear. "I've never been drawn to a man. I … well, I've never been with a man at all." Her cheeks colored. "I suppose I sound like a harlot, but my feelings say otherwise. Well, that's confusing, because my feelings—my *physical* feelings—tell me to come to you at night, after everyone is asleep. Is it so terrible to have those feelings, Mr. Applewh—Wilbur?"

Patsy's height allowed her breath, sweet from brushing her teeth, to caress Wilbur's cheek. Fine curls of red hair twined at her temples. Lovely eyes, framed by arched brows and long lashes, drew him closer, and an urgency he hadn't felt for Catherine in too long surged through him. Blinking furiously, he pulled away from her hand to answer her question. "Your ardor—I mean your affection—is appreciated, both for myself and Maurea. However, my values keep me from submitting to you. Please don't take that as an affront. I've come to admire you also."

She answered with a slight smile and nothing more—a woman who knew it was only a matter of time before she won him over.

Ahead of them, Maurea stopped on the sandy rise. As the breeze fluttered blonde hair across her forehead, she looked back. "You're right, Papa! It's much better here than from inside the house!"

As she ran down the rise toward the ocean, Wilbur placed his hand to his chest to check his heart. It felt like it was skipping a beat each time her precious little toes slung sand into the air.

"You have a wonderful daughter," Patsy said.

"I do," Wilbur said, trying not to cry. He didn't say the rest. *At one time I thought I had a wonderful wife. Now, except for Maurea, I have nothing.*

They followed her, stopping as she chased a flock of sanderlings northward up the beach. When it was obvious they wouldn't catch her, they sat on the slight rise above the surf line, marked by a fringe of seaweed and bits of sea shells. Watching her now and then, Wilbur didn't worry. The only other people on the beach were a young girl about Maurea's age with long, black curls, evidenced by the sun highlighting them. Two women, both sitting at the base of the slight dune, must've been with the girl, so she was fine too. Let Maurea meet a child her own age. She didn't have any friends yet, so she needed to make some, whether they were in Corolla or in Richmond. Truth be known, Wilbur preferred she make friends here. Any friends in the hustle and bustle of Richmond, in Catherine's chosen territory, might not be friend's at all, not if they had parents like Catherine.

"Come on, Mommy and Daddy," Chester said, waving them to the door. "You said we'd go to the beach for my birthday, and it's time to go."

Folding a quilt for sitting on the beach, Mommy laughed. "It's not like we haven't been going since you were born."

"Now, now, Alice," Daddy said, donning his blue hunting cap. "Our young man is five-years-old today, as you well know. He deserves to have his way."

"I never said otherwise, Abner, as *you* well know." She tossed him the quilt. "Hold that while I put my shoes on."

"It's sand, Mommy," Chester complained. "You can walk in the sand barefoot, like me and Daddy."

"She doesn't like sandspurs," Daddy said.

Mommy joined them at the door. "I didn't think about them until I stepped on one. I don't take any chances now."

The threesome left for the path that led though the live oak trees and passed the Currituck Lighthouse. They waved at one of the keepers at the top, cleaning the huge Fresnel lens with a cloth.

Chester loved the tall lighthouse, its wind-worn bricks a powdery red beneath his fingertips when he brushed them against it near the back. At a place taller than he could reach, Daddy had pointed out a loose brick one summer. Apparently the cement hadn't set properly, causing the brick to jut out like a loose tooth. Chester wondered if it could be pulled like a loose tooth too.

Minutes later they were climbing the slight rise to the beach. Beyond it, the surf thudded to the sand instead of thundered. Chester liked it when the wind wasn't bad. That meant he could wade up to his ankles in the foamy water.

At his first steps forward, he realized Mommy and Daddy weren't with him. Puzzled, he looked back at them. Both smiled and waved him on, saying it was his day to enjoy without them slowing him down. At this, he ran as hard as he could, eyes focused on the surf, lacy white with foam.

"Hello, boy!" a girl's voice yelled from his left. He had never seen a girl like this one, or either her appearance from the other girls he'd seen in Corolla was different enough to cause his astonishment.

As if she lived in the sun, every inch of skin visible was tanned. Dark hair down her back framed a narrow face and a slender nose. The only response to such an appealing stranger was to raise his hand and yell hello too.

Puffing hard, she stopped a few feet away. He decided to let her rest before he said anything else.

"Hello!" another girl's voice yelled from behind him.

He looked past her and then past the first girl. Both were with grownups, so they hadn't just fallen out of the sky like angels, although they both certainly looked like angels.

The yellow-haired girl wore her hair in a ponytail, and it had bounced back and forth as she ran, like the tails of the wild horses when they galloped. Her eyes, though, drew him like the sea, so green he could hardly stop looking at her. Like Mommy and Daddy had taught him when meeting someone he didn't know, he offered his hand. "Hello. My name is Chester."

Instead of letting the yellow-haired girl shake his hand, the black-haired girl grabbed it. "I'm Mirlande." Frowning, she pointed at his left hand. "Did you get hurt?"

"That's not nice," the yellow-haired girl said. She shook his hand. "I'm Maurea. Papa says it means little snail." She paused. "I'm not trying to be mean. What happened to your hand? It's different from everyone else's."

"I'm not mean," Mirlande blurted. "I just want to know."

Maurea offered her a smile. "I'm sorry. Papa says I'm too much like Mother sometimes. I like your name." She faced Chester. "I like yours too, Chester. Did you hurt your hand? It *is* very different from everyone else's."

"Mommy and Daddy said our insides are more important than our outsides."

Mirlande giggled. "Our insides are like what fish have—yucky guts."

Maurea giggled too, but Chester didn't. Mommy and Daddy taught him special lessons, and this was a special lesson too. "I don't mean that," he said, a little too loud. "I mean if we're nice or not."

Both Maurea and Mirlande stopped giggling. Mirlande's eyes focused above Chester's. "What happened to your head?"

"His forehead," Maurea corrected.

Chester grew tired of these questions, but since these two girls weren't trying to be mean, he told them he was born like this. They nodded. Then Maurea touched his arm. "Tag! You're it!" and streaked off down the beach.

Mirlande gave chase but soon slowed, so Chester did to. "She's too fast," Mirlande said.

The man and the woman Maurea came with were waving her toward them, so Chester dropped to his knees in the sand to pick up a sea shell. As soon as Mirlande's knees touched the sand beside him, the woman with the cloth wrapped around her head came striding across beach. "Get away from that monster," she said, waving Mirlande toward her. "He's a crab boy. See that hand of his?"

Mirlande stood. "He's nice, Auntie."

The woman grabbed her by the arm and dragged her away, leaving Chester to wonder what made her insides so mean. He didn't feel like playing anymore, so he shuffled through the sand back to Mommy and Daddy. They had been sitting on the quilt. Now they were lying down, so he did the same.

The wind blew harder. Dark clouds flew by like the sails of ships, except these sails were black. The ocean's soft murmur changed to a roar. A wave crashed down to wet their feet and make them scramble up and away from the churning surf, dragging the quilt after them. Mommy and Daddy laughed but Chester didn't. Why had that woman—a woman he had never met—call him names like monster and crab boy? He couldn't help how he was born, and his hand and forehead didn't make him a monster.

The wind turned cool, raising gooseflesh on his arms. Daddy said a storm was coming. Mommy said they better go home. Chester agreed. He loved them more than he loved himself and couldn't stand to think of a life without them. They said all things die, even them. If they were gone, he would rather be gone too.

On the way home, he considered the yellow-haired girl, Maurea, and the dark-haired girl, Mirlande. Something about Mirlande scared him at first, but she seemed nice a few minutes later. Maurea scared him at first too, when she snapped at Mirlande for asking about his hand. For some reason, he felt like he was a fish, and they were two gulls pulling him apart.

Having slowed while thinking, he hurried to catch Mommy and Daddy. They would never pull him apart like a fish. They would all go home and stoke the fireplace and have supper, and Daddy would carve a decoy and Mommy would talk about pelicans and how they would dive into the water and gulp fish in their beaks. Chester grinned. In their beaks like the flabby double-chin of the man at the general store.

But maybe he would get to see the two girls again one day. He could be wrong about them scaring him. Like him, they just might need a friend too.

Fling

Lying in bed, still damp with sweat from her and Alex's exertions, Catherine plucked the cigarette from his lips. After a deep inhale, she released the smoke. It rose in a lazy gray haze to the ceiling of the less than stellar hotel room he had rented for three nights in Kitty Hawk.

With his fingers, he swept his hair, black and thick, back from his forehead. His dark eyes, half open, appraised her. "For someone who chastised me for buggery that time, you seem to have changed your mind. Either that or my inheritance changed your mind. You refused my advances until I mentioned the Andino family fortune."

"Oh, money is nice, as it always is." Catherine exhaled a second cloud of smoke. "Had I known you would be so gentle in bed, I might've consented before Wilbur came along." She returned the cigarette to his lips. Then too, if she had consented, she wouldn't have married Wilbur and Maurea wouldn't exist. She could do without Wilbur, but she wasn't sure about Maurea. Time would tell—time and the matter of punishing him by making Maurea into the spitting image of herself.

Alex returned the cigarette to her and yawned. "You've worn me out. Wake me in an hour or so. I'd like to shower before lunch."

Saying she would, Catherine rose to don her silk robe. At the salt-smeared window facing the beach, she took the cigarette from her lips and sighed. Because life offered so little satisfaction, she failed to understand why she had found it in the arms of anyone other than Wilbur. As gentle as Alex, a good father too, something in Wilbur vexed Catherine. Perhaps it was his innate goodness, learned from his Christian parents. Perhaps it was the words of love he had smothered her with not long after they met.

Feeling anger heat her cheeks, she stubbed the cigarette out on the water stained windowsill, a result, no doubt, from windblown seawater during an Outer Banks hurricane.

What made her react with anger, she didn't know. Regardless, she couldn't control it, so there was no use trying. She didn't aspire to any religion, which flung her non-existent moral compass to the four winds. She didn't aspire to motherhood, which flung her non-existent love for Maurea away as well. She almost sputtered laughter. And forget being a wife. No man would ever attempt to own her again, especially if the payment were words of love and having a child, regardless of agreeing with Wilbur to do so.

In the graying horizon beyond the window, black clouds scurried by. Huge raindrops splattered against the glass. Two beachcombers, a man and a woman braving the chilly November day, hurried to their room, pants legs and a dress flapping around ankles, hair like blown cobwebs. And their smiles, such disgusting things, chins wagging in laughter. That's how Wilbur expected her to be with him, but that's *not* what he got.

Alex softly snored. He was the third man since the marriage. The first two were dull creatures like Wilbur, boring in bed with their own needs. Alex pleased her before he pleased himself, something she had been looking for. In the days after she and Wilbur met, he had succeeded in pleasing her. For some reason she didn't understand, the marriage ruined her desire for him, which ruined his desire for her. She didn't care for that. A man had to make her his universe, at least in bed, and he had given up. Thank goodness her father had taught Wilbur the tobacco business before he and her mother had drowned on the ship to Europe. Thank goodness Wilbur's parents had drowned also, prudish creatures that they were, always talking about morals and character and doing the right thing. What fun came from morals? What amusement came from character? What excitement came from doing the right thing, whatever the right thing was supposed to be. If Wilbur's parents hadn't drowned, what an even more boring life with him it would've been. Catherine could hear what they'd say when they got to know her better. "Wilbur didn't tell us about your lack of religious affiliation, Catherine. Exactly why do you feel that way? Did someone turn you against God at one time or another? You can tell us, Catherine. If someone did something to you, that must be it. The only way to overcome it is to place it in our heavenly Father's hands." Who were they to act as if they cared in any way whatsoever? Although they never got the chance to ask her those questions, how she despised them for judging her.

Lightning brightened the ocean, startling Catherine into blinking her eyes and jerking back from the window. Thunder followed, rolling and booming like kettle drums in a symphony orchestra.

She returned to the bed. How could it storm in November? She wasn't religious, but she believed in premonitions. The last time lightning and thunder had created such an occurrence in her life, her and Wilbur's parents had met their end. Who would meet an end now?

Moaning, Alex rolled over and opened his eyes. "Still up?"

Catherine didn't care to mention his family, but it was something to get her mind off the weather's premonition. Before she could do so, he sat up, lit another cigarette, and blew a smoke ring. "How's that husband and daughter of yours?"

"I was about to ask you about your wife and son. Do they mind your trips to the beach?"

He pinched a sliver of tobacco from his lower lip and flicked it away. "Oh, I tell them I'm on a business trip like I always do." He puffed again. Smoke drifted from his parted lips. "Did I tell you Con will be five soon?"

"Why do you call him that?" Catherine asked, truly curious. "Constantine has much more of a ring to it. It's very Greek, after all."

"Our blood may be Greek but our family isn't." More smoke drifted from his lips. "As I'm sure you've noticed, we've lost our accent."

"Will you teach him the shipping business?"

Ash fell from the cigarette to the sheet covering Alex's chest. "I really don't care to talk about them," he muttered, looking away.

Catherine didn't say how he had broached the subject of family by mentioning hers. She recognized guilt creeping into his voice, or rather, weakness. So far she was happy with him, could carry on like this for who knew how long. Yet she despised weakness in a man. Wilbur's weakness for love was an example. If Alex ever claimed love, she might as well murder him and start over with someone else.

He set the cigarette in the ash tray on the nightstand, caressed the rise of her hip through the robes' blue silk, tugged the tie loose and caressed her again.

Although she accepted him once more, Maurea and Wilbur remained in her mind's eye. *Catherine, I don't understand how you can do such a thing? Where's your respect, if not for yourself, then for Maurea and I? Mother! Who's that man? Have you no shame?*

Catherine dug her fingernails into Alex's broad back. Like when Eve allowed the serpent to seduce her with the promise of knowledge, Catherine used seduction to prove how easy it was to make weak men forget their wives and children. Even Wilbur, with his pious self, would, no matter how long it took, eventually succumb to Patsy's allure. After all, that's why Catherine had chosen her. Then his doting daughter would discover how men were meant to be used instead of loved.

Irene

Aydlett, North Carolina
2011

At the porch table with coffee and oatmeal, Maurea considers the kayak. It floats in the high tide, tied to a leftover post from the last bones of a pier that lived here who knows how long ago. She prefers to think of any wooden structure as having lived. After all, it was a tree in its former life.

The last spoon of oatmeal clots her throat. Sips of coffee ease it down.

Something is wrong. The air, maybe, or maybe it's the humidity, thick as summer fog but invisible. Her gray hair is in a bun pinned to the crown of her head. The nape of her neck tingles with something. It's not apprehension. It's a feeling she hasn't felt since—

She fetches the radio from beside the sink and returns to the porch, sits and twists the knob savagely. It's an ancient thing. The wooden cabinet's finish is sticky to the touch. If she sniffs it hard enough, she swears she can smell jazz and big band from the 1930s. Music from before then and after doesn't move her. Mrs. Knight's piano playing didn't move her. The nostalgia of the 30s is what moves her, when she lived in the depths of denial as deep as the Atlantic.

Static, static, and more static. It's as if she's returned to 1930, until a modern voice tells the weather. "Tropical Storm Irene has formed 120 miles east of Martinique. It's too soon to forecast the track, but residents of both the Gulf and east coasts of the United States should be aware of the possibilities of a landfall."

Maurea clicks the switch off.

Possibilities.

The word pauses on her lips. Young girls believed in possibilities—young men too—then narcissism's bitter standards, sadly shared by many such as her mother, ruined those possibilities. Little did the narcissists know who the true monsters were, and it wasn't a young boy who once roamed Corolla.

The next day, August 21, 2011, in the Caribbean Sea, Irene gains strength. The circulation grows larger. It moves over St. Croix. It tracks west-northwestward. Its center crosses the eastern shore of Puerto Rico on August 22. It becomes a hurricane soon after.

Maurea wrestles a step ladder from beneath the rear deck. In turn, she takes it to the windows around the house and closes the storm shutters, leaving one facing the Currituck open so she can watch the hurricane's progress.

If Chester taught her anything, it was when a storm was coming. Irene may dance in the Caribbean Sea, waltz over Cuba, Foxtrot over Florida, Jitterbug into the Gulf of Mexico, but it will eventually Twist the Outer Banks into a knot of broken trees, flooded houses, and shattered vacations.

On August 24, Irene nears Hispaniola. That afternoon, sore from securing the shutters and the porch furniture, Maurea ignores the heart attack symptoms and goes to bed early. She doesn't need much more time, but if she knew what she needs to do with that time, she'd rather know exactly how much time she needs. She manages a smile at this bit of twisted logic. Like anything, it makes sense if you give it enough thought.

During his morning stroll beneath the live oak limbs beside the highway in Corolla, Chester overhears a couple on bicycles talking about a tropical storm forming near Martinique. How he missed the feeling in the air—the same feeling he had taught Maurea so long ago—he doesn't know. Another couple passes. The tropical storm is called Irene.

He grins at the name. She'll be a fine dance partner when she hits the Outer Banks, and he *knows* she will hit the Outer Banks.

At home, he somewhat secures what's left of his parents' shack. It's on a rise, so the sound's storm surge won't touch it. The wind, though, is another thing altogether. Since the grove of thick-trunked live oak trees circles the house, and since their twisted limbs wrap around the four walls like protective arms around a loved one, everything should be all right.

Done with his work, he visits the family cemetery behind the house. While working at Corolla Island, he scrimped and saved to honor Mommy and Daddy with headstones to match the two for his dead siblings. He has an idea who, but someone has prematurely honored him with a headstone too. Inscribed into the granite, a canoe and the profile of a Labrador Retriever's head bracket a single word: *Beloved.*

He wonders where Mirlande is buried. Victims of tragedy rarely rest, but if anyone deserves to rest, she does.

That night he visits an indoor mall. In a coffee shop, locals scoff at Irene. In a restaurant, tourists talk about leaving. In a book store, he enjoys the first chapter of a book already at home, *The Diary of Carlo Cipriani.* Concerning a fictional account of how the first herd of Spanish horses could've arrived in Corolla in the early 16ᵗʰ century, including the tragic reason for the main character, Carlo, leaving his home in Spain, it's quite the page turner.

In the same coffee shop the next morning, Chester listens as the TV announcer says Irene, now in the Caribbean Sea, has gained strength as the circulation grows. She then moves over St. Croix. She then tracks west northwestward. Her center crosses the eastern shore of Puerto Rico on August 22. She becomes a hurricane soon after.

At home again, Chester closes storm shutters. Scowling at the rotten wood that crumbles in his hands, he knows it's the best he can do.

If Daddy taught him anything, it was when a storm was coming. Irene will eventually twist the Outer Banks into a knot of broken trees, flooded houses, and shattered vacations.

On August 24, the coffee shop TV announcer says Irene is nearing Hispaniola. That afternoon, sore from the work at home, Chester feels a sharp pain in his chest and shuffles to the marsh to watch the sun set over the Currituck.

Something stranger than Irene is happening, and he doesn't know what it is. Regardless, he doesn't need much more time, but if he knew what he needs to do with that time, he'd rather know exactly how much time he needs. He manages a smile at this bit of twisted logic. Like anything, it makes sense if you give it enough thought.

Pete

Corolla, North Carolina
1914

In the floor of the Pinkham household, the Labrador Retriever puppy squatted. As yellow urine puddled beneath the yellow behind, Chester pointed. "Why is he squatting?"

Trying not to laugh, Abner grinned regardless. Along with a new puppy and a sunny April day, yet another thing was filling his heart. His six-year-old son—smart as the proverbial whip—had gotten good at noticing things.

In a rocking chair with her knitting, Alice shook her head. "Wipe that up before it soaks into the wood and smells."

Abner did so. He threw the rag in the fireplace and returned to Chester's side. The puppy was the last of a litter from one of his hunting friends. Like Abner, his friend also guided the wealthy northerners who flocked to the Outer Banks in the fall, like those millions of ducks and geese flocked here.

He knelt beside Chester and patted the pup's yellow head. "Your pup is a girl. Do you have a name for her?"

"Why's she skinny? I see her ribs."

"She was the runt of the litter."

"I'm small. Am I the runt?"

Abner hated it when his son questioned his size. Time and time again, he and Alice had told him how his self-worth had nothing to do with his size. "No, Son, you're not the runt."

Chester raised his left hand. "My hand is little. Is it the runt?"

"Your hand is how God made you," Alice said. "That's all you need to know."

As with all these discussions about Chester's differences, his brown eyes didn't seem to believe what he was told. "But why—"

"That's enough," Abner said, standing. "You're just the same as anyone else where it matters" —he touched the center of Chester's chest with a fingertip— "in your heart. Just be kind like we tell you and everything will work out."

"Okay," Chester said, his somber voice betraying his disbelief. He patted the pup's head. "What's a good girl's name, Daddy?"

"That's your responsibility."

Chester grinned. "Yours is wiping pee. Mommy said so."

Abner returned the grin. "Not if I'm fishing or hunting or guiding hunters. Then it's yours."

"When can I go on the boat with you and the hunters?"

The question somewhat surprised Abner. Chester accepted duck and goose on the table, but he frowned when their limp bodies were brought home after a day's hunt. He even helped pluck them, but he didn't care for the specter of death when it removed the animation of flying or preening or quacking or honking waterfowl.

"We'll see," Abner said, consoling his son. "Those men take hunting seriously. A boy your age in the boat might upset them."

"I'll be good."

"Let's name your pup. Show me how responsible you are. Then we'll see about you going out with the hunters."

"Can we walk to the water? It might help."

"A fine idea," Alice said. "Then I can knit in quiet."

Abner and Chester donned jackets and hats against the chilly morning. Outside, the pup sniffed the path to the sound and the trees on both sides, scurrying back and forth with its tail pointed straight up. Chester asked if she was looking for ducks. Abner said she was too young. Chester asked if she was hungry. Abner said his friend had just fed her.

At the sound, the path split. To the right, it continued north. To the left, it continued south. Both paths were created by locals fishing, hunting, or by lovers seeking a special sunset moment to share. Abner and Alice had done so in the early years of their marriage. Although those times were few and far between now, their memories filled the spaces: wavelets whispering in the marsh, Red-winged Blackbirds perched on swaying cattail heads, dolphins leaping and beads of water illuminated with scarlet sunlight. The daddy in Abner hoped for a relationship like that for his son one day. Despite his outer differences, his heart was as true as an Outer Banks sunrise.

The pup bounced onto the pier and ran to the end, barely stopping in time to avoid tumbling into the water. Chester ran after her, his shoes pattering the wooden boards. Abner joined them at the end. His son knelt to pat the lab's head, then tilted his head upward, brown eyes visible beneath the brim of the old hunting cap. "Let's name her Goldie."

Abner nodded. "An excellent name from an excellent son for an excellent pup. I knew you could do it."

Goldie's ears perked up. She twisted her head from beneath Chester's hand and ran to the side of the pier, eyes searching. Chester asked what she saw, and Abner peered into the marsh.

"It's a pelican." Craning his neck forward, he peered again. "Looks like a young one."

Chester craned his neck too. "It's a brown one. How old is it?"

Deep within a patch of marsh, the pelican flapped. "Let's see," Abner said. "It might be hurt."

The pelican splashed again, this time adding a strident squawk. Goldie ran from the pier, yipping, followed by Chester and Abner. At the water's edge, the pup barked and barked. Abner picked her up and gave her to Chester. "Hold her while I check that bird." It was only a few steps into the marsh. When Abner arrived, he verified the bird's young age, likely a late fledgling from last year, evidenced by its white underside, neck and head. "It's hung in some fishing line," he said to Chester. "I'll see if I can untangle it."

"Pete!" Chester yelled as the bird squawked again and again. "Let's name him Pete."

Abner freed one wing. "What if Pete's a Priscilla?"

Chester giggled. "How will we know?"

The other wing came free. Abner stuffed the fishing line in his pants pocket. He expected the pelican to fly away, but it didn't.

"Why won't it fly away?" Chester asked.

Abner nudged the bird. It flapped and squawked but stayed put. "It might be too weak from not eating. We haven't come to the pier in a few days."

With Goldie in his arms, Chester ran up the inclined path to the house and soon returned to tell Abner he had put Goldie inside while they fed Pete, whose meal was leftover shrimp from supper last night.

"Well," Abner said, removing his cap to scratch his head, "that might work." He carried the now silent bird to shore and held its beak open while Chester dropped shrimp after shrimp inside. The beak tilted back, and Pete squawked again. "I think that did the trick, Son." He moved a few steps away. "Come over here and let's see what Pete does." The pelican turned its head sideways, eyed father and son, and waddled toward them. Abner winked at Chester. "We started the day off with one more member of the family, and now we've got two."

Chester pulled a handful of shrimp from his jacket pocket and fed the pelican. "Son," Abner said, "your mommy won't like your jacket smelling like shrimp."

Chester dabbed his hands in the sound and wiped them on his pants. "I put minnows in my pockets. She doesn't smell them."

Abner knew what he meant. Chester often came home with anything from minnows to shells to rocks in his pockets. Even at six, he loved to ramble the path along the sound, and since no hoodlums were welcome in Corolla, he was safe.

Chester pointed south. "I catch minnows there, Daddy. Maybe Pete can catch some."

Abner knew the place, where the marsh had washed away in the last hurricane. He followed Chester and the pelican waddling behind him. At the spot of open water, Chester felt around with his fingers like a raccoon felt around for oysters. Several minnows, their silver sides reflecting sunlight, darted out of the water, and Pete started gulping. Each time he did, the skin beneath his lower beak expanded and contracted.

Down the path toward the south, a laugh drew Abner's attention. A man about his age, dressed in slacks and a nice shirt, took a pipe from his teeth. "My, my, we've left Richmond and arrived in Corolla to find a maritime circus."

A girl of about Chester's age walked to his right. She wore her blonde hair in a ponytail, and her striking green eyes crinkled with humor.

To the man's left, possibly his wife, a young woman with red hair covered a laugh, then lowered her hand. "I've never seen anything so funny in all my life, Wilbur." Her yellow dress, reaching to her ankles, offset the red hair worn in a bun on the crown of her head.

The girl ran up to Chester. "I remember you, Chester."

Wilbur touched the brim of the derby shading his eyes. "Wilbur Applewhite. This precocious child is my daughter, Maurea."

"And I'm Patsy," the redhead said.

Abner touched the brim of his hunting cap. "Abner Pinkham. You've a lovely family, sir."

Patsy's cheeks colored. Wilbur glanced at her, then returned to Abner. "Patsy is Maurea's governess. My wife is at our cottage with a headache. We came down from Richmond for a few days."

Abner recognized the crisp voice, possibly one of the wealthy hunters who came for waterfowl. He tilted his head to one side. "Have we met by chance? I guide hunters for waterfowl in the fall, and you seem familiar."

Wilbur's eyes widened. "I think you're correct. I came down a lot with my father before he and my mother died. His name was Theodore. Hers was Elizabeth."

"Ah, yes," Abner replied, happy to recall the former client. "I'm sorry, you say they died?"

"Yes, quite a few years ago. Do you still guide? I've been thinking about hunting again. Get out and enjoy nature, you know." He nodded toward Chester and Maurea, who were watching Pete gulp minnows. "Like those two are enjoying nature."

"Pardon me for interrupting," Patsy said, "but how does Maurea know your son?"

"I remember now," Chester said, turning toward them. "It was on the beach."

Wilbur faced his daughter. "I don't remember that."

"You and Patsy were talking, Papa. That's why."

"Oh." He faced Chester. "It's nice to meet you, young man. Tell us about this hungry pelican."

"Pete was stuck in some fishing line."

"You're saying he's grateful enough to not fly away?"

"I guess."

"I suppose we should go," Wilbur said, touching his hat brim again. "Abner, I'll remember you when I decide to try duck hunting again. Do you live nearby?"

"We're the next house along the path. It's up a rise, you can't miss it. If you send me a letter to the post office with the date you'd like to go hunting, I'll be ready."

Wilbur turned to leave, but Maurea pulled his tweed jacket. "Papa, can I visit Chester sometime? It's not far."

"Maybe when you get older. Six is too young."

"I'm six too," Chester said. "We can go to school together."

"That's what I do," Patsy said. "Besides, like Wilbur already said, we live in Richmond."

"Why can't we live here?" Maurea asked her father. "I like it here."

"I *have* been thinking about coming more often. Maybe we'll come enough to enroll you in school this fall."

"Good," Chester said. He held Abner's hand. "I need more friends."

Like a man who understood Chester's statement, Wilbur knelt beside him. "I suppose I know why." He touched the center of Chester's chest. "Who you are is in your heart. Never let anyone tell you any different."

"My wife and I tell him that too," Abner said. "As you might know, the world—and people—can be cruel, even to children. We're teaching him about character. A person with a strong character is confident enough to ignore cruel words from cruel people."

Wilbur stood. "Truer words have never been spoken." He patted Chester's shoulder. "Listen to your mother and father, all right? If you do, you'll grow up to be a fine young man with a fine family."

Maurea took Chester by his smaller hand. "Then we can get married. I like pelicans."

Wilbur chuckled. "It takes more than pelicans to make a good marriage." He glanced at Patsy. "I should know." He touched his hat brim again. "Good day."

Chester watched them leave. "I like them, Daddy. Maurea's eyes are like the ocean."

Although they were nice, Abner wasn't sure *how* nice. Wilbur was a gentleman, no doubt, but his glance at Patsy, when he said it takes more than pelicans to make a good marriage, was troubling. If his wife was at home with a genuine headache, that was one thing, but some of the stories from wealthy hunters were filled with wives using headaches as an excuse to ignore their husbands. Maurea, though, was sweet as could be, but some of those wives with headaches, also according to their husbands, were raising daughters to be headaches too. Still, a husband played an equal part in raising his children as well, so they should share the responsibility. Thank the good Lord that he and Alice did that with Chester.

On the way home, Chester in the lead with the pelican waddling behind him, Abner wondered more about the Applewhites. Of course he'd like to earn a wage to take Wilbur hunting. He might even like Chester and Maurea to get to know each other. Maybe they could do so in school first, around other children Chester should get to know. It was entirely too soon to think about him marrying, but a local wife, one willing to take on the struggle of living on the Outer Banks, would be the better choice than one from the city, who might not realize what she was getting into.

At the bottom of the path to the house, Chester stopped. "Daddy, why did Pete's Mommy and Daddy go away?"

Abner hadn't expected this question. "Pete's old enough to take care of himself. That's what living things eventually do."

His son's brown eyes blinked once, twice, and once again. "Will you and Mommy ever go away?"

"No, Son, but you'll want to have a home and a family of your own one day."

"One day long away, right?"

"Yes."

"Can my house be beside yours?"

"Your wife might not like that."

"I'll find one who will."

"Oh?" Abner said, trying and failing not to grin. "Do I have to guess who that is?"

"I'm not telling." Grinning himself, Chester poked Abner's stomach. "It's a secret."

Meeting Mr. Pinkham and his son pleased Patsy, for it would give her yet another opening to praise Wilbur. Like waves grinding a sea shell into sand, enough praise would wear even *him* down. Mrs. Applewhite had been explicit. "Wilbur's as prudish as his parents were, but I'm certain you can do it. It may take months or even years, but I want Maurea to see the truth about men. They are to be used and tossed aside."

Although Patsy had nodded, a twinge of guilt had pricked her soul. Wilbur really was a good father, and the only reason he couldn't be a good husband was because Catherine wouldn't let him.

On the path by the marsh, Maurea ran ahead, blonde ponytail bouncing along her shoulders. Lighting his pipe, Wilbur shared a soft smile, and Patsy returned it.

She didn't understand Mrs. Applewhite. She had a fine husband, a wonderful child, and the comfort of wealth through a thriving tobacco business. Most women would feel blessed to have all those things. Regardless, Patsy had come from a broken home. Her mother and father would drink themselves into oblivion every few nights. When they didn't do that, they fought until one or the other, or both, drew blood. This led to an older brother and sister leaving Patsy to fend for herself at age sixteen. Since her parents would only earn enough money to buy spirits, plus the minimum for food, Patsy resorted to prostitution, either that or starve in her own bedroom in a Richmond tenement house.

Thank goodness she had turned her life around. She had done well in school, so she put an advertisement in the paper as a tutor. Mrs. Applewhite's response, when they met instead of sending mail, had been with an approving eye and what could only be described as an evil smile. She didn't explain these things until several paychecks had been able to tempt Patsy into pursuing Wilbur. Then, when his attributes as a father and husband had become apparent, the hope of love had begun to burn in Patsy's heart, prompted as well by her guilt at taking money to ruin him.

Wilbur removed the pipe from his teeth and blew a smoke ring. The quickening breeze dissipated it as if it were a fading spirit. "Thank you for walking with Maurea and I, Patsy. I've come to appreciate your company."

"I appreciate your company too, Wilbur." She hesitated. Admit her true feelings or not? Up until recently, she had only been interested in making a paycheck and doing as Mrs. Applewhite had instructed. She gazed up into Wilbur's eyes. Truth sometimes hardened the heart, but she believed the truth about her previous life might soften the heart of this wonderful man. Blinking away tears, she shared the shame of having terrible parents, plus the worse shame of resorting to prostitution to sustain herself with food and clothing.

While Wilbur listened, he alternated between puffing the pipe and clenching his teeth. Done with her story, Patsy readied herself to be fired.

"Well," he said, removing the pipe, "were I a young woman in your predicament, I might resort to the same thing." He placed a gentle hand on her shoulder. "Don't give it another thought. You studied hard and redeemed yourself. Seeing the errors of our ways is a mark of character."

Patsy's mouth fell open. Although she admired this man for so many things, could she be falling in love with him too? She touched his sleeve. "You're too kind, but ..."

"What is it?"

"I'm sorry for saying I would do anything to comfort you concerning Mrs. Applewhite's mistreatment of you. I disregarded your marriage vows. I'll never do so again."

Wilbur squeezed her shoulder. "As we both know, my marriage is a sham. I stay because of Maurea." He took his hand from her shoulder and pressed her forward in the small of her back. "Let's go before my little snail leaves us."

Patsy could never have imagined this moment—the lovely sheen of the Currituck to her right, this wonderful man to her left, their footfalls silent in the sandy path. She looped her arm within Wilbur's. "I'm still sorry. Please don't tell Mrs. Applewhite of our talk."

Removing the pipe from his teeth, Wilbur chuckled. "And ruin the only comfort I have besides Maurea? Perish the thought."

Ahead of them, Maurea stopped. "Come on, slow pokes. We can tell Mother about Chester and Pete."

Wilbur waved at Maurea. "Come back here. I need a word."

Puffing from her run, Maurea returned, her shoes flinging sand. "What, Papa?"

Wilbur released Patsy's arm and stopped. "I've told you how secrets aren't always a good thing. What I haven't told you is secrets are sometimes necessary to avoid arguments."

"Oh, you mean Mother won't like Chester and his family because they're not like us."

The comment broke Patsy's heart. According to Wilbur's downcast eyes, it broke his too. He knelt before his daughter. "I know, I know. We've heard enough of her comments to know her views on people she thinks are beneath her."

"I love her, but— Well, I don't like her very much." Maurea's green eyes found Patsy. "You make Papa smile. Don't stop doing that." She took Patsy by the hand and looped her arm within Wilbur's. "It's good to have a friend. I like Papa having a friend."

Ignoring how she would get her dress sandy, Patsy dropped to her knees and hugged Wilbur's precious daughter. "And you're my friend too, Maurea dear. I'm so happy I met you and your papa." She stood. "Let's get home so I can plan us a nice supper."

As they continued along the path that eventually turned toward the Atlantic and the cottage, the morning's events amazed Patsy. Not only had Wilbur accepted her despite a less than optimum past, Maurea had accepted her as a friend for her papa. The only problem now was Catherine's scheme to ruin her husband. How that would be dealt with, Patsy didn't know, but she didn't intend to let it happen—no matter what.

At the cottage, the presence of the new model 30 Cadillac—Wilbur said he liked its blue paint because it reminded him of the ocean, and the convertible top because he loved the sun and wind on his face—said Catherine hadn't driven anywhere. For this trip, to facilitate coming more often, he purchased the car and hired a man with a barge to bring it over, leaving another car in Currituck for the return drive to Richmond. The man said the salt air would rust the fancy car in no time. Wilbur ignored him at first. Then he said the first car the same man had brought over had lasted long enough to sell to a fisherman who wanted to travel further south and haul his catch back to sell to wealthy northerners on vacation.

Maurea brushed sand off her shoes and climbed the steps. Before doing the same, Patsy gave Wilbur a quick peck on his cheek. "I'm so grateful, Wilbur."

"I am too," he said, flushing a glorious shade of pink. "Not only are you lovely to behold, your intelligence is lovely too. I'm sure you've noticed, but Catherine doesn't care for deep subjects. She prefers new hats and dresses and shoes to books. When she's away like she often is, I hope we can spend more time together discussing more interesting subjects than what the fashions are in New York and Paris."

Patsy agreed, adding, "All I care about is having my backside decently covered. I wore enough ragged things as a child, thank you very much. As far as I'm concerned, of all the attitudes, the greatest is gratitude."

Wilbur's noble brow furrowed. "That's a very good saying. Who said that?"

Patsy grinned mischievously. "Why, I said that. Don't you know by now how intelligent I am?"

As if he wanted to kiss her, Wilbur licked his lips. "I certainly do know now. It's a *very* good saying." He raised a palm to her cheek. "I wish—"

The rusted hinges on the door above squeaked open, startling them apart. "Patsy," Maurea said, "Mother says to come to her room." The door squeaked shut.

Since they were partially hidden by the steps, Patsy dared to palm Wilbur's cheek like he just had hers. "I wish too, Wilbur. I wish too."

She followed him up the steps. Inside, he went to the basin to wash his hands while she went to Catherine's bedroom, where she was told to close the door. "Did you enjoy your stroll with my husband?" Catherine asked, her voice filled with contempt. "You were gone long enough."

Still wearing a lace nightgown, hair cut in a bob, Patsy's employer sat on the bed and crossed her legs, both impossibly long and impossibly white from staying indoors and never wearing knee-length shorts like Maurea did in Corolla during the summer.

Tempted to cross her arms in defiance, Patsy did nothing. Appear meek and compliant and bide her time. If Wilbur came to love her, they would take Maurea away from this madwoman who appreciated nothing and no one.

"I'm doing as I'm told, Mrs. Applewhite. That's why Mr. Applewhite pays me."

"You thought I couldn't see you just now out the window. You and Wilbur looked rather cozy." She pointed. "On my dresser you'll find a check. Since you're following my instructions so well, you deserve a bonus."

Patsy took the check without looking at the sum. Then she decided she must, for appearances' sake. "I appreciate this, Mrs. Applewhite. You're very generous."

"What I'm generous with is my husband. I have the feeling you're falling for him. If you like the kind of man who'd rather be controlled than not, you're welcome to him when I divorce him. However, I can't do that until Maurea learns what a weak man she has for a father. Sleep with him if you must, but don't let her see it until she's old enough to know what you're doing. I want the impact to destroy her. Then she'll come to me for answers, and I'll be happy to give them to her." She fluttered a hand toward the door. "You can go. I'm driving to Kitty Hawk for the night. Perhaps you can talk Wilbur into your bed while I'm gone. If so, demand a prophylactic. The last thing you want is a brat ruining your happiness."

In her room, Patsy started to tear the check to shreds but stopped. The best way to enact revenge against such a terrible excuse for a woman was to save her money in order to escape with Wilbur and Maurea one day. No doubt she'd take the tobacco factory from him, so they would need all the savings they could get.

School

Feeding the chickens, Mirlande poked her lips out. Mommy wanted her to go to school but Auntie said no. She could've gone last year, but Auntie said she could learn everything she needed right here with them. As expected, since it was the first day of school, the bell at the one-room schoolhouse rang through the still September air.

She returned the bag of chicken feed to a wooden box that had washed up in the sound one day. Mommy said if they closed the top, it would keep bugs and rain and animals out.

With fishing poles in hand, Mommy and Auntie came outside. "We're going fishing at that place we caught those flounder," Mommy said. "Get your shoes on and come along."

Mirlande rubbed her stomach. "My tummy hurts."

Auntie made an ugly face. "That's what you get for eating too much of that candy I stole from the store."

Afraid Auntie had guessed her plan, Mirlande rubbed her stomach again. "I might come later. I'm going to the outhouse." She left for the outhouse, tucked in the woods behind the big house, and slammed the door without going inside. After several groans, she peeked around the house. Mommy and Auntie's tall forms were walking up the path. Smiling broadly, Mirlande put on her shoes and ran in the other direction, toward the still ringing school bell.

It took several minutes of hurrying beside the marsh and through the twisted trees to get there. By the time she arrived, the bell in the steeple, like a church steeple, had stopped ringing. Watching the two windows on both sides of the door, she crept through the sandy yard, up the steps, and cracked the door open to peek in. Eyes wide, she ran away to hide amongst the trees surrounding the school. She had never seen so many boys and girls at one place at one time. If she went in, the thought of all those staring eyes would send the heat of embarrassment into her cheeks.

Forming a V, a flock of pelicans glided over her head toward the ocean. Like most days the breeze arrived, rustling the tiny leaves on the trees.

Mirlande sat on one of the limbs hanging next to the sand. The children also wore better clothes than her, just a tattered dress that Auntie had taken from a trash can beside some person's home. She hadn't brushed her hair either, so it hung in tangles around her shoulders and down the middle of her back. If she went in that school, the children would point and laugh until she ran home in tears.

"Good morning," a voice said through the partially open schoolhouse door. "If this is your first day at school, I'm Miss Sanders, your new teacher. The voice sounded nice, unlike someone who would tease anyone about their clothes or hair. Then again, she was a teacher, not a mean child.

The teacher's voice continued, but Mirlande barely heard it. Her opinion of mean children came from the time a boy caught her at a window of his home. Mommy and Auntie had bad colds, so they hadn't been fishing or crabbing or scrounging in trash cans for food. Although Mirlande had fried their eggs that morning, her stomach was empty before noon. They usually had bread or bacon, but Auntie's cold had kept her and her money at home.

On the way to the store and its trash can to see what she could find, Mirlande detoured to follow the aroma of fried chicken. Licking her lips, she let the delicious smell draw her like a chicken neck tied to a string drew one of those blue crabs in the sound. Up ahead, not too far from the store, the open window of a house allowed the crackle and pop of frying chicken to announce its location. Lowering her head, Mirlande crept to the trash can beneath the window. As she raised the lid, hoping for something as wonderful as fried chicken, the front door of the house squeaked open and slammed closed, and a boy rounded the corner of the house. "I seen you you trash eater! Git outta here!" He turned his head over his shoulder. "Paw! It's that gal again! Git the shotgun!"

Mirlande whirled and ran back home, vowing to never look through a trash can beneath a window again.

The teacher's voice droned. The day warmed. Regardless of her fear at being seen by the children, Mirlande wanted to stay for lunch. Maybe one or two would be nice enough to offer a taste of something. She left the tree limb to sit behind it and lean against the trunk. Like a lullaby Mommy sometimes sang, the leaves rustled louder now, hastened by the quickening breeze.

This place called Corolla, with the sound on one side and the ocean on the other, seemed like an island. Once, when Mirlande was walking the path along the sound, she followed another path where it entered a section of twisted trees. Strange tracks in the sand suggested a creature with feet that made holes instead of footprints. Eyes focused ahead, she eased along, the hair on the back of her neck prickling with both fear and curiosity. Maybe these creatures were some of Auntie's monsters or maybe not, but seeing them would tell the tale.

Step after step she crept forward. One low tree limb resembled a lion in one of Auntie's stories about Africa. Another resembled an elephant. Yet another resembled a zebra, except— Mirlande's mouth fell open. This zebra's hide was brown instead of black with white stripes. Then, one after another, more zebras appeared from within the trees and brambles. Some wore black hides. Some wore brown and white hides. Mirlande giggled. They weren't zebras. They were horses.

From within the group of horses, a pony raised its head to watch her. Unlike the grown horses, its mane resembled a hair brush. It waggled its head and whinnied. The grown horses snorted and stomped their hooves. Then, in a blur of colorful hides and raised tails, the horses galloped deeper into the twisted trees.

Mirlande pressed both hands to her chest, where her heart mimicked the sound of those pounding hooves. How she longed to ride one of them along the beach, hooves splashing white foam, maybe with her future husband riding another horse at her side.

The schoolhouse door slammed open, startling her. Crouched behind the tree trunk, she watched boys and girls stream outside with brown paper bags. How had the time passed so quickly? Maybe she had fallen asleep and had dreamed about the horses. Mommy and Auntie hadn't come looking for her, so they might still be fishing.

"Looka here!" a familiar voice yelled from behind her. "It's that trash eater!" Mirlande turned to run, but he blocked her way, kicking sand at her. "Trash eater, trash eater! Git on outta here, trash eater. We got no trash fer the likes of you!"

From behind Mirlande, a boy ran over. "You stop that! She's my friend!"

111

A girl joined him. "She's my friend too. Leave her alone!"

The mean boy drew back his foot to kick sand again, and the other boy grabbed a rock from beside the base of the tree. "Don't even think about it."

"Aw, ain't no one scared, crab boy. Drop that rock before I hit you with it."

The boy—Chester, Mirlande remembered—raised the rock, and the other girl—Maurea—grabbed his arm. "You can't do that, Chester. You'll get in trouble."

Chester dropped the rock and looked back at the girl. "You better go." As she ran across the wagon track, he faced Elmo Parker. "If you want to call someone names, Elmo, I'm right here."

Elmo came closer. Several other children circled them. "Crab boy," Elmo said, sneering. "You ain't nothin' but a big-head crab boy. Yo momma was a crab an' yo daddy was a whale. Whatcha gotta say 'bout that?"

Chester laughed. "Say it again, it's funny."

"What?"

Maurea laughed. "Elmo Parker, you smell like fish guts."

Elmo shoved his chest into Maurea's chest. "If you won't a girl, I'd knock your teeth out."

Chester grabbed the rock again. "And I'll knock *you* out."

"You an' what army, crab boy?"

The schoolhouse door creaked open, revealing Miss Sanders. "What are you children doing over there? Chester Pinkham, you put that rock down!"

The circle of children scattered. Chester dropped the rock. Elmo skulked away to sit on a tree limb and open his lunch bag. The teacher went back inside the schoolhouse.

"You shouldn't have picked up that rock," Maurea said to Chester.

"Elmo shouldn't have said what he said to Mirlande."

Maurea picked up their lunch bags and led him to another tree limb near the wagon path in front of the schoolhouse. The bags crinkled open, followed by wax paper. Chester ate his bologna sandwich and drank water from a Mason jar. Maurea ate a ham sandwich and drank sweet tea from something she called a Thermos.

"Why did you laugh when Elmo called you those names?" she asked. "Didn't it make you mad? You got mad when he said he would knock my teeth out."

About to drink water, Chester lowered the jar. "Sticks and stones. That's what Daddy and Mommy said."

"What about sticks and stones?"

"They'll break my bones but names can't hurt me. It's called character."

Maurea took a bite of sandwich and swallowed. "I don't understand?"

Chester loved the slow way she said things. Understand came out smooth and syrupy: "Ondastayund." He grinned. "I like the way you talk, Maurea."

"Okay, but what's character?"

"It's when you know words can't hurt you." He patted his chest. "When words can't hurt your heart. Rocks are different, rocks can hurt. I just laugh at words." He raised his left hand. "Mommy and Daddy said mean people would say things about my hand and my head. That's when they told me about character."

"I'm still sorry they're mean to you," Maurea said after drinking tea. "Would you really knock Elmo out?"

"He's a scaredy cat. Didn't you see that dumb look on his face?"

"You mean when you told him to say what he said about your mother and papa again?"

"His brain got frazzled. He didn't like me having character."

Chester watched Maurea eat silently, apparently satisfied about his explanation of character. He remembered when he and Daddy met her and Mr. Applewhite and Patsy last year, by the sound with Pete. Not a day went by when he didn't think about her, but he also thought about the dark-haired girl they met on the beach that time, the girl Elmo had called trash-eater, whose name was Mirlande. She had come to the beach with two ladies instead of a lady and a man. Chester didn't know what to make of it until Daddy, having seen them at the general store, asked the post office clerk about them.

"The pastor said they're from Haiti," the clerk said as he gave Daddy the mail. "The older woman is the younger woman's Aunt, I think. I know the little girl calls her Auntie, so maybe she's her great aunt. They stay in that old shack where the pastor used to live. Keep to themselves except for digging in trash roundabout."

Daddy thanked him and took the mail home. His motto was if you can't say anything nice about someone, don't say anything at all, and Chester loved him for it. Too bad Elmo didn't have a daddy who taught good lessons like that. He was a gruff old man who, according to rumors at the general store, bullied his wife and children. No wonder Elmo turned out like he did.

Finishing the last bite of his sandwich, he elbowed Maurea. "Look."

On the other side of the wagon track, Mirlande waved.

"Her dress is torn," Maurea said. "She's very pretty."

114

"You weren't here for school last year," Chester said, facing Maurea. "She didn't come then either. I guess her mommy won't let her come to school."

Maurea held up a sandwich and waved Mirlande over. "Maybe she'd like some lunch."

Mirlande hurried over. "I'm not hungry, but thank you. Thank you both for stopping that boy, he's mean."

"He's just a big mouth," Chester said, taking a bundle of waxed paper from his lunch bag. He offered Mirlande a cookie. "It's oatmeal. Mommy makes them with raisins."

Mirlande took a bite. "Mmm," she said, still chewing.

"This is my first year at school here," Maurea said. "I went back home last year. I'm seven, are you seven?"

Chewing more cookie, Mirlande nodded. "Do you know how to read?"

"We're learning," Chester said, raising the Mason jar for water.

Mirlande finished the cookie. "Mommy taught me the alphabet, but I can't read."

"She won't let you come to school?" Maurea asked.

"Auntie won't."

Maurea drank tea and put the Thermos away. "Maybe you can come next year." She tilted her head to one side. "Do they know you're here now?"

"They're fishing." Mirlande looked up at the sky. "I better get home before they come back."

Behind Chester, the bell rang to end the lunch period. On the way to the school house, he faced Maurea. "Mirlande's nice, but she should come to school so she can learn to read."

Nodding, Maurea said nothing. Something in her eyes said she might think Mirlande was nice, but not *very* nice. Chester had noticed that look before, when she talked about her mommy, which she didn't do much.

When the teacher went to the chalkboard, she drew a map. "This, children, is Germany. In case your parents haven't mentioned it from stories on the radio, or from hearing people at the post office or the general store, there's a war in Europe."

Chester shot his hand up. "Miss Sanders, Daddy said the Germans sank the *Lusitania* in May. Do you think America will join the war?"

Miss Sanders erased the map. "I certainly hope not, Chester. I certainly hope not."

Discovery

Sheriff Maurea Sandifer here again. I hate to break up this story's timeline, because doing so can make a reader feel disjointed. Regardless, Chester's life couldn't have been any more disjointed, and I hope to help readers feel more empathy for him by writing in what might seem to be a disjointed way.

In this short chapter, we begin our murder case with the discovery of the bodies in the Corolla Island boathouse, and in the next chapter, we meet Amos Sandifer, my great-great grandfather.

I'll leave you to it.

Corolla, North Carolina
1928

After breakfast with the other servants at Corolla Island, Constantine Andino's butler waited by his employer's bedroom door to be called. Although "Con," as Constantine's friends and family called him, usually slept late on rainy days, no snores could be heard from the other side of the door. The butler agreed with Constantine's nickname. The man had certainly conned his fiancé, the beautiful Miss Maurea Applewhite.

117

Following orders, he waited another thirty minutes, evidenced by glances at his pocket watch, before opening the door. Oddly, the bed was still made. Not oddly, the butler had seen Con last night on his way to the boathouse. Not oddly as well, he had also seen the sheen of moonlight reflecting off the flowing black ringlets of the young woman Con had been meeting there, no doubt to do things a woman should not do with an engaged man. In fact, both of their heads had been visible at the edge of the boathouse porch, proven by Con's thick, black hair, slicked back and also shining in the moonlight. Their embrace had also been visible before they escaped into the privacy of the boathouse. They had even paused to look at the beam of light from the Currituck Lighthouse, a short walk away.

The butler checked his pocket watch again. Con had wanted to leave for New York first thing, and the boat to the North Carolina mainland would arrive soon. He packed Con's luggage, leaving out a suit if needed, and took an umbrella downstairs to the front porch for the rainy morning. A search around the house revealed nothing. Since the Knights weren't here, and since they allowed the Applewhites to stay when they pleased, and since neither Wilbur, Catherine, nor Maurea were up yet, the butler left for the only logical place to find Con, in the boathouse with his mistress.

As the butler started toward the raised bridge to the right of the boathouse, he caught a glimpse of the blue hunting cap worn by Chester Pinkham, the Knight's hired hand. About a hundred yards north, standing in the path by the sound, the young man raised his hand to wave. He then faded into the marsh and cattails, both swaying in the wind.

Thinking Chester was waving to someone else, the butler turned to watch the guest room windows of Corolla Island, in time to see the curtain in Maurea's room close. Some of the other servants had mentioned their relationship. Miss Rose, the cook, said they were mere friends. The groundskeeper, who Chester worked with, said they were friends too. The butler, though, had seen them leaving the house on one occasion after midnight, so he had his doubts. Friends don't sneak around like lovers. Lovers sneak around like lovers.

With the rain pelting the umbrella, the butler hurried to the back of the boathouse porch. The door was ajar. Not caring to see Con and the woman in a compromising position, he knocked and waited. No rustling of clothes. No fearful whispers. He knocked again and waited. Rain pattered harder on the umbrella. The metallic aroma of water filled the air. In the lagoon, wavelets lapped against the dock's pilings. At times, if the wind blew hard from the east, one might hear the Atlantic surf pounding the beach. Today it was a distant murmur.

Throwing possible embarrassment aside, the butler opened the door. He didn't consider himself the squeamish type, but at the sight of blood-soaked hair and wide-open eyes, he whirled around to vomit in the sand outside the door.

Done retching the breakfast of coffee, toast, and scrambled eggs, the mixture leaving a multicolored mess on the ground, he ran to the house. Someone must be told.

Crossing the bridge again, he stopped at the sound of an engine slowing down, barely heard above the increasing patter of rain. The boat coming for Con was entering the lagoon. He ran back to the boathouse. When the boat was close enough, he jumped aboard, breathing hard from all his running. "Murder," he gasped. "Two people have been murdered."

119

Sheriff

Currituck, North Carolina
1928

At his office near the Currituck County Courthouse, interim sheriff Amos Sandifer cradled the telephone. The electric chair had sent another murderer to his grave, and he didn't know how he felt about it.

He sipped coffee made by Sandra, his secretary, and lowered the mug to the battle-scarred desk, its edge marked with burns from many a cigarette butt. How many cases had his predecessor considered while sitting here? On the edge facing him, knife cuts evidenced either confusion, apprehension, or satisfaction at another criminal sent either to prison or jail, where he or she wouldn't harm another victim again. In the case of released prisoners, some learned their lesson and some didn't. If the crimes were heinous enough, the criminal demonic enough, the repeat offenses numbering enough, why not set their cruel behinds in the electric chair to keep them from harming more innocent victims?

Beyond his open office door and the windows bracketing the department door, past a grove of oaks, the shimmering waters of the Currituck Sound beckoned.

He hadn't wanted this job any more than his wife had wanted him to take it. Aside from his love for her and their twin ten-year-olds, Larry and Harry—Harry was already talking about being a sheriff and passing the desire to keep Currituck County safe to his children—his other love was commercial fishing. Nothing excited Amos more than seeing filled nets hoisted into the stern of a boat. Now his boat, the *Angela,* named after his deceased mother, was being rented to another fisherman. At least it was making money, so there was that.

He grimaced from the injury he took in The Great War, a German bullet that removed a fair amount of his right calf muscle. As much as he loved fishing, common sense overcame desire. If he couldn't do all the work on a boat because of his injury, not just captain it, it was best to rent the *Angela.* Thank the good Lord for Susan waiting for him until the end of the war. Their marriage and their boys had eased the pain of seeing friends kill and being killed in the trenches in France. He'd even thought of writing a book about the war, but reliving it might've driven him insane. War is what happens when good people—people with morals and honor—do nothing to stop people who believe they have the right to force their opinions down everyone's throats, no matter how destructive they are.

Without meaning to, a habit from checking his head for a wound after a near-miss from an exploding artillery shell, Amos ran a hand through his bristly crew-cut. At least his injury didn't keep him from earning a wage for his family, and if this interim position turned into a permanent position, so much the better. If not, he might consider captaining his boat again. When it came to caring for a family, a man had to do what a man had to do.

He went to the reception area, refilled his mug, and faced Sandra. "Where are my two deputies? Have they decided against the new guy on his first day?"

Sandra peered over the Raleigh newspaper. Her blue eyes crinkled above readers perched on the tip of her nose. "Not a peep out of either one. Good thing the jail is empty."

"You mean it's a good thing you don't have to feed a prisoner," Amos said, adding a hint of humor to his voice to let Sandra know he was joking.

"I just started this job last month," Sandra said, *not* adding any humor to her voice. "Besides, no one said I had to."

"I'm joking, Sandra." Amos sipped coffee. "Don't worry, we'll figure it out."

Sandra raised the paper. A moment passed. She peered over it again. "Who's this county's coroner now? Ours retired last week."

"Something else to figure out." Amos rubbed his chin. "Hmm, how are you with a scalpel?"

Sandra raised the paper once more. "I don't even filet a fish."

In the gravel lot outside, a car joined the other two. With a flurry of gangly legs and arms on his tall, thin frame, Bill Timms resembled a scarecrow more than a deputy. He slammed the car door and hurried inside. "Sorry I'm late, flat tire got me." He looked from Sandra to Amos. "It's just me and you and Sandra, Amos. Ed took a job in Norfolk."

Longtime friends with Timms, Amos should've known better than to think he'd abandon him. "Norfolk, huh? He's welcome to it. I'll take peaceful Currituck County over Norfolk any day of the week."

On Sandra's desk, the phone rang. "So much for peaceful Currituck County." She turned the phone toward Amos. "Welcome to your first call."

Amos raised the handset. "Currituck County Sheriff's Departme—"

122

"Amos, this is Ted, down at the docks. A crabber just towed a fellow in, ran outta diesel. He's got a crazy butler onboard. Says two people been murdered over at Corolla Island, that fancy place them Knights built."

"I know who built it, Ted, it took long enough. Why, the barges with the building materials only stopped running at night." Amos hesitated, disgusted with his habit of friendly talk. Being interim sheriff, he needed to get down to brass tacks. "What's this about two people being murdered?"

"A man and a woman. The man—he's a rich New Yorker named Constantine Andino—is the butler's boss. The woman is a local. The butler didn't say who she was. Some rich folks are stayin' at that place. The butler didn't tell them so they wouldn't leave. You need to get over there right away before they do. The bodies are in the boathouse. Nobody's likely to go there in all this rain. You still need to hurry. There's a murderer runnin' loose in Corolla."

"I'll be right there." Amos cradled the phone. "Durn, Bill, we got a double homicide on our hands." He filled Bill and Sandra in. At the deputy's first question, Amos raised a hand to stop him. "Hold off on the questions until I get back. The boat the butler is on ran out of diesel. I'll use it once it's filled up again."

He faced Sandra. Her eyes blinked like a woman who hadn't heard of such a thing as a double homicide in this quiet county. "Not a word to anyone, Sandra. I'll be back soon as I can, hopefully with a suspect." He faced Bill. "That means you too. Take care of things while I'm gone. I've gotta be the sheriff and the durn coroner to boot."

Proposal

While mending one of Mirlande's dresses by lamplight, Lovely waited for her and Auntie to fall asleep. After so many years of not calling that woman anything because she claimed to have not been named when she was born, it seemed "Auntie," created by Mirlande, had stuck. Lovely despised the name like she despised the woman. As far as she knew, they weren't even related, their only link being Hazel, Lovely's dead mother. Even if they were related, she wished they weren't.

She rose from the rickety ladderback chair and checked the pair for the even breathing of sleep.

"That creaking chair would wake the dead," Auntie said, snapping her eyes open. "What do you want?"

"I'm checking my stitches." Lovely raised the dress in front of the kerosene lamp. "Can't I check my stitches? You complain about my stitches, so I thought I better check them."

"I complain more about you talking too much. That doesn't shut you up, does it?"

Lovely draped the dress across the chair, raised her hands and yawned. "Aren't you sleepy? Our summer squash came in nicely. I'm glad Jeff gave us those seeds."

"They came in *too* nicely. My back aches from picking them." Auntie raised up on her left elbow. "You talk to Jeff too much. He comes from the back of the store every time we go there."

"He's a hard worker," Lovely said, trying to change the subject. "He hopes to run the store one day."

Auntie dropped to the pillow. "Lies and more lies. He'll just be another Creole bastard like the one that raped you."

Behind Lovely's back, she clenched her right hand into a fist. One day—maybe one day soon—she would break Auntie's jaw for her. Then she would starve to death instead of trying to ruin Lovely's chances at love.

"Fix that shirt I wore today." Auntie yawned and rolled over. "The sleeve is torn."

Mirlande gave a little snore and rolled over too.

Instead of risking the creaking ladderback, Lovely waited until Auntie's breathing hinted sleep before she left the shack.

Outside, the air of the July evening had cooled slightly. In the light of more stars than she had ever seen, she hurried to the path by the sound and picked up her pace, anxious to meet Jeff at the beach.

If his words of love were sincere, his promises of them marrying and him providing a home and a father for Mirlande as well, only a fool would refuse him, and Lovely didn't consider herself a fool.

Oh, she had been a fool when she allowed the Creole into her bed back in Haiti. When Auntie caught them, the jealous woman got the idea of rape into her head and wouldn't let it go. The thing was, as Lovely knew, Auntie had wanted the Creole for herself, and she couldn't stand him wanting anyone else, like when he had wanted Hazel.

Puffing for breath, Lovely paused to get her wind. Recovered, she continued along the path toward her and Jeff's special place.

Like she had wanted to leave Haiti for America, she wanted to get away from Auntie. She had bided her time since Auntie kept her money—well, Hazel's money—hidden, preferring to dig clothes and food out of people's trash. Lovely met Jeff one afternoon at the store this way. His sad smile upon seeing her suggested a good heart, which was affirmed when he gave them the summer squash seeds when planting time came.

Lovely didn't believe Auntie's stories about Hazel at first, but the Creole confirmed them on walks around the plantation. "She loved money," he said. "I asked her once if she slept with all those men to get enough money to get out of Haiti and to a better life. She snorted like a pig and said, 'As you know, you bastard, I love men like I love money. If they're willing to pay me well for a few minutes of my time, who am I to argue?'"

This lesson taught Lovely what *not* to be in life. She wanted a decent man, a decent home, and a decent father for Mirlande. If they stayed with Auntie and her voodoo dolls, who knew what might happen.

She turned right, taking the starlit path to the beach. Here and there in the sand, horse droppings marked why this section of beach was special to her and Jeff.

Every other step or so, worry joined her excitement. Jeff had said news reports from his family's radio spoke of the possibility of America entering the war in Europe. If so, German submarines, as difficult as it was to believe, might attack these very shores. Lucky for Jeff, although he didn't claim it as such, a broken arm as a child from falling out of a wagon, plus a bad reset by his father, would keep him from fighting.

Seeing no need for war, Lovely was glad. When she and Auntie returned from fishing, and while Auntie cleaned them, Mirlande pulled Lovely aside and told her how she had visited the schoolhouse. She added how embarrassed she was because of her clothes and her hair, but said she had made two friends. Lovely asked if she wanted to go again, to attend class instead of sitting outside, and Mirlande said no. Since that was the case, a marriage to Jeff would allow for new clothes that wouldn't embarrass Mirlande so she could attend school. Lovely ended the conversation by saying to keep it a secret from Auntie, to which Mirlande happily agreed.

At the beach, Lovely climbed the slight incline, marked by footprints. Sitting at the bottom of the incline, Jeff turned at the sound of her bare feet shuffling in the sand. "There she is. I was afraid you wouldn't make it."

Lovely sat beside him. "I had to wait for Auntie to go to sleep." She lay her head on his shoulder, and he slipped a hand around her waist.

"It's a pretty night with all the stars, but you outshine them all, Lovely." She kissed his cheek and snuggled into his warmth, and he pulled her closer. "I know we talked about getting married, but—"

Lovely jumped up and knelt before him. "Please" she said, nearly in tears, "please don't ruin our dreams."

"How can I do that when I love you so much?" He opened his hand to reveal a ring. "Will you marry me when things get settled after the war? I want to start our lives together in peace, not in a world gone crazy with killing." He took her hand and slid the ring on her finger. "I promise, we'll get married soon as we can. I know you need time to break it to your aunt too. She'll hate to lose you."

Relieved at his proposal, Lovely wiped tears, kissed his cheek, and sat beside him again. "I don't care what she hates." She looked Jeff in the eye. "And don't dare suggest her living with us. Like I told you, I only came here with her to start over, and now I am."

Jeff patted her knee. "Now *we* are. I'm looking forward to being a dad to Mirlande. She's as sweet as you, but a lot shyer."

"That's from Auntie's influence. She would keep us in a cave if she could. She hates everyone, especially men."

"We can talk about better things, you know." He slipped his fingers into hers. "Like our honeymoon."

Lovely admired Jeff for his willingness to be a father to Mirlande, but she admired him as much for avoiding the topic of physical intimacy before marriage. Among men, he was a rare man, and she loved him for it. Yes, the wait to see if America joined the war might take a while, but Jeff would be worth it. "Do you think the war will last long if we join it?" Lovely asked, hope and fear making her voice rise.

"I hope not," Jeff said. "Like I said, there's been talk of German submarines attacking ships off the coast if we do join, and that would stop those rich northerners from coming here to hunt. I want to build us a nice house, so I'd rather wait until they come back after the war. They'll be ready to spend money then, and the store will be ready to rake it in."

Lovely thought that made sense. Jeff had even said she could work in the store if she wanted and draw a wage. She wasn't sure about that. The first thing she wanted was a brother or sister for Mirlande. Maybe that would help her shyness with school. She needed to learn to read and write, something neither Lovely nor Auntie knew how to do well. Oh, they could scratch a few letters and read enough words to get by. Given enough time in school, Mirlande could even teach Lovely, who was too embarrassed to tell Jeff about her lack of education.

As far as Auntie, who would rage about the marriage and being left alone, sure to add how Jeff just wanted a beautiful woman for his bed and to wait on him hand and foot, she could go to the devil.

Irene

Maurea wakes to August 25 without any symptoms of a heart attack. Making coffee, she scoffs at the possibility. Making eggs, she shoves it from her mind. Crunching whole-wheat toast, she even laughs. She's a tough old bird, having survived worse than a silly hurricane.

Dishes done, she goes to the porch with the radio. The sky is indigo. The yard is green. The Currituck shimmers gray in the rising sun. The radio is silent because she hasn't turned it on. From somewhere in Aydlett, the aroma of bacon rides the breeze from the north. A pair of Red-winged Blackbirds flits over the cattails and continues south.

The sun seeps from the sky and warms her brow. She thought she slept well but apparently didn't. Her eyelids lower and rise, lower and rise.

The binoculars on the counter beside the toaster tempt her. Across the sound, the distant red tower that probes the night with its finger of light tempts her. To its right, the distant yellow rectangle of Corolla Island tempts her, where twin tragedies ruined so many lives.

It's been years since she cried over it all, or has it? Did she cry last night? When she woke, the dry pillow said no. Did she cry yesterday? The lack of tissues anywhere in the house or in the trash says no.

She fetches the binoculars and returns to the porch. Inside the eyepieces, mascara darkens the lenses. She's almost 103 but has existed a thousand years. How long must she be penitent? How long must remorse eat at her soul? She deserved a fraction of the blame but not all. Mother—that immoral wretch— deserved most of it, if not every single bit of it. Each and every one of her evil schemes and calculations led to those twin tragedies. Had those schemes been given a chance to be revealed all those years ago, not only would she have deserved a seat in the electric chair, she would've deserved a seat in hell.

Maurea raises the binoculars over her shoulder. If she were a teenager again, with a strong right arm, she could easily throw them in the sound. She starts to go closer to do exactly that, but the fear of never focusing on the place where some of the most tender moments of her life occurred makes her lower them beside the radio.

Like two black eyes, the knobs stare. Like a weather announcer's mouth, the speaker wants to tell her to drive the Buick inland to escape Hurricane Irene.

"No," Maurea whispers, breathy and barely audible. "I've run my entire life, and I won't run anymore."

On August 25, Chester decides against worrying about Hurricane Irene and returns to the book store near the coffee shop for a copy of *If the Sunrise Forgets Tomorrow*. By the same author as *The Diary of Carlo Cipriani*, this book takes place on Ocracoke Island in the early days of World War II, when German U-boats sank ship after ship along the North Carolina coast. As he knows, they did the same thing in The Great War, but not with the same deadly statistics. Fortunately, only ten ships were sunk off the North Carolina coast in the first world war. In the second, nearly 400 went down in flames, littering beaches with bodies and wreckage.

If the Sunrise Forgets Tomorrow includes the sinking of the British trawler HMS *Bedfordshire*, refitted with guns and men to help patrol the North Carolina coast. Four men washed ashore on Ocracoke Island, where they were buried and remain there today. As the pages turn, Chester laughs at the main characters, twin eighteen-year-old sisters Virginia and Ruby Starr. Although they're dealing with family tragedy, they're an amusing pair, arguing one moment, sincere the next.

He returns home to continue reading. When the sun sears down straight overhead from the August sky, evidenced by the heat building in the shack, he leaves for a stroll to Corolla. If he hears any news about Irene, so be it. If not, so be that too. He's ready regardless, but it would be nice to have an idea of the strength when it hits.

At Corolla Island, the yellow paint glares brightly. Atop the Currituck Lighthouse, tourists mill around the black-painted walkway. Below, more tourists form a line. A woman raises a camera. A man wipes beads of glistening sweat from his forehead with the back of his hand. A little boy asks how tall the lighthouse is. A little girl says she wants to go swimming at the beach. A husband says he'd rather be fishing. A wife says she'd rather be shopping. A couple reading an Outer Banks tourism guide stare at each other. "I didn't know two people were murdered in the boathouse at the Whalehead Club," the man says. "In 1928," she says, tapping the page with a fingertip. "They think the murder weapon was a brick because of the indentions in their skulls, how awful." The man looks at the page. "A young man and a young woman in the prime of life, how sad."

Chester approaches them. "I was nineteen back then. I live here. I know all about it."

The woman turns the page. "Oh, look. Everything's half-off at those huge beach stores we see everywhere." The man nods. "Good. I need a new beach chair."

Disgusted, Chester wonders why he tries talking to anyone.

Beside Highway 12, walking in the shade of the live oak trees, his attitude improves. Like him, walkers, joggers, and bicyclists enjoy the day.

At the coffee shop, the TV is off. At the restaurant, patrons concentrate on lunch: seafood, salads, burgers, etc. Tourists love many things at the Outer Banks, but one of their favorites is eating.

He returns to the Currituck Lighthouse. As a boy of three, he wanted to be a lighthouse keeper, but decided he didn't care to work on the lighthouse with all of its upkeep, which would lessen his time outdoors.

He strolls around, snaps a twig from a tree for his teeth, and strolls some more. Before he realizes where he is, he's staring at the hole in the back of the lighthouse. Six feet up, like the empty socket of a pulled tooth, the black hole where the one red brick once was hastens the hint of a memory.

He wishes he hadn't shown it to Maurea, who told her mother about it. Including himself, three humans had teetered on the edge of dying in the electric chair, yet they were all guilty in one way or another.

Chester leaves for home. Like a child's balloon, he's deflated, depressed. Why can't he go on to either his reward or his punishment and be done with it?

To his left, the reflection of Corolla Island boathouse in the lagoon laughs at him until he can't ignore it. The best thing to get his mind off of it is to retreat to one of his many treasured memories of Daddy.

Hunt

A hand shook Chester's shoulder. "Rise and shine, Son."

Chester blinked until his eyes focused. Darkness filled the windows. A glowing lantern sat on the kitchen table. Shimmering embers in the fireplace filled the stone hearth. Over them, hanging from a hook, a coffee pot steamed. Although his body was warm, his head and nose, the only parts of him not covered with two quilts, were cold. Kneeling at the fireplace, Daddy turned strips of sizzling bacon in a cast iron pan, filling the house with hickory-smoked aroma. Chester sat up. "It's too early to rise and shine."

Daddy kept turning bacon. "It's not too early for a surprise, is it?"

"It's November." Chester rubbed his eyes. "Christmas is in December."

"Your birthday is in November." Daddy faced him. A length of black hair fell across his forehead. "Are you ready to be eight?"

In a burst of white, like the limbs of a pine tree, frost etched the lower left edge of the window to the right of the door. The site made Chester shiver. "It's too cold to rise and shine too."

Daddy set the pan of bacon on the oak table, beside a plate of scrambled eggs. "Get dressed and eat. You've been asking about this for a long time."

Curious about Daddy's promise of a surprise, Chester yawned and crawled out of bed, shivering at the touch of the cold wooden floor against his warm feet. He had wanted one of the ponies from the wild herd, and Daddy had never said if they could get one or not. "Are we getting a pony while it's asleep?"

"We're not getting a pony, so stop asking," Daddy said sternly. "This is something else you've been worrying me about." He poured coffee. "Put on your warmest clothes and two pair of socks. Get out your stocking hat too, and your mittens. Don't forget your long underwear."

Chester started to ask if they were going to the North Pole to visit jolly old St. Nick but didn't. Whatever Daddy was planning was serious. Dressed as instructed, except for his coat and mittens, he sat at the table. "Is Mommy coming?"

"Someone is. Not her."

Chester rolled his eyes. "One of the elves?"

"Whose elves?" Daddy asked, sitting down across the table. "Oh." He grinned. "No, we're not going to the North Pole."

"Why is it a secret?"

"It's a surprise, remember? Fill your plate and eat. You'll need it where we're going." Daddy filled a plate for Goldie. Grown now, she padded over from her bed in a corner and gobbled it down, then drank water from her bowl near her bed.

Bacon crunched. Eggs were peppered. Coffee almost scalded lips. On the frigid window, frost formed a limb on the white pine tree.

Chester yawned again. "Let's save my surprise for another day and go back to bed."

Daddy put the empty dishes in the basin and took two hand-carved duck calls from the fireplace mantle, and Chester jumped up from the chair. "You're finally taking me duck hunting?"

Daddy nodded. "Not so loud, you'll wake your mommy. Get on your mittens and hat. It'll be cold out on the sound."

Chester and Goldie followed him out to the pier, illuminated by starlight, where Daddy's skiff waited. Daddy didn't have his shotgun, so he was going to guide someone. Just as Chester started to ask who, footsteps thudded in the path to his left, the one coming from the south. "Morning, Abner. Morning, Chester. I've been looking forward to this for a while."

Chester whirled toward the familiar voice. "Hey, Mr. Applewhite. It sure is cold."

"That's what I told Maurea before I left Richmond yesterday. She said to tell you hello."

Daddy took Mr. Applewhite's shotgun while he climbed into the skiff. "Got us a clear night, Wilbur. As cold as it is, I hope we see plenty of ducks at sunrise."

Chester climbed in and sat at the bow. Goldie jumped in and joined him. Their breaths formed white clouds in the freezing air. Chester pulled Goldie close, hoping they would warm each other. "How does Maurea like school in Richmond, Mr. Applewhite? She told me she would go there this year, but Patsy is still staying with y'all."

"She likes school better here. Yes, she's quite fond of Patsy. As far as my name, call me Wilbur. I don't even ask my workers at the factory to call me Mr. Applewhite. I'm not a man for putting on airs."

"What's that?" Chester asked, curious about such a strange phrase.

Daddy untied the skiff from the pier. "It's not acting like those boys that make fun of your hand."

"Like bullies?"

"It's people who think they're better than other people."

The explanation made sense. Chester liked having character. He enjoyed watching boys' faces get red when he ignored the names they called him, like crab boy and big head. They thought they were better than him. Most of them left him alone now, but he still hadn't made any friends. He often wondered about Mirlande, the girl who came to school that one time last year. He also wondered where she lived. She seemed like someone who could use a friend, maybe even a friend like him.

"I see your canoe," Wilbur said. "Not quite the thing for duck hunting."

Daddy set the oars in the locks. "Chester loves it. Maybe he can take Maurea out one day."

Wilbur looked away and back. "I hate to bring this up, but with all the talk about the war in Europe, I doubt it'll be one day soon. I'm friends with a politician in Richmond. He says there's talk of the Germans sending submarines to the east coast to sink freighters. I never would've believed it until I heard about the *Lusitania*."

"I hope it won't come to that," Daddy said, pulling the oars.

Both men said nothing more. They were concerned parents, worried about their children and their country like Chester knew he would be worried if he were a parent.

Behind Wilbur, far, far away, the first hint of day lay a pink ribbon along the horizon. Flashing every twenty seconds, the beam from the Currituck Lighthouse brightened the walkway at the top.

The oars dipped and rose, dipped and rose. Droplets of water dribbled into the Currituck with each stroke. When they were about a half mile to the north, Daddy steered the skiff into a clump of marsh near a mound of black muck. It would only be visible in low tide, which it now was. The huge expanse of water loved hiding its secrets.

With the skiff secure inside the circle of marsh grass and cattails, Daddy threw out several decoys. Weights on strings tied to their bottoms kept them in place. He and Wilbur peered into the lightening sky, their breaths puffing in twin rods from their nostrils.

"I love it here," Wilbur said. "If I don't see a single duck, it's still worth coming."

A whir of wings somewhere behind them made them twist their heads around. "Just a single," Daddy said, his voice louder than it should be in the quiet of dawn.

In school last fall, Maurea told Chester about her father hunting with his father here as a boy, including how his father and mother, who would've been her grandfather and grandmother, had died when a hurricane sank their ship before she was born. He couldn't imagine losing Daddy and Mommy. If that happened, he might as well crawl into one of their graves and be buried too.

On the horizon, the pink ribbon transformed to orange. In its center, a burst of yellow light marked the sun. To the south, a swarm of black dots against the brightening sky neared another clump of marsh. Shotguns boomed. Ducks fell. A dog splashed out to retrieve them.

In Chester's arms, Goldie whined. Daddy started training her at six-months old. He said she loved moments like this.

In the darkness of the western sky, the dots scattered and faded. From the south, more dots came. This group moved toward Corolla and then turned west, heading straight for this clump of marsh.

Daddy raised a duck call to his lips. Chester knew these calls, known as greeting calls, sounded like *kanc, kanc, kanc*.

The black dots, now veering north, turned toward them again. Daddy lowered the call. Goldie whined again. Wilbur raised the shotgun, a black stick against the ever brightening sky. The dots became plump bodies, wings ablur. Chester's breath clouded before him. To the south, more shots destroyed the silence. The ducks slowed and dropped to extend their webbed feet toward the still water near the decoys, and Chester waited for the blast of Wilbur's shotgun. Instead of shooting, he lowered it. This started the ducks into the air again, where they faded to black pinpoints heading north.

Wilbur sighed. "I'm sorry, Abner. With all the killing in Europe, I'd rather enjoy the simplicity of this beautiful morning and do nothing but watch those amazing birds. I hope you don't mind."

Daddy softly chuckled. "I understand completely. When we get back, I'd like to show you something."

Chester knew what Daddy meant. He was going to show Wilbur his decoys, more art than something to attract ducks on a hunt. They were amazing, each feather carved to perfection, especially the Wood Duck hanging over the bed.

More black dots came, eventually filling the sky. Daddy called them in like the first ones. By the time the sky fully brightened, hundreds of Mallards, their heads green against the gray Currituck, spread before the hunters in a blanket of feathered folly. Trying not to laugh, Wilbur called them that since he refused to shoot. Perhaps sensing the innocence in the nearby humans, the ducks ignored the soft chuckles. Wilbur took a Thermos from a bag, filled three mugs, and passed two to Chester and Daddy.

To the south, shotguns boomed again, joined by more to the north and to the west, where hunters were hidden in the marsh near Aydlett.

As if they were of one mind, the Mallards surrounding the skiff whirred into the sky. Daddy raised anchor, retrieved his decoys, and returned the oars to the locks.

Still in the bow, still about to freeze, Chester pulled Goldie close once more.

Since America might join the war soon, when would he see Maurea again? He wondered what she was doing now, on a November morning in Richmond not long after dawn. He imagined her blonde hair scattered on her pillow, her eyes fluttering open. Patsy might be cooking bacon and eggs and planning some pastime for her young companion.

Something strange about the family occurred to Chester. He had never met Mrs. Applewhite, and Maurea rarely mentioned her at school. He knew of families like this in Corolla, knew of arguments and talk of divorce, knew of reconciliation and children happy again.

Maybe he was overreacting. Maybe Maurea's family was as happy as his.

But with another round of shotgun blasts to the south, he doubted it.

Sitting at the dresser, Maurea gave Patsy the hair brush. "I wonder if Chester went hunting with Papa and Mr. Pinkham?"

Patsy raised the brush to the blonde tangles. "I'd rather stay in bed on a cold day like this."

Maurea enjoyed Patsy's company. Few friends at school understood how she enjoyed the Outer Banks. Whenever she mentioned it, they frowned and asked what was so special about it when it had no clothing shops and theatres like in Richmond. They especially loved silent films like *Vagabond*, starring Charlie Chaplain; *Snow White*, starring Marguerite

Clark; and *Habit of Happiness,* starring Douglas Fairbanks. Maurea could barely stomach those. Her favorite, *20,000 Leagues Under the Sea,* drew her in with its oceanic theme.

Of course, Patsy took her to the theatre. Papa was usually tired from work, and Mother didn't care to go anywhere except out with friends, whoever they were. She had done so last night, stumbling home long after Maurea, who had gotten up for the bathroom, had gone to bed. Strong drink was probably involved. Mother was even shushing herself in the hall outside Maurea's door, on the way to her own bedroom, now apart from Papa's.

The arrangement confused Maurea. Mother ignored any questions about it, while Papa said she slept better alone. Patsy said Papa slept better alone too, though how she knew this was a mystery. Perhaps they were closer than Maurea thought. She could understand it. After all, he and Mother rarely said three words to each other in a day.

Patsy set the brush on the dresser. "There we are, pretty as a picture. What would you like for breakfast?"

Patsy cooked on weekends because Cook stayed home with her family. Maurea enjoyed the arrangement. Cook was just Cook while Patsy, much closer to Maurea's age than Cook's fifty-something, was a dear friend.

In the dresser mirror, Maurea admired her blonde tresses, green eyes, and full lips. Older friends shared stories of kisses, so she wondered how it might feel to kiss a boy. The wondering would only last seconds, until the idea of mouths and teeth colliding made her frown.

In the hall, on the way to the stairs, she noted Mother's closed bedroom door and much louder snores than usual. Patsy said to tiptoe to avoid waking her. They crept down two flights of stairs and entered the kitchen. Copper pots and pans hung from hooks over a large oak table. Knives filled a butcher block. A new gas stove and range gleamed brightly in white enamel, recently replacing a wood cookstove. Although they still had an icebox, Papa said an inventor was working on an electric model.

Patsy opened the icebox, and Maurea pondered the selection. She loved blueberry pancakes, but blueberries weren't in season. She loved biscuits with honey, but they were out of flour. She loved sausage and eggs, but they were out of both. "Cook hasn't been shopping," she said. "I'll wake Mother for some money."

After plodding up the stairs, she tapped on Mother's bedroom door, which, not being fully closed, opened enough to see inside. Hardly believing the sight of Mother in bed with a dark-haired man who wasn't Papa, the source of the loud snoring, Maurea closed the door. She blinked in confusion. Mother and Papa weren't close, but this was a serious betrayal, more serious than coming home late.

Despair flooded Maurea's veins and her knees gave way. If not for the wall at her back, she would've fallen down.

But could there be an explanation? Did her parents have what some of her friends said was an open marriage? No, Papa would never, ever do such a thing.

Composing herself with a cleansing breath, Maurea left for the kitchen. No options existed to explain this situation. She couldn't approach Mother for the row it might cause, and she couldn't approach Papa because he might not know about it. The best thing to do was to keep quiet, nor to even share it with Patsy, who, by her words of praise for Papa's role as a loving father, might be destroyed by the news as well.

In the kitchen, Maurea said she didn't care to wake Mother for the money, so she and Patsy decided on oatmeal and coffee with plenty of sugar and cream, for they both disliked it black.

As they ate, Maurea wondered about Papa and his hunt, but she wondered more about Chester. He was such a sweet boy, protecting her and Mirlande like he had done last year at school. Like he had said, a person's value was in the heart, not in their appearance, such as with his oversized forehead and his small hand without all of its fingers.

Done with their breakfast, Patsy washed dishes while Maurea dried them. Halfway along, Patsy turned on the radio in the corner. In the middle of a newscast, the announcer spoke of the war in Europe and the possibility of America joining it.

Maurea despised these events. Papa said if America joined the war, they couldn't visit Corolla until Germany surrendered, and no one knew how long that might be. She and Chester and Mirlande would likely be much older by then, and those lost years might be special ones.

Patsy changed the channel. Static crackled until an announcer played a song called *Somewhere a Voice is Calling* by John McCormick. His high tenor penetrated Maurea, making her miss the sweet boy called Chester Pinkham. With his ideas about the heart, he might understand Mother and Papa's relationship, because Maurea surely could not. Even so, she would never tell him. To do so would mortify her with embarrassment.

The song ended, followed by more news. Done with the dishes, Patsy turned the radio off. Leaning toward the window behind it, she spread the curtains. "I wonder who a taxi is picking up down the road? He certainly has a headful of dark hair."

Maurea knew who he was. They must not have heard him sneaking down the stairs and going out the back door.

Drying the last dish, she was tempted to take it upstairs and bash it over Mother's head. How could she betray such a wonderful man as Papa? He would never do such a thing, not in a million, billion, trillion years.

War

When Jeff Barnett entered the Army enlistment center in Norfolk, he considered himself a traitor. Not only had he lied to his father about going to Norfolk to look at some new merchandise for the store, he had told Lovely he couldn't join the service because of his broken arm. Although the traitor part bothered him, it bothered him more with how the United States had entered the war against Germany on his birthday a few days ago, on April 6, 1917. Since then, all he could think of was killing Germans. The need was drilling into his brain like the cancer that had killed his mother when he was just a boy.

Plenty of other men with his anger over the war were in line just inside the door. He joined them and waited, wondering if his arm would be a problem, not even hearing the questions asked of the men in front of him. It was as if he were standing on the beach at Corolla, the rush and roar of the waves drowning all sound, leaving nothing but his desire to kill Germans for taking him away from his beautiful Lovely.

How had he, nothing but the son of the owner of a general store on the sandy strip of nothing on the Outer Banks of North Carolina called Corolla, managed to find a woman like Lovely?

More importantly, how had he found someone like her to love him like he loved her? He ran his fingers through his hair. And here he was, about to betray that love by doing the very thing be said he wouldn't do.

The line dwindled. Men clenched their hands into fists. One said he hoped every last German would die a horrible death. Jeff didn't want every last German killed, just their leaders and the soldiers who followed their insane ideals.

But how could he do this to Lovely? He wanted to marry her, to take care of her and Mirlande, to give them all the happiness they deserved, to have a family of their own, to celebrate Thanksgiving and Christmas and all the birthdays they could manage, on and on and on and—

"Name?"

"Sorry," Jeff said, realizing he was daydreaming.

"Son," the uniformed man seated at a table said, his tone sharp, "you ain't begun to be sorry. Tell me your name."

"Jeff ... Jeff Barnett."

"Middle name, Jeff Jeff Barnett?"

"Sir?"

The man shook his head. "How about your IQ? I'd say it's in the single digits."

"No middle name, sir."

The man filled out a line on a form. "What's wrong with your arm?"

"I broke it and my dad didn't set it straight."

"You can forget combat. What are you good at?"

"I work at my dad's general store. I know inventory."

"Good deal. We need plenty of pencil pushers in the Army. If you pass your physical, which you should for pencil pushing, be back here in three days to take the bus to boot camp."

With the physical passed and his signature on the dotted line, the situation fully dawned on Jeff. Now he had to tell Lovely, and he didn't know how in the world he would do that.

Aboard his father's lobster boat he bought cheap at auction, he fed throttle and left the dock at Norfolk, for the long ride down the Elizabeth River to the Intracoastal Waterway to Corolla.

Despite his choice to enlist, he felt good about it. Even if he couldn't fight, he would be serving his country. Maybe Lovely would understand. At least he would return to her after the war, and they could marry then.

The trip dragged on in the narrow waterway. He moved aside for larger boats, tooting the horn and waving from the tiny cabin as he did. His growling stomach and pocket watch signaled lunchtime, but he didn't have the appetite to eat the ham sandwich and can of pork 'n beans he had packed in a cooler, along with a Dr. Pepper to wash everything down.

Despite the soothing purr of the diesel engine, the wash of water along the bow, the turtles sunning in rows on dead logs, and the aroma of the sometimes black water tinged with decay, dread at Lovely's possible reaction loomed large in Jeff's troubled mind.

He opened the Dr. Pepper and took a cold, fizzy swallow.

Then there was his father's reaction.

Jeff's lie was sure to create a rift in their relationship. Pops, as he called him, expected him to record inventory, order inventory, and run the store on weekends, when Pops went fishing or hunting. To say he wouldn't be happy was an understatement.

Upon entering the Currituck Sound, he kicked the throttle up a notch. Might as well get home and get it over with.

Diesel exhaust erupted from behind the cabin. The engine chugged louder. The bow cut the Currituck. The water churned at the stern. Regardless of the sensation of more speed, the miles still passed slowly, especially when a flock of gulls winged by.

Passing the Currituck County Courthouse to the right, its two-story building a red-brick smudge in the distance, he wondered if anyone was in the nearby jail. If Lovely didn't understand his need to serve the country, she might wish he was there.

Monkey Island soon came into view. Hardly more than sand, marsh, scrub brush, and a decent forest, the small island was once used by the Pamunkey Tribe for a summer hunting and fishing camp.

After Monkey Island, the red-brick Currituck Lighthouse to the forward left of the bow made Jeff clench his teeth. Time to dock and take his medicine from Pops. Then, as planned, he would meet Lovely on the beach tonight.

At the edge of the marsh, where Lovely was trying to tempt a crab into grabbing the chicken neck she had tied to a string, the sound of a boat motor made her look up from the clear water. Jeff, easing his father's boat to their pier, was back from Norfolk.

Along with catching crabs, she had caught and cleaned two speckled trout. Time to cook supper and clean up. What young lady wanted to smell like fish when she was going to see the man she loved tonight?

Inside with the bucket, she showed Auntie her catch. "Can you boil the crabs? I need to wash the fish smell off my hands."

Mirlande, now eight and getting prettier all the time, looked up from the table, where she was sewing a tear in one of her dresses. "I can cook the crabs." She put the sewing away, took their drinking pail to the well, and returned with it full. Within minutes the crabs were turning red in a pot on a used white-enameled wood cookstove, recently installed by the pastor.

Auntie set a cast iron pan on the stove and added bacon grease. When it started to smoke, she added the trout, which sizzled deliciously.

At the well with soap, a cloth, and a towel, Lovely washed her face, under her arms, and all around her sweaty neck. A bath in the sound would've been perfect, but she had bathed yesterday, and she didn't want to make Auntie suspicious. She had already mentioned the extra baths, narrowing her eyes as she did. If one thing about the tricky woman was true, it wasn't wise to make her suspicious.

Enjoying the coming twilight, Lovely dried her face with the towel. Although Auntie claimed she could kill people with her voodoo dolls, Lovely didn't believe it. Regardless, Auntie loved having her own way, and those hatpins of hers could kill if used in a vital place, such as the heart.

She did seem fond of Mirlande, who wouldn't be the least bit happy if Auntie took a hatpin to the doll she called the "Lovely" doll. Of course, Auntie only mentioned it when Mirlande wasn't within earshot.

Inside, Mirlande was picking the crabs. At the stove, Auntie turned the sizzling fish and looked back at Lovely. "You bathed yesterday. If I didn't know better, you were planning to meet one of these men around here."

Lovely draped the towel and cloth over one of the ladderback chairs to dry.

"Why are you wasting our soap?" Auntie asked.

"I told you, to get the fish smell off my hands."

"Then why's the hair at your neck wet?"

"Can't I wash my neck if I want to?"

Auntie pointed the fork she was using to turn the fish at her. "Mind what I say. If you've got a man around here somewhere, you know what'll happen." She touched the tip of the hatpin in the cloth wrapped around her head.

Mirlande, who had been looking back and forth at them, swept a length of curly black hair behind her ear. "Why can't we go where people are? There's a church and a school and—"

Auntie pointed the fork at her. "They're nothing but monsters, like that boy on the beach and that Creole bastar—"

"Enough!" Lovely screamed. "You're a cruel woman and I wish I'd never met you. If anyone in Corolla is a monster, you are! I want to meet people and live a normal life. If I have to keep living in this miserable house with you, I might as well be dead."

Mirlande ran to Lovely and wrapped her arms around her waist. "Don't say that, Mommy, please don't say that. I don't want to be here alone with her."

Lovely regretted her outburst. Not only could it make Auntie suspicious, it might make her suspicious of Jeff, who Lovely spoke with at the store more than anyone else. "Don't worry," she told Mirlande, taking her hands from around her waist. "I'm just in a bad mood. We all get in bad moods at times." She looked at Auntie. "Please forgive me. We do argue too much, you know."

Auntie plated the fish. "All I know is you shouldn't waste our soap. I work hard digging it out of trash cans."

Lovely told Mirlande to set the table. If the talk with Jeff went well tonight, maybe she would bring up the subject of getting married before the war ended. She didn't need a big house or anything fine. All she and Mirlande needed was a man like Jeff who sincerely cared for them.

The trout tasted bland because Auntie refused to buy salt. The crab meat tasted like it always did. Beef or pork would be a welcome change, but Auntie wouldn't buy that either. The only reason she bought bacon was because she wanted it.

When the dishes were washed, Lovely lit a kerosene lamp and set it on the table. Mirlande opened her letter book. "When can I learn to read?"

Auntie, who was looking through her sewing basket, snorted. "Books are worthless."

"You have a book in your basket," Mirlande said. "I've seen you reading it."

"It's best you ignore what I do, little girl. Best for both you and your mother."

Lovely slid her chair next to Mirlande. "I wish we had paper and pencils. I know my ABCs, but I haven't tried making them very often." She swept back that same unruly length of hair behind her daughter's ear. "I'd like to learn to read too. Maybe Jeff can order a book to teach us."

"Not if I have anything to say about it," Auntie grumbled.

Lovely said nothing. Revisit the ABCs with Mirlande, wait until she goes to bed, and hope Auntie does too. Then meet Jeff and see if she can talk him into marrying her now instead of after the war.

Impatience

Sitting by the window in her room, Maurea set her elbows on the sill, set her chin in her upturned palms, and huffed a hard breath.

Although the window was open, no breeze stirred. She was tired of the August heat, tired of the war, tired of not doing anything fun like going to Corolla and seeing Chester. Oh, certainly Papa had gone hunting last fall, ignoring her pleas to go with him. That wasn't fair at all. Then, after his talk of how roast duck made such an excellent supper, he hadn't brought a single duck home.

On top of that, Mother had gone to New York for Thanksgiving, and since Cook was with her family, this left Patsy to roast the turkey. Papa, always considerate, helped with the dressing and gravy. They both boiled green beans and butterbeans with a slice of ham hock in each pot, and the combined aromas of their roasting and simmering meal made all their mouths water. Maurea made pecan pie with pecans from the trees in their back yard. Finally, when the table was set and the food was steaming in platters and bowls, they all held hands while Papa said grace.

"Dear Lord, grant our country strength in this time of war. Keep our young men safe on the battlefield. Give them rest and food. Give them courage to fight the evils in this sad world of ours." He squeezed Maurea's hand. "As well, Lord, let our loved ones on the home front know how precious they are to us. They bring us joy with their smiles and cheered hearts with their laughter. Also, Lord, please bless this food for the nourishment of our bodies. In Christ's name we pray, amen."

Maurea snapped her eyes open, not because she couldn't wait to eat, but because she had wondered if Papa had squeezed Patsy's hand like he had squeezed hers. Although they had released one another's hands, they were smiling at each other until they realized Maurea was watching them. "That was a nice blessing, Papa. I appreciate our loved ones too, especially the ones who didn't run off to New York for Thanksgiving."

Papa placed a slice of turkey on Maurea's plate. "Now, now, Little Snail, don't be too harsh. I don't begrudge her those trips if it makes her happy."

Maurea hadn't forgotten the dark-haired man she saw in Mother's bed. Try as she might, no decent excuse came to mind, so when a school friend explained what she called "The Birds and the Bees," she assumed Mother was a loose woman with no morals, and she despised her for it. Regardless, she couldn't tell Papa for fear of breaking his heart. Thank goodness he had Patsy. Without her to spend time with, he might whither in this oppressive heat like the vegetables in the small war garden they had planted in the side yard, where it would get plenty of sun.

The realization that she needed to water the garden snapped Maurea from her Thanksgiving memories. Wearing a white summer dress, barefoot, her hair in a ponytail, she hurried down the stairs and to the kitchen. It being Saturday, Papa and Patsy were planning supper for today and tomorrow. Whether Mother, always in her room, ate with them or not, one never knew until she sat at the table, sometimes smelling of strong drink.

Opening and closing cabinet doors, Papa faced her. "What would you like for supper, Little Snail? This war has made beef and pork scarce."

"Fish too," Patsy said, closing a cabinet door. She faced Papa. "Didn't you say the Pinkhams kept chickens? I could do with roast chicken."

"And eggs over-easy for breakfast," Papa said, a dreamy look in his eyes. "I'll be so glad when this war is over."

Maurea snickered. "Are you tired of asparagus from our garden yet? I am."

"Count your blessings, Little Snail. Those foods we miss are feeding our men on the front."

Although Maurea understood the need to feed the men, she didn't say so. The nightly radio reports reminded her of that very thing. "When will the war be over, Papa? I want to go to Corolla and see Chester."

"I'm not sure, but it seems it's drawing to a close."

"I hope it's soon," Patsy said, gazing at Papa. "I loved our time there." She faced Maurea. "With you too, of course, Maurea dear."

Patsy's attentive smile at Papa hadn't escaped Maurea's notice. "Do you like it better when Mother is away? I do. She never goes to the beach."

"She used to love the outdoors," Papa said. "I suppose her tastes changed."

"When, Papa?" Maurea asked, sincerely wanting to know.

He pulled a chair from the table and sat. "It's not your fault, so don't dare think it. She seemed to change after you were born."

"But you didn't change."

"I certainly did not." He paused. "Well, except I fell in love with my darling daughter."

Maurea smiled at the sentiment, until a terrible thought popped into her head. "Is she jealous of me?"

Patsy went to her. "If she is, she shouldn't be. I'd love nothing more than to have you as my own daughter."

Eyeing Patsy, Papa cleared his throat. "Maybe she'll come around one day, Maurea. All we can do is pray for her." He went to the radio and turned it on. "Let's have some music to lighten our mood." After finding a jazz song, he returned to the cabinets and took out a can. "We can make fried fish cakes with this mackerel. Maybe it will remind us of Corolla."

Maurea stuck her tongue out and left for the garden. She didn't like fish cakes. At least they had ketchup in the icebox. With enough ketchup, she could eat fish *scales*.

While she watered the plants drooping in the afternoon sun, she wondered about Chester. How was he and his family dealing with the war? Since they had chickens and eggs and a garden and fish and shellfish from the sound, they should have enough food. Mr. Pinkham hunted ducks and geese, so maybe Mrs. Pinkham preserved some of the meat by canning it, like Cook did with their extra vegetables.

Maurea put the hose away and went to the tire swing beneath the pecan tree in the back yard. She and Chester had talked about visiting the Currituck Lighthouse. Since Papa had never taken her, maybe Chester could take her during the next visit. He was always so thoughtful and kind. During the few months she spent at the one-room Corolla schoolhouse, they often spoke of the beach and the sound and all the wildlife living at both. Although Pete the pelican had reached maturity, he visited on occasion, no doubt for the fish Chester would catch and feed him. His next favorite animals were dolphins. Bottle-nosed and slick-sided, gray and offering what resembled a toothy grin, they sometimes circled the green canoe when he paddled it out into the sound. Delighted at the idea, Maurea made him promise to take her to see them one day.

The thought formed a warm kernel of hope in her heart. She would be ten in November, and ten was only a few years away from when young ladies and young men started thinking about each other in terms of romance instead of friends. Papa demanded college first. Mother said it wasn't necessary. Maurea wasn't sure. Fancy dresses and parties and strong drink didn't appeal to her like it did to Mother. Papa often said happiness was a state of mind, arrived at by being one with God's natural world, and Maurea agreed. Who needed money and belongings when you lived within sight of the sound and a short stroll from the beach, and you had a loving relationship like Chester said his parents had?

Maurea turned round and round, twisting the tire swing and the rope until she raised her feet to twirl beneath the pecan tree. Who needed college and money when she could marry a nice boy like Chester Pinkham and live near both the sound and the sea? She certainly didn't need expensive things, nor did she care to become a sinful woman like Mother, sneaking a strange man into her bedroom.

When the swing stilled, she returned to the kitchen, where Papa was handing Patsy a handkerchief. "That was quite the sneeze. Are you coming down with something?"

She wiped her nose. "Some people in the market were coughing. My cashier said something is going around."

"I've heard talk of it on the radio," Papa said, waving the handkerchief away when she offered it. "Maybe the flu season is coming early."

"Dadburnit," Daddy exclaimed, his cheeks turning red. "I come to the store for flour and get news of another U-boat sinking a ship in North Carolina waters." Shaking his head, he returned to Mr. Barnett. "I suppose all the men died too."

"Not all," Barnett said. "The radio said John Midgett's life-saving crew at Chicamacomico saved some of them. It was the British tanker *Mirlo.*"

"Well, at least they saved some of them," Daddy said, shaking his head again. Wallet in hand, he set his elbows on the counter. "Now, about that flour ..."

Chester recognized the impatient tone in Daddy's voice. He hoped the news about the flour from Mr. Barnett would be better than the news about the *Mirlo.*

"Still out of flour," Barnett said. "I guess our boys overseas eat lots of biscuits, God bless their poor souls."

"Amen to that," Daddy said. "How about a bolt of denim for Alice? Chester's outgrowing his pants."

"Out of that too," Barnett muttered. "Sure will be glad when this war is over and things get back to normal."

Chester went to the counter. "I bet Jeff's ready to come home. Has he called lately?"

"Once a month or so, Chester. He's as busy keeping inventory of bullets as our boys are shooting them." Barnett rubbed the side of his nose. "Have y'all heard anything about some kind of illness on the mainland? A fisherman stopped by the other day for bait. I do have that, you know. He said lots of people are sick, some even dying."

"I haven't heard anything," Daddy said. "What kind of illness is it?"

"Kinda like the flu but worse." Barnett sounded truly concerned. "Some people get over it," he continued. "Some get where they can't breathe. They wheeze and cough 'till they pass on. Some pass fast. Some pass slow. Like I said, some get over it."

Behind them, the brass bell over the door rang, signaling a patron's entrance. Leon Smith came to the counter. "Hello, Abner. I hope you and yours are well."

"We are, Leon. How's the family?"

"Lucille's got a terrible cold. The rest are okay."

"A cold?" Mr. Barnett's eyes widened. He backed away from the counter. "What kinda cold?"

"Just a cold," Leon said. "Runny nose, sneezing. You know, just a cold."

"No fever?"

"No."

"No cough?"

"No."

"No wheezing?"

Leon's nostrils flared like a man tired of all the questions. "No, why?"

Mr. Barnett explained about the illness on the mainland. "That's why."

"Well ..." Leon said, dragging it out, possibly to make a point, "she doesn't have any of that stuff." He took a dollar from his wallet and set it on the counter. "I need a bottle of cough syrup."

Daddy backed away from him, grabbing Chester by the collar and pulling him back too. "You just said Lucille wasn't coughing."

Mr. Barnett took a bottle of cough medicine from one of the shelves behind him and tossed it to Leon. "Keep your money. You can pay me when none of y'all are sick."

Mumbling under his breath, Leon stuck the dollar back in his wallet and slammed the door behind him.

"I swear," Mr. Barnett said. "The last thing we need in Corolla is some kind of flu germ killing us all."

On the path to home, minus the flour, Chester looked up at Daddy. "Do you think Lucille will die?"

"We all die," Daddy said. "It's just a matter of when the good Lord takes us."

Daddy had said this before. "Every wild thing dies too, like ducks and geese and fish and … well, everything." Still, Chester didn't like it when people died. Those men on the *Mirlo* died, and they were far away from their home in England. Some might wash ashore. If so, they should be found and buried. The others, though, would live on in all the sea creatures that fed on them. The thought was both sad and not so sad, such as when Chester thought about Mommy and Daddy dying one day. Hopefully, that day would happen a long time from now, after they had lived a good life and seen their son married and with children.

At the bottom of the path, where they turned south to go home along the sound, Daddy glanced at him. "I know what you're thinking, Son. Your mother and I aren't going anywhere. We want to see you married one day. You're a fine young man, so I know you'll marry a fine young woman. We know you'll raise your children like we raised you, with plenty of character. Never let anyone control how you feel about yourself. Your hand and head might be different, but your heart is one of the kindest I've ever known. Always do the right thing. Always do your duty too, like the men who are fighting for this country, and you'll never let anyone down."

Smiling at Daddy, Chester caught a movement behind them. In a white dress, hair down to her waist, ankle deep in the sound, Mirlande waved.

He returned the wave, and she tossed a chicken neck tied to a string into the water, no doubt to catch a crab.

Once he had thought Mirlande might need a friend. Although he had a few friends now, they were only school friends. None ever visited him and none ever asked him to visit. The worst kind of alone is thinking you aren't alone when you really are.

At home, Daddy told Mommy about the sickness on the mainland. She waved it off as landlubber talk. They didn't have a radio, so they couldn't verify what Mr. Barnett said. Maybe it *was* landlubber talk. Chester couldn't stand the thought of being more alone than he already was.

Supper was sliced tomatoes, fried summer squash, and corn bread from the last of the corn meal. Mommy said they were getting low on grits. Daddy said the store was out of those like it was out of flour and denim. Both were glad the sound wouldn't run out of fish and crabs. Mommy said she had plenty of duck preserved in Mason jars, plus they could always fry a hen when it stopped laying and let some of the eggs hatch into more chickens.

Drinking the last of the milk, Chester wiped his milk moustache and frowned. He didn't like it when Daddy chopped a hen's head off with the ax. After he did, as he held it by the legs, it flapped like it was trying to fly to Heaven without its head, still there on the chopping block.

While Mommy washed dishes and Daddy worked on his latest decoy, a Canada Goose, Chester took Goldie for a walk along the sound.

Daddy had trained her well, for she stayed close to Chester's right side. The pink tongue hung from her mouth as she panted in the hot, humid air, the air that sometimes stilled at the start of twilight.

Out on the sound, a fish splashed. Moments later, a V of pelicans flew from toward the Atlantic and curved north toward Monkey Island, possibly to rest for the night. Maybe Pete flew with them, maybe not. Like Daddy had said about marrying, maybe he had a family of his own.

Goldie woofed and wagged her tail. Up ahead, Mirlande was sitting on a huge log that had washed ashore. "Hey, Chester," she said softly, shyly. "Does your dog bite?"

Chester continued until he arrived at the log. "Goldie's a good girl. The only thing she bites is fleas." He patted her head. "Don't worry, she swims all the time to drown them. Do you want to pet her?"

"I never petted a dog."

"If you let me hold your hand, I'll help."

Mirlande offered her hand. Chester took her by the wrist and gently rubbed her palm along Goldie's head. "See how soft her fur is? It keeps her warm when she swims for a duck." He released Mirlande's wrist and knelt to lift Goldie's paw and spread her toes. "She's even got webbed feet like a duck to help her swim." Chester giggled. "I thought I heard her quack one time. What do you think?"

Mirlande shared a shy smile. "I think you're silly." She patted the log beside her. "You can sit beside me if you want to."

Chester did, telling Goldie to sit. Instead, she lay at his feet and rested her chin on her paws.

"I like this time of day," Mirlande said. "Mommy and Auntie fuss after supper, so I come out here."

Chester understood. Mommy and Daddy rarely argued, but when they did, he went out to watch the sound too. He couldn't get enough of either it or the ocean. Although he felt alone at times, the ocean and sound made him feel like he was part of everything around him, part of the rush and roar of the waves, part of the hiss of the surf when it spread a blanket of white lace on the sand, part of every living thing that had lived and died since the time when things started living and dying.

Mirlande was watching the sun dip into the horizon. It was directly beyond her face, and the golden light blended with her hair, illuminating the individual strands of the individual curls. She turned to face him. "Do you ever get lonely?"

Chester didn't know how to answer such a question when she asked it. Her voice, soft as a morning breeze in the marsh, seemed to hover around him. If he tried to answer with the thoughts he'd been having about the ocean and the sound, he felt like he might burst. Some thoughts were best shared with a loved one, and he didn't know who he might love one day. Realizing this was true, he could only answer simply: "Sometimes."

Accepting his answer, she turned to watch the sun complete its dive into the distant tree-lined horizon, leaving an orange glow that turned to purple and then to black overhead, where the first star of the night winked into view.

Mirlande slid close and leaned her head on his shoulder. Her hair smelled like fresh air and sunshine. Before Chester knew what he was doing, he had put his arm around her thin shoulders, and he wasn't lonely at all.

Done with his shift at work, Jeff Barnett left for the mess hall and took a filled tray to a table. Time to celebrate with some corned beef hash, two slices of bread, and a glass of powdered milk. His discharge papers had arrived this morning, and he would head home to Lovely tomorrow.

Swallowing a bite of the hash, he winced at a sharp pain in his throat. It was probably from yelling at his assistant for losing some paperwork. It would get better as soon as he took a good lungful of his beloved Outer Banks air.

Sheriff

As the boat with interim Sheriff Amos Sandifer aboard it chugged across the Currituck Sound, the red-brick form of the Currituck Lighthouse materialized out of the gray curtain of rain.

Sandifer rubbed his chin. Although he had served in The Great War, which meant getting to know his fellow Army soldiers, he wasn't sure how to question the wealthy folks at Corolla Island about a double homicide. He patted his back pocket beneath his raincoat. At least he had remembered his notepad, and he wasn't so dumb he couldn't ask questions. The weight of the gun on his right hip comforted him. And if anyone got rowdy, they could talk to the barrel of his .38 revolver.

Regardless of his growing confidence, when the yellow structure of Corolla Island emerged from the rain, his nerves got the better of him. Unfortunately, that was nothing compared to when he saw the boathouse, where the butler on the seat beside him said two people had been murdered.

The diesel engine's rumble slowed. The boat eased into the canal, beneath the arched bridge to the left of the pink boathouse, and into the lagoon. No lookie-loos had gathered from Corolla, so maybe the bodies hadn't been discovered by anyone in the main house yet. Beyond the boathouse and a second bridge that led over another canal, which circled the yellow leviathan of Corolla Island and its copper-shingled roof, a 1926 Packard and a 1927 Cadillac parked by the house suggested the wealthy visitors were still here.

Telling the boat's driver to tie up and stay for his return, Amos climbed out. The butler, his face as white as the proverbial sheet, climbed out behind him and said he wasn't going inside. Amos faced him. "I need a witness. Do you understand?"

The muscles in the man's throat tightened with a hard swallow. "I ... well, I suppose."

Inside the boathouse, Amos cursed under his breath. He needed a coroner and a camera, and he had neither. No doubt the wealthy folks might have a camera, but he wasn't ready to alert them to their dilemma. Ignorance sometimes led to loose lips and gossip, and gossip led to a suspect or suspects, whichever the case may be.

He faced the butler. "Did Mr. Andino have a camera?" The butler nodded, pleasing Amos, but when he asked if the butler could slip inside and get it unnoticed, he shook his head, saying everyone would be awake by now, and they would ask questions. Amos let it go. He would take notes and use Andino's camera later, after he broke the news to everyone concerned.

Dim light made dimmer by the cloudy day entered the windows of the boat house. The smell of rain permeated the air. The bodies were fully clothed, so the man, dark haired and handsome, and the woman, stunningly beautiful with a headful of long, black curls, could've been friends, lovers, or, as some liked to say, strangers passing in the night. Amos doubted that. Concerning young men and young women, sex could cause all kinds of mischief.

He started to kneel for a better look but needed more light. A lantern sat on a shelf, near a stack of folded cloth bags. He asked the butler what they were for, and he said hunters carried their ducks in them to the house to be plucked.

Amos lit the lantern with his lighter—he really needed to stop smoking—and knelt by the man. He lay on his stomach, his face in profile. Blood, now dark with time, pooled beneath the back of his head. Probing fingers decided the murder weapon had corners and was used once. The wound wasn't very deep. When it came to head wounds, it didn't take deep to kill. Since the wound was on the back of his head, the killer had likely snuck up behind Andino before turning his or her attention to the girl. Amos asked the butler if he knew the girl's name.

"I must've forgotten it in all this hullabaloo. I think it's Mirlande. She was friends with Maurea and Chester."

"And they are?"

"Maurea is Maurea Applewhite. She was engaged to Mr. Andino. I don't know anything about Mirlande except she lived nearby." The butler paused. "She might've been romantically involved with Chester."

Amos wiped the sticky blood from his hands with one of the cloth bags, took the notepad and a pencil out, and noted the butler's statement. "And Chester is who?"

"He works here as a handyman. He's very smart. He was born different. His left hand is like a crab's claw. It's smaller than the right too. His forehead is like the bow of a ship—proud."

Amos stopped writing. "How do you mean?"

"Very high, like Moby Dick's head."

Making a mental note to learn more about Chester, Amos knelt by the girl. She lay on her back, her face tilted to one side. Dark blood pooled here too. He eased her head over and winced. The single wound to the center of her forehead, the same as the one on Andino, might've killed her. If not, the wounds on the left side of her face, left unrecognizable, would have.

More notes followed, including the names of everyone in the house, their appearance to identify them before the questioning, how they were related, and how the killer likely hated this girl. Not only did he or her want her dead, he or her had tried to destroy her beauty. Maybe she fell with the destroyed side of her face up, and the killer pounded away until satisfied. Amos held the lantern closer. A smudge of sand on the right side of the girl's forehead told the tale. Done with the grizzly task, the killer had kicked the girl there, knocking her head over and hiding the destroyed side of her face.

Done with his notes, Amos searched the floor and the shelves and underneath the duck bags for the murder weapon. The only thing interesting was the stack of duck bags askew, as if someone had pulled one off the top in a hurry. He faced the butler. "I've been to Corolla a time or two, but that's it. Does it have an icehouse? I need to preserve the bodies as well as possible until I can get them to the mainland and have a coroner examine them."

"Perhaps at the general store," the butler muttered. "I'm not sure."

Amos set the tip of the pencil to the pad. He should've already done this. "Name?"

"I've never seen the place."

"Not the store's name, *your* name."

"You suspect *me?*" the butler asked, his voice squeaking.

"I suspect everyone until a verdict is reached."

"I suppose I can see that. It's William Best."

Amos wrote the name above his statement and put the pad away. "All right, Mr. Best. Did you drive Mr. Andino here in one of those cars by the house?"

"The Packard. He had it brought over on a barge. The Applewhites did the same with their Cadillac."

Amos closed the boathouse door behind him, noting how the rain had stopped. "Drive to that store and see about an icehouse. It should have ice, so buy all you can. If I have to, I'll put the blocks around the victims and chip some ice on top of them."

Without a reply, Mr. Best left for the Packard. As Amos left for the front porch of Corolla Island, a curtain in one of the five dormers opened, revealing the face of a blonde woman of about forty. Before he took another step, she snatched the curtain closed. Suspect number one, Amos guessed, likely the wealthy—and lovely—Mrs. Applewhite. Older women chasing younger men happened every day, but a mother chasing—and possibly killing—her daughter's fiancé because of jealousy? How rotten was that?

Irene

Taking her morning walk through Aydlett, Maurea remembers that day like it was yesterday.

Sheriff Sandifer gathered everyone into Mrs. Knight's piano room and had them sit, saying to remain calm because he had some bad news. Thank goodness the Knights were in Europe. Otherwise, the shame of it all would've embarrassed them to no end.

Although Sandifer said he had taken the butler's statement, naming everyone in the process, he started by asking their names and comparing them to what he'd written in his notepad, just to make sure nothing was missed. He began with Wilbur Applewhite, Catherine Applewhite, and Maurea herself. When he asked the servants their names, Miss Rose, the cook, perked up. "Where's Mr. Andino and his butler, William?" Sandifer said he would get to that, then wrote the servant's names: Miss Rose the cook and Miss Timson the maid. "Now," he said, appraising everyone, "where's this fellow named Chester, the handyman?"

"He's at home," Maurea said.

"He should be here," Mother said, her tone hard.

Sandifer eyed her. "Is there something you'd like to share, Mrs. Applewhite? I saw you looking out the window just now."

J. Willis Sanders

Like a fish dying on a pier, she opened and closed her mouth. Finally closing it and snorting a breath, she lowered her head. "I have nothing to say."

"Please," Papa asked the sheriff, "why are you here?"

Sandifer closed the notepad. "Mr. Best is running a sad errand. He's gone to the store for ice to cool two bodies in the boathouse. He found Mr. Andino and a young woman named Mirlande there dead this morning."

Maurea Stood from the sofa, her face paling. "Con? Dead? I don't— How did— And Mirlande too?"

"Of course her too," Mother hissed. "I tried to tell you but you wouldn't listen."

Anger seared Maurea's blood. "That's because you're a liar and a slut, and I've been wanting to tell you that for years. If anyone was trying to take him from me, it would've been you."

Papa heaved a deep sigh. "Now's not the time to air the family laundry, Maurea."

Regardless of his and Patsy's relationship, Maurea wished she were here to get him through this, but she was taking care of a sick friend back in Richmond.

Papa straightened. "Sheriff Sandifer, I suppose we're suspects. You couldn't be more wrong in thinking that. We're good, upstanding people."

"Not that deformed freak Chester Pinkham," Mother growled. "He and that Mirlande person were involved. He found out about her and Con and killed them."

"I can't believe Con is dead," Maurea sobbed.

Papa patted her shoulder. "There, there, buck up, Little Snail. Life gives and life takes. We must make the best of it, come what may."

Miss Timson raised a trembling hand. "I have something to say."

Sandifer opened his notepad. "Go ahead."

"I saw Mrs. Applewhite talking to Mr. Andino on the front porch last night. She came inside and he went around back. A few minutes later, Maurea went out the front door—I suppose she didn't see me—and met Mr. Andino. I saw her walking around the house through the windows until she met him. Then—"

"Lies and more lies," Mother said through clenched teeth.

"If I were you, Mrs. Applewhite," Sandifer said, "I'd keep quiet now that we know *exactly* who's lying." He scribbled in his pad. "Go ahead, Miss Timson. You were about to say something?"

"I was. After Maurea and Mr. Andino spoke for a moment, she went to Chester. He was down by the edge of the sound. They talked for a moment as Mr. Andino watched. Chester left for the path by the sound north of here. Mr. Andino lit a cigar. Maurea spoke to him for a moment and went upstairs. I continued dusting because I was behind from helping Miss Rose with all the meals and cleaning. Mr. Andino then went to the front porch. To me, if I may say so, I thought he was waiting for someone."

Scribbling madly in his notebook, Sandifer stopped to turn the page. After more scribbling, he looked up at Miss Timson. "Did you see him meet Mirlande at the boathouse?"

"No, sir, I didn't. Everything I told you is what I saw. I kept working until dark. I went to bed soon after."

Sandifer eyed each person in turn. "Can anyone corroborate this information?" Everyone's head shook. "Does anyone have anything to add?"

Wiping tears, Maurea took a deep breath. "Chester and I have been lifelong friends. He had asked Mirlande to marry him and she agreed. This was last month. Then we all came here to celebrate my engagement to Con. On other visits here, I had seen him and Mirlande talking more than I thought acceptable. Last night I confronted him. He admitted to meeting her here a while back, but said their relationship hadn't become physical. He said he would stop seeing her. Yesterday morning I told Chester everything. He wanted to be here when I confronted Con. He was overwrought after. I went to him that night to comfort him. He walked me to the end of the path by the sound this morning. He waited there until I got inside and waved to me at my window. I assumed Con was in bed. Since—" Maurea sobbed again. "Since he and Mirlande were in the boathouse, I assumed wrong."

On the return walk through Aydlett, all these memories running through her mind, Maurea weeps bitterly. What a mess she has made of her and Chester and Mirlande's lives. Now, at the end of her own life, she has no idea how to atone for it. As far as Con, it seemed he sincerely cared for Mirlande, not if he hadn't seduced her. As far as Mother—

Maurea halts her thoughts. Mother is surely in hell, where she belongs.

At home, she refuses to turn on the radio for news of Irene. Lunch is chicken noodle soup from a can and a ham sandwich. She even drinks a glass of red wine. If she's going to continue living, she might as well eat to keep up her strength. One day— one day soon—atonement will come whether she wants it or not.

In Corolla, Chester leaves the coffee shop and his one weakness: cinnamon doughnuts. He loves both enough to live on the delicious aromas alone. Once he came in with some change he found in a vending machine in the mall. He jingled it in his hand

and offered to pay for the smell of their food with the sound of his money. The cashier didn't get the joke.

The TV is broken and the tourists are quiet, so there's no news of Irene. The line at the lighthouse is quiet too, so there's no news there either. It's the same with the tourists at Corolla Island.

Chester ends up at the sound, where he and Mirlande sat on the log all those years ago, and it all comes rushing back like a dying woman's scream in the night.

He remembers Sheriff Sandifer finding him at home and questioning him. He remembers going with him to Corolla Island and helping him and the butler stack blocks of ice around Mirlande and Con, including covering them with some of the duck bags and chipping ice onto them with a screwdriver from a shelf. He remembers crying so much he had to go outside to vomit. He remembers the hate in Mrs. Applewhite's eyes and the pity in Wilbur's. He remembers the sheriff taking their car keys and demanding everyone stay until he said they could leave.

Most of all he remembers the way Maurea blinked over and over at him, possibly from recalling the magical times they shared before things went so terribly, utterly, completely insane.

He wades into the sound. The water warms him up to his knees. The midday sun reflects off the surface, and he shades his eyes. Off to the north lies Monkey Island, and the memories of one of the best—and worst—days of his life. He wades back to the sand, falls to his backside, and weeps.

Contagion

When Jeff Barnett returned home, he didn't tell anyone about his sore throat. It was just a cold. The most important thing was hugging his dad and kissing Lovely and waiting on the increasing numbers of customers at the store because of the end of what people were calling The Great War. The first customers to welcome him were Abner and Alice and Chester Pinkham, happy for his return and for the bags of flour brought from the Army storage depot.

That night, anxious to see Lovely, he hurried to the beach, having left a note under a rock near her home for such an occasion.

No sooner than she slid down the dune on bare feet, he covered her face with kisses, murmuring how much he had missed her, how much he wanted to marry her, how much he wanted to be a father to Mirlande.

They made plan after plan. They would tell his father and Mirlande. To hell with the aunt. They would live in his bedroom until the increased revenue from wealthy duck hunters and frugal beachcombers helped them afford to build a house.

By the time he got back home, he had a fever. By the time his fever was too high to ignore, he was coughing. By the time Dad woke up to see what all the noise was about, Dad knew it was too late for both of them. He put a Closed sign in the front window of the store and returned to his son's room to wipe his forehead with a washcloth and wait for him to die. Around midnight his throat burned. Around one he was feverish. Around four he wrote a will leaving the store—whenever the damn flu bugs were gone off the shelves and walls—to his brother in Illinois.

Jeff wheezed his final breath at exactly 6 a.m. Barnett wondered who would bury them. If the undertaker didn't die, he would bury them in the Barnett family plot, him on one side of his wife, Jeff on the other.

Sometime later, sweating proverbial bullets in bed, hocking mucus, his entire body on fire, Barnett struggled to roll over to check the windup alarm clock. He knew he would die before his blurry vision could focus on both hands at the same time.

With Daddy to get some cough medicine for Mommy from the store, Chester pointed at the Closed sign. "Mr. Barnett is never closed in the mornings. I wonder what's wrong."

"I don't know," Daddy said. "Hardly anyone is out in town today." He rubbed his throat. "Let's get home. I don't feel too good."

Chester had a tickle in his throat, but it wasn't bad. On the way home, Goldie at his side, he remembered Leon Smith saying his wife, Lucille, was sick. Although Daddy had seemed worried when he pulled Chester back away from the man, he later said he didn't believe the flu could be as bad as Mr. Barnett had said it was.

They found Mommy in bed with a fever. Daddy held her head up and gave her water. His throat muscles tightened as she swallowed and winced. She said she should get up and make lunch. He said to stay in bed, he would take care of it. Instead, he went outside and closed the door behind him.

175

Goldie went to her bed in a corner and lay down. Her amber eyes darted back and forth, back and forth, as if she sensed something was seriously wrong. Chester went to the window. Daddy, with both hands over his face, his shoulders shaking, was crying. Chester ran outside, fear chilling his blood. "Daddy, is it like Mr. Barnett said?"

Daddy lowered his hands and stepped back. "Stay away, Son. I don't want you to catch it."

The last thing Chester wanted was to stay away. If Mommy and Daddy were going to die, he wanted to die with them. Being lonely from not having friends was one thing, but being alone when most of the people in Corolla might die was another. He faked a cough. "My throat hurts too. You, me, and Mommy can all go to Heaven together. You said we all die when God calls us. He must be calling us."

Daddy cupped Chester's cheek with his hand. "My strong boy filled with character ... what would your mother and I do without you?"

They went inside to check Mommy, who was asleep. Goldie lay curled up on the foot of the bed, whining now and then, amber eyes blinking. Daddy had a coughing fit, so Chester faked one too. Mommy and Daddy might go to Heaven first, but he wouldn't be far behind. Daddy told Chester to watch Mommy while he worked in the garden. This seemed like a strange thing to do if he thought they all were dying.

Chester went to Mommy and touched her forehead. On a hot summer day, old folks would say it was hot enough to fry an egg on a sidewalk. Chester didn't know what a sidewalk was, but Mommy's head might've been hot enough to fry an egg. Through the window on the back of the house, which faced a grove of the twisted live oaks, Chester could see Daddy digging with a shovel. The garden was on the side of the house, not the back, so he didn't know—

The reality of his family's situation made him burst into tears. Daddy was digging their graves.

After a few more sobs, Chester dried his eyes with his shirtsleeves. He would be ten in three months, and Daddy had just said he was a strong boy with character. That meant it was time to grow up.

He got a shovel from a shed on the garden side of the house and joined Daddy, who had dug one shallow grave in the soft sand and had started on another, piling the sand to the side of the hole. When he saw Chester, he dropped the shovel and dropped to his knees to sob on his boy's shoulders. Despite trying to grow up, Chester dropped his shovel and sobbed too.

Amidst his cries, he wondered if Maurea and her parents were sick or dying, and if Mirlande was sick or dying too. He hoped not. He couldn't imagine a world without all those people in it and looked forward to seeing Maurea again.

Daddy pulled away to wipe his eyes, followed by a coughing fit. "I'm just digging two graves. You're my good, strong boy, and God isn't ready to take you yet. If your mother and me die, roll us out of bed and onto a blanket. Then you can take turns dragging us out here and rolling us into our graves and covering us with sand."

Sobbing again, Chester shook his head. "I don't want to be alone, Daddy. Please don't—" He wiped his nose. "Please don't leave me alone."

Daddy hugged him, then held him at arm's length. Tears filled his eyes. The black length of hair stuck to the sweat on his forehead. "God will always be with you. I doubt anyone will come out of their houses until this flu is over. You know how to fish and shoot ducks when they come. Your mother has plenty of vegetables from the garden canned, and we have duck in Mason jars too. You can catch crabs too, okay?"

"What if I can't drag you and Mommy out here? My hand isn't as strong as the other one."

"I'll tie a knot in the blankets and tie a rope around it. Then you can tie the rope around your waist. We're not big people, you can do it." Daddy finished the second grave and stuck the shovel in one of the piles of sand. Taking Chester by the hand, they went inside.

Daddy checked Mommy again. She was still asleep. He started to show Chester all the food and the shotgun and the shells and the fishing rods but didn't, saying he already knew where everything was. "Just do the best you can, Son, and that will be enough." He swayed back and forth and dropped into a chair at the table. "Bring me some water, Son."

Chester brought the dipper from the pail. Daddy tried to drink but coughed and said his throat was too tight to swallow. "I better get to bed. I pray your mother and me can beat this thing, but I don't know."

He asked Chester to take his boots off for him, climbed in bed and pulled the covers up. Despite the hot August day — almost September now — he said he was about to freeze.

The day dragged on. In the distance, thunder boomed and echoed over the sound. A storm was coming from the east, where they always came from on these scalding summer days.

Twilight followed. Both Daddy and Mommy slept. Chester cried again because his throat felt better. Still, he would be Mommy and Daddy's good, strong boy filled with character. No matter how, he would make them proud and live to have a wife and family of his own.

The thunder boomed louder. He took ham from the icebox and made a sandwich, washed it down with cold water from the well instead of the warm water from the pail.

Night came, signaled by lightning brightening the mainland's distant shore. Like a dark giant striding closer while throwing spears of light, the storm pressed toward Corolla. As Chester lit a lantern, a gust of wind rattled the window panes facing the sound. Huge drops of rain struck like sleet. Fearing hail, Chester opened the door and held the lantern up to see. It was only huge drops of rain splattering the sand in the path to the sound.

He touched Mommy's forehead and almost cried with relief because she felt cooler. Then he noticed her slitted eyes and her still chest, and he let out a keen wail. Daddy's forehead was still hot. Chester dropped to his knees, clasped his hands together, and prayed and prayed and prayed.

Daddy gasping and his hand reaching brought him upright. "I'm here, Daddy," Chester said, grabbing his hand. "I've been praying as hard as I can. Please don't leave me, Daddy. Please don't leave me."

"You're my good strong—" Daddy sucked in a wheezing breath. "You're my good, strong boy. Always do the right thing. Always do your duty like our soldiers did. You do that, you'll be … you'll be …"

His hand fell from Chester's grasp, and that same keening wail erupted from Chester again. He was a sea gull that had lost its mate. He was a dolphin that had lost her baby. He was a whale that had lost its song.

Lightning lit the windows, almost blinding him. A tree exploded, clattering wood against the side of the house. Chester's ears rang from the blast. He had to escape death, and the only way he knew to do that was to run to the ocean.

He burst through the door and into the pelting rain and tore off into the night, that same keening cry surging from within his heart. On the path south, he used the lightning to find his way. When he cleared the trees, he followed the finger of light from the lighthouse. As he passed it, he almost stopped to take that loose brick from its home six-feet up and bash his own head in, but he was too short to reach it.

Running on, heart hammering in his chest as if it hoped to escape the cage of his ribs and fly to Heaven to join Mommy and Daddy, Chester used the lightning to find his way until he arrived at the beach. Now partially offshore, the storm blew its winds toward him, creating huge swells that rolled and crashed to the sand, almost drowning out the thunder.

That keening cry erupted from his throat again. He jerked his clothes off and ran to the surging surf, sobbing unlike any time in his entire life, and threw himself into the roiling water white with foam.

The undertow sucked at his body. It pulled him deeper into the darkness, only turning aquamarine when lightning brightened this watery world. He stayed under as long as his burning lungs would allow it, then kicked himself upward. When his head cleared the water, a wave flipped him over and over again. Salt water stung his sinuses. Sand scoured his back. His arms and legs ached from the struggle, so he staggered to shore.

Standing in the surf, lightning flashing, thunder rolling, he raised his arms to the sky and screamed at God for taking Mommy and Daddy and for destroying his life. He screamed again and again, wishing his throat would erupt like a volcano in one of his books, until his life's blood would flow like lava over his deformed body. He faced the ocean again and stumbled into the surging surf, intending to end it all. Having regained his breath, he kicked with conviction, and a set of teeth gripped his foot. Goldie had come for him, his only link to life now. He turned toward shore, his faithful friend beside him. On the beach, he hugged her and thanked her, loving the wet-dog smell and her rough tongue licking his face as she whined with concern.

The storm had moved offshore. Chester dressed. Goldie took his hand in her mouth and led him home. They both curled in the corner on her bed. He needed to tend to Mommy and Daddy, but tomorrow was another day. Other than praying over their graves, he had no idea what it would bring.

In the kitchen, illuminated by a pool of yellow light from an oil lamp on the table, Maurea added a piece of a jigsaw puzzle into its matching place. The electricity going out in Richmond because of a passing storm used to be exciting, now, not so much. It was nice, though, because she and Patsy and Papa were spending time together. Mother, of course, had retreated to New York to escape what people were calling the Spanish Flu. Thank goodness Patsy's sniffles had just been a cold.

In the daytime, few of Richmond's citizens moved about. On occasion, a car or a horse drawn wagon went by, visible through the mansion's tall windows. The shrouded bodies, wrapped in sheets in the wagons, gave Maurea nightmares. At night, many of the windows in the houses along the street were dark, either from dead residents or those who had fled like Mother. The day Patsy sniffled, Papa went to the market and bought all the food he could to prepare for the rumors of a devastating sickness. All they could do now was to stay inside and wait for it to end, while so many other people died.

Patsy inserted a piece into the puzzle and sighed. "I wish we knew how long this monstrosity of a situation will last." With fluttering lashes, she faced Papa. "Not that I mind the company."

He studied a puzzle piece. "What was that?"

Maurea touched his hand. "Patsy said she likes our company, Papa."

"Oh," he said, studying another piece. "I quite agree." He faced Maurea. "I wonder how your mother is faring. I'd send a telegram if I could get out."

Maurea didn't care how Mother was doing, likely laid up in bed with that same dark-haired man. She had no scruples, no morals, no nothing. Although it was clear Papa and Patsy cared for each other, they wouldn't dare share a bed unless he and Mother divorced. They possessed fine Christian values—the same values he taught at home—making sure they attended church before the flu ruined everything.

Papa chose another piece, studied it for a second, and inserted it into the puzzle. "I know I keep bemoaning the fact, but I certainly will be glad when both the war and this flu is finally over. At least the war seems to be winding down. With God's grace, it'll be over soon."

He was referring to the radio reports about the war, Maurea knew. Announcers were saying Germany was running out of resources, and the citizens were growing more disgruntled every day.

Maurea took a puzzle piece from the table. "When can we go to Corolla, Papa? It feels like we haven't been there in forever. Besides, you left Patsy and I here when you went duck hunting."

Papa chuckled. "And you haven't let me forget about it since, Little Snail."

"I'd like to go myself," Patsy said.

Papa took his pipe from the ash tray and started cleaning the bowl with a pocket knife. "We're not going anywhere until the war and the flu are over. Who knows how Corolla is faring under both. Despite its remote location, I imagine many of its citizens are suffering the same as the rest of the country."

Raising another puzzle piece to study, Maurea dropped it. "Not Chester and his family, Papa. Please don't say it."

"I hope not, sweetheart. God calls who He will when he will, and there's nothing we can do about it." He cupped Maurea's cheek in his palm. "You're my good, strong girl like I've taught you to be. Have faith and say your prayers. Perhaps Chester and his family will greet us when we return."

Trying not to cry at her lack of faith, Maurea returned to the puzzle. Who might be dead or dying at Corolla? Who might the Currituck Lighthouse's revolving finger illuminate for the undertaker's shovel next?

She wished she knew, prayed she could know, prayed Chester, his family, and sweet, shy Mirlande were safe from all harm.

At the edge of the sound, taking in the scent of rain-washed air from the storm last night, Mirlande raised her eyes to the bluest sky she had ever seen. She usually loved it, usually breathed the sweet aroma of clean air in deeply, usually thanked God, who Mommy, despite Auntie's complaints, had taught her about. God might paint the sky blue and create a storm to freshen the air, but He couldn't mend broken hearts.

Mommy's heart broke when she went to the store to see Jeff.

She had told Mirlande about him weeks ago, giving her hope for a normal life with a loving father instead of a fearful life with Auntie.

At the store, so Mommy said yesterday, two men with rags tied over their mouths were loading Jeff and his father into a wagon. Their bloodless skin and unseeing eyes and sagging mouths needed no explanation. Expecting Mommy back soon, Mirlande waited at the end of the path. She expected her to come running, expected them to plan a wedding, expected them to pack their meager belongings and flee from Auntie.

As Mirlande had learned, expectations that might fill the heart with happiness rarely happened. Neither her nor Mommy were princesses in a fairy tale, although Auntie could certainly be an evil step-mother.

Between terrible, coughing sobs and moments of calm, Mommy explained what had happened, leaving Mirlande as cold and numb and as lost as if she could never hope for a happy moment again. Not only did sadness fill her, anger did also. Knowing Auntie, she might've made a voodoo doll for each and every person in Corolla and had stabbed them through the heart with her hatpin.

The only thing to fear after Mommy came back from the store was when Auntie might strike at Mommy, and if she would be her last victim or not. Mommy had died in the night, holding Mirlande's hand. All the while, Auntie kept saying it was just a cold, not to worry. All the while too, she fiddled with one of her voodoo dolls, humming as if a wish she had made was coming true.

Having gotten her cry out, likely the first of many, Mirlande left the sound and went inside. Mommy needed a nice burial, and she intended to give her one. While Auntie slept, she searched her sewing basket for a needle and thread to sew

Mommy in her blanket. Rambling in patches of cloth, she reached down where the spools of thread usually were, at the bottom of the basket. When she pulled a spool of thread out, a doll—a Mommy doll—came tangled with it, a hatpin deep in the middle of her chest.

Despite Auntie's evil nature, Mirlande never believed she could kill Mommy, but she was clutching the evidence in her hand. Mommy mostly wore ragged white dresses to her ankles, so Auntie had dressed the doll the same. Auntie had started wearing black dresses to her ankles years ago, with a dark blue wrap around her head. With black cloth from the basket, Mirlande wrapped the doll's body to her knees. With blue cloth from the basket, she wrapped the doll's head. She pulled the hatpin from the doll's chest and raised it. Once she did this, she would be a heartless killer like Auntie, but the time for worrying about such things had faded with Mommy's last breath.

Clenching her teeth in rage, Mirlande drove the hatpin through the doll and into the table. In the rocking chair by the wood stove, where Auntie was asleep, she jerked forward with a coughing fit. Then she hocked mucus streaked with blood and fell into the floor. Raising a hand, she waved Mirlande over. "Water, Lovely. Bring me some—" She swallowed, evidenced by her swollen neck tightening and relaxing. "I need water."

Mirlande stood from the table. "Mommy is haunting you already, and I'm glad. You're a bad woman. I wish Mommy had never met you." She went outside for a handful of sand and returned to mix it with a dipper of water. When she knelt to offer it to Auntie, the dark eyes were glassy and blank, and the chest rose no more.

Mirlande spat in her face. "How do the fires of hell feel, you old witch? You killed Mommy but I killed you. I hope you suffer like you made us suffer."

Inside her chest, rage compressed her heart. Auntie had died and ruined the trick with the sand, but there were other ways of revenge: hatpins into her eyes until they struck bone, a mouthful of sand until it spread over her face, sticks from one of those crooked trees lit in the stove and shoved up her nose until the smell of burnt flesh filled the air.

Done with her revenge, Mirlande felt her heart loosen again. Now she could bury Mommy.

Because of the corn shuck mattress that tended to poke a person, they kept a sheet and a blanket on it. Mirlande pulled the sheet up and lay the sides and corners over Mommy. Using the thread and needle, she sewed the sheet closed, stopping at her cold chin. Small hands caressed the pale cheeks. This beautiful woman, kind and caring, was a fine mommy, but no words would come because none seemed fitting enough to properly express the feeling of loneliness engulfing Mirlande.

Where three people once lived, now there was one. The pastor rarely visited. He hadn't collected the rent in a month, so he might be dead. Actually, every person in Corolla might be dead, leaving Mirlande truly alone. Regardless, she needed to bury Mommy.

At the edge of the sound, she cut cattails with a butcher knife and lay them in the sand. Mommy loved how the wind whistled and rustled in the sea oats, so some of them were gathered. The last things were in the house on a shelf over Mommy's bed. Mirlande gathered the collection of sea shells: white cockle shells, translucent amber jingle shells, and several large oyster shells made up the bulk. There was one large conch, spiraled with a pink mouth. Mommy had learned the names from Jeff.

Although she was a small person, Mirlande had trouble dragging her behind the house, stopping several times to catch her breath and to let her thudding heart rest. Thanks to the soft sand, it didn't take long to dig the grave. Mirlande did her best to ease Mommy into it so she would lie face up. Mommy rolled instead. Mirlande got in the grave and adjusted her flat, lay the cattails on the sheet, then the sea oats, and climbed out to scatter the shells over the body.

Standing at the head of the grave, Mirlande again tried to think of something to say. When nothing came to mind, she sang a song Mommy would sing when they, just the two of them, visited the beach together.

My daughter, my daughter, my daughter you see,
Seek not a love from the men of the sea,
Find a poor hunter, or a gardener who toils,
And he'll be a fine father, when the wind it doth roil.

The song ended. Mirlande thought it was too short, so she sang the last verse of *Amazing Grace,* Mommy's favorite. She said amen and sewed the sheet closed over Mommy's face. She covered the bundle of cattails, sea oats, and shells with sand. They would see each other again. She just hoped it wasn't soon.

That night, because Auntie would soon smell, she drug the body out to the edge of the sound. When the tide went out, she drug her into the water, where the high tide would take her away.

Supper was a piece of cornbread and some leftover pinto beans. In the garden, green tomatoes were ripening. In the chicken house, hens were laying. In the sound, fish would take a worm on a hook. If nothing else, Mirlande would eat.

Jeff had given them toothbrushes and paste. Mirlande used both and went to bed, praying to God to please allow Mommy into Heaven, and to please forgive a child for murder.

Birthdays

On November 28th, 1918, Mother, to Maurea's dismay, returned from New York and held a birthday party. "It's your tenth," she said, having come inside from a taxi. "I wouldn't miss it for anything in the world."

The party consisted of Maurea, Mother, Patsy, and Papa. The neighbors not suffering with or killed by the flu weren't ready to leave their homes to be around people for longer than a few minutes. The party also consisted of a venison roast Papa got from one of his employees, plus canned green beans, mashed potatoes with gravy, and a cake without candles Patsy had made since Cook was still staying at home like most everyone else. For a present, Mother gave Maurea the one item of her clothing she coveted, a blue silk robe. "It's a bit too large," Papa said.

"She'll fill it out in no time," Mother said. "I was a late bloomer, especially in the bust. My Maurea will transform into a butterfly exactly like me."

Patsy cut her eyes at Mother as if to say, *You're still an ugly caterpillar, you worm, leaving your family for so long during this flu epidemic.*

Papa cut his eyes at Patsy the same way, as if to say, *Now, now, Patsy. We know she's an adulterer unlike us. She can always get the flu and set us free.*

Maurea blinked. What an imagination she had. She faced Papa. "I want to go to Corolla for my birthday."

"It's too soon, Little Snail. You must stay inside your shell until the flu is over."

Patsy swallowed a bite of cake. "Thank goodness the war is over. That means no U-boats will sink ships like the one the radio said." She faced Papa. "What was the name? Mir something."

Having eaten a bite of cake, Papa raised a napkin to his lips. "The *Mirlo*. It was a British tanker."

Sighing, Mother tightened her lips, refreshed with red lipstick after the meal. "Can't we talk about something else? I heard quite enough about the war while I was in New York." Her green eyes, darkened with mascara, brightened. "I heard some gossip while I was away. That hunt club in Corolla, the Lighthouse Club, might close next year. It's the place south of the lighthouse."

"I'd buy it if I had the money," Papa said. "Dad and I hunted with them when I was young. It's quite the place, 2200 acres."

"Well," Mother said, leaning forward conspiratorially, "another rumor—a delicious one at that—says Edward Knight is courting—"

"Ah," Papa said, interrupting her. "His father patented the sleeping car for trains, and he has interests in sugar, amongst other things. Word has it that his son spends money better than his father makes it."

"Which won't matter when Mr. Knight marries the woman he's seeing," Mother said.

"I understand she enjoys waterfowl hunting like he does," Papa said. "She has plenty of money of her own. Maybe she and Knight could afford the Lighthouse Club. The other clubs don't let women hunt. She could do so then."

"A friend told me about her." Mother paused for effect, knowing someone would ask her to explain. When Papa did, she continued. "Her name is Marie-Louise LaBel. She's French Canadian and much younger than him. Twelve years to be exact."

"I see nothing wrong with an older man marrying a younger woman," Patsy huffed. "I'm sure such men do so to get away from their wives who don't appreciate them."

Maurea imagined the rest. *And who abandoned what should be a beloved family by retreating to New York during a flu epidemic.*

Mother arched a plucked and combed eyebrow at Patsy. "Why, Patsy, whosoever do you mean? Do you have knowledge of such a woman and such a husband? Do they have a child, perhaps? A daughter, perhaps?"

"I'm just speculating," Patsy said. The red bow of her full lips pressed into a thin line. "Can't I speculate?"

"If you do so silently. Loose lips sink ships." Mother cocked her head to one side. "Who said that? Didn't someone say that?"

"Not that I know of," Papa said. "It would be wonderful for a campaign against gossip during a war. Maybe someone will use it for the next one. God forbid it happens."

The talk ended. Maurea finished her cake, thanked Patsy for baking it, thanked Papa for the venison and, as much as it galled her, thanked Mother for the robe.

Upstairs, she raised it to her nose. It had been washed, thank goodness. As wild as her imagination was, she could imagine Mother wearing it while she carried on with some man in the act of the Birds and the Bees.

The revulsion passed. Maurea undressed completely and donned the robe. The shimmering fabric felt cool and enticing, like a second skin embracing her. Other than Mother's philandering, the meaning of the Birds and the Bees meant nothing to Maurea. She could, however, see the appeal if a lover's fingertips felt like silk, cool and inviting while caressing every inch of her body.

Fueled by the descriptions of the Birds and the Bees from her friend, sinful thoughts filled her mind. Why didn't her cheeks flair hot with shame? Why didn't she fling the robe out the window? Why, when she knew these imagined sensations were what Mother experienced with that man in bed that time, did her curiosity not wane instead of growing stronger?

Tears burned Maurea's eyes. No matter how hard she might try otherwise, it seemed she was destined to become Mother.

Having found a bag of flour in a cupboard, Mirlande made biscuits. The ice in the icebox had melted. She was too afraid to go to the store for butter and the ice to keep it. Searching through canned vegetables, she found a jar of honey. Mommy talked Auntie into buying it, saying she wanted Mirlande to taste the sweetest thing in the world, like her dear daughter.

With a single biscuit on a plate, honey running from its browned top and down its sides, she took it to Mommy's grave and sat on an old wooden bench she had dragged outside. Many an hour had been spent here talking to Mommy since she died. Auntie liked to keep up with dates for some reason. At least the calendar she bought from the store this past January said Mirlande had been alone three months, and it was now her birthday.

She nibbled the biscuit. Licking the sticky-sweet honey from her lips, she held the biscuit out toward the mound of sand. "It's your turn, Mommy."

Mommy took a pretend bite. "Oh, my, it's delicious, Mirlande. You did such a fine job of making your own birthday cake."

"Thank you, Mommy. Would you like some more?"

"Not right now. How have you been since I went to Heaven? Do you eat enough?"

Mirlande nodded.

"Do you drink enough of our good well water?"

Mirlande nodded.

"That's a good, strong girl." Mommy paused. "I know you worry about what you did to Auntie, but you shouldn't. She was an evil woman. She hated people without taking the time to know them, particularly men. She was jealous of me because a man cared more for me than for her. It hardened her heart worse than it was already hardened. We should always give people a chance. I've shown you people in Corolla who are different than us. Remember Tobias, the man who's black as night?"

Mirlande nodded.

"He gave us fish that time when none were biting. He has a good heart."

"I agree, Mommy. He was a very nice man."

"That's exactly right. Remember the Italian woman who gave us bread when she caught us looking through her trash?"

Mirlande nodded. "She was nice too. You said the same thing about Mr. Chen and his family. I thought their eyes looked funny."

"No, you said they were slanted and wondered why. His wife said they were Chinese. Then she gave us some of their roast duck. You see, being a good person is in the heart. You'll never see it on the outside, so you have to get to know a person so you can learn who they are on the inside."

Mirlande remembered Elmo Parker, the boy at school who called her a trash eater. His sneering face and mean voice could be seen without getting to know him. She stood. "I better wash the dishes. I love you."

Inside, Mirlande finished the biscuit and washed the dishes. How did ten-years-old feel? She was taller, her hair was longer, and she was skinnier, but that was because she hadn't felt like eating after Mommy died. Although people had started moving around Corolla, some of that movement had been the undertaker burying people. It was now duck hunting season. Whatever had killed Jeff and his daddy must still be killing people on the mainland, because no one came to hunt ducks or geese. Every sunrise, to keep from feeling lonely, Mirlande watched them fill the sky. Whether in long strings, short strings, small flocks, big flocks, or in V shapes, they came quacking and honking every morning.

Done with the dishes, she decided on a twilight walk along the sound. Wearing Mommy's threadbare flannel coat with a quilted liner because hers was too small, she changed her mind and turned from the path toward the beach. She liked the beach because the waves talked to her, which made her feel less lonely.

Afraid a keeper would see her at the lighthouse, she stayed inside the twisted trees. At the sandy road rutted with wagon wheel tracks, she stopped at the smell of bacon frying in a house somewhere upwind. Nostrils flaring, mouth watering, she could see lights in the windows of a house down the road. The longing to be with someone made her take a single step toward it, then no more.

At the beach, she sat at the base of a dune. Between her and the surf, ghost crabs—so Mommy called them—scuttled to and from their holes, pausing now and then to pick at a bit of seaweed or shell.

A cold wind blew across the beach, chilling her legs. Not only had she outgrown her coat, she was outgrowing her dresses. Mommy's would fit a little loosely, but that was fine. The last thing she wanted was to wear Auntie's clothes.

Footsteps thudded over the dune behind her. A stick went flying onto the beach. A yellow dog ran after it but stopped when it saw Mirlande. Afraid it would bark, she hurried to a thick clump of sea oats to her right as fast as she could and squatted down behind them.

Over the dune came Chester Pinkham, the boy who had stopped Elmo Parker from calling Mirlande a trash eater that day at school.

Like Mirlande, he was taller. She wondered where his Mommy and Daddy were. For his sake, she hoped they hadn't died from whatever had killed Jeff and his daddy.

The dog barked at her. "Get the stick!" Chester yelled. "There's nothing in those sea oats but a crab."

Wagging its tail, the dog got the stick and took it to Chester. He threw it again, this time up the beach, away from Mirlande. She had been shivering, either from the cold or from the fear he would find her. Since she longed for the company of people, her fear made no sense. Maybe it was because she hadn't been near anyone for three months.

Happy Birthday to me, she thought. *If I keep being scared, I'll be alone until I die at this sandy and salty place.*

Goldie brought Chester the stick. Walking north, he threw it again. She was good company, but dogs weren't people.

Like the surf washing over a shell, sadness washed over him. He left the beach and took the path for home. By the time he got there, darkness filled the windows. He hadn't even noticed the sunset over the sound, and he always noticed the sunset over the sound. He hadn't taken the canoe or Daddy's skiff out since the flu hit. Doing it alone was no fun.

Inside, he took off his jacket, lit a lantern, and added wood to the fireplace. Goldie curled at his feet as he sat in Daddy's rocking chair. Mommy's chair was empty. He tried to imagine her in it but couldn't. Loneliness was bad enough, but being alone on his birthday made him wish he had died with Mommy and Daddy.

No one in Corolla had come. Maybe someone remembered seeing him and Daddy at the store with Jeff and thought the flu had killed them all. He didn't mind as much as he thought he would. Few people looked him in the eye for very long before they either looked away or looked at his hand. When would they learn that the most important part of a person was on the inside instead of the outside? Maurea and Mirlande knew that from the time they met on the beach so long ago, until they had last been together at school. Were children born with good characters and changed as adults? No, Elmo Parker answered that question by calling Mirlande a "trash eater" and by making fun of Chester's hand and head. Still, it seemed more adults were meaner than children were mean, at least when it came to looking different.

With the lamp dimmed on the nightstand, Chester undressed and pulled the quilt up to his chin. Goldie stayed by the fireplace. When the flames burned to embers, she would curl up on the foot of the bed.

This reminded Chester of how, when he was little, he would get between Mommy and Daddy in bed, in what he called his "cuddle hole." He had never felt so safe and loved in all his life, and he wished Goldie were a person instead of a dog. Paws were okay, but arms were better for hugging.

The flames died. The embers crackled and popped. Goldie stayed by the fireplace, lightly snoring. Even she had abandoned him.

Sometime in the night, the bed sank beside him. Cold feet touched his legs, and an arm slipped around his waist. Maybe Mommy and Daddy—now in angel form—had come to comfort him, and for the first time since they had died, the sweetness of their love surrounded him in his dreams.

Companion

Chester woke to the smell of something cooking. Goldie couldn't cook, so maybe, like with Mommy or Daddy holding him in bed, he was imagining it.

Plates clanked to the table. Mommy's old pewter silverware followed. Chester's mouth watered. Imaginary food couldn't do that. Well, imagining pancakes did. He loved pancakes.

Rubbing his eyes, he sat up in bed and gawked. Watching a pancake bubble in a pan on the cast iron grate over the glowing embers, Mirlande was squatting by the fireplace. She flipped the pancake with one of Mommy's spatulas. "That boy's gonna sleep all day," she mumbled. "We've got chores to do."

Chester didn't know what to think about any of this. "Did you sleep with me last night?"

Mirlande looked over her shoulder at him. "I was lonely. I didn't see your Mommy and Daddy, so I thought you were lonely too." She added the pancake to a stack on a plate and took it to the table. "I didn't see any syrup. I went back and got some honey. Do you like honey?" Mirlande turned around. "You can get dressed. I won't look."

Chester put on denim coveralls and a yellowed button-up shirt. "Okay." Sitting on the foot of the bed, he added socks and boots. "I don't see Goldie."

"She scratched at the door. I let her outside." Mirlande sat at the table. "I guess you wonder why I'm here. You know, other than being lonely."

Chester sat across from her. "Was it the flu? Lots of people have died."

"My Mommy died." Mirlande put a pancake on her plate. "Auntie left when people started getting sick. Did your—"

Goldie scratched the door and Chester let her in. He gave her a pancake, and she took it to her bed in the corner. He returned to Mirlande. "My Mommy and Daddy died too. I buried them behind the house."

"I buried Mommy too," Mirlande said flatly, as if her mommy's death had stolen a part of her heart. A faraway look dimmed her green eyes. "I'm sorry I slept with you. I'll leave after we eat."

Since Mirlande had lost her mommy, Chester understood why she had slept with him. After all, Mommy and Daddy's deaths had stolen a part of his heart too. He started on his pancake. Mirlande had made coffee, which he sipped. He didn't like being alone either, and her embrace in the night had comforted him with remembrances of Mommy and Daddy.

He swallowed another bite of pancake and so did Mirlande. Goldie, curled in her bed, fell asleep.

Chester was ten now. The flu might've killed Maurea, and his eyes stung at the thought. If so, the only other person who might care for him was Mirlande. Mommy and Daddy married at eighteen. They were very, very happy and in love. Chester wasn't sure about that kind of love. He loved Goldie, but it wasn't the same. Mommy and Daddy sometimes smiled at each other and talked in low tones while holding hands. In bed, illuminated by the glow of embers in the fireplace, they sometimes kissed longer than with a simple kiss goodnight.

Although Daddy had explained what he called The Facts of Life, including how people made love to confirm and share their love, Chester didn't want to do that. Then again, Daddy said he might when his voice deepened and when hair starting growing in places where hair never grew.

He waited while Mirlande drank coffee. "How old are you?"

She lowered the cup. "My birthday was yesterday. I'm ten."

"Really?" Astounded, Chester blinked several times. "My birthday was yesterday too. I'm ten, like you."

"That's good," Mirlande said, apparently unimpressed.

Chester remembered something. "When I woke up, you said we had chores. What did you mean?"

Chewing a bite of pancake, Mirlande swallowed. "Mommy didn't keep a clean house. Auntie minded but I didn't. I think the flu might've come from a dirty house. Your house is dirty."

Chester knew the flu came from the mainland. Regardless, Mirlande was right. He and Goldie had tracked sand in. Dust coated Papa's decoys. Cobwebs hung in corners. He was tempted to joke about getting married if they were going to clean the house.

Mirlande narrowed her eyes. "Why are you looking at me like that?"

"Mommy and Daddy got married when they were eighteen, so we—"

"No, Chester. I like sleeping with you because I'm lonely, but Mommy loved someone and he died. It hurt her heart. I won't hurt like that."

"Mommy and Daddy loved each other and died too." Chester paused, hoping to find the right words to explain his feelings. "Mommy and Daddy were happy for a long time. I want to have what they had."

Mirlande took their plates to the basin. "You can have that with somebody else. I'll leave if you want it with me."

Chester took the coffee cups to the basin. Mirlande's eyes were wet with tears. He placed a gentle hand on her shoulder and turned her toward him. A single tear tracked down her cheek. Her eyes searched his, possibly in hopes of finding someone who understood her feelings like he wanted her to understand his. "The flu took people we love," he said softly, solemnly. "Our hearts hurt for them. I want you to stay. I won't talk about getting married, but I liked it when you held me last night. It reminded me of Mommy and Daddy letting me sleep with them. His eyes grew wet too. He placed his other hand to her other shoulder and she came to him, pressing her chest to his while holding him tight. Together they cried for all the lost people—her Mommy, his Mommy and Daddy, and all the people in Corolla who either had died or lost loved ones—but he couldn't cry for Maurea. She couldn't be dead, or he might as well be dead himself.

The warmth between them grew from an ember to a flame. A strange heat flared in the pit of his stomach, then died. Maybe it was a hint of what Daddy had said about the physical feelings married people had for each other. Chester kissed Mirlande's forehead and pulled away. "I hope you feel better. If not, we can hug anytime you want to."

Saying nothing, she left with the pail and returned with water to heat over the fire for the dishes. He got more wood and stoked the fireplace. Evidenced by frost on the sparse grass growing in sandy spots around the house, where the sun pierced the spaces between the twisted live oaks, winter was coming. It was time to sharpen Papa's ax and chop firewood. He told Mirlande so and she agreed, adding how she would clean the house.

Seated on the bench Papa made for securing blocks of wood while he transformed them into waterfowl decoys, Chester filed the ax. Like when he had slept with Mommy and Daddy, he looked forward to sleeping with Mirlande. What would happen, though, when their feelings—The Facts of Life feelings—overcame them like the hint of them had started to overcome him when they had hugged?

Mirlande dried the dishes and put them in the cupboard, threw out the dishwater and returned with the empty basin. She sat by Chester and kissed his cheek. "I'm sorry I can't love anyone. I might one day." She wrapped her arm around his waist and leaned her head against shoulder. "Do you understand?"

He nodded. "It's okay. We're too young to think about it anyway."

She kissed his cheek again, got Mommy's broom and swept the sand into a pile by the door. When she opened it to sweep the pile out, cold air blew in, flaring the fire and making Goldie whine.

For some reason Chester didn't understand, fear twisted in his guts, and the ax and file clattered to the oak floor. Mirlande glanced his way but said nothing. Beyond her, down the hill that ended at the gray waters of the sound, Maurea waved him toward her. He rubbed his eyes. No, it was his imagination, because he could see straight through her body to the marsh and the cattails. Despite rubbing his eyes, she was still there, beckoning to him.

Wait for me, Chester. Mirlande isn't right for you and I am. You'll see one day. I'll come and show you what love is.

The blonde hair and green eyes intensified. The white dress faded away, revealing silky skin and feminine curves. Below her navel, like a nest of straw made by a Red-winged Blackbird, a similar nest drew his eyes. Night fell, yet the full moon illuminated her, now wearing a shimmering robe of the darkest blue he had ever seen.

This is how I'll come to you Chester. This is how we'll learn what true love is.

Sheriff

In Mrs. Knight's piano room, sitting in a chair brought from the dining room, Sheriff Sandifer sipped a second cup of coffee, provided by Miss Rose. Chester seemed like a nice young man and Maurea seemed like a nice young woman. Mr. Applewhite seemed extremely sincere. His wife, on the other hand, seemed coldhearted to the extreme. How the two got together was anyone's guess.

Like earlier, except with the addition of Chester, everyone sat around the room. Miss Rose had fed them lunch in the kitchen. Amos loved coffee, which was why he had asked her to pour him another cup. He also liked to sip and watch the expressions of everyone involved in this case. Who knew some simple clue that might lead to another clue? If he recognized that clue, could he use it as a wedge to make someone share yet another clue? If so, could he drive the wedge in deep enough to make someone bend until they eventually broke? Only time would tell—time, more questions, and getting the bodies to the mainland for the autopsies.

Mr. Applewhite cleared his throat. "My business. I need to get back to Richmond."

Softly crying now and then, Maurea lowered a handkerchief from her eyes. "What about arrangements for Con and Mirlande?"

"His father should be told," a red-faced Mrs. Applewhite demanded. "Immediately."

"The weather station has a telegraph," Chester suggested. "Poor Mirlande had no family."

Mrs. Applewhite snorted derisively. "Trash like her don't have family."

Amos raised an eyebrow. Mrs. Catherine Applewhite was still suspect number one. Maybe the feel of the electric chair—the hard wood against her back, the straps tightening around her wrists and ankles, a cold head from it being shaved for the voltage to burst from the copper cap into her brain—would remove the arrogance from her attitude.

He opened his notebook. "Mrs. Applewhite, your daughter, the butler, and Chester's stories don't match yours. I've explained the victim's injuries. Since someone hated the young woman enough to do that to her, and since you have voiced a particular hatred for her, I'm tempted to arrest you now on suspicion of a double homicide."

Mrs. Applewhite clenched her teeth. Nothing but a little squeak of outrage issued forth from her thin lips, now missing the red lipstick.

"Be that as it may," Amos continued, "I've sent a telegram to Mr. Andino's father and am waiting for a reply. The bodies must be taken and autopsies done."

The maid looked toward the hall and back. "Someone's knocking on the front door. May I see who it is?" Amos said she could. She returned moments later with a woman of about forty-five, who said she might have information pertaining to the case or she might not, but she would feel terrible if she kept it to herself.

Amos eyed the crowd for reactions. Chester stood and gave a little bow with his head. "It's good to see you, Miss Sanders.

It's been quite a few years since those days at the one-room schoolhouse."

"I'm married, Chester. It's Mrs. Elliott now." Her face paled. "I ... you were such a good boy. I hate—" With a handkerchief from her purse, she quieted a sob. Under control again, she lowered the handkerchief and faced Amos. "When Chester was in the second grade, I saw him—"

In a flurry of her dress, Maurea bolted up from the sofa. "That was so long ago. It has no bearing on this, no bearing at all."

"I'll be the judge of that," Amos said. "Please sit so Mrs. Elliott can speak. This is obviously weighing heavy on her mind."

"What about the murder weapon?" Mr. Best, the butler asked. "You never said what you think it is, only that you couldn't find it."

"It was a rock," Mrs. Elliott said. "A boy named Elmo Parker used to bully Chester about his hand and head. It didn't seem to bother him. Elmo eventually stopped, so I didn't add fuel to the fire."

"Why do you think it was a rock?" Mr. Applewhite asked.

"Yes," Mrs. Applewhite chimed in. "I'd like to know that myself." Unlike earlier, when Amos mentioned how her story had been debunked, she seemed more confident.

He faced Mrs. Elliott and raised his pencil to the pad. He supposed the butler had gossiped while getting the ice, and the gossip had blown through Corolla like a hurricane. "Please continue," Amos urged.

Mrs. Elliot gave a slight nod. "One day Elmo must've been bullying Chester. It was lunchtime. I let the children eat outside when the weather is nice. I heard loud voices and went out.

Chester was about to hit Elmo with a large rock. I'm sure it would've killed him if he had."

"That was twelve years ago," Chester said, his tone neutral. "You have a good memory."

"I was about to stop him," Maurea said. "He told me later he was just trying to scare Elmo."

Chester chuckled. "It worked. He never called me names from then on."

Amos penciled Mrs. Elliott's story. "Do you have anything to add?"

"What about this Elmo person?" Mr. Applewhite asked. "Maybe he can confirm Mrs. Elliott's story."

"He died during the Spanish Flu," Miss Rose said. "Quite a few died at the end of 1918."

"My parents included," Chester said. "Mirlande's mother died also."

Amos remembered what the butler had said about Chester and Mirlande having a romantic relationship. "You seem to know a lot about her."

Chester eyes darted toward Maurea and back. "A few months after our parents died—we were only ten—Mirlande showed up at my home one night. We were both lonely. We did what was natural for two children who had lost their loved ones to do."

"You started having sex," Mrs. Applewhite spat.

Mr. Applewhite's mouth fell open. "Oh, Catherine, what a horrible thing to say. They were only ten years old, for pity's sake."

"Oh, shut up, Wilbur," Catherine huffed. "He's a monster like in that stupid book you made me read, Frankenstein something or other. Why you let his deformed self be friends with Maurea, I'll never know. The world hated Frankenstein and I hated

Frankenstein. He was just a perversion like Chester is a perversion."

"I remember you saying that about the book," Mr. Applewhite said. "Since that was all you got out of it, I knew better than to discuss it with you. Here's a clue—Frankenstein wasn't the monster at all." Mr. Applewhite waggled a finger in her face. "The monster was a superficial world filled with people exactly like *you.*"

Simultaneously, the cheeks of Mrs. Elliott, Miss Rose, and the maid flared crimson. Maurea's did also, but not from shame. With the speed of a striking water moccasin, she jumped from the sofa, where she'd been sitting between her father and mother. "Mother, you are—I don't have the words to describe how vile you are. How me, Papa, Patsy, and Cook put up with you all these years, I have no idea." She strode across the cork floor to a chair beside Chester and sat.

Again, Amos raised the pencil to the pad. "Who's Patsy? Is she here and I don't know it?"

"She's my husband's strumpet," Mrs. Applewhite blurted. "We've something of an open marriage, although Maurea didn't realize it until a few years ago."

Turning red-faced himself, Mr. Applewhite faced Amos. "Patsy is at home with Cook. She was Maurea's tutor and is now our maid." His chin lowered and raised. "I admit to loving her. When a man is married to a woman like my wife, his soul is scoured clean of love. Patsy rekindled it in me, and I'll be forever grateful."

Amos made his notes. What a nightmare of a case: loneliness bringing two children together because of the Spanish Flu, adultery in the guise of a something called an "open marriage," and a past witness who said Chester was going to kill a bully with a rock. On top of that, Maurea, who was engaged to one of the murder victims, was defending young Chester. How deep did their relationship go? He needed to get them away from this crowd and speak to them individually. Only then might he get to the bottom of his first murder case as interim sheriff of Currituck County, and that included having the bodies seen by a coroner. Still, he had another question to ask Mrs. Applewhite, and who knew how she would answer it.

He stopped writing. "Mrs. Applewhite, what kind of relationship did you and Mr. Andino have?"

"What kind of ridiculous question is that?" She looked at her hands in her lap. After a pause, she raised her defiant chin again. "I was going to be his mother-in-law. That's the full extent of our relationship. How dare you suggest otherwise."

"It seems you were more than that to him," Amos said. "Tell me why you were seen with him at the boathouse a few nights ago—in a passionate embrace?"

She stood from the sofa, eyes blazing, looking around the room. "Who said that?"

"It doesn't matter who said it," Amos replied. "What matters is it happened."

"Absolutely true, Sheriff," Mr. Applewhite said.

Maurea rose from the chair beside Chester, slowly walked to her mother, and slapped her so hard that the sound echoed around the room like a gun shot. "I've been wanting to do that for years. It felt as good as I thought it would. You were sleeping with him, weren't you? You make me sick."

"Now, now," her father said. "Don't hurt your hand."

The slap had knocked Mrs. Applewhite off balance, dropping her to the sofa. She straightened, tucked several loose strands of blonde hair behind her ears, and glared at Amos. "I was hugging Con because he was going to stop seeing that Mirlande woman and marry Maurea. Whoever said that garbage about a so-called embrace didn't see anything other than a simple hug, did they?"

Amos flipped the notepad's pages back to the butler's answers. He had only said they embraced. Certainly he would've mentioned anything more. "No, that wasn't stated."

"So much for *that* accusation," Mrs. Applewhite said.

The answer disappointed Amos. She had been his most promising suspect, but not anymore. The key was the motive, such as who hated Mirlande enough to beat her face with whatever the murder weapon was, and the best way to discover that was to get the bodies to a coroner.

Irene

Chester rises from the sand beside the sound and wipes his eyes. He should've known better than to look at Monkey Island. Some memories are best left hidden behind a curtain of denial.

It's night. A fingernail moon hangs in the sky. Although it's August, he feels a chill. How long did he sit crying? An hour? Five? Seven? A thousand? Maybe he's in Purgatory, waiting his judgement.

At home he lights a lantern and collapses to the bed. Above him, the Wood Duck hangs from its fishing line. Below him, the sheet is cool against his naked body. Within his mind, blue silk tempts tears. How long must he remain here? How long must he suffer?

Morning finds him at the coffee shop. The aroma of cinnamon doughnuts fails to cheer him. The TV on a counter has been replaced with a huge LED model hanging from a wall.

It's August 24. The weather announcer says Irene is leaving Hispaniola and is strengthening. Chester leaves. Let Irene come. Let it blow and howl and scream out its rage upon the Outer Banks and Corolla. He will welcome it with open arms like he did with all the others since December 1928, when he was arrested for the murder of Con and Mirlande.

No, he thinks. It was later when he welcomed the hurricanes, after they released him from prison. Did they release him? His mind is slipping. There's no other explanation for it.

211

Home again on the bed. The door is open. The wind sways the Wood Duck. He goes to Mommy and Daddy's graves. His stone waits. He's as ready as he's ever been. When will it happen? When will it come? If Maurea's alive, when will she come?

He lies with his head near his stone. Where is Mirlande's grave? Sheriff Sandifer took her and Con's bodies to the mainland for autopsies. His father came to claim the body after, evidenced by a gruff voice yelling in the yard outside the jailhouse that Chester Pinkham would cook in the electric chair if it was the last thing his lawyers ever made happen. A person in jail isn't privy to certain information, but Chester was privy to *that* information. He didn't blame the man. He would feel the same way if he were a father.

He leaves his headstone and goes inside to sit on his bed. The open door frames the sandy path to the sound and the gray waters perfectly, like a black and white photograph of his life in stark contrast to the love he still feels.

He goes to the sound and takes the path north. Having never visited Mirlande's house, he wants to. One step, two steps, three. He can't do it. His grief turns him around to visit his own grave again. Beside it is a simple wooden cross made of two boards he pried from the outhouse. Upon the horizontal board, gray with age and lichen, one word is carved: Goldie.

The bastards caught her when he went to the store. She was asleep on the pier, and they beat her to death. Chester didn't care to hate, but whatever Corolla citizens killed her after the murders and before the arrest deserved the fires of hell.

He found her by the sound. Because of her age, her muzzle was gray and she was missing teeth, but oh how she still loved to swim the Currituck. A further description of her death is too painful to release from the recesses of his mind.

He touches the tip of the cross. "How's my old girl? I'll be there soon, I'm sure. Maybe Mirlande is keeping you company."

The thought helps take Chester north, along the path by the sound again. Mirlande's house is nothing more than a few rocks left from the foundation. The rest must've been washed away by a sound side storm surge from a hurricane. If her mother's grave had a marker, it's gone too.

At the back of the foundation, near where the grave might be, he bows his head. "I'm sorry I couldn't—" He weeps. "All she wanted was to be loved." He weeps again. "I'm sorry."

The Corolla Cemetery calls him. Here, after so many years, he is drawn to Mirlande's grave like steel to a magnet. The simple stone says: "Mirlande 1928." It's not enough, but to add anything more would destroy him.

At the bottom of the path to his house, he recalls his green canoe. From there he recalls the trip to Monkey Island. No tears this time. If he must recall that day, it's best to start in the summer of 1919, when Wilbur, Patsy, and Maurea returned after the war.

She came on a Saturday morning. He was sitting with his feet hanging off the pier, a fishing pole in his hand. To his right, perched on a piling, Pete's experience with line-caught fish made him eye the water expectantly. To Chester's left, Goldie's experience with ducks made her eye the sky expectantly. What a picture they would make.

From the south, something yellow caught his eye, and that something was a barefoot Maurea's hair, golden and streaming in the sun. Wearing blue shorts past her knees and a white blouse tied at her waist, she came running toward him along the path, waving wildly.

He put the pole down. Pete took flight. Barking, tail wagging, Goldie ran to Maurea, Chester right behind.

Instead of stopping to greet him, she ran right into him, hugging him and turning him in circles. "Oh!" she laughed, "I missed you so much!" She stopped turning and kissed him right on the mouth. "I missed you *this* much!" Then her bright eyes darkened. "I'm sorry, I wasn't thinking." She ran up the path and looked up the hill toward his house. "I'd like to say hello to your parents, but ..."

Chester went to her. "The flu took them last August. It took Mirlande's mother too."

"What about her aunt?" Maurea asked. "You told me she had an aunt, didn't you?"

"She left before the flu started. Mirlande didn't say to where."

Maurea blinked. Her eyes filled with tears. "I wish I had been here for you both." She blinked again. "Where's Mirlande? You're both alone, you should be together. No one should be alone."

Chester certainly agreed with that sentiment. "You're here. Does that mean you didn't lose anyone?"

"We're fine. Mother ran off to New York, but she's fine. It's just me and Papa and Patsy on this trip." Maurea patted Goldie's head. "Hello, Goldie." She faced Chester again. "I saw Pete fly away. I guess all my caterwauling scared him."

"You scared me too," Mirlande said, coming down the path from the house. She went to Chester's side. "We're not alone now. You can leave if you want."

"I'm sorry about your mother," Maurea said. "Chester told me what happened."

Chester didn't care for Mirlande's attitude. In the time after they lost their parents, she had become more and more possessive of him, even to the point of pushing Goldie off the foot of the bed when they went to sleep.

Mirlande looped her arm into Chester's arm. "We're all right now. You just go on back to your wealthy papa. We do fine without money. All we need is each other."

Chester pulled his arm free. "Stop being mean. Maurea is our friend. Don't you remember that day at school, when she was nice to you?"

Mirlande's green eyes, usually wide and observing the world, narrowed. Without a word, she stomped away and went up the path to the house.

"I'm sorry about that," Chester said. "I guess losing her mother makes her afraid of being alone again. How long are you staying?"

"A week. I can't wait to go to the beach."

"I like going at night with a lantern. Have you ever been at night?" He tried not to grin. "That's when the sea monsters come out." He raised his left hand and touched the two fingers to his thumb. "They're like me. One hand is normal, but the other one isn't."

Frowning, Maurea shook her head. "You really shouldn't joke about your hand."

"God made me this way," Chester said.

"Would you change it if you could?" Maurea asked.

"God did it for a reason. If it's good enough for Him, it's good enough for me." Chester tapped her nose with a fingertip. "Your nose is kind of long for a girl. Would you change it if you could?"

Maurea leaned over to see her reflection in the sound. "You're right, it *is* kind of long. I never noticed until now." She whirled around and dug her fingers under Chester's arms. "I saw you grinning about the sea monsters. That means you're teasing about my nose."

Chester ran into the sound and threw water at her. She ran in and did the same thing to him, and they both laughed.

In the doorway of Chester's house, Mirlande spat in the sand. If little Miss Rich Girl didn't leave soon, a voodoo doll with yellow hair might hurry her along.

Chester stopped splashing Maurea. "Okay, that's enough. Let's go out on the beach tonight. Will your daddy let you?"

"As long as he can see the lantern. I've seen those crabs you call sea monsters. They're gross."

Chester shoved her shoulder. "Scaredy cat. I bet you scream like the little girl you are when they run across your toes."

Maurea shoved him back. "I'll have you know I'm growing up now." She pushed her chest out. "See my bosom? Girls can grow bosoms at ten years old."

"You're ten?" Chester asked, surprised. "Mirlande and me are ten too. When's your birthday?"

"November 28."

"Ours is too, how about that? It's like we're tied together in some strange way."

Maurea tapped her chin with a fingertip. "It *is* strange, but it's no stranger than my bosom growing at age ten."

Chester shoved both hands in his pockets. "I thought I had one in here somewhere." He took out both hands, pinched the thumb and index finger of his right hand like it was holding something, and brought it close to Maurea's chest. "Hmm. Hmm."

She slapped his hand down. "What are you doing?"

"I'm trying to find your bosom with my magnifying glass. You must need glasses. Your bosom doesn't exist."

Maurea twisted her lips to one side. "It will one day. Then you'll dream about ... well, you know what you'll dream about."

Chester snickered. "More like nightmares."

She tousled his hair. "Enough of our foolishness. When I see the lantern coming to the cottage, I'll come out and meet you."

She skipped away, and Chester admired her long legs. More than that he admired her humor. Mirlande had next to no humor, preferring to clean the house or walk the beach or the path along the sound in silence. She even refused to play fetch with Goldie. She wouldn't be happy about tonight. He'd have to make up a story so she wouldn't be suspicious, or maybe he could go after she went to sleep, as she always did soon after dark.

At the cottage, Maurea went to the deck. Papa was reading a newspaper from Richmond. Patsy was reading a recipe book. "Well, well, Little Snail," he said as she sat in an Adirondack chair. "How's our friend Chester and his parents?"

Maurea's happiness faded. "Oh, Papa," she said, eyes brimming with tears.

"There, there," he said, dropping the paper to take her hands. "I suppose your tears mean the flu took them. What a shame. I greatly admired Abner. I'll always treasure my hunt with him and Chester."

Pulling away to wipe her tears, Maurea nodded. "Remember Mirlande, the girl I told you about that day after school? Her mother died too. Her and Chester are staying at his house. They seem to be doing well."

"I'm glad they have each other for company then," Papa said, picking up the paper.

Patsy's mouth fell open. "For Pete's sake, Wilbur, they're children like Maurea. Would you let her live by herself like that?"

"They're fine," Maurea said.

"Do they go to school?" Patsy asked, her tone incredulous. "They simply *must* go to school."

"I didn't ask," Maurea admitted, wishing Patsy would let the subject go.

"It isn't any of our affair," Papa said. "If they must go to school, the officials here will see to it."

Patsy returned to the recipe book. When Papa raised the paper, Maurea stopped him. "Chester and I are going out on the beach tonight. You don't mind, do you?"

"As long as I can see the lantern, like with your other forays onto the beach. Will Mirlande go as well?"

"I'm sure she will," Maurea lied, not wanting Mirlande to go at all. She had missed Chester more than she thought she would. Although she enjoyed coming to Corolla for all of its diversions—the beach, the sound, the lighthouse she hadn't climbed yet—she enjoyed it more because of Chester. His boyhood was fading, visible in his confident smile while he teased her. He seemed to pluck a string inside her, the same as how the blue silk robe plucked her string of curiosity about the Birds and the Bees. Perhaps she would try another kiss tonight and see if he responded more than earlier—she smiled at the thought—and see if it plucked her chord of curiosity about the Birds and the Bees even more than the blue silk robe.

When the glow of the lantern appeared in the path to the cottage, Maurea, waiting by Papa's car, crossed her arms. "You're late, Chester Pinkham."

Coming closer, he stuck his tongue out at her. "Neither Daddy nor I used a pocket watch. We tell the time by the sun and our growling stomachs. A man has to eat, you know."

Maurea regretted her joking. "I'm sorry about your parents. It must've been terrible for you."

"Goldie helped keep me company, and I keep Mirlande company."

"She didn't want to come?"

"She goes to bed early."

"What about Goldie?"

"She's curled up in her corner with her tail over her nose."

The door up the steps squeaked open on hinges rusted by salt mist from the ocean. "Chester, please accept my condolences," Papa said solemnly. "If you recall, I met your mother when your father showed me his wonderful decoys after our hunt that time. She was as fine a person as he was."

Chester looked up the steps. "Thank you, Mr. Applewhite. I'm glad your family is all right."

"Please call me Wilbur, my boy." He took a pipe from his teeth and gestured toward Maurea with it. "Don't let my little snail scream your eardrums out when she sees those ghost crabs."

The door closed. Maurea grabbed Chester's hand and led him to the beach. They stopped just above the roiling white surf. In the circle of yellow light from the lantern, bits of shell and seaweed marked the low tide line.

"You got lucky," Chester said. "We didn't see any crabs." He squatted to study a shell.

"Are you going to school?" Maurea asked. "I suppose it was closed during the flu."

"No one makes me." Chester stood. "Besides, I know enough to catch fish and crabs and grow a garden and raise chickens for eggs."

Maurea wondered if she should ask a question that had been on her mind. Of all the boys she knew, none made her think of it. "I'd like to attend college one day. Have you ever thought of it?"

Chester looked into the sky. His dark hair fell from his high forehead. He waved his small hand upward. "The stars are my college." Lowering his hand, he faced Maurea again. "And the ocean and the sound too." He paused as if thinking. "And the sunrises and sunsets. I can't forget them, or the ducks and geese and the dolphins. I love the dolphins."

"But there's more to life than all that," Maurea said.

Lantern light illuminated Chester's raised eyebrows. "Like what?"

"Museums and mountains and books to start. Do you have a favorite book?" Maurea poked his stomach. "Or can you even read?"

Chester poked her back. "We were in second grade, remember? That means I can read."

Maurea strolled a few steps away, then turned to face him. "Uh-huh, you read comic books."

"You joke too much." Chester looked at the sky again. "I can read the stars."

Maurea joined him. "You mean the constellations." She pointed. "That one's Ophiuchus. He's holding a snake."

Chester snickered. "That's you. You hiss like a snake when you tease me. I bet you'll bite me like a snake one day and kill me."

Maurea ignored him. "That one's Hercules."

"He sounds like a hero," Chester said, his voice serious. "He faced Maurea. "You're a mean snake and I'm the hero. I'll tame you and protect you when other people try to kill you."

Maurea took the lantern and went to the rise of sand above the surf. She set it down and asked Chester to sit. She then sat in front of him and, taking his hands, wrapped them around her waist. "I like the idea of you being my hero."

A breeze, soft and warm, was blowing along the beach. Out on the horizon, a distant light marked a ship. From behind them, the finger of light from the lighthouse beamed out to sea and paused twenty seconds before doing so again. Maurea loved this place, but she couldn't see living here. Maybe she could if she traveled elsewhere now and then, but Chester seemed like one of those twisted live oak trees, feet rooted in the sands of Corolla, never to be moved. Only time would tell—time and seeing how their relationship went as they grew older, when the pull of the Birds and the Bees became much more insistent than it was now.

Maurea turned her head to look back at him. The lantern light gave his brown eyes a yellow hue. "What did you think of my kiss today? I didn't know I was going to do it. I was just so happy to see you."

"You kind of surprised me," Chester admitted.

A silent moment passed, followed by another. "Did you like it?" Maurea finally asked. Chester said nothing. Maurea whirled around to face him on her knees and hold him by his shoulders. "If you didn't like it, can I try again? It won't be a surprise this time."

She started to kiss him, but Chester turned his head. "We're too young, okay?"

"So we can when we're older." Maurea turned him back to face her. "How *much* older? Girls mature faster than boys. I need to know."

"What's the hurry?" Chester asked, truly curious.

Maurea frowned "Are you saving yourself for Mirlande? She sure is pretty. Do you think she's pretty?"

Chester shrugged. "I guess."

Maurea didn't mind that. At least he was thinking about things like the Birds and the Bees. "Promise you won't kiss her before you kiss me." With a fingertip, she made a cross on her chest. "Cross your heart."

Chester did so. "Are you happy now?"

She grabbed his hand and pulled him up. "Get the lantern and let's run. I want to feel like we're those long-legged birds that run up and down the beach looking for something to eat."

Chester got the lantern. They ran along the beach, her holding his smaller hand and screaming when a ghost crab almost zigzagged across her feet. Chester loved her, she just knew it, and one day they would share their first real kiss here at Corolla.

Behind the dunes, crouched and peeking through a wall of sea oats, their stalks rustling in the breeze, Mirlande watched Chester and Maurea run along the beach. She envied the yellow hair, envied the simple dress, better than anything she had ever worn, envied how the girl didn't care if the hem got wet or sandy.

She spat into the sand at the base of the sea oats and muttered a curse she had learned from Auntie. One way or another, the yellow-haired girl—she wouldn't dare say her name—needed to go away. Maybe she could find Auntie's book of spells in the old shack they had once shared. Then she could make a voodoo doll with which to hex the girl. Auntie was dead and didn't need it anyway.

She left the sea oats, crouching while she followed them up the beach. Yes, one way or another, the yellow-haired girl needed to go away.

J. Willis Sanders

Irene

Maurea wakes to August 24. The radio weather announcer says Irene is leaving Hispaniola and is strengthening. The sky is still clear, but the outer bands of the hurricane will arrive eventually. Like the storm of her life she feels descending upon her, she has no doubt of its impending arrival.

Breakfast is two soft-boiled eggs in a new-fangled invention called an air-fryer. Set the temperature at 275. Cook for ten-minutes. Cool in ice water and peel. Add salt and pepper, whole-wheat toast and coffee. Delicious.

Done with the dishes, she refills the mug and goes to the porch with the binoculars. A cold front came through last night. The cool air and crisp smell leaves her refreshed. Deciding to view Corolla and all the memories it holds, she raises the binoculars. A turn of the focusing knob sharpens Corolla Island's yellow rectangle. Another turn sharpens the red tower of the Currituck Lighthouse. Does she dare? She eases the binoculars north. Although one last turn sharpens Monkey Island's trees and brush, it's still just a low smudge, tinted green and brown in the distance. Hidden by the few trees and brush, the hunt club and its outbuildings have gone to ruin.

The binoculars clatter to the porch floor and a lens pops out. This isn't the first time this has happened, so she has another pair. It usually happens when she sees the black-painted walkway atop the lighthouse. Then again, she didn't focus on it this time.

Does she dare recall that day at Monkey Island or not? To get clarity on a life—or lives—gone so wrong, sometimes a person must revisit those times that caused—cause—the greatest pain and the greatest regrets.

It was the last week of August, before her senior year in high school started. She and Chester were seventeen going on eighteen, their birthdays only three months away. She, Papa, and Patsy had spent every summer since 1919 in Corolla, and it was now 1926.

The day began like any other, with her running to see Chester and Goldie. Up the path to the house, Mirlande might stick her head out the door or not. Maurea never knew what she would do.

Chester was taller and broader. He seemed permanently tanned from fishing, working in the garden, and tending the grounds as a shirtless handyman at Corolla Island, where Papa had recommended him for the job to the Knights in 1925, when their extravagant retreat was completed.

The summers from 1920 until 1926 had been amazing, filled with walks along the sound and the beach, even a visit to the herd of the wild Spanish horses roaming the area, apparently the remnants of either a shipwreck or a failed colonization attempt in the early 16th century. More than a few times they sat by a fire on the beach at night. Sometimes Patsy and Papa joined them, sometimes not. Sometimes they sat by their own fire alone while Maurea and Chester watched from the cottage's deck. Chester never mentioned their relationship, but Maurea was happy about Papa having such a good friend to ease his mind as he approached middle age.

On the nights she and Chester sat by the fire alone, they sometimes held hands. When they reached fourteen, she might sit between his legs and lean back against him. He never complained, only saying he loved the smell of sunshine and salt air in her hair. His hands were usually clasped in her lap. When they turned sixteen, she would twine her fingers within his, then raise his hands to her lips to kiss his palms. When she did this, she would make sure to brush his palms against her breasts when she returned his hands to her lap. From seventeen on, she made sure to forgo a bra for nights like this. If she pressed firmly enough against him, the memory of the blue silk robe would transform her once tentative emotions into a roiling sea within the pit of her stomach.

On these nights as well, she had the feeling Mirlande, who always refused any invitation, was watching from behind the dunes. If so, so be it. She had Chester to herself for most of the year. If she didn't want to share him during the summer, preferring instead to let him spend time with Maurea, it was her loss.

Then came the canoe trip to Monkey Island and everything after, when things went so horribly, terribly, wrong.

The night before on the beach, after they both kicked sand over the fire, Chester took Maurea's shoulders in his hands. Just when she thought they would share their first real kiss, he slid his hands down and squeezed her arms. "I was going to ask you something, but your muscles feel kind of flabby."

In the dark now, with only the stars to dimly illuminate his face, Maurea couldn't tell if he was grinning or not. "We could always kiss," she said. She licked her lips to make them shine in the starlight. "I'm sure my lips are as firm as you've dreamed they are."

He chuckled. "Well, I have dreamed of that," he said, his voice deeper than when he was twelve, when it started changing.

The suggestive tone of it sent a shiver along the nape of Maurea's neck. How might his lips feel there, on her throat, on her shoulders?

"Aside from admitting my deepest, darkest, thoughts," Chester continued, "I'm asking you out on our first official date. All you have to do is bring something to eat and drink for a canoe trip to Monkey Island."

Maurea loved the idea. She hadn't mentioned going to college since the first time. Because this would be their first date, maybe she could talk Chester into leaving this salty, sandy place to be with her. Surely Papa would let him live with them and give him a job at the tobacco factory. If so, she might not attend college. Marrying Chester, having a family, and living in Richmond near Papa would be amazing. As far as Mirlande, what she did was up to her.

"Well," Maurea said, patting the firm muscles of Chester's stomach, "I'll have to come up with something to satisfy my man, won't I?"

He grinned. Starlight clearly revealed his teeth this time. "What a suggestive question, Little Snail. The answer might draw you all the way out of your shell if we're not careful."

They parted at the cottage, him striding away in a pool of light from his lantern, her running up the steps.

Papa's pipe glowed in the dark living room. "I do believe two young people are smitten." He set the pipe in an ash tray on the end table beside him. "Is that the case, Little Snail? You and Chester looked quite cozy by the fire."

Maurea hoped he couldn't see exactly *how* cozy. She sat by Papa on the sofa. "I care about Chester a great deal, but I wonder if he would leave Corolla for Richmond."

"What about college?" Papa asked, concern coloring his voice. "Don't tell me you're ready to settle down and start a family."

"Would you give him a job if I were?"

"You know I would. He's a very bright fellow. He might make a fine supervisor or manager, after he works his way up the ladder, of course."

Maurea was glad Papa had confirmed her faith in him. She couldn't think of anything he wouldn't do for her, or anything that would ruin her faith in him. Thanking him, she hugged his neck and got ready for bed.

The next morning, as the sun rose from the horizon like a ball of fire steaming up from the ocean, Maurea left to see Chester. Passing the lighthouse, she waved at a keeper going inside. She had always wanted to climb it and see what Corolla looked like from such a height. Maybe Chester would ask the keeper after the canoe ride.

He and Goldie were waiting on the pier. Maurea held up two paper bags, one inside the other to help keep their food cool. "I've got baloney and cheese sandwiches and a Mason jar of lemonade. For desert, we can have leftover sugar cookies Patsy and I made yesterday."

"I'm disappointed." Chester helped her into the wobbly canoe. "I was expecting caviar and champagne."

Maurea took the seat toward the front. "What do you know about that, Chester Pinkham, out here on this overgrown sandbar?"

"I'm smart is how," Chester said, tapping his temple with a fingertip. "I even taught Mirlande to read and write. She's pen pals with a woman her age. She met her on the beach last year. I haven't met her. She says she's nice."

Maurea set the bag at her feet. "Where'd you get the books to teach her?"

"Daddy and Mommy liked to read about all kinds of things. Daddy even had some books on waterfowl hunting with pictures of the ducks he used to make decoys." Chester untied the canoe from the pier. He picked up a paddle and gave Maurea one. "We'll get there quicker if you help." Goldie lay sleepily on the pier, eyes half-open. He told Maurea she usually went, but he would let her stay home this time.

Paddles dipped and raised, dipped and raised. The Currituck, as some of the area old timers would say, was "flat cam," meaning it was flat calm. The bow of the slender craft cleaving the water spread an easy wake out to the sides. The rising sun behind them intensified the color of Maurea's hair hanging down her back. Chester loved it when she sat against him on the beach at night, loved the silky feel of those soft strands against his face, loved the smell of fresh air and sunshine and salt air residing there. He hated to admit it, but he especially loved it when she brushed his palms against her breasts. Regardless, he didn't care for how it made him feel. Due to Mommy and Daddy's moral teachings from the Bible, he wanted to wait until marriage before he shared physical intimacy with a woman. Sometimes, though, he understood how the biblical David felt when he was attracted to Bathsheba, and he was afraid Maurea's beauty might cause him to fail like David had failed. Who would've ever thought the deformed crab boy with the whale head would have a woman like Maurea, as gorgeous as an Atlantic sunrise, interested in him?

Then there was Mirlande, as sultry as a Currituck Sound sunset, who likely had feelings for him too. She stirred the same feelings in him as Maurea did, possibly even to the same degree as Bathsheba stirred them in David.

"Whew, I'm getting warm." Maurea stopped paddling, took a ribbon from her shorts pocket, and tied her hair into a ponytail. This revealed her slender neck, which made Chester lick his lips with the need to kiss her there. Paddling again, she looked over her shoulder at him. "You're mighty quiet back there, Mr. Pinkham."

"Well ..." he said, hesitating, "I guess I'm enjoying the view."

"You guess?" Maurea's lips thinned into a knowing smile. "I think you know what view you're enjoying. You just won't say so."

Chester pointed beyond her. "I'm enjoying the way the western sky stays cobalt blue before the sun gets too high, and the way the water reflects all that." He paused to keep from laughing. "I'm also enjoying the way your flabby arms jiggle when you paddle."

"Huh," Maurea said, splashing him with the paddle. "You'll pay for that when I get you on land, you salty boy. I'm firm all over and you know it."

Chester knew it all right. She had spent the last two years making sure his hands knew it too. Although he wanted her, he wasn't sure if he loved her. It didn't help matters when she mentioned him leaving everything he loved in Corolla to go to college. He felt a kinship with the salt and the sand, the fish and the horses, the ducks and the geese. Next to not losing Maurea, the last thing he wanted was to leave his home. Mommy and Daddy had raised him to appreciate the simpler things in life, and he intended to always live simply. Some of Daddy's hunting magazines had articles about the wealthy people who came here for waterfowl, including some of the cities they were from—New York, Philadelphia, Washington, D.C., and Richmond—where Maurea lived. He wanted no part of skyscrapers that blocked the sunlight, crowds that filled the sidewalks, nor concrete covering the good earth that should have trees and grass instead. If he and Maurea fell in love, and if she insisted he leave his home, the ensuing argument might be heard all over Corolla.

The bow of the canoe scraped the sand of Monkey Island. On shore, he led her to the shade of a grove of live oaks not far from the sound and spread a quilt for them to sit. She lay back, propped on her elbows. "Papa said some wealthy men have bought this island and plan to build a hunt club for waterfowl."

Chester winked. "They're no wealthier than you."

She slapped his arm. "Hush. We might be wealthy but we're grateful."

Chester winked again. "Grateful is good." He touched one of the paper bags. "Baloney and cheese sandwiches?"

"Sorry. I didn't think about bringing breakfast food when I made them."

"I don't mind," Chester said. Sitting cross-legged at her feet, he ran a fingertip along the sole of one. She jerked her foot back, jumped up from the quilt, and pushed him down to straddle him. That same surge of need as when she brushed his palms across her breasts became all too apparent. Full lips, green eyes like the sea, tanned face from the summer sun, the sweet smell of some kind of perfume, the curve of her bosom peaking from the top buttons of her shirt, the realization because of the thin, white material that she wasn't wearing a brassiere—all of it combined to make him squirm out from under her. "Let's eat before they get here."

"Before whom gets here? I thought this trip was just for us." Maurea offered a sandwich.

"'Whom?'" Chester asked, taking the sandwich. "Oh, I forgot. I'm on my first date with a city girl."

Maurea rolled her eyes. "Shut up. Who are we waiting for?"

"You'll know when you see them." Chester unwrapped the sandwich.

Bites of baloney and cheese with tangy mustard were washed down with lemonade, followed by crunchy sugar cookies. Done, Chester got up. When he took his shirt and pants off, revealing a pair of boxer shorts, Maurea strangled on the lemonade. "If I had known you wanted to make love, I would've worn a sexy nighty."

He lifted her by her hand. "You're sexy as you are. Since you're not wearing a brassiere, keep your shirt on. If you're wearing underwear, take your shorts off."

Maurea did so, revealing legs long and tanned. She wanted to wrap her arms around Chester's neck and press herself against his muscled body but didn't. Before the day was over, she intended to bring up the subject of a job at Papa's factory, and that was more important than a kiss.

Guessing Chester wanted to swim, she waded into the cool water of the sound and turned to face him. "Why did you invite someone else here? You must not care who sees us half naked."

Chester joined her. The wet shirt revealed more of her than he wanted to see. No, to be honest, he loved seeing her this way, all wet and lovely and entirely too seductive. Lucky for him, his friends were arcing out of the water and coming closer. He pointed. "What do you think?"

Maurea whirled around. "Dolphins? I love dolphins! I didn't know they were in the sound like in the ocean."

Chester patted the water. Two dolphins broke off from the rest and swam over, raising their bottle-shaped noses to look at the two humans. He took Maurea's hand and placed it on the slick, dark skin. "I call them Maurea and Chester. Dolphins don't usually mate for life, but I think they have."

The fact that he had named the dolphins after them thrilled Maurea. He must love her like she loved him. If so, he would follow her wherever she went, including all the way back to Richmond.

The splashing of escaping baitfish, their slender shapes silver in the sunlight, took the dolphins back to their friends.

Maurea hugged Chester. "I'll always remember this, Chester." She looked up into his brown eyes. *Please kiss me,* she begged in her mind.

He raised a palm to her cheek. "I hope you know how special you are to me, Maurea. After Mommy and Daddy died, I swam in the ocean in a storm. I wanted to be with them, but Goldie came for me." He pulled Maurea to his chest. "I'm really glad she did."

They went to the quilt and lay down. Chester propped himself on his elbow and gazed into her eyes. He kissed her forehead, her nose. Then, ever so lightly, he kissed her lips.

The roiling emotions in the pit of Maurea's stomach became a hurricane. She parted her lips and kissed him fully. *This is love,* she thought. *I can't wait until we get married and move to Richmond and start our own family.*

Before his need overwhelmed him, Chester ended the kiss. "Well, I'd say we've had an interesting morning. I have another idea if you're game."

Glad their kiss hadn't ended the day, Maurea agreed. They dressed, gathered their trash from lunch, and paddled back to Corolla. Chester tied the canoe to the pier. Goldie wasn't around. Chester said she might be asleep behind the house in the shade. He said he'd take care of the trash later. Maurea said he could keep the jar. He took her by the hand and tugged her along the path leading toward Corolla Island. Just as she was ready to complain about visiting the place where he worked, and where Papa and Mother sometimes went as a diversion from Richmond, Chester took a left toward the lighthouse. "I asked the keeper yesterday if we could climb all those steps. Can your flabby leg muscles handle it?"

"Hush. You like my legs and you know it."

"Regardless," he said, grinning at her, "one of the keepers said to take our time. They're caught up on maintenance, so they went to Norfolk with their wives to do some shopping."

Maurea liked the idea. Sharing more kisses at the top of the Currituck Lighthouse would be a great way to end her last day at Corolla. If Chester admitted to loving her, and if he accepted Papa's job offer, off to Richmond they would go tomorrow morning.

As they neared the brick building attached to the base of the lighthouse, Chester detoured to the back, where he nodded upward. "See that loose brick? I heard it's cursed."

"How so?" Maurea asked, taking the brick out and looking at it.

Chester laughed. "If a person takes it out and doesn't put it back in ten seconds, the curse will ruin their life. One, two, three, four ..."

Maurea dropped the brick. "Oh, shoot!"

"... five, six ..."

"Will you shut up and help me? It's stuck."

"... seven, eight—eight and a half ... "

"Chester!"

Chester shoved the brick back into place. "Ah, just in time."

Maurea slapped his chest. "You are so mean, Chester Pinkham!"

"And you are so easy, Maurea Applewhite."

She looked at her hands. "That brick is rough. I even broke a nail."

Running for the lighthouse entrance, Chester looked back over his shoulder. "Better catch up, you pitiful city girl!" With his head start, he had to wait at the bottom of the spiral stairs, each coated with black paint, including the handrails.

Maurea joined him, breathing hard from her run. "Why are the bricks inside painted white?"

"To make you ask that question," Chester said, winking at her.

She slapped his behind and started up the stairs, the metal steps ringing as their feet pounded each one. Round and round they went up the narrowing lighthouse. Here and there, tall, slender windows let in sunlight. Nearing the top, breathing hard, they slowed to a reasonable pace, until they went out on the metal walkway, painted black like the stairs.

As Maurea leaned against the metal railing, the wind blew the strands of hair that had come loose from her ponytail. "Oh, my, I can see the whole world from up here. There's Corolla Island. There's the marsh before you get to your pier. It's amazing."

Chester slipped his hands around her waist. "You sure are."

Taking the biggest chance of her life, Maurea turned within his arms. "I'm glad you think so. In case you didn't know it, I've fallen in love with you."

Chester kissed her. "I love you too, Maurea. More than I ever thought possible."

She pulled away. Excitement sent a flush of heat into her cheeks. "We're going home tomorrow. Papa will give you a job.

If you do well, and I know you will, he'll make you a manager. You and Goldie can stay with us until we find a house and get married. I can't wait to start a family. Isn't it wonderful?"

Gradually, almost imperceptibly, Chester's mouth fell open. "I already told you, I don't want to leave here. Everything I love is here except you." He paused as her own mouth dropped open. "I don't want to work in some factory," he continued, trying to not let anger creep into his voice. "Not even for your father. I'd die in a city. I need the sun. I need the sand. I'm just as much a part of this place as it's a part of me."

"I ..." Maurea blinked once, twice, and once again. Her eyes brimmed with tears. "But you said you love me. You should be willing to do anything for me and not hurt me in any way." She didn't say the rest: *Like Papa wouldn't hurt me in any way.*

"It will hurt me when you leave, what about that?" Chester asked. "No, don't answer. Mommy and Daddy always told me marriage was about compromise. I took you to Monkey Island because they went there when they were young. They said it was a magical place, so I hoped it would be magical for us. Now you want to ruin it." Maurea had lowered her head while he was talking. He leaned down to look her in the eye. "I don't like fighting. We can talk about it more before you leave."

"What's there to talk about?" She shoved him away. "You made your choice."

Chester couldn't believe what had happened. One minute everything was great. The next it was shot down like a duck out of the sky. He had wondered about something when she first mentioned him going to Richmond, but he was afraid to accuse her of it. If she loved him, it might be why she wouldn't live in Corolla.

"Be honest," he said, hoping she wouldn't overreact. "You don't want to give up your father's money. That's why you want to live in Richmond."

She drew back her hand as if to slap him. "I can't believe you said that. I don't need a lot of money, but I don't want to raise our children in what amounts to a shack. I like visiting here, but I can't live here. The sand gets in everything. The salt air rusts everything. There's only one store with just the basics. There's no theatre or department stores. It's like living on an alien planet." She paused. Her nostrils flared. "We're going home tomorrow. I start my last year of high school next month. If you're not at the cottage in the morning with Goldie and a suitcase, I'll enroll in college next year and you'll never see me again."

Fear swelled in Chester's heart, but anger overwhelmed it. "People who love each other don't make demands. I wouldn't do that to you and you shouldn't do it to me."

"Shut up," Maurea said, the anger clear in her voice. "You just want a woman you can push around like Mirlande. If she knew more about the world than just Corolla, she'd leave too." Maurea left for the door to go down the lighthouse stairs. She stopped to face him. "Like I said, if you aren't at the cottage in the morning, it's over."

As she left, Chester kicked the metal railing. She was more stubborn than any wild horse he'd ever seen, making demands and giving ultimatums. Yes, he loved her, but they were too different to make it work. What a fool he'd been to think they could.

After a bout of tears, anger forced them away as Maurea walked to the cottage. She loved Chester—was *in* love with him. He'd be at the cottage in the morning. She *knew* he would.

The climb up the steps felt like climbing a mountain. Inside, she expected Papa and Patsy to be on the deck, but they weren't. In the hall, on the way to her room, she stopped at the most heartbreaking sound she'd ever heard coming from behind Papa's closed bedroom door—the same soft moans Papa and Mother used to make in bed while making love, but now he and Patsy were making love.

She started to shove the door open and call her a whore and him an adulterer, but she couldn't see them that way. In addition to her and Chester breaking up—and now this—her life was ruined.

Then again, if Chester met them in the morning, she could salvage that part of her life. She would put up with Papa and Patsy long enough for Chester to take the job at the factory and save enough money to build their own house. It didn't have to be fancy and expensive. It just needed to be somewhere besides Corolla.

In bed, she finally broke down in tears, muffling her sobs by pressing her face into her pillow. She had no idea what the morning would bring, but it better be Chester waiting with a suitcase, Goldie beside him.

At home, Chester found Mirlande at the fireplace, stirring a huge pot of stew. The smell told him the ingredients included vegetables from the garden and beef he had bought with money from working at Corolla Island. "Why so much?" he asked.

She set the lid on the pot, put the spoon on the fireplace mantle, and faced him. "You look sad. Maurea didn't like the canoe?"

"We, uh … she's going back home tomorrow. She starts high school next month." Chester raked his fingers through his dark hair. Maurea had to come back. Except for living in a world of concrete and asphalt instead of sand and trees and the Atlantic and the Currituck nearby, life without her would be worse than any nightmare he could imagine.

Mirlande took an envelope from her dress pocket. "Do you mind if I take the barge to Currituck tomorrow? My aunt wants me to visit for a week. That's why I'm making more stew than usual."

Chester glanced at the envelope. "I didn't know your aunt was living in Currituck."

"Oh, I thought I told you." Mirlande shoved the envelope back in her pocket. "She went to Haiti and came back."

"I thought that envelope might be from your pen pal." Chester dropped to the bed. Mirlande leaving for a week was a good idea. He needed time away from anyone but Goldie for a while.

Mirlande came over and rested her hand on his shoulder. "Are you sure you're all right?" She studied him carefully, eyes narrowing. "You look like something's bothering you."

"It's just the shock of …" Chester couldn't tell Mirlande the truth about him and Maurea without upsetting her, and she'd been through enough when she lost her mother to the flu. "I guess it's the shock of losing someone. You know, like when I lost my mommy and daddy and when you lost your mommy."

"You still have me and Goldie," Mirlande said, rubbing his shoulder. "You know we'll never leave you." She got a galvanized tub from a corner. "I'll heat some water for our baths. I want to be clean for tomorrow, and you've got sand all over your legs and feet."

Chester agreed that baths were a good idea. Between working at Corolla Island and fishing, he could smell pretty sour by the end of a day.

When the tub held enough steaming water for Mirlande to bathe, he sat on the pier with Goldie. Part of him wanted to have a good cry, but part of him didn't. Maurea had made her choice. Now she would have to live with it like he and Mirlande would have to live here together. He had never thought about them getting married except when they were ten. At least she didn't complain about Corolla like Maurea did. She enjoyed fishing and cooking and sharing the chores. Ever since she'd started writing her pen pal, she had gotten along with Goldie better, even letting her sleep on the foot of the bed at times. He wasn't immune to her beauty either. More than once he'd watched her bathe, like David watched Bathsheba bathe. Although shame heated Chester's cheeks when he watched her, he couldn't stop. With defined lips and a strong nose, bronzed skin and a tall, slender figure, she touched his inner longing to discover how it would feel to share physical intimacy with a woman.

Wrapped in a towel, her hair in one too, she opened the door. "Your turn!" she yelled down the path.

She didn't get as dirty as Chester, so he used the same water, now lukewarm. While he bathed, she lay facing away from him on the bed, reading an old newspaper of Daddy's with an article about a new skyscraper in New York. Curious about architecture, he liked re-reading how it was built. Mirlande sometimes asked what he thought it would be like to go to the top of one of those buildings. He said he'd rather go to the top of the lighthouse. The view of the sound and the ocean and the marsh beat looking at nothing but concrete, which was what the picture showed. She didn't say whether she agreed or not.

Done with his bath, Chester dressed and dumped the water outside. He was tempted to return to the pier and wait for his old friend, the sunset. At least Maurea hadn't ruined that for him like she had the dolphins. Depression would likely set in when he saw them again.

At Papa's work bench, he sat on the custom-made seat and set his latest decoy in his lap. His attention to detail wasn't as fine as Papa's, but it wasn't bad. The wealthy hunters coming to Corolla Island now saw the value in collecting decoys, paying a fair amount for everything Papa had made. Chester couldn't part with the Wood Duck hanging over the bed, another old friend like the sunset, as well as a remembrance of his parents.

As he carved one eye, Mirlande came over. "I'm sorry about Maurea leaving." She hugged his neck and kissed his cheek. "I meant it when I said I'll never leave you. I hope you know that."

Chester looked up at her. "I'm glad we found each other when we lost our parents. Living alone is hard. Goldie's good company, but she isn't a person."

Mirlande left to check the stew, the aroma of which made his mouth water, and started making biscuits.

The Mallard's eye took shape, then the other one, then the slitted nostrils. Dimming light through the window signaled late afternoon. Sometime later, an empty stomach and a handful of wood shavings in a pile by Chester's feet signaled suppertime.

Mirlande took the Dutch oven from the embers in the fireplace and plated the biscuits. "I got some butter and honey from the store this morning. I love biscuits with both."

Intent on carving the curve of the Mallard's beak just so, Chester nodded. He enjoyed sharing the money he made, both from working and selling decoys. Mirlande said she didn't know her father, and he felt like something of a father to her, except for watching her bathe, of course.

She buttered the biscuits and filled bowls with stew, added glasses of water and said supper was ready.

Although Mirlande felt sorry for Chester, she had seen this day coming for years now. The rich girl with the yellow hair had led him along until she had no more use for him. It was a good thing. Otherwise, the voodoo doll with the yellow string on its head would've been stabbed with a hatpin by now. Regardless of the situation—Mirlande's pen pal understood it perfectly—it was best to not place all her hopes on loving Chester Pinkham. She longed to see more of the world than Corolla, and her pen pal was willing to help with that. When they met on the beach this summer, the headful of thick, black hair, the strong jawline, and the crisp accent had infatuated Mirlande. Before the week was over, they were taking long walks on the beach at twilight while talking of all the amazing things to see and do in the world, such as skyscrapers in New York, movies in theatres, and dancing in music halls. The pen pal had even taught Mirlande a few steps, saying she was a natural, and how lovely she would look in a dress made to fit her tall, slender body, especially in high heels, with just enough makeup to accent her smokey green eyes. When Mirlande asked why the pen pal was here, the dark eyes laughed. "Oh, my family wants to take up shooting ducks, so we're getting a firsthand look at some of the hunt clubs in the area." Following the remark, the twilight walk ended with them trading addresses. The night before the family left, the pen pal softly kissed Mirlande's cheek, then promised to never abandon her like Chester was doing for whatever girl had him under her thumb. Mirlande missed the attention, unlike any Chester had given her. Still, the pen pal was away and Chester was here. She didn't want to ruin their relationship, so she needed to act quickly.

He took a biscuit from the rest. Before he started eating, Mirlande held his hand. "You must've forgotten the blessing.

Let me." Chester bowed his head and closed his eyes. She did neither. "Dear God, thank you for this day and thank you for Chester." She squeezed his hand. "I'm thankful for him in every way. He's kind and gentle and would make a wonderful father and husband. He works hard to provide for us and Goldie. I don't know what I would do without him. Please bless this food for the nourishment of our bodies, amen."

Chester released her hand. "That was very nice, Mirlande. I'm thankful for you too."

They ate silently. The red haze of the setting sun dimmed in the doorway, casting crooked shadows from the crooked limbs of those crooked trees lining both sides of the path, all the way down the hill to the silver waters of the sound.

The stew made for a savory meal. The buttered biscuits with honey made for a sweet dessert. Mirlande donned her flimsy, white nightgown for washing the dishes—not because it was hot, which it was, but because Chester and Maurea's parting had likely left him in need of a woman. Like Auntie sometimes told Mirlande's mother, "To be an intelligent woman in the world, we need to know how to bend men to our wills. I don't like it, and it's a last resort, but using our bodies is sure way to control a man."

At the basin with the dishes, while Chester returned to the decoy, Mirlande lowered the collar of the dress until the firelight bathed her brown shoulders with its yellow glow. "It's hot," she said. "Can you open more windows?"

Chester got up. "Good idea. That screened wire I got from when they built Corolla Island works great for keeping the bugs out."

Mirlande was grateful too. She loved listening to the crickets chirp and to the gentle wash of the Currituck Sound in the marsh, but not while mosquitoes buzzed near her ears.

He opened the remaining windows. As he returned to the workbench, she caught him looking at her, like a fly caught in a spoonful of honey.

Done with the dishes, she stood by the bed and stretched. The nightgown rose, revealing her brown legs, tempting the fly with honey again. Of course she wore no brassiere. Of course he noticed through the thin material of her nightgown, yet his work on the decoy continued, now within a circle of light from the lantern on the work bench.

In bed, Mirlande listened to the crickets chirping and to the sound lapping against the shore. More importantly, she listened to Chester's soft breathing, hoping he was thinking of her instead of the yellow-haired girl.

The crickets stopped chirping. The first drops of a gentle rain whispered on the tin roof. The aroma of it entered the windows.

Chester lowered the wick on the lantern, evidenced by the darkening room beyond Mirlande's closed eyelids. His clothes rustled as he draped them across a chair. The bed sank as he climbed in next to her. When he finally breathed evenly with the rhythm of sleep, she placed her hand on his chest.

In that misty place between dreams and nightmares, Chester felt Mirlande's hand on his chest. She had done this before, possibly from loneliness. Then she pressed the full length of her body against him, and he realized she was naked. Like a snake suffocating a marsh rabbit, desire coiled within his gut, compounded by the memory of his and Maurea's kisses at Monkey Island.

Mirlande tilted his face toward her and kissed him. "I want you, Chester. Don't you think it's time?"

And just like that, she thought, *the honey smothered the fly.*

Pen Pal

Dear Mirlande,

I can't tell you how glad I was to read your last letter. I'll meet you at Currituck as planned. We'll then drive to the nearest train station and see New York. Of course, like I promised, I'll take you shopping. I'm sure you'll look lovely in anything, but we want to make all those New York women as jealous as possible.

I hope you won't mind us not visiting my parents. You never met them, but they'll bore you to tears. I have a place of my own anyway, with an extra bedroom for you, of course.

I can't wait to see you. We'll dine out, see the sites, and visit a theatre or three.

Pack light, my dear, for we're about to have a wonderful week in New York.

All my love,
Your pen pal.

Pen Pal

Dear Con,

I can't wait to see New York. I'm so happy we have an entire week together, and I look forward to making all those New York women jealous in whatever clothes you think will do that.

Don't worry about me meeting your parents. I'd rather it just be us for the coming week.

The theatres sound wonderful. Would you believe I've never seen a movie? I guess you would, considering where I live.

As planned, I'll meet you in Currituck.

See you soon!

Love,
Your pen pal.

Patience

Richmond, Virginia

Sitting at the vanity in her bedroom, Catherine scowled at what time had done to her complexion. In the mirror, the bags under her eyes were the worst. Makeup could hide a lot, but it couldn't hide sagging, puffy skin.

Patsy, however, at thirty-one, was still the picture of youth and vitality, evidenced by Wilbur's weekly forays into her bedroom when they were here instead of Corolla. Of course they did the same thing there, so it was just a matter of time before Maurea learned to loathe her father. Yes, it was taking longer than expected. Still, the trap had been set, and it was only a matter of time before lust sprang it. And since the threesome had arrived home from Corolla yesterday afternoon, and since Maurea's eyes had been red from possibly crying, it was only a matter of time before she broached the subject with the only person in the household who hadn't been committing adultery in Corolla, her dear, understanding mother.

Someone knocked on the door. "Breakfast is ready," Patsy said, it being the weekend without Cook.

Catherine grinned. "I'll be right down, Patsy." She didn't say the rest. *Ready to take part in the downfall of both you and my philandering husband as soon as possible.*

On the way, she met Maurea standing in the upstairs hall, head down, arms crossed. Taking hold of her shoulders, Catherine studied the green eyes. Could it have finally happened? Had her patience paid off?

"Why, sweetheart," she said, attempting the sincere tone she had practiced endlessly, "what in the world is wrong? You appear to have lost your best friend."

Maurea pulled away. "Like I would tell you about it if I did. All this is your fault, Mother. You drove him to it."

Catherine took a step back. "Drove whom to what?"

"I don't want to talk about it."

"So, you've finally seen the depths of depravity your father and Patsy can stoop to, is that it?"

The full lips, not thinned with time like Catherine's, parted. "You know about— How long has it been going on?"

"Let's have breakfast on the patio. Nourishment always helps a person consider things more clearly, and you've much to consider concerning your father and Patsy. It will also give us privacy for our discussion."

In the kitchen, Catherine asked Patsy to bring their food and two cups of coffee to the patio. Wilbur hadn't come down yet, which was just as well. He didn't need to be suspicious. Let the proverbial chips fall where they may. If Patsy was suspicious, so be it. Plans were made and plans were laid. Soon to be ensnared, Maurea was a fly buzzing near a spider's web, and said spider was Catherine Applewhite, Black Widow extraordinaire.

Behind the huge mansion, as the spider and the fly sat in wicker chairs at a wicker table, Patsy brought their food and left. Surrounding the table, a marble patio gleamed in the morning sun. Over their heads, a huge cloth umbrella, golden in color, naturally, shaded them. On the mansion's red brick walls, ivy formed a lattice of green leaves. On its roof, slate shingles wet with dew shimmered brightly. On the trellis at this end of the swimming pool, roses wafted sweet seduction. Catherine risked the slightest of smiles. Money couldn't buy happiness, but it most assuredly could make a down payment.

Head down, the fly stared at her breakfast. The spider waited, sipping coffee. Don't push. Let her start the conversation. Then she's more likely to—

Maurea raised her head. "I don't know why I'm out here. You're worse than he is."

Catherine didn't smile, but she certainly wanted to. "How do you mean, dear?"

"I saw you with a man in your bed. It was sickening."

"Oh, I see. Naturally, you assumed the worst." Catherine dipped toast in the center of a poached egg and nibbled. "You should know better than to assume. You can only trust your eyes. I suppose you saw your father and Patsy at the cottage ... well, you know."

"I heard them in the bedroom. I didn't dare go in."

Maurea sipped coffee and Catherine did too. Now that her daughter was loosening up, evidenced by sipping coffee and now putting orange marmalade on toast, the plan would ease into place.

"About this man you saw me with ... I remember that because he's a dear friend who was going through a hard time. I was in the kitchen getting a midnight snack, and he came to the back door. He was having business trouble. He had a gun, and I was afraid he would harm himself. The only way I could calm him was to get him to sleep. I didn't want him to sleep alone. You can understand the serious of the matter, can't you? I couldn't let him commit suicide."

Maurea's nostrils flared. "You could've made that story up."

"No doubt I could. Finish your breakfast. Then I'll prove what happened."

Catherine continued with her meal. Part of her—an infinitesimal part—regretted creating such a rift between Maurea and Wilbur. She had thought she loved him when they were young, but the fire went out of the marriage when Maurea was born. She couldn't explain it at first. Eventually, though, home life bored her. Compared to New York, Richmond was a mole hill against a mountain, and she was meant for mountains. Perhaps she wouldn't completely tear asunder the father-daughter relationship. Maurea was her flesh and blood, which meant she needed a husband to keep her entertained instead of one to fill a house with selfish little brats who constantly expected her to wait on them hand and foot. I'm hungry. I'm thirsty. Can you read to me? Can you help me with my homework? If she'd considered those things soon enough, she would've had a back alley doctor root the little worm out of her womb and been done with it.

Done eating, Catherine told Patsy to get the dishes. She then took Maurea to her bedroom, particularly to the telephone on the nightstand, which she offered to her. "If you'd like to verify what I said, feel free to call that gentleman."

"And do what?" Maurea's cheeks turned crimson. "Ask him if he's sleeping with my mother? I'd be mortified."

Catherine sat on the edge of the bed. "I'll call, you listen. Bring my vanity chair over and sit." As Maurea brought the chair over, the line on the other end rang until Alex answered his home office number, where he usually retreated after Sunday breakfast. For Maurea's sake, as well as for a few planned code words for this expected situation, Catherine added a few pleasantries before getting to the heart of the matter, including a fake name for the rest of the plan. "I do hope you're doing well, Maurice. You know, from that dreadful business some time ago." Waving Maurea closer, Catherine tilted the handset away from her ear.

"Yes, Catherine, dreadful business, thank you for asking. I took your advice and am seeing a doctor about my stress." Alex, the perfect actor, paused. "How's that daughter of yours? Is she ready to visit New York instead of Corolla? A friend of mine has a handsome son about her age. She might enjoy seeing the sites with him."

Catherine forced herself not to smile. Alex was even disguising his voice for when she took Maurea to New York to meet Con. What a pair they were, as devious out of bed as in. "Oh, we'll have to see because of high school. Perhaps we'll take the train up one weekend. I better ring off for now. I'm so glad you're doing well. Forgive me for not calling sooner."

Maurea's red complexion had returned to normal. Catherine cradled the phone "I hope that raises your opinion of me a notch."

Maurea moved the chair back a bit. "I suppose, but you stay in New York more than you stay at home. Why *is* that?"

Faking seriousness, Catherine sighed. "I admit I'm not a happy woman, dear. I also admit I've driven your father into Patsy's arms. Our mistake was getting married before we knew we were a good match. I enjoy things he doesn't, like the night life in New York. He's satisfied to sit with a book. I'd go insane if I did that. It's like going to Corolla—who wants all that sand and salt and boredom? He reminds me of your friend there, Chester. I couldn't abide such a dreary existence, never knowing when the next hurricane might blow my home away."

Upon hearing Chester's name, Maurea lowered her gaze to her hands in her lap. From some of the stories she'd told over the past few years from her visits to Corolla, Catherine thought she and Chester were getting close, and she didn't like it one bit. However, it seemed something had happened between them. She cupped Maurea's chin and raised it. "I'm sorry. You'll be going to high school soon, so you won't see your friend until next summer."

"I ... well. Yes, I suppose that's true. I haven't thought about it much because of Papa and Patsy."

"Life goes on, dear. What if we visit New York next weekend for a shopping spree? If we have time, perhaps the dashing young man that Maurice mentioned will accompany us to a Broadway show? I so enjoy a Broadway show."

Maurea shrugged. "I guess."

Catherine slid the phone closer on the nightstand. "Let me call Maurice and have him make plans. Go check your wardrobe for anything you might need. We'll shop to our heart's desire next Saturday. Then we'll enjoy supper and a show that night and catch the overnight train back here in time for you to rest before your first class on Monday."

In her room, Maurea sat on the bed. She didn't know whether to believe Mother's story about the man. Nevertheless, she needed to get away, both from Papa and Patsy and to think about something other than Chester.

In Corolla, when he hadn't met her with his suitcase and Goldie, she had to ask Papa to let her out of the car to vomit, even turning away so he and Patsy wouldn't see her cry. In the car again, when he asked what was wrong, she said breakfast hadn't agreed with her. Thank goodness she hadn't mentioned Chester coming with them, other than when she'd mentioned it to Papa the day before. He didn't raise the subject, so he must've thought it was just one of her whims that didn't work out. After that, the ride home had been the longest of her life. She really loved Chester, and she thought he loved her too. Of course it was wrong to give him an ultimatum, but it was for his own good as well as hers. If he had agreed, they would've had a much better life in Richmond than in that sandy and salty sliver of nothing called Corolla.

Then again, criticizing his home wasn't fair. After all, she had enjoyed Corolla too over the years. But live there? No, not at all.

Lying on the bed and holding the pillow close as if it where Chester, she wondered how he felt now. Did he regret his choice? Was he as upset as she was? Or, Heaven forbid, had Mirlande comforted him in bed last night? He had mentioned them sleeping together because of their loneliness as children after their parents died, but after the debacle of yesterday, could he have found a different kind of solace in her arms? No doubt Mirlande was beautiful. In fact, she was more beautiful than any woman Maurea had ever known.

A picture of them together wove itself into her mind—their kisses and caresses, their legs entangled. Mirlande rolled Chester over to sit astride him, closing her eyes and throwing her head back like Patsy had probably done when she'd been with Papa. Their combined moans of pleasure, again, like those of Patsy and Papa, echoed around the room.

A combination of anger and pity flooded Maurea, both from Mother denying Papa physical intimacy and from Patsy providing it. Maurea knew she would forgive him eventually. She would even forgive Chester and Mirlande eventually. Right now, however, right this very moment, it was entirely too soon. As far as Mother, only time would tell. Until then, her actions would spell her fate. The most important thing was to go to New York next weekend to escape the hurricane of emotions roiling in Maurea's muddled mind.

Tossing the pillow aside, she rose from the bed and went to her wardrobe. She opened the oak doors and shoved racks aside with a clatter. Some new dresses would be nice, as well as shoes and hats, maybe a purse or three.

At her vanity, she applied lipstick and rouge, then pinned her wavy blonde hair back at the temples, like Mother wore hers. Not bad, not bad at all. Maybe the young man in New York would approve.

Aftermath

In bed, with Mirlande's leg draped over both of his, her chin snuggled into his neck, her hand on his chest, Chester didn't know how to feel about what was happening between them. Like a nor'easter's gale roaring through a grove of live oaks, confusion roared through his mind. He had always tried to do the right thing, had always tried to have character like Mommy and Daddy had taught him. Unfortunately, when Maurea left a month ago, the only thing that eased his anguish was Mirlande. At least she hadn't said she loved him yet. She would expect him to return the sentiment, and he would never love anyone except Maurea.

Then there was the issue of Mirlande getting pregnant. Although he had questioned her about it one night when they started kissing, his need for her soon erased that concern as if it had never existed. After more kissing and caressing and soft moans of pleasure, the now familiar wave of satisfaction washed over him like the summer-warm waters of the Atlantic. Of course he would love a child. Of course he would care for Mirlande. Sadly, for them both, that was all he could offer. Then a week ago, when her monthly cramps curled her in bed, it had relieved his fears.

After their lovemaking, though, his mind would return to Maurea. What was she learning in high school? Was she thinking of him, or was she trying to let go of their shared past that refused to release him from its grip? As lovely as she was, the boys would be after her—boys who might offer a nice home in Richmond, nice clothes to wear, a car to drive, a normal hand and a normal forehead. Being so perfect, she had amazed him by ignoring his deformities.

But his hand and forehead didn't bother Mirlande either, and her perfection was unsurpassed. For her, pleasing him in bed came as naturally as breathing. To even think of it made him want her again.

He ran his fingertips along her waspish waist, trailed them along the rise of her hip, and his need circled in strengthening trails of tingling adrenaline at the base of his spine.

Moaning, she woke and kissed his cheek. "Mmm, that feels nice, but I need the outhouse. What if you gather the eggs and scramble some for us?"

Chester said he would, and Mirlande ran outside naked. He dressed and returned with the eggs. She dressed and started the coffee. Leftover biscuits warmed in the pan after the eggs were done completed their meal.

Chester fed Goldie two cold biscuits and some leftover crabmeat while he ate.

"Can't she stay outside?" Mirlande asked. "It smells like wet dog in here."

He patted Goldie's head. "I like that smell."

"I don't mind her inside in the winter." Mirlande nibbled a biscuit. "Why can't she stay out in the summer and come in at night?"

"We tried. She scratched on the door, remember?" Chester stopped eating and faced Mirlande. She had stopped complaining about Goldie a while back, so something might be on her mind. "Is something wrong? You don't seem like yourself."

"My aunt asked me to visit again. I thought you might miss me." She took eggs and swallowed. "Do you mind?"

Chester didn't mind. He might like to visit the mainland too. "What if I take off from work and go with you?"

In the middle of a sip of coffee, Mirlande coughed. Chester gave her one of the cloths they used as napkins and patted her back. "Are you okay?"

"My coffee went the wrong way." Red faced, she wiped her mouth. "You need to work. Fall is coming, and—"

"That's right," Chester interrupted. "Mr. Knight asked me to check the basement for mice. After that, Mrs. Knight wants me to check the copper shingles after that last nor'easter." Chester spooned honey on a buttered biscuit. "How long will you be gone?"

"A week, like last time."

"What's your aunt's name? I don't think you ever told me."

"Alice— No, I mean Susan. Alice is your mother's name." Mirlande took her empty plate to the basin and returned to kiss Chester's cheek. "You're very sweet to not mind. I'll make sure you get a nice reward in bed tonight."

Chester wondered about the name mistake but let it go. Everyone made mistakes. He sure had, by giving in to the lust he never knew was inside him.

Done with breakfast, he took the plate to the basin and buried his face into Mirlande's hair at the nape of her neck. She had bathed last night, and the sweet smell of the shampoo he had bought her filled him with the aroma of roses.

She took his hands and wrapped them around her waist. "We can if you want to."

He kissed the back of her head. "I better go fishing. I'd like fried flounder for supper." At the door with his fishing tackle, he patted his leg. "C'mon, Goldie."

When the door closed behind Chester, Mirlande smiled. She had never known making love could be so amazing. Auntie made it sound like torture, by the way she described all men, not just the Creole in Haiti, the one she called a bastard. In secret, Mommy said not to listen, because all men weren't bad, and Jeff was proof.

Life was strange. One minute Mommy and Jeff were alive and planning to marry, the next they were gone. At least Auntie was also gone. Good riddance to evil rubbish, and good riddance to the yellow haired girl being gone too.

Mirlande finished the dishes, filled the galvanized tub with water heated over the fireplace, and piled her and Chester's clothes in the doorway to wash, preferring to do so outside to keep from sloshing water on the wood floor.

Thank goodness she had reminded Chester about his work. Otherwise, she would've been forced to write Con that she couldn't go with him to New York again.

What a fine gentleman he was. With hair thick and dark and wavy, intense blue eyes and a complexion as dark as Mommy's, he put every man in Corolla to shame. Unlike them, he smelled of cologne where they smelled of fish or sweat or both. His nails were always clean as well, and he wore pressed trousers and shirts, usually adding a bow tie and something he called a sport coat.

On their first night in New York, after they'd spent the day shopping in stores called boutiques, he told her she looked like a queen. He'd taken her to a hair salon first, making sure the women didn't remark on her threadbare dress. Then they bought dresses and skirts and blouses and shoes and hats, each fitted perfectly by an in-store tailor. When they entered a theatre lobby, the people getting popcorn had gawked. When they strolled the sidewalk after, both men and women stared.

When they arrived at a restaurant, the man who seated them asked who the lovely actress Con had on his arm was.

Every day brought more surprises, more restaurants, more movies, more strolls, several in Central Park. Every evening they returned to Con's high-rise apartment, where they drank champagne while watching the flickering lights of the city.

The entire time, Con never made a single romantic move, although he did kiss her hand when he said goodnight at her bedroom door.

As Mirlande plopped a wet pair of Chester's pants into a tub of cold water to rinse, she felt a twinge of guilt about lying to him. Like Con, he was a gentleman, although he didn't look the gentleman. Still, ever since they made love the first time, he would ask her to sit on the pier some nights to watch the sunset, her on the edge with her bare feet hanging off, him behind with his legs against hers, his hands around her waist. He'd point out a Blue Heron flapping low in the distance, a Red-winged Blackbird fluttering in the cattails, the black fins of several dolphins rising above the surface of the sound. After a few of those nights, she began to wonder if she loved him, or even if she knew what love was. She didn't think it was fancy clothes or cars or New York theatres and restaurants, but those things certainly appealed.

Con's father owned a shipping company, and he was learning the business. He said his mother and father hadn't mentioned grandchildren. Truth be told, Mirlande wasn't ready for children either, but she hoped to be one day. Chester would make a wonderful father—gentle, kind, patient—but Con seemed to enjoy the material side of New York too much for Mirlande's taste. In Central Park, for instance, when she mentioned the flowers and the trees and the lake, he kept talking about the places they would go and the shows they would see, plus, more importantly, the people who would gawk at the handsome young man and the gorgeous young woman. From her time with Chester and Con, Mirlande had learned one important fact of life: for some people, being seen is more important than just being.

She added the last piece of clothing to the rinse water and stirred everything. Could she be happy here with Chester, tending to the daily work that sometimes became drudgery? Her cracked hands, sunburnt cheeks, and mosquito bitten arms and legs said no, while her heart said maybe. Then again, the fancy clothes, the delicious food, and the astounding skyscrapers of New York said maybe as well. Eventually, she might have to choose one or the other. When or how that time might come, she had no idea.

Sheriff

Having brought the bodies of Mr. Andino and Mirlande to Currituck, then to neighboring Camden County for the coroner, Amos waited impatiently in his office for the phone call with the autopsy results. Bill and Sandra waited too, unable to grasp who could murder two people so violently. Mr. Andino's parents were in Greece, so a telegraph from their butler in New York had said before Amos left Corolla. As directed, the Applewhites and their daughter were still at Corolla Island. Chester, of course, was at his home, with directions to not leave the area. How this murder case would play out, Amos didn't know.

At his desk with his third cup of coffee, not including during breakfast at home, he finished sharing his notes with Bill. "Have you ever heard of such a thing, Bill?"

Sitting across from Amos, Bill lowered his own cup. "It might help to find the murder weapon."

"I agree," Amos said, trying not to grunt it out. Bill tended to state the obvious. "I hope the coroner can at least give us an idea of what it is," Amos added.

"What about a motive?" Bill continued. "Someone really hated Mirlande. According to your notes, it sounds like Mrs. Applewhite was having a fling with Andino. If so, and if she found out about him and Mirlande, that's a motive." Bill sipped coffee. "What about Mr. Applewhite? Maybe he found out about the affair between his wife and Andino."

"I can't see it. He seems like a nice fellow and a good father." Amos flipped a page. "Huh. I didn't think about this at the time. I told you Chester was engaged to the girl. When I showed him her body, he was so upset he threw up. Then later, he actually laughed when the school teacher—"

Bill snapped his fingers. "That's right. She said that Elmo boy almost got his head bashed in by Chester, and Chester laughed about him never teasing him after that. How can someone who just saw the body of his fiancé laugh about anything?"

Amos wrote that question in his notes. Chester needed to explain it. Depending on the murder weapon, and if such a thing was at his house, he might have to explain that too.

Sandra came in. "Amos, what's the chance Miss Applewhite committed these murders as an act of passion?"

Amos peered up at her. "Have a seat, Sandra. Looking up at people for too long puts a crick in my neck."

Sandra pulled a chair over from beside the wall. "It's like this—I'm a woman, and if my fiancé was cheating on me, I might kill him, but I'd beat the woman's face to a pulp."

"Not me," Bill said. "The one who did me the most wrong would be my wife. She's the one who promised to love me, not the guy cheating with her."

"You're not a woman," Sandra said. "Some of us might think that way, but not all of us. Miss Applewhite might think my way."

Amos considered this conundrum. Maurea Applewhite might've been jealous enough to beat Mirlande's face in, but she didn't seem the type. The uninjured side was certainly beautiful enough to attract any man and to make many a woman jealous.

As far as crimes of passion, Chester, who was engaged to Mirlande, could've done like Bill said and beat her face in, but he didn't seem the type either. Amos sat squarely on the fence with this subject. If he caught his wife and her lover together, he would be tempted to shoot both right between the eyes.

Shaking his head, he grunted a dissatisfied sigh. "I can see three people committing these murders—the two Applewhite women and Chester. After that, I don't know what to think."

Sandra returned the chair to the wall. "Did you tell the coroner to check the wounds before doing the full autopsies? They take a while. Maybe he could give you an idea about the weapon if he checks the wounds first."

"Good idea, Sandra," Amos said, snatching the handset from his phone. "Maybe you'll get a raise for that fine bit of detective work."

"Well," Bill grumped, "I'd already thought about it but hadn't said anything."

Amos dialed. "But your coffee isn't as good as Sandra's either."

Sandra left the room as someone answered the phone. "Camden County Coroner's office."

"This is Sheriff Sandifer over at Currituck. Can I speak to the coroner?"

"Yes, sir. Just a moment."

A pair of high heels clicked on a floor and clicked back, this time joined by the thudding footsteps of a man. "I was just about to call you, Sheriff. I decided to debride the wounds for foreign material first and found something strange. I think your murder weapon is a brick. I know you said the weapon had been taken, but were there any bricks around?"

The only bricks Amos knew of were the ones in the Currituck Lighthouse, and they were all cemented in place. "Not any loose ones. What makes you think it was a brick?"

"I found particles of a red brick in the wounds. The courthouse here is made of red brick. The janitor gave me one of the extras stored in a shed out back. I scraped it with my pocketknife for a sample and checked it against what I got from the wounds. It's a perfect match under a microscope. You find that brick, you'll find your murderer. If you're lucky, he or she—as the case may be—might've been in too much of a hurry to get the blood and hair off. Any idea where it might be?"

Amos said he had some places in mind and asked the coroner to continue with the autopsies, adding a quick thank you before cradling the phone.

Bill's bushy eyebrows scrunched together. "A brick's kind of heavy. Could a woman do what was done to those two folks with a brick?"

"She could if she were mad enough," Sandra said, sticking her head in the door. "I know I could."

Amos noted the coroner's finding in his pad and stood. "Hold down the fort, Bill. I've got a brick to find. The *one* red brick, that is."

As he started toward the docks, Sandra came out and yelled for him to come back. He did, listening intently as she said the coroner just called to say he'd found no semen in the woman, including how that meant she hadn't had sex recently, although she had been sexually active.

Boarding a friend's motorized skiff, Amos wondered about Mr. Andino and Mirlande's relationship. Maybe Miss Applewhite and Chester had told the truth about the victims parting ways. If so, the motive had just switched to the antagonistic Mrs. Applewhite. Regardless, he needed to find that brick and any clues concerning it.

Con

At one of the windows of his high-rise apartment, Con sipped cognac. Fifteen stories below, on the black asphalt of Fifth Avenue, headlights pierced the darkness. Horns blared. Street lights glowed. Crowds strode the sidewalks, both coming and going. New York City, where all the important people were doing all the important things.

And he despised every bit of it.

He downed the cognac and went to the bar to refill his glass. Instead, he lit a cigarette and returned to the window in time to see lightning transform the sky into a blinding sheet of whiteness.

And just like that, New York City disappeared.

No, as much as he despised New York, he loved it too. "Con the Conman," so his contemporaries called him. "No better place to hunt women than on the streets of New York."

And that was what he despised as well as loved. After seducing more women than he could recall, it was in his blood.

And then he had met Mirlande, which made him hate himself even more. Although her innocence had revealed his own character to himself, meaning he wouldn't dare touch her unless she begged him because he was such a rotten human being, it didn't lessen his need for other women, nor his need for wealth and prestige.

"It's time you settled down," Dad had been saying for the last year, since Con had been seeing Maurea Applewhite. "She's a fine girl from a fine family." To Dad, of course, "fine" meant any family with money.

On the other hand, Mom had heard the rumors of her son's philandering. "If you're not careful," she often complained, "some husband or boyfriend will catch you, and that will be that. Go ahead and propose to Maurea. You need a wife to straighten you out."

Con considered them damnable hypocrites. Not only had Dad been bedding Mrs. Applewhite for years, Mom sometimes joined in. They were the talk of certain bars in some of the less than ideal areas of New York. Maurea even thought Dad looked familiar when they met, no doubt from catching a glimpse of him sneaking out of her house one morning after bedding her mother, who probably said he was the milkman or some such garbage. Yes indeed, damnable hypocrites, the both of them.

Lightning flashed again, this time stuttering with indecision. Where would it strike next? What was the highest point to expend its energy? If anyone deserved it, Con knew he did. He had just returned from a long train ride from North Carolina, having left Mirlande to return to Corolla, and he was going to propose to Maurea next weekend.

Oh, she would make a fine wife all right, but she would make a shallow wife as well. Like her mother, she had learned to love New York's night life after her first visit, plus expensive clothes and fancy automobiles and fine restaurants. Unlike her mother, though, she had never mentioned sleeping together, while Catherine, when she attended Con's eighteenth birthday, had seduced him in her own hotel room, after saying she had drank too much and would he please drive her to the room and see her up the elevator. Of course he had been willing, not knowing about her and Mom and Dad at the time.

Then there was Dad's shipping business, one of the bright spots in Con's life. Nothing suited him better than working in a company that shipped goods all over the world, and it would eventually be his.

The ember on the tip of the cigarette reddened. Smoke left his nostrils and drifted upward in two lazy lines. Lightning brightened the horizon again. Thunder followed seconds later.

Of all the people in this specific circle, Con admired Wilbur Applewhite the most. He mentioned the Bible often, said the blessing before meals, and often told Con in private how he would make a fine son-in-law. Wilbur's love for the Outer Banks, Corolla specifically, had him talking about its waterfowl hunting, along with the amazing sunrises over the Atlantic and the sunsets over the Currituck Sound. "After you pop the question," he said one afternoon when the women were out shopping, "we'll have to celebrate with a stay at Corolla Island."

Con already knew of the place from his visit there, and from Mirlande. Her story was quite tragic. The aunt and mother had escaped a coffee plantation in Haiti, and Mirlande was born in what amounted to a shack in Corolla. Then she lost her aunt and mother in the Spanish Flu epidemic. After that, because of loneliness, she had befriended a boy with a deformed hand and forehead, who had lost his parents to the flu as well.

Con sensed a connection between her and the young man. Mirlande even admitted to having romantic feelings for him, but she wasn't sure if she wanted to spend the rest of her life in Corolla. Con didn't mind this nugget of information. It wasn't like he could love her. To him, she was an innocent child whose eyes brightened at dresses and restaurants and sidewalks filled with rushing New Yorkers. But she brightened the most in Central Park. Yes, she was a child when it came to New York, but when it came to nature, she was an adult. This was when she shined for him, when temptation said to slip into her bedroom and show her what being a woman was all about.

Maurea, however, was a child for every minute of every day. One day he would show her what being a woman was all about also, whether she wanted it or not. She would want it, though, because deep down, all women like her wanted it, wanted everything to be about them, wanted a man to bow and scrape and tell them how lovely they were in their fine dresses and makeup. Unlike them, Mirlande refused makeup to hide her glowing complexion. Then, before they left for Corolla, when she left the fancy clothes in her bedroom closet at Con's apartment, she donned one of her ragged dresses and came out smiling, the small cardboard suitcase in hand. "Now," she always said, "I'm back to the real me, and I couldn't be happier."

Con refilled the glass with cognac, finished it and the cigarette and got ready for bed.

The engagement to Maurea was just as well. If Mirlande continued coming to New York, his dark side would overshadow her light side. A man with tastes like his, tastes for a woman's tender flesh, couldn't hold those tastes at bay for long. Besides, his and Mirlande's worlds, as alien as the earth and the moon, would drive them apart eventually. Either that or he would corrupt her like his world had corrupted him, and he would never, ever, allow that. During the engagement trip to Corolla Island, he would break the news to her. How she would take it was anyone's guess, but it was for her own good.

Perhaps her friend Chester would comfort her. From her descriptions of him and their life together, he was the better man.

Irene

At the coffee shop, sitting in his usual booth opposite the TV, enjoying the aroma of caffeinated dark roast, Chester waits for a weather report about Irene. A commercial spokesperson invites tourists to enjoy a boat ride on the Currituck Sound to see the dolphins. Chester wishes he could throw a rock through the screen. The commercial ends. The weather announcer speaks. His voice is tense.

"Today, August 26, Hurricane Irene's circulation has expanded and the pressure continues to fall. All indications point to a landfall along the southern coast of North Carolina, possibly near Cape Lookout. Anyone along the southeast coast of the United States should pay attention to local forecasts and be prepared to evacuate."

Chester leaves the coffee shop. He's lived these forecasts before. Irene will scream into southern North Carolina and hug the sound until the center of circulation cuts right across Corolla. He doesn't need to watch the rest of the forecast to know this. He feels it in his bones, feels it in the way the fine hairs on the back of his neck prickle with apprehension, feels it in the way the hot blood surges through his veins, like a scalding crimson tide about to engulf him.

At houses along the oak-shaded shoulders of Highway 12, vacationers load vehicles with suitcases and fishing gear. A girl of about five-years-old cries about going home. A woman complains about missing what's left of her vacation. A man groans about his cancelled fishing outing to the sound. A boy wants to build a sand castle.

The children glance cautiously at the old man walking by. The adults do not. Children, whose souls have yet to be blotted with evil, notice everything.

Vehicle doors slam. Reverse lights brighten. Engines roar. Tires squawk. Exhaust fumes stink. Except for die-hard residents and business owners hammering plywood over windows, Corolla will soon become a ghost town.

At the rear of the lighthouse, Chester regrets the empty hole where that one red brick once hung like a loose tooth. The keeper told Daddy about it. Daddy told Chester about it. Chester told Maurea about it. Maurea might've told her parents about it. Secrets sometimes exist for everyone to see. It's just a matter of finding them.

His mind slips from the past to the present and to places in between. He's home again, lying in bed. Above him, the Wood Duck decoy's glass eyes glint in lamplight.

Outside Corolla Island, after he and Maurea had discussed Con and Mirlande's relationship—innocent it seemed because he had freely admitted it—they planned to let them say goodbye that night. Not long after Mirlande left Chester, Maurea came to him. Beneath her dress she wore a blue silk robe. She joined him beneath the Wood Duck decoy. Without a word he slid the robe from her shoulders, kissing her there. They would never have this chance again, and they would make the most of it. Over and over again they made love. Over and over again they cried at the betrayal of a world gone insane, of a world where people, no matter how hard they tried, grew selfish with want instead of simply having gratitude for ideals like love and family, as well as just waking to the inspiration of a new day, when the sun rises over the Atlantic, or at twilight, when it sets over the Currituck.

Time became an afterthought, and both were surprised when dawn brightened the windows. Maurea dressed and kissed him one last time. It was then, as he still lay in bed, that he realized she wasn't a virgin. Although Mirlande had been a virgin, evidenced by a spot of blood on the bed after their first time, she must've ignored any pain. Maurea, however, must've been sleeping with Con, for no blood was visible anywhere, and her passions had proven she wasn't inexperienced. For years, Chester had hoped to be her first and only lover. He also hoped now, though it was beneath him, that she never enjoyed sex with Con for as long as she lived. Asking himself if he could enjoy the twin vengeance of her having his baby first instead of Con's, he dressed.

Maurea asked where Mirlande might be. Chester said she might be walking the beach to get her thoughts together about never seeing Con again. At the edge of the woods near Corolla Island, he waved as planned when Maurea appeared in the window of one of the yellow dormers. She returned the wave—their last wave. Except for Sheriff Sandifer getting everyone together to ask about Con and Mirlande's deaths, he might never see her again. Then the sheriff took the bodies to a coroner and came back the next day, as Chester was burying Goldie next to Mommy and Daddy.

Amos Sandifer's footsteps made no noise in the sand. When he rounded the corner of the house, he cleared his throat and took his hat off. "What in the world happened to that retriever?"

Chester raised his left hand. "For most of my life, people have either been afraid of me, or hated me, or both. A few were ok, but not many. My folks taught me to have the character to ignore insults." He knelt by Goldie, trading tears for anger. "But this is too much." He kissed her head and placed her in the grave. When the sand covered her broken body, he told the sheriff to come inside, expecting him to be here for a reason.

Chester poured two cups of coffee. "I guess the coroner has something."

The sheriff took the offered cup. "What's the chance you'll let me search your home without a warrant? I can get one, but I'd rather this go smoothly."

Chester downed the lukewarm coffee. At the bed, he pulled several envelopes from under the mattress and set them beside the sheriff's cup. "This is how I found out about Mirlande and Con. When Maurea and her family came the other day, I told her. I'm sure you'll want to read them. They're in order from the time she started writing him to the last time she went with him to New York. I knew she had a pen pal, but she told me she was visiting her aunt."

The sheriff read everything. "These seem pretty innocent, but I doubt a young man and a young woman could spend so much time together and nothing physical happen. What do you think?"

Chester knew the sheriff's point. "Right. If I admit to thinking they were sleeping together, I'm a suspect because of what the killer did to her face. Only anger would do that."

"And jealousy," the sheriff said, returning the letters to the envelopes. "You realize I need these for evidence." Chester nodded, and the sheriff slipped the notes into his pants pocket. "I had an interesting talk with one of the lighthouse keepers. It seems you knew about a loose brick on the backside of the lighthouse. When we went to take a look, it was gone."

Chester studied the sheriff. He wasn't sure, but doubt seemed to cloud the man's eyes. "And you think that brick was the murder weapon."

"I have reason to think that, yes."

"But you won't tell me why."

"The prosecutor will tell your attorney. He'll tell you."

"And you think I did it because I knew about the brick."

"Do you have a better candidate? Your fiancé had some kind of relationship with Con, and you found out. It also seems you had some kind of relationship with Miss Applewhite, yet she was engaged to the same man your fiancé was seeing. Given all that, I'd say you had plenty of motive for murder."

Chester said nothing. He didn't care to be executed or spend the rest of his life in prison, but he didn't want anyone else to either. The world had corrupted Con and Mirlande. In a way they deserved what had happened, but one person, according to one of Mirlande's letters he had burned, deserved it more. Catherine Applewhite, according to Con, personified the depths to which narcissism could reach. She was corrupt to the core, loving nothing but men, money, and herself. Why he had chosen to share this information with Mirlande, Chester didn't know, but if Catherine was sleeping with Con, her jealousy of Mirlande could've provided a motive. Of course, she wouldn't have been jealous of her own daughter. She had likely introduced Con to Maurea to corrupt her as completely as she had corrupted herself. After all, misery loves company, and anyone who thinks happiness comes from money is miserable whether they know it or not.

Sheriff Sandifer took a pair of handcuffs from his belt. "Unless you have a better candidate, tell me why I shouldn't put these on you right now."

Chester considered the question. If he told the sheriff that Maurea might've told her mother about the brick, it would implicate Maurea, and she had as much reason to kill Con and Mirlande as he did.

Then again, if he went to trial and was found guilty, he'd be better off dead than to spend the rest of his life in prison. Add to that how Maurea had decided she couldn't live in Corolla, what was the use of living anyway? Without either her or Mirlande—or even Goldie—or the chance of any other woman loving a deformed man, what happiness did life offer?

"Well?" the sheriff asked, offering the handcuffs.

On her porch in Aydlett, Maurea watches the first bands of Irene circle in from the south. Intermittent clouds, like dark arms ready to embrace her, spit rain. Wind gusts chop the Currituck into whitecaps and rattle the limbs on the trees in the yard. Leaves tear loose from the branches to form a cloud of swirling green confetti, its smell similar to cut grass. Marsh and cattails bend until some break, then stand upright until the next gust hits.

Could Chester still be alive like she's still alive? Is he waiting in Corolla for her to change her mind about marrying him like she had hoped he would change his mind about moving to Richmond all those years ago?

Life leads along the strangest paths. One minute you're doing the right thing by accepting the proposal of the man your parents want you to marry. The next you're making love to the man who holds your heart in his hand. Or as you hover above him, waiting for that knot of exquisite pleasure to release, is he focusing on a Wood Duck decoy hanging from a length of fishing line? Or on a school of dolphins swimming toward him in the Currituck? Or—worst of all—on a dark-haired woman whose beauty surpasses that of a light-haired woman from Richmond, Virginia?

That last thought makes her get the .22 pistol and aim at the bobbing cattail heads. Her hand trembles. She squeezes the trigger. The cracking report and the gray cloud of gun smoke is dispersed by the wind. A miss, another, another. She reloads the pistol and puts it in her purse for looters after the storm.

Staying inside because of the increasing rain, she hits the TV remote for the weather. A commercial says to take a dolphin tour in the sound. She considers putting a .22 bullet through the screen.

Something bangs against the house, and a tree limb blows past. The Currituck is surging. Dark water floods the yard. Lightning brightens the sky. Thunder cracks and booms. Wind whistles around the corners of the house. Another limb blows past.

It's a good thing she parked the Buick a half-mile inland. It's a good thing she closed all the storm shutters except one. It's a good thing the house is on a stilted foundation to let the storm surge pass beneath it. It's a good thing the heat pump is on a stilted platform too. If you live on or near the Outer Banks long enough, you adapt to its struggles. If not, like those people who attempt to drive their non-four-wheel drive vehicles on the beach from Corolla to Carova, you get stuck, and you don't want to get stuck on an Outer Banks beach in a hurricane.

Even through the walls of the house, the humid air settles around Maurea like a warm, wet blanket. The energy of the Atlantic is coming closer, drawn into Irene like a lover drawing someone close for a kiss.

Maurea's memories of clear days and raised binoculars return. To the east, the Currituck Lighthouse's red brick form is a thin, leafless tree with a black top, as if lightning has struck it, leaving a burnt and blackened stub where the Fresnel lens and black-painted walkway is located. The yellow paint and copper roof of Corolla Island is a festering sore, the shingles tinted green with aged patina.

Fear trundles in her gut. She shouldn't be here, shouldn't be so stupid, shouldn't continue hoping for death, should've gone inland to ride the storm out in Elizabeth City.

"No," she whispers through trembling lips. "Death will come when it comes, and the sooner the better."

Guilt from the time after Chester's arrest rips through her as if it has just happened. Sheriff Sandifer brought him to Corolla Island in handcuffs. He took everyone's contact information for the trial and said they could leave.

Papa hung his head. Mother snorted laughter. Maurea fainted and woke in the car hours later, every bit of strength emptied from her anguished heart. Then, a month later, when Papa was away on a business trip, she awoke sick for three mornings. Mother took her to a supposed doctor—supposed because his office was located in a rundown building and he wore a stained suit instead of a white doctor's smock. His nurse's credentials—a red rag wrapped around her oily hair, a non-descript dress hanging from her thin frame, a black mole to one side of her thin lips, the stench of cigarette smoke exiting her flaring nostrils—inspired even less confidence.

As Mother spoke to the doctor, it struck Maurea that she knew him well. He asked Maurea to undress and lie on a wooden table. The nurse covered her with a sheet, placed a cloth mask over her mouth and nose, and had her count backwards from 100. *What a curious treatment for vomiting,* Maurea had thought.

In profile, a scarf hiding permed hair, Mother stood in the doorway. Between puffs on a cigarette, she muttered something about getting rid of a worm, confusing Maurea even more.

Then, although it wasn't time for her monthly cycle, she woke at home with stomach cramps and bleeding. The next day, Mother left for New York. That afternoon, when Patsy lay a cool palm to Maurea's scalding forehead, she gasped and ran from the room, screaming for Papa, who must've come home from his business trip in the night. Maurea told them about the doctor. Papa cursed. He and Patsy took her to the hospital. As Maurea improved from the infection, she realized Mother had taken Chester's baby from her, because she hadn't slept with Con recently.

At home again, Papa settled her in bed. "I'm so sorry, Little Snail. I didn't know you and Con were … well, you know. I suppose it's your mother's influence. I never should've let her take you to New York and get you mixed up with that crowd." Maurea started to ask why he stayed with Mother but didn't. He did so because, despite his relationship with Patsy, he was a good and honorable man.

This completed her forgiveness of both of them. Life is too short to live without love. She had abandoned her love with Chester, and any chance of having it again was gone.

Then the trial came. Papa didn't mention the results and Maurea didn't ask. Some things are better left unknown. If not, the pain might drive a person insane.

But for the briefest of moments, clarity brightens the years, until it's shoved back into the womb of despair. If not, if the truth is embraced, the resulting regret cannot be borne.

What is love anyway? Mother said it was the most worthless of emotions, while Papa said it was the most worthwhile of all of life's endeavors.

The wind and the waves, the distant flash of lightning and the dull keen of thunder, the endless ache of a heart that once knew love and tossed it aside—all those things combine and part again and again, until Maurea Lynn Applewhite goes out into the rain and wind and raises her tear-stained face to the blackened sky and screams.

Atop the dune east of the lighthouse, as Chester revels in the whistle of sea oat stalks thrashing against each other, he whirls toward the mainland.

This is the first time the pull of a hurricane has been overridden by anything, much less the sound of a distant scream. He cups his hand to his ear. Maybe it was a waking dream. Maybe it was a drunken tourist? Maybe it was—

Lowering his hand, the realization of who it is drives him to his knees. The climax is nearing. The devil will receive his due.

He faces the Atlantic. Waves build. Aquamarine transforms to gray. Crests transform to curling, crashing echoes slamming into eardrums.

Chester kicks off his boots. He sheds clothing like a pair of impassioned lovers beside a waiting bed. He stumbles down the dune. The surf covers the beach with blowing foam. His ankles wear it like whiskers, then his knees, and then he dives into the Atlantic like a nail of flesh and bone driven into the coffin of his life.

Salt burns sinuses. Sand blurs vision. He tumbles in the undertow again and again, is forced down until the need to breathe claws him to the surface. One inhale and he's driven down again. The impossibility of a 102 year-old man swimming in the Outer Banks surf during a hurricane adds silent laughter to his dilemma.

Feet find purchase. Sinews and tendons flex. Ancient muscles tighten. He pushes upward to find the wind driven surface once more.

Chester hears the scream again. He cocks his head to one side. Or is it the wind? Or is it his imagination? Or is it a combination of both?

Done with those questions, he body surfs a wave to the beach and stands, the length of him wrapped in yellow foam. A memory raises his hands to the sky, and like so many times before—*endless* times before—he screams.

The One Red Brick

Aydlett, North Carolina
2011

The day after Irene, Maurea's kayak has been swept away. Marsh and cattails are flattened. The yard, soaked by the storm surge, squishes beneath her tennis shoes as she gathers tree limbs and piles them by the road for removal. When she's done, she drives the Buick home. The electricity is out, so there's no TV to see how Corolla faired. She tries the radio. The batteries give out seconds later and she has no more. She's not a good survivor. She should've bought one of those whole-house generators by now.

Lunch is a can of tuna and a plastic bottle of water while she stands on the porch. The humidity's ozone scent is gone, replaced with air scrubbed crisp clean by Irene. Binoculars reveal the Currituck Lighthouse and Corolla Island. Edward Knight's art nouveau masterpiece still stands.

Two days later, the electricity flickers on that afternoon. Maurea celebrates with a glass of iced tea while watching Irene's damage on TV. Several sections of Highway 12 on Hatteras Island have been washed away by the Atlantic. The wind blew the sound both inland and toward the western shore of the Outer Banks. In one photograph, supplied by a Nags

Head local, the water has retreated from beneath soundside piers, leaving nothing but barren sand and several pools of water. In another photo it covers everything, including the piers. A helicopter crew surveys the damage. Several oceanfront houses have been claimed by the surf. Rainwater stands in low-lying roads. Two inlets have been cut through Pea Island. On roofs up and down the Outer Banks, shingles are missing. Trees are down. Power lines dangle. South of Oregon Inlet, along Highway 12, construction equipment repairs breaches in the dunes. Despite the mandatory evacuation, homeowners and businesses remove plywood from windows. In Avon, Rodanthe, Waves, and Salvo, along with some areas of northern Dare County, the storm surge climbed as high as twelve feet. Lives are mangled. Lives are destroyed. The Outer Banks is still here. Vacationers will return.

Done with the tea and the TV, Maurea sets a ladder on the front and rear gutters and inspects the roof. All is well—maybe Chester is looking out for her. If the invisible brick wall of her fear will allow her to drive to Corolla, she's tempted to try. Then again, while the Outer Banks heals, she should wait for their birthdays. She's never tried that, so maybe it will work.

Down from the ladder, she raises the binoculars. Corolla Island, now the Whalehead Club, gleams yellow in the crisp sunlight. Of course, contrasted against the brilliant blue sky, the red-brick monolith of the Currituck Lighthouse maintains its grip on the shifting sands. It never hurts to see if real is real.

Maurea sets the binoculars on the porch table and drops to a chair. Not long after she moved here, she visited the library in Elizabeth City to search the records for what happened during Chester's trial. Rumors said he might change his plea from innocent to guilty. Rumor's also said the prosecutor was against it. He wanted Chester to fry in the electric chair, and a guilty plea would likely be made to avoid it and eventually get paroled. Although Maurea had stopped reading there, hope that he was alive filling her heart, she ordered a headstone to be placed beside Abner and Alice's graves. It was the least she could do to honor the memory of all those wonderful times she and Chester had shared so long ago. Then again, as she well knows, she's always been good at doing the least.

While at the library, she also researched Sheriff Amos Sandifer, who had written a book entitled *Chester Pinkham: The Personification of Character*. It covered Chester's life in Corolla, how he loved the area, loved all of its creatures, how his greatest love would remain anonymous. Amos said people would know anyway from the rumors. Chester said he didn't care.

"We talked hour after hour in his jail cell," the sheriff wrote. "I wanted to set him free even though I would lose my job. The Great War made me see the evil in the world. Then World War II took one of my sons and made me see evil for what it is, the result of small people with small hearts who love no one but themselves. The biggest mistake Chester made was loving other people too much. The rest of the guilt fell squarely on the shoulders of those whose evil affected his life, his sweetheart's life, and the lives of Mr. Andino and Mirlande. I could easily go on but won't. My wife would kill me if I got sued for slander. Suffice it to say, narcissism, not the love of money, is the root of all evil."

Maurea had thought long and hard about this passage. After the abortion, she wanted to have it out with Mother, who had moved to New York permanently. Papa, God bless his soul, still refused to divorce her, so, when Patsy became pregnant, Maurea gave them her blessing.

Upon arriving at the apartment building and Mother's door, she didn't need to enter to know what was happening. The combined moans of Mother and Con's parent said it all.

Maurea promptly went outside and vomited. This was the evil that had affected her and Con. Whether or not it had affected Mirlande, she would never know. In a way she seemed innocent, in a way not. The ability to murder definitely dwelt behind her green eyes, possibly from how Elmo Parker had called her a "trash eater." No doubt others in Corolla had done the same thing, like they had bullied Chester about his hand and forehead.

Yes, the little old lady from Richmond, now in Aydlett, had allowed narcissism to destroy her life, but the love of money had played a part too. Then again, the love of money stems from narcissism. When a person thinks the universe revolves around him or her, they think they deserve everything it has to offer whether they're willing to earn it or not. Maurea knew that was her in a nutshell, because she had wanted Chester and her life in Richmond too. Chester—sweet, gentle, insightful Chester— knew the things of the world, like with so many couples before them, would take the place of love eventually. In Corolla, however, the things of the world are replaced with the simplicity of sunrises, sunsets, and making love beneath a Wood Duck decoy—the sweetest time she has ever known.

Maurea pours more tea. Seated outside again, she wonders about Chester changing his plea. The rumor died without verification, and she didn't have the heart to read whether he got the death penalty or not. She also wonders about the one red brick. The prosecutor had opened his case by saying the murder weapon was a brick taken from the bottom of the Currituck Lighthouse. Yes, the brick was gone, but both the prosecutor and the sheriff felt the case was strong enough without it for an arrest. Then, when the prosecutor revealed how particles of a brick were in the victim's wounds, adding how the particles matched an unused brick one of the keepers had given him from the construction of the lighthouse from 1873 to 1875, plus how he had seen Chester studying the brick on more than one occasion, it seemed the young man was doomed.

From the sheriff's book, Maurea thought Chester could've been found innocent. Some of the jurors knew Chester's father from when he guided duck hunts, and they said the young man would've never fallen in love with a landlubber from Richmond. The prosecution's motive for murder, however, being in a jealous rage because he knew about Con and Mirlande through his letters to her, might've swayed them. How the Applewhites and the Andinos got out of testifying, Maurea never knew. More than likely, both families had pulled some political strings to avoid the embarrassment, and Con's mother and father weren't nearly as broken up about their son's death as they should've been, more evidence of the evils of narcissism.

From the north, little more than a dot above Carova, a clattering helicopter jars Maurea from these thoughts. It circles above the community, impossible to see clearly from so far away, and continues south toward Corolla. When it nears the lighthouse, the red and white markings identify it as from the U.S. Coast Guard. It circles Corolla Island. Satisfied, the pilot steers toward the beach to inspect million-dollar homes and, in some cases, multi-million dollar homes.

Maurea realizes it took quite a while to learn to enjoy the simple life in Aydlett, but seeing the sun rise over the Atlantic every day helps. Such a thing makes a person feel insignificant. Then you realize how much influence you have over the lives of other people. That influence can be positive, negative, or in-between. Negative is easy. Mother and the Andinos made negativity an art form. Affecting people positively is extremely difficult. Nobody's perfect, but we can try our best, which is where the in-between comes in. It's still difficult, but it starts when you realize you're human. Then, if you want to truly be the in-between, you realize your moral borders must include forgiving yourself for your mistakes, but only as long as you don't continue making them. Oh, we do continue making them, but trying lessens them exponentially.

The ice in the tea has melted. Maurea tips the glass toward the woods across the sound, where Chester's house should be. "Here's to you, Chester. I think you'd be proud of the woman I've finally become." She drinks and laughs, almost strangling herself. "Hey, it only took almost 103 years. Maybe we'll celebrate on our birthdays next month."

Leaning his elbows against the black-painted railing at the top of the Currituck Lighthouse, Chester laughs at an unheard joke. He doesn't know what's so funny, but laughing seems as natural as swimming in the Atlantic during a hurricane, which is laughable in itself. Swimming in the ocean is okay, but sand in your underwear is *not* okay, which is why he undresses during a hurricane, as well as to keep his clothes, heavy with water, from taking him to the bottom. Yes, he's felt like sinking into the depths of the ocean from time to time, but the belief that he needs to see another sunrise never abandons him. Since that's the case, maybe his last eighty-three years in Corolla, living alone and without love, haven't been wasted, and his sacrifice will be justified in the end.

Aside from such serious thoughts, he always feels good after those swims, fresh and clean like the air, scrubbed free of the summertime heat and humidity by a hurricane. Like his varying mood, though, this feeling, as he well knows, won't last for long.

What keeps his heart light is imagining Goldie running on the beach, or swimming after a duck, or taking one of Mommy's biscuits from his hand under the table, then Daddy doing the same thing as Mommy frowns, and then both him and Daddy smiling when she does it too. Pete perched on the pier piling waiting for a fish brings back good feelings, especially when Goldie would yap at him as a pup, not understanding what kind of dog had such a big mouth. Enormous flocks of ducks and geese filling the sky is another source of satisfaction, particularly with Snow Geese and Tundra Swans. Seeing dolphins is hard to take. Some days he enjoys them, some days not. Existing in a loveless vacuum is more difficult than he imagined. Still, living in Richmond not only would've killed his soul, it would've killed his and Maurea's marriage. He regrets so many things, but he regrets losing her the most.

Regardless, she's nearby, evidenced by her scream. No doubt she's in as much pain as he is. He hopes their birthday will settle things. If not, he's not sure how much longer he can wait. Besides, his headstone behind the house should've been used ages ago.

Circling the lighthouse walkway, he ignores Hurricane Irene's damage to Corolla. His home sustained a few more leaks, a few more loose sheets of rusted tin on the roof, a few more loose boards on the walls. At the height of the storm, its category one winds pushed the Currituck Sound halfway up the hill, stealing the canoe, the skiff, and the pilings left from the pier. He doesn't mind much. Imagination can perform miracles, and he can imagine everything and everyone he cares about, to the point of making them real anytime he wants.

On the ground again, walking the path along the sound, he whistles for Goldie. Asleep on the pier, the specter of his imagination raises her head and blinks sleepy eyes. Then she comes running, ears flopping, tail high, grinning her toothy grin. He kneels to hug her, buries his face in her thickly furred neck, loves the precious aroma of dog smell, even if she isn't wet. She pulls away and licks his face, and he tells her how much he's missed her. She yips in reply, runs off and comes back with a stick to play fetch.

Like people, if dogs are raised in a loving family, they know nothing of evil. Oh, some go astray like people—some even to the point of becoming evil—but a good start is a good start no matter what the species is.

Throwing the stick, Chester can't help but wonder why Goldie, in all of her youth and bouncy exuberance, chose to return now in his imagination. He doesn't know, but he's grateful beyond words. Maybe she's an early birthday present. After almost 103 years, eighty-three of them spent alone, he's earned it.

His friend, Amos Sandifer, thought he had earned plenty. Except for being away from his home and everything he loves, Chester enjoyed his time in jail while sharing his life story with Amos, as his pencil filled several pads with information.

"How did you deal with having a deformed hand and forehead?" Amos asked.

With a grin, Chester tilted his head to one side. "Define deformed, Amos. Can you?"

Amos raised his pencil and tapped his chin with the eraser. "Well, I'd think it was obvious. Aside from how you look, you can't do everything other folks can do, like I can't run because of the bullet I caught in my leg in The Great War."

Chester grinned again. "Let other folks worry about themselves. What matters is what *we* can do. Plenty of other folks aren't—I'll use your word for it—deformed—but they refuse to acknowledge the abilities they *do* have. We've all got something to offer. It's just a matter of figuring out what that is."

Nodding, Amos wrote a few lines. "Makes sense to me, Chester. Makes sense to me." The pencil stopped scratching. "I 'spose kids teased you. How did you deal with that?"

Holding a cup of coffee, Chester sipped. "By not letting them get to me. I couldn't control them, but I could control me. I just laughed in their faces. When they figured out I didn't care what they said, they left me alone."

"What about that time in school, with Elmo—"

"Elmo Parker," Chester said, recalling that day. "It wasn't about me, it was about him calling Mirlande a trash eater." Sitting on his bunk, Chester rested his elbows on his knees. "You see, most people—Mirlande was one of them—live too close to their hearts. The least little thing injures them, even words. What matters, like Mommy and Daddy taught me, is having character. When you have character, what other people say doesn't matter. Like a lot of people, Mirlande hadn't learned that yet. I think she would've if she'd gotten the chance."

Chester didn't say the rest. *Like Maurea would've learned if she'd gotten the chance.* She got the chance from her father, but her mother's evil ways ruined her. That might've been because she was her mother's daughter. If she had been Patsy's daughter, things would've turned out differently.

"Speaking of chances," Amos said, looking at him with sad eyes. "Do you mind telling me if you're guilty? I hate to think I've grown fond of a murderer."

Chester winked. "Smile when you say that, Sheriff, so I can tell if you're joking or not."

Amos didn't smile, but he did raise the pencil from the pad. "Just between you and me, did you do it or not?"

Chester said nothing. He had considered changing his innocent plea to guilty for second degree murder. He could argue that because he could imagine finding Mirlande in Con's arms and how it would've made him feel after all their nights beneath the Wood Duck decoy together.

"You don't have to tell me if you don't want to," Amos said. "I just thought you might like to get it off your chest."

Again, Chester said nothing. He had written Wilbur Applewhite to ask if he would keep up the property taxes on the house and land so he wouldn't lose it if he got less than a life sentence. Wilbur promptly wrote and said considering the circumstances, he would be glad too. Of course, Chester knew what Wilbur had meant. He thought Chester hadn't implicated Maurea because he believed her mother's evil ways might've given her the ability to kill in a jealous rage. Chester never confirmed anything. He simply sent a thank you note, adding how he hoped everyone was well. With his home safe from the county taking it, he might return there eventually. What happened after that depended on Maurea. She might come and she might not. It was entirely up to her. She might come when she learned how to enjoy the simple life. Still, like him, she has a debt to pay for her part in the direction their lives have taken. The key is if she realizes it or not.

Chester sipped his cooling coffee and faced Amos. "Where's your faith, Sheriff?"

Amos laughed. "Ain't that the truth. Tell you what, I found it in a trench in France in The Great War, how about that?"

"Glad to hear it. As you well know, there aren't any atheists in foxholes." Chester paused to get serious. "I'm also glad you made it back. You've been a good friend, and I need all the friends I can get. If the trial goes bad, will you take care of things for me?"

The cords in Amos's neck tightened with a hard swallow. His eyes misted over. "I will," he said, his voice breaking. "I sure don't want to."

Chester finished the conversation by telling Amos it was his duty, the same as his duty in the war and his own duty to do what was right after what happened to Mirlande and Con.

At his feet with the stick, Goldie nuzzles his hand and whines. He throws the stick in the sound. As she swims after it, she fades away, leaving nothing more than the wake of her passing on the silvery surface of the water, sparkling with sunlight.

Chester tries to reimagine her, but it doesn't work. He does the same for Pete on the lone pier piling, but it doesn't work either. Closing his eyes, he starts to imagine Mirlande, but that makes him cry. Then he imagines Mommy and Daddy. In the canoe, both young, both feeling that first blush of love, they pause their paddling toward Monkey Island and wave. Chester is afraid to wave because they might fade like Goldie. They fade anyway.

At home again, he leaves the door open and lies in bed, hoping the breeze off the Currituck will bring the Wood Duck decoy to life once more.

What does a person do when most of their life has been spent as a decoy for the red brick of hate pulsing inside people's chests? Children like Elmo Parker sneered and said, "Crab boy. You ain't nothin' but a big-head crab boy. Yo momma was a crab an' yo daddy was a whale." They also called Mirlande a "trash eater," and likely worse things Chester hadn't heard. It wasn't just children like Elmo either. Plenty of adults had looked at the boy with the deformed hand and head as if he were something that should've been thrown into the Atlantic when he was born. No doubt they thought the same thing about the two women from Haiti and the child born to one of them.

Chester rolls over in bed to face the rear wall of the house.

The red brick of hate has been growing since 1928. Not only did a second world war prove it, numerous other wars and conflicts prove it, including the September 11, 2001, attacks in the United States, resulting in the loss of 2,996 innocent souls. Many governments choose power over compassion, greed over gratitude. What's worse, some governments allow the criminal element to flourish. Then those criminals victimize the populace at will, forcing citizens to flee their homes for other countries. People everywhere are forgetting who they should be—good on the inside so their outsides won't matter. Because of how Chester and Mirlande were ridiculed, they were aware of this ideal. According to the TV in the coffee shop, their opinions don't matter to an increasing number of people.

Hot tears roll from Chester's eyes. He misses Mommy and Daddy. Despite people like Elmo Parker, life was much simpler when they were alive. Most of the people in Corolla knew it too. All they needed for a smile was a golden sunrise, a roof over their heads, a kind word from a loved one, and a crimson sunset at the end of the day. Anything else was an unnecessary luxury.

Some vacationers know these things now. A boy wants to build a sandcastle. A girl does too. They don't care if they get sand in their bathing suits. A man fishes in the surf. He doesn't care if the bait is gone or not. Just breathing in the salt air and feeling the sun on his face is enough. His wife fishes with him. She's pregnant but hasn't told him yet. She'll surprise him tonight after supper. Chester would love to be there, would love to be him, would love someone—anyone—to be her.

Similar stories reach across the county, the state, the country, the world. There's hope yet, despite the red brick of hate pulsing in many a chest.

The room darkens and brightens. Days come and days pass. Goldie jumps on the bed but can't rouse her miserable friend. Whining with sympathy, she fades away. Abner and Alice take turns whispering that'll it'll be all right, to be patient. Their son doesn't stir. They fade away also. Mirlande lies beside him, hugs him tight. He's such a fine man, yet she failed him. She kisses his cheek and leaves to walk along the sound. Mommy and Jeff join her. Auntie does not. She's in the place where the people live who haven't learned to extinguish the red brick of hate smoldering in their chests. Con is in that between place. He realizes why he loves the things of the world, but he can't get past his lust for controlling women. Mirlande was trying to change him, to be his friend, to end how he considered himself superior to everyone around him. He might learn eventually. To be in that between place, never knowing how long it will last, not quite knowing why he's there, might be a worse torture than the place where Auntie is.

A cold wind whistling through the cracks in the walls wakes Chester. Rain patters the tin roof. Through the open door, down the path to the sound, the Currituck is as gray as the sky. Wearing Daddy's hunting coat and hat, he goes to the coffee shop. The news announcer says it's November 28. Chester realizes he, Maurea, and Mirlande, if she were alive, are 103. He doesn't know how to feel about it, doesn't know if it means anything or not.

A TV commercial says it's not too late to visit the Outer Banks. Many enjoyed Thanksgiving last week, so what better time to make plans to enjoy Christmas than now.

Not that Chester has an appetite to start with, but the commercialism ruins even his enjoyment of smelling coffee.

On the way home, he passes the old one-room schoolhouse he attended, which now houses the Corolla Wild Horse Fund's Museum. Just up the road, he visits Island Bookstore, a larger store than the one near the coffee shop. Here he looks for more books by the author who wrote *The Diary of Carlo Cipriani* and finds one called *The Coincidence of Hope.* The back cover description says it's about a young man who died in World War II. Although he still exists as some kind of spirit, his greatest hope is to find out what happened to his girl in Nebraska after he died.

Chester, the old man no one notices except children, his coat and hat damp with rain, his hair steel gray, his wrinkles many, sits in a dim aisle with his legs crossed and reads.

As the warmth of the store permeates his coat, the memories of similar days at home, with him either in Mommy's or Daddy's lap, soon permeate his mind. Flames dance in the fireplace. Burning wood crackles. The occasional pop of a knot softly explodes, sending out the aroma of hickory or oak. The smell of fried flounder fills the air after supper. Rain taps the tin roof, or moonlight glints off wavetops in the sound. If he's very lucky, secure in his family's loving arms, crickets sing him to sleep while the warmth of the fire bathes his face like the warmth of their love bathes his heart.

Chester's a fast reader. He almost absorbs the story. This book goes even faster because the scenario is so similar to his own. Like Joe Matthan, the main character, Chester lost the love of his young life at an early age, and he seems to be wandering in time in hopes of returning to her or, in Chester's case, her returning to him.

Several chapters bring tears, particularly the part where Joe's girl, Elaine Johnson, receives the telegram that says he was killed. Although tears wet the sleeves of Daddy's old hunting coat, Chester reads on and is rewarded with a satisfying ending, something he hopes he and Maurea and Mirlande will earn.

As he closes the book, the soft patter of a child's shoes comes close, and he realizes he's sitting in the children's books section. Rounding the shelves lining this aisle, the spitting image of Maurea at five-years-old, when she, Chester, and Mirlande met the first time, stops, and Chester smiles. "Hello there, young lady."

The girl looks around the shelf of books to her right, possibly for one or both of her parents. "Mommy, there's an old man here." She turns her head back around quickly, yellow ponytail bobbing, to face Chester.

No one comes. Mommy must be busy. Chester takes a book from a shelf. "This was my favorite when I was your age. My mommy and daddy read it to me all the time. Do yours read it to you? It's called *The Wonderful Wizard of Oz.*"

Brilliant green eyes blink. "Oz?"

"That's right," Chester says, his tone encouraging.

"They don't read to me." The girl's plaintive tone, filled with longing for someone to read to her, breaks his heart.

He swallows to stop a sob, then pats his lap. "I'd love to read to you, sweetheart."

The girl sticks a finger in her mouth, no doubt wondering if it's okay. Then she comes over and plops in Chester's lap, which makes him almost cry again. Swallowing a sob once more, he opens the book and reads. As he does, his heart compresses in his chest. He had wanted a family and children, or at least one.

Joe Matthan wanted a family too. His story was satisfying, so there's that.

Chester finishes chapter one of *The Wizard of Oz*. At the counter, blocked by shelves, two women talk about taking a tour to see the Wild Spanish Mustangs. One says she wants her daughter to see them. Chester sets the girl on her feet and offers her the book. "Go tell your mommy you want her to buy this book and read it to you. I bet she will."

The girl takes the book, politely chirps, "Thank you," and patters toward the counter. Mommy buys the book. She and the clerk speak in low tones. The door slams as if she's in a hurry to read to her daughter. Chester smiles. He loves good parents like he loves his own.

He shelves Joe's story and slips from the store unseen. Down the road is the one room schoolhouse he attended until the Spanish Flu hit. No one seemed to worry about him after that. Then again, most people only paid him any attention as a boy because they knew Daddy and Mommy. After they died, people completely abandoned any pretense of caring about the Crab Boy with the deformed hand and head, the product of a whale and crab mating.

Head down against the November breeze, hands in pockets, he shuffles toward home. Above him, the twisted live oak limbs clatter. It's strange how they don't lose their leaves, which resemble dragonfly wings, until spring. It's as if they are out of sync with the rest of the world, which is exactly how Chester feels at 103. He should've died a long time ago. What was that chore he wanted the sheriff, whatever his name was, to do? Yes, he's out of sync with the world, or either he's going insane from living alone for— What's 103 minus his age when he got out of prison? He would need to know his age then to complete the math, and he can't even remember that.

He considers slipping into the rear of Corolla Island—the Whalehead Club he should say—and walking the rooms, but it's closed for the season. It's just as well. If he recalls seeing Maurea there, beautiful in a fitted yellow dress to her ankles, blonde hair piled on top of her head, green eyes flashing as she spoke with other wealthy guests, the sleeves of Daddy's coat will be soaked to the elbows.

He considers going to the rear of the lighthouse, but the empty hole, like an incised cancer, will haunt him even more than it does now.

As he walks home, Goldie trots up the path with a stick in her mouth. How can that be when she died so long ago? Maybe it's like the song he heard from a passing car's radio in 1971, it's *Just My Imagination*.

Wagging her tail, Goldie whines. Chester ignores her. Her yellow form fades until the stick falls from her mouth to the sandy path.

He's at the top of the lighthouse, unsure how he got here. Across the sound, as the sun drops below the horizon on his birthday, a distant pinprick of light winks on in a house in Aydlett. Could that be Maurea? Chester mournfully shakes his head. It's time to forget his dreams. If she doesn't come tonight, he'll use his headstone and be done with it.

Maurea turns on the lamp by the chair in the living room and sits. She and Chester are 103. Mirlande would be too if she had lived. Imagine living so long and seeing so many things and so many changes, not all of them good. Nostalgia grips her. What's wrong with a two-parent family when both are good people? She's a product of a two-parent family, when one is good and one is as bad as it gets. Yes, Papa wasn't perfect, but he had good reason not to be.

The darkness deepens. The walls flex as the house breathes in and out, in and out. The heat pump whines on. Air from a floor register flutters a curtain.

Maurea's sigh mirrors her home's sigh. Unlike when fear gripped her at the thought of driving to Corolla, it draws her there now. She's a dolphin swimming toward Chester, and she still loves him more than she can say. Her purse and keys are on the kitchen table. She's dressed in jeans, an old sweater, walking shoes, and a jacket. Her white ponytail hangs from the opening in a baseball cap. She just needs to get up, crank the Buick, and drive.

Then why doesn't she?

One reason is she's afraid of what people will think of her. Chester would say she did the right thing by driving there, so why worry?

She goes to the sliding glass doors. Beyond the porch, beyond the flattened cattails, beyond the sound, the light flashes at the top at the Currituck Lighthouse. Twenty seconds later it flashes again, and she expects it to illuminate her for the part she played in what happened at the Corolla Island boathouse so long ago. Oh, she's guilty, just like so many other people are guilty. The difference between her and them, if she drives there tonight, is it acknowledges her guilt. Then again, those other people are dead now, so maybe, with their last breaths, as their hearts slowed and their vision blurred, they acknowledged their guilt and asked forgiveness. She doubts it, especially for Mother and Mr. and Mrs. Andino. Narcissism is the refuge of a person with no regard for anyone else.

In the Buick, she leaves Aydlett. At Grandy, on Highway 158 east, a peach Flurry would've tasted great in the summer, when the Grandy Market was open for the season.

The headlights illuminate four lanes of asphalt. Millions of vacationers drive this road every year, not only passing the Grandy Market, but passing, and sometimes stopping at, golf courses, fishing tackle stores, restaurants, a vineyard, and more farm stands like the Grandy Market.

Eighteen miles later, when the Wright Memorial Bridge appears in the headlights, Maurea's throat tightens. Can she really do this? She knows she's needed to for most of her life, so it's about time. Regardless, the thought of what will happen makes her tap the brakes. Then she hits the accelerator. What better time to do this than on her birthday, as well as on Chester and Mirlande's birthdays.

The bridge, nearly three miles long, welcomes drivers to the Outer Banks with expansion joints that make vehicles rise and fall as they cross them. On the horizon, lights from homes and businesses sparkle. To the north, because it's a moonless night, the Currituck Sound is a sheet of black water. To the south, the Albemarle Sound is the same. Drivers come and go. If not for the glare of their headlights, untold numbers of stars would be visible in the sky.

When the Buick reaches the end of the bridge, Maurea's mind goes blank. She processes no visual input except Highway 12 north, until the flash of light from the lighthouse beckons her onward.

An hour after she leaves home, she parks at the one-room school house, still there after all these years. She loops the purse strap over her shoulder and walks through the woods. Now the stars brighten her way. Now the path is clear. Now she knows what she needs to do.

Approaching Chester's house, she hardly recognizes it. Vines cover the entire back wall. A twisted oak limb lies on the rusted tin roof. The window on the southern side is shattered.

Inside, the Wood Duck decoy still hangs from the fishing line, but one wing is broken. The roof has been leaking. Black mold lattices the front wall. The bed has been torn apart, likely by animals.

Using the flashlight on her phone, Maurea peers into dark corners. "Chester? Are you here? It's Maurea. I'm sorry I haven't come by now." Nothing. Not a sound. Not a whisper.

Chester peeks in the open door. She's finally come. After all these years she's finally, really, actually here. Words fail him and it's just as well. He wants to see what she'll do, preferably without his influence.

She calls a few more times and heads for the door, pauses at the bed to muffle a sob. He takes advantage of the phone's light aimed at the bed to slip around the other side of the house nearest the woods. The light goes to the left. As silently as a ghost he follows. She stops at the four headstones, touches his parent's headstones. Standing before his, she collapses with it in her arms and weeps. He expects words of apology. Like when she left him, she ruins his expectations all over again. Will she ruin them one last time, or will she—

She goes to the trunk of a tree in the woods, sets the phone beside her and begins to dig. She does so slowly at first, then franticly, throwing sand like Goldie would've done. She shines the light around, surrender on her face. She goes to his headstone and lies beside it, takes a gun from her purse and shoots herself in the temple.

Chester cradles her head in his lap and rocks the fragile body. He's too stunned to cry. He thought she might do something like this, but he's too stunned to cry.

Goldie runs up the path from the pier. Mommy and Daddy come from inside the house. Mirlande comes from toward the beach and kneels beside him. The plain white dress covers her bare feet. The waterfall of dark hair flows across her shoulders and down her back. To see it all, he imagines himself a few steps away, imagines the full moon's light piercing the twisted limbs of the live oak trees and the shadows splayed on the group of people circled around him. No one says anything. Mommy kisses his cheek. Daddy squeezes his shoulder. Goldie licks his face. Mirlande hugs his neck. Then they fade away into the darkness.

He kisses Maurea's lips. What words can change anything now? What words can erase the past? What words can change the people who set this tragedy in motion?

None can.

To escape the grief exploding in his chest, he imagines himself on the beach at five-years-old. It's a beautiful day. The sun warms his brow. The waves crash softly. Gulls cry. The scent of salt air is a balm to his young soul. His new puppy, Goldie, bounces beside him. The tip of her red tongue shows between black lips. Her paws sling sand. Her excited yips pierce his eardrums. Her tail thrums the air. What a joy she is.

"Hello, boy!" a girl's voice yells from his left. As if she lives in the sun, every inch of her skin is tanned. Dark hair down her back frames a narrow face and a slender nose. The only response to such an appealing stranger is to throw up his hand and yell hello too.

Puffing hard, she stops a few feet away. He decides to let her rest before he says anything else.

"Hello!" a yellow-haired girl yells from his right. She wears her hair in a ponytail. As she runs, it bounces back and forth like the tails of the wild horses when they trot along the surf. Her eyes, though, draw him like the sea, so green he can hardly stop looking at her. Like Mommy and Daddy taught him, when meeting someone he doesn't know, he offers his hand. "Hello. My name is Chester."

The yellow-haired girl shakes his hand. "I'm Maurea." She waves at the black-haired girl. "What's your name?"

"I'm Mirlande."

"I never heard a name like that." Maurea shares a sincere smile. "It's *very* pretty."

"I like your name too," Mirlande says sweetly. "My name means shining sea. What does your name mean?"

Maurea nudges a whorled shell with her toe. "Papa said it means little snail, kind of like that shell."

Chester introduces them to Goldie. They pat her head and ruffle her neck fur.

He then looks up and down the beach. No adults are here, and that seems okay. He tells both Mirlande and Maurea he likes sea shells. With him between them, they set off along the beach. Here and there, one squats and holds up a shell. The other two squat to study it, saying how pretty it is. They do this again and again, endlessly stuffing shells into pockets.

Chester's heart feels as if it will burst from happiness. Neither Mirlande nor Maurea asks about his head or his hand. It's as if he's as handsome as they are beautiful.

But then something from his past—or is it his future—says to think again. True beauty—the beauty that counts the most—comes from the inside, and that's what he's enjoying right now.

They find shell after shell. They play tag. They swim in the warm waters of the Atlantic. They never grow old. They never need to eat. They sleep when they're tired. They wake when they're refreshed.

But is it his imagination? Would it be so bad if it isn't? Would it be so bad to roam Corolla with Mirlande and Maurea and

Goldie for eternity, forgetting the tragedy that brought them together called The One Red Brick?

He answers his own question by picking up another shell and studying its spiraled whorls. To escape her guilt, Maurea had withdrawn into her shell. Mirlande, despite her guilt of lying to him about Con, chose to be a shining sea of calm and forgive Maurea for killing her. Yes, he had seen Maurea bury the brick before they made love, and because he understood her faults, understood her jealousy, understood how he felt when he found Con's letters to Mirlande, he couldn't condemn her for what she had done.

Maurea tugs his hand. "You know what you have to do."

Mirlande tugs his other hand. "You have to, Chester. It's the only way."

Chester realizes they're right. He should've done it a long time ago. He lets them lead him back to his home while Goldie runs ahead. They pass the lighthouse, pass the boathouse, pass Corolla Island. Then they walk the path along the sound and climb the hill to his—now their—home.

During the walk, a strange sensation fills him, and he realizes it's pure knowledge entering his mind. Each and every moment of Maurea and Mirlande's life is visible to him—all those things that molded them into adults who made mistake after mistake. He wonders if they know all the things that shaped him as well, but there's no need to ask and no need to relive those things—not even how Maurea's despicably evil mother murdered their child.

Still, thanks to the little girl he read to recently, he knows the joy of fatherhood. He can either dwell on the bad or dwell on the good. It's best to dwell on the good ... and the innocent.

Behind his home, they kneel by the body of the old woman who came to admit her guilt. One at a time, gently, reverently, they kiss both cheeks. Chester says a prayer of forgiveness. He goes inside for the cloth bag beneath his bed and returns with The One Red Brick. Maurea touches it. "You hid it. You thought I might come."

He nods solemnly. "A good person can only take so much guilt. We either admit it or let it destroy us. You wanted to put the brick by your head to let whoever found you know you were guilty, not me. It doesn't matter now. None of it matters now. I loved you so I protected you. I still love you now."

Mirlande comes close. "What about the car? People will come."

"Let them come," Maurea says. "I don't care what anyone thinks. What matters is I finally did the right thing."

Chester uses sand and spit to clean the dried blood and black hair off the brick. "And we have one more thing to do."

They go down the hill to the path by the sound. A few steps in front of them, Goldie trots along, wagging her tail. Chester knows they'll return home. They'll live in the crumbling house and sleep beneath the Wood Duck decoy, where Goldie will keep them company.

At the lighthouse, the brick fades from his hand and solidifies into the hole. No one will know how it got there. After so long, he doubts anyone will care.

He looks around. He's as alone as he's ever been. He must've imagined everything except Maurea's death and returning the One Red Brick to its place in the Currituck Lighthouse.

During the walk home, stars fill the sky. Maybe everyone he loves is waiting for him there.

At the fireplace, no warmth rises from the ashen embers. Has he ever lit a fire in the eighty-three years he's been here alone? He looks around his home, empty for far too long. Then he shuffles around slowly, intently running gentle fingertips along the things of his past—Daddy's decoy making tools, Mommy's books, Goldie's bed in the corner—tender caresses to press everything to his ancient heart. He considers lying in bed to recall making love to Mirlande and Maurea. To do so would gut him, and he needs his resolve.

Behind the house, circled by the live oaks, their limbs twisted in the direction of the prevailing winds like indecisive fingers wavering between the guilty and the innocent, he lies beside the body of the old woman—for that's all Maurea is now, a lonely old woman like he's a lonely old man—and takes the gun from her clenched hand, presses the barrel to his temple, and pulls the trigger.

Forgiveness

Sheriff Maurea Sandifer here again. This is the last chapter, and I'm sure readers have plenty of questions to be answered.

First, I hope the tragic story of Chester, Maurea, and Mirlande's lives have left the same indelible mark on your heart as it has on mine, and especially, on my great-great grandfather's heart.

Second, I admit I started writing this book as the standard murder-mystery combined with the love story of Chester and Maurea. Yes, much of it is exactly that kind of story, influenced by the eternal theme of the conflict between good and evil, personified by Catherine's evil of influencing Maurea.

Regardless, this book revealed something else about Chester, Maurea, and Mirlande that I didn't see coming. Sure, I wrote in the last chapter how—as children—they forgave each other. Could that have really happened, or is it just wishful thinking by me, someone who wants a hopeful ending to this sad story filled with heartache?

To what I imagine is the first question you'd like answered, at the beginning of this book, why didn't I find Chester's body beside Maurea's body? The answer is coming, but I need to cover a few other things before then.

To what I imagine is the second question you'd like answered, did Maurea kill Con and Mirlande, and did she hide the brick near Chester's home as the last chapter suggests?

Well, I admit that I wrote Chester seeing her hiding the brick near his house as fiction, which, if it weren't fiction, would mean she was the murderer after all.

However, what if Catherine Applewhite killed Con and Mirlande and buried the brick near Chester's house to frame him?

Yes, I know I said the brick being buried near his house is fiction. Bear with me. More is coming concerning it.

As far as Catherine, I can see her committing the murders. I can also see how Chester—if he saw either Catherine or Maurea burying the brick near his house—might refuse to reveal the guilty party. After all, even after Maurea spent the night with him, he knew it would be their last, and he had nothing left to live for. Since that was the case, why put her through a murder trial? And since he knew putting Catherine through a murder trial would be an unimaginable ordeal for both Maurea and Wilbur, he wouldn't do that either.

What a testimony to as good, and kind, and as decent a human being who has ever roamed the Earth, one who, as I mentioned at the beginning of this book, embodied so much goodness that any of his faults were hardly worth mentioning.

What's that you ask? What about the business of the brick being buried near Chester's house? And why, since I keep saying it was fiction, do I seem so sure it happened?

For starters, it begins at the beginning of this book, when I was standing over the body of Maurea Applewhite. Now, though, it includes the ongoing connection between her Chester, and Mirlande.

Yes, I said "ongoing," even after the tragedy that unfolded at the Corolla Island boathouse so many years ago, and now, even after all of them have died.

I know, I know. Why didn't I mention finding Chester's body beside Maurea's body at the beginning of this book? Don't worry, I wouldn't leave that out for all the flounder in the Currituck Sound, and I love flounder.

In the Currituck County sheriff's office, done with the investigation into Maurea Applewhite's suicide by gunshot, I skim the book Amos wrote.

However morbid the story might be, it still intrigues me, especially because of the supposed sightings of the ghost of Chester Pinkham, which began not long after his execution in the electric chair in 1930. Sometimes he's an old man. Sometimes he's a boy of about five. Sometimes his dog, Goldie, is with him. Sometimes he's walking along the sound. Sometimes he's walking along the beach. Sometimes he's paddling a canoe. Sometimes he's on the walkway of the Currituck Lighthouse. Sometimes he's roaming the rooms in the Whalehead Club. Never, ever, not once, has he been seen near the boathouse.

Other than a time or two, one thing never changes—except for Goldie, he's utterly, completely, and miserably alone, sometimes red-eyed as if he's been crying.

At the time of Maurea Applewhite's suicide, which happened before I finished writing this book, I wasn't sure if I believed in ghosts. Still, those people saw something, and I wanted to find out what it was.

As far as the sightings when Chester wasn't sad, one happened on his and Maurea and Mirlande's combined birthdays—their *last* combined birthday before her suicide that night. One of the clerks at Island Bookstore called to say a woman and her daughter came in. As she and the woman discussed tours to see the Wild Spanish Mustangs, her daughter browsed the children's section. A while later, she took a copy of *The Wizard of Oz* to her mother, saying a nice man read some of it to her, and would she buy it and read the rest. The clerk, familiar with Chester's ghost, asked the girl what the man looked like.

"He's very old," the girl replied.

"Is he thin?" the clerk asked.

"Yes," the girl said, her voice rising a bit. "He's *very* thin."

The clerk nodded. "Is his left hand smaller than his right?"

"Yes," the girl said, a note of sadness in her voice. "It doesn't have as many fingers, either."

The mother, likely thinking the man was some kind of pedophile, stomped to the aisle and returned, white as the proverbial sheet. "I ... he ... there's no one there."

"He died a long time ago," the clerk said. "He likes to read, so this isn't the first time he's been here. I'm sure your daughter made him very happy."

The mouth of the girl's mother fell open. "Are you saying he's a ghost?"

"He's lonely," the clerk asserted. "We have a book about him if you'd like to read it. The sheriff of Currituck County wrote it in 1946."

The woman paid for *The Wizard of Oz*, grabbed the girl's hand and hurried from the store, mumbling something about how her family needed to vacation somewhere—*anywhere*—else.

Every time I think of this story, I laugh. Then I'm tempted to cry.

Concerning Amos's book and the notes in his personal copy, he thinks Chester offered Mirlande's letters from Con as evidence of his guilt to protect Maurea Applewhite. If not, why did the elderly Maurea Applewhite commit suicide beside Chester's grave? Guilt could do that—guilt from her letting him take responsibility for what she, or her mother, had done, guilt for Maurea not visiting him on death row, guilt for not even writing him. Chester might've preferred she make a clean break from him. After all, she had decided against marrying him and living in Corolla. Since that was true, if she killed Mirlande and Con, it was because of spite and jealousy. Chester, raised by his parents to have the character to scoff at a world that would shun him because he was born different, didn't care for spite and jealousy. Regardless, he loved her completely, even dying for her, or her mother, in the electric chair.

I rise from my desk and go to the window that faces the Currituck Sound.

Maurea's will left her property to the descendants of her father and a woman named Patsy, names and addresses included. Only one request needs to be fulfilled, and it's happening now. She's being buried beside Chester, having set aside enough money in an IRA to pay the property taxes in perpetuity.

Despite this tragic story of love, jealousy, and murder, it hasn't ruined my desire for marriage. I'm dating a wonderful man named Ted, and I expect a proposal any time now. We've agreed to start a family soon. If we have a daughter first, I'll name her Mirlande. The young woman, killed in the prime of her life, deserves to live again, if in name only.

Gazing through the window at the shimmering waters of the Currituck Sound, turned golden by the setting sun, I feel the weight of The One Red Brick on my shoulders. No doubt Amos, Harry, and my dad felt the same weight, convinced Chester was innocent, saddened by how Maurea's mother must've been evil to the core to destroy her daughter's innocence by dragging her down the same path to ruin she had so freely chosen, evidenced by her willingness to destroy her own marriage while poor Wilbur clung to it, possibly while hoping, against all odds, they could find love again.

Twilight settles over the sound. In homes and businesses north and south of Corolla Island, now the Whalehead Club, pinpricks of light flicker on.

For myself, Sheriff Maurea Sandifer, I believe in justice. Now, though, after Maurea Applewhite's final admission of guilt by suicide—if that's what it is—I hope justice consists of not one, not two, but three ghosts roaming happily instead of sadly along the sound, the beach, and anywhere else in Corolla they desire. Four if I count Goldie, and Goldie definitely counts, having been tragically killed by malcontents so long ago. Chester and Maurea and Mirlande deserve their peace, deserve to have the burden of The One Red Brick lifted from their now innocent souls.

As far as The One Red Brick and how I knew where it was buried, I feel no guilt for covering the hole Maurea Applewhite dug beside that tree, evidenced by the hole itself and her sandy hands. Yes, I know I said the brick being buried near Chester's house was fiction, but I did find a hole there. Nor do I feel any guilt for brushing Maurea's tracks to the hole away before the coroner arrived. The 103-year-old woman, pitifully lying dead beside Chester's grave, tears still shining on her cheeks, her head in a pool of darkening blood, deserved no more indignity.

Another question at the time concerned the location of the brick, and I found it after the coroner left, returned to its hole in the Currituck Lighthouse. Yes, Maurea could've taken it there before returning to shoot herself, but there were no footprints leading away from her body, only to it. This meant the only other person who knew where it was buried took it there, which meant Chester Pinkham must've known where it was buried.

Maybe he saw a disturbance in the sand the day after the murders. Maybe he saw footprints and found the brick. Maybe he saw either Maurea or Catherine bury it. Maybe Maurea saw her mother bury it, and, as much as she despised her, she couldn't tell anyone because of what it would do to her poor father, who still, deep down inside, loved the person his wife used to be. No one will ever know, because none of this information was passed on, either verbally by Amos or in his book.

One thing is fairly certain. Since Chester didn't take the brick to the lighthouse before his arrest, because Amos's notes said it wasn't there when he looked, the only other possibility was Chester's ghost took it there on the night Maurea shot herself, hoping to ease her burden of guilt even more than suicide had.

Other questions, of course, remain, never to be answered. Why did either Maurea or Catherine choose the brick as a weapon? Why walk all the way to the lighthouse for it? Why bury it beside that tree behind Chester's home? If Maurea committed the murders, one can never know the workings of a distraught mind. If Catherine committed the murders, it was to frame Chester. Since he nobly consented to his arrest, the issue of finding the murder weapon became a moot point.

Suffice it to say, eighty-three years later, none of that matters now.

Outside my office window, the night deepens. In a sudden burst of brilliance, the Currituck Lighthouse powers on, leaving a few final questions to contemplate.

Whose evil will be pointed out next? Better yet, whose innate goodness—like Chester's innate goodness—will it illuminate?

Or is the evil of what happened in 1928 well on its way to becoming commonplace in a world where people care no more for each other than to murder without regard as to how—like with either Maurea or Catherine—it creates more problems than it solves, symbolized by the tragic circumstances of The One Red Brick?

Regardless of the seriousness of the question, the answer brightens my mood.

Like Chester Pinkham, whose parents taught him to have the character, not only to ignore bullies, but to have the perspective to understand even those who betrayed him, people exist who are willing to see the good on the inside, where character resides, regardless of how people appear on the outside.

That's all anyone can ask. Unfortunately, it takes a mirror to delve into a person's heart, and it seems fewer and fewer people are willing to dive that deeply into their own reflections.

I imagine Chester in the electric chair. I imagine the leather straps snug around his wrists, ankles, and chest. Attending the execution, Amos Sandifer, that era's Sheriff of Currituck County, made sure not to overtighten the straps. Chester had already suffered enough pain in his short life, although he had done his best to cherish every moment of it, from each sunrise over the Atlantic to each sunset over the Currituck, to the smallest, most insignificant shell, to the largest, most significant ideal of being a good and decent person.

Before the final declaration of the execution was read, Sheriff Sandifer shook Chester's hand. He didn't write in his book if they shared a smile, but I like to think so. They also likely shared a cascade of tears wetting their cheeks, hands clasped, unwilling to let go until the black hood covered the innocent young man's head, his chest rising and falling like a hurricane's storm surge pressing against the sands of the Outer Banks of North Carolina.

Were his loved one's gathered around him, hands on his shoulders to see him through his ordeal? Did Abner and Alice say how proud they were of him for doing the right thing? Did Mirlande tell him how much he meant to her? Did Con beg his forgiveness? Did Wilbur study the ticking hands on his pocket watch as they approached 12:01 a.m.? Did Goldie curl in Chester's lap and whine while waiting? Did Catherine roll over in bed, away from her latest conquest to light a cigarette and smile at the looming death of the twin to Frankenstein's monster? Beside Wilbur, did Patsy turn from her pillow to comfort him with soft words of assurance, kissing his forehead as it lowered when the pocket watch ticked to 12:02?

I finger tears from my own eyes.

And what of Maurea Lynn Applewhite? Where was she and what was she doing when those 2000 volts exploded into Chester Pinkham's brain, ending the life of the sweetest, most generous, most forgiving man she had ever known?

And would ever know.

The cynical part of myself—the Sheriff Maurea Sandifer part—doesn't care where Maurea Applewhite was and what she was doing when Chester died. Maurea's actions, though, influenced by her mother, led directly to Chester's death, so that tends to infuriate me. However, the part of myself that admires Chester for doing his duty *does* care about Maurea.

He loved her without question. He knew her to the depths of her soul—the good and the bad, the forgivable and the unforgivable—and he forgave her regardless.

Darkness fully shrouds the Currituck. In the glow of the streetlights outside my office window, a misting rain begins to fall. I call Ted and tell him I love him. He returns the sentiment, adding because he knows how close I am to this case, he hopes I'm okay. I say I am, adding how I feel like taking a drive. He doesn't ask where because he likely knows. This is love. This is trust. This is commitment. This is what a great marriage requires. This is something too many people have forgotten.

Yes, I'm being preachy. After what my family and I have had to live with over the years, bearing the guilt for Amos's part in executing what he—and we—believed to be an innocent man, I hope you can find it in your heart to forgive me.

Now that that's out of the way, let's get on with my drive and the end of this story.

I lock my office door and climb into the Chevrolet SUV. The windshield wipers clear the mist. As the engine warms, the defroster clears the December chill from inside the glass.

Passing the Grandy Market, closed for the season, I wonder if my namesake liked peach flurries. Crossing the Wright Memorial Bridge, I wonder if her head bobbed with each crossing of the expansion joints like mine does now. Gazing left and right at the black expanses of the Currituck and Albemarle sounds, I wonder if she noticed the uncountable number of stars in the sky, even if they weren't hidden by clouds like they are now.

When the flashing finger of brilliance from the Currituck Lighthouse slices through the darkness above me, I continue toward the end of Highway 12. Here, vacationers can head north in their four-wheel drive vehicles, either to fish, hunt for shells, see the famous Spanish Mustangs, or to vacation in Carova. Instead of driving north, I stop when the road ends and the sand begins and park with the headlights aimed at the Atlantic. The combined mist from the rain and the crashing waves forms swirling, drifting images in the low-beams. Some are round. Some are thin, Some are short. Some are tall. Some are—

I hit the high-beams and blink. Near the water's edge, partially hidden by the mist, the faint figures of three children and a dog turn to look at me. Then they run away into the night.

Was the boy's hair dark, a length of it hanging over his high forehead? Was one of the girl's hair dark as well, long curls to her waist framing her face? Was the other girl's hair blonde, falling along her shoulders like sunlight shimmering on the Atlantic? The dog, though, the dog was definitely a Golden Retriever.

For ten seconds, the burn of adrenalin attempts to purge my disbelief. "No," I whisper. Despite my hopes of Chester, Maurea, Mirlande, and Goldie roaming Corolla as ghosts, happy instead of lonely, it just can't be.

Or can it?

I kill the engine and the headlights. Wearing a rain slicker, a ball cap, and aiming a flashlight, I trek toward the Atlantic.

If it can't be, why did I come here?

Ghost crabs scurry by. Some zigzag. Some dive into holes. Some rear back and wave their claws defiantly. Some dine on clumps of seaweed tangled with the pink shells of mole crab remains.

The mist wets my cheeks and eyelashes. It tastes of salt and smells of ozone. The breeze from the west chills the nape of my neck and the back of my ears. The sand crunches softly beneath my shoes.

I near the crashing surf. Along the sand, the flashlight's beam moves side to side. Here's an oyster shell. Here's another, but it's broken. Here's a perfect Scotch Bonnet, fairly common on the Outer Banks. Here's the broken spiral of a whelk. A single, tiny barnacle clings to it.

Fear rips up my spine, and I drop the flashlight. The beam shines across the beach, revealing what frightened me—a line of children's footprints heading south. Before I can pick the flashlight up, childish giggles circle me, and a dog whoofs playfully. Fingertips brush the slicker and the giggles grow louder, tempting me to scream. I grab the flashlight and stand to shine the beam all around.

Nothing. No children. No dog.

My knees tremble. I drop to the sand on my behind. I want so badly to believe Chester, Maurea, and Mirlande are here, happy instead of lonely, and all I've done is to allow my overactive imagination, plus a desire for a positive end to this story, to make a fool of myself.

Huffing a hard breath, I pick up the flashlight, When I turn to leave, I stop when the beam reveals a pile of shells on the rise above the surf. I go to the pile. The circle of light from the flashlight shudders.

Along the rise, the prints of three small behinds and three sets of footprints are pressed into the wet sand. Beside where they sat, handprints tell the tale. Three children were sitting here.

To the south, a dog whoofs playfully.

I study the handprints. The two sets to the outside are normal, but the left hand of the set in the middle is—

I shake my head, hardly believing what I'm witnessing.

Yes, the left hand of the set in the middle is smaller than the right, and, miraculously, it has two fingers and a thumb.

This time, fear doesn't rip up my spine. This time, I don't drop the flashlight. Instead, I smile as large as when Ted will propose.

Not only are Chester, Maurea, and Mirlande here, happy instead of lonely, Corolla is their version of Heaven.

I take one perfect Scotch Bonnet from the pile and speak into the night. "I'll leave the rest for y'all, okay?" I have to smile. My voice likely carries the same soft, southern drawl as Maurea Applewhite's voice.

The dog whoofs. Out of the darkness, a stick lands a few feet away, and a boyish laugh follows. I throw the stick back and the dog whoofs again. The clouds part. A shaft of moonlight reveals four misty forms running down the beach. The clouds close.

Only now do I realize what the theme of this story is about. It isn't a murder mystery. It isn't a love story. It isn't even an illustration of the evils of narcissism.

It's about one of the most difficult things a person can do, which is to admit their guilt and to ask for forgiveness.

Let's consider Maurea's mother, Catherine Applewhite.

In the final moments of her life, before she sent a bullet through her brain, did she regret how she treated Maurea and Wilbur?

I think we know Maurea admitted her guilt and hoped for forgiveness before she pulled the trigger at Chester's grave, so why can't Catherine have that same consideration?

Yes, that's a hard thing to do, but imagine how hard it was for Chester to sacrifice himself in the electric chair.

When we're born, we're destined to make mistakes, but we're often influenced by the world we live in, or by people who claim to care for us, or by people who actually *do* care for us. Maurea's mistake of not trying to live with Chester in Corolla was influenced by her mother. Mirlande's mistake of lying to Chester about Con was influenced by her aunt. Chester's mistake of loving Corolla to the point of not considering Maurea's offer of marriage and a job in Richmond was influenced by his parents.

Yes, they seem like simple mistakes, but they led to the murders of two young people in the Corolla Island boathouse, which means Chester, Maurea, and Mirlande share the guilt for the parts they played in their story.

No, that's not true anymore. They no longer share the guilt because forgiveness has lifted it from their shoulders, placed there by the evils—and the burden—of The One Red Brick.

This realization fills my eyes with tears of gratitude. I only wish my relatives, both those who served as sheriff of Currituck County and those who took such an interest in this story like my dad, were here to share this experience. Then again, Dad will just have to read this book, won't he? I can't wait to hear what he has to say about the ghost stories in Corolla being true.

In the SUV again, on my way home, inspired by the ghosts of two children who lost their precious lives so long ago, and by the one who asked for forgiveness by taking her own life on her 103rd birthday, I have two final thoughts.

One is how people might be compared to grains of sand. Like every person in Chester's story, we ebb and flow with the tides, always seeking, always hoping, always dreaming. We do those things in our search for significance. Most of all we do those things to simply be accepted for that special spark of light that makes us who, what, and why we are—not just grains of sand scattered on a beach, but recognizable stars within the universe of every beach ever known—a single shining star shining brightly of our own accord, waiting for another star to drift within the ebb and flow of the tide until it joins us, never to part for eternity.

Being a sheriff, and the person who finally put my dad's idea about giving people the benefit of the doubt to paper, the second and final thought is much more personal. I roll it around inside my mind until I have the words just right, and they need to be just right to honor those three children who now run along the beach in Corolla, and wherever else they might choose to roam.

Forgiveness is one of the most significant ideals a person can practice. Forgiveness mends relationships, saves marriages, prevents wars, and ends hate.

As bright as the stars, as illuminating as the sun, as deep as any ocean, to set aside hate, to set aside blame, to set aside the wrongs of the past in the name of hope, is likely the most shining example of humanity's existence.

Sheriff Maurea Sandifer
Currituck County, North Carolina
December, 2011

ABOUT THE AUTHOR

J. Willis Sanders lives in southern Virginia, with his wife and several stringed musical instruments.

With eighteen novels completed and more on the way, he enjoys crafting intriguing characters with equally intriguing conflicts to overcome. He also loves the natural world and, more often than not, his stories include those settings. Most also utilize intense love relationships and layered themes.

His first idea for a novel is a ghostly World War II era historical that takes place mostly in the midwestern United States, which utilizes some little-known facts about German POW camps there at the time. It's the first of a three-book series, in which characters from the first continue their lives.

Although he loves history, he has written several contemporary novels as well, and some include interesting paranormal twists, both with and without religious themes.

He also loves the Outer Banks of North Carolina, and he has written four novels within different time frames based on the area, what he calls his Outer Banks of North Carolina Series. Yes, more novels set in the area will be written.

Also, he enjoys learning about the variations of Amish culture, which inspired his Eliza Gray and Clara Engelman series.

Other hobbies include reading (of course), vegetable gardening, playing music with friends, and songwriting, some of which are in a few of his novels.

To follow his work, visit any of these websites:

https://jwillissanders.wixsite.com/writer

https://www.facebook.com/J-Willis-Sanders-874367072622901

https://www.amazon.com/J-Willis-Sanders/e/B092RZG6MC?ref_=dbs_p_ebk_r00_abau_000000

Readers: to help those considering a purchase, please leave a review on Amazon.com, Goodreads.com, or wherever you bought this book.

Your recommendations help authors more than you may realize.

Made in the USA
Columbia, SC
21 May 2024

35577095R00209